THE BRIDGE

MOONLIGHTING
WITH THE WEREWOLF

USA TODAY BESTSELLING AUTHOR

CINDI MADSEN

Fighting For Her Series

Until You're Mine

Until We're More

Heart In The Game Series

The Wedding Deal

The Mistletoe Trap

Getting Hitched Series

Just One Of The Groomsmen

Always A Bridesmaid

Catch And Release Groom

Turnaround Ranch Series

A Cowboy Never Quits

Hope On The Range

Stand-Alone Novels

Cinderella Screwed Me Over

Just Jilted

Lights, Cowboy, Action

12 Steps To Mr. Right

Taking Care Of The Target

Nailed It

Runaway Christmas Bride

Country Hearts

Sailing At Sunset

Verity Sloan: Supernatural Investigator

Young Adult Novels

Cipher Series

Cipher

Rift

Resolution

Standalone

All The Broken Pieces

Losing Romeo

Demons Of The Sun

Operation Prom Date

Hell High

CHAPTER ONE

Kerrigan

WHAT WAS AN INDEPENDENT, former city gal to do after signing up to be a backwoods veterinarian?

As far as proper procedure, I was still in the dark, but I'd found my way into the local bookstore, where I'd discovered —and purchased—a copy of the *Backwoods Survival Guide*. No shit, there was a ginormous book dedicated to that very subject. Not to complain, as it'd been super-duper informative thus far, but the "Practical Advice for the Simple Life" tagline seemed like false advertising, as the advice was neither practical nor simple.

The town name seemed to be a misnomer, too, as I'd seen all of zero waterfalls during my first week in Guadalupe Falls, Massachusetts. What I had seen was an abundance of extra tall, spiky pines with a side of oak and birch trees. The waitress at the local diner cheerily informed me their tiny town sat smack dab in the Bridgewater Triangle, which was "a total hotbed for paranormal activity." Suddenly the sign welcoming people to town, with its caricatures of Bigfoot, aliens, and a Pac-Man ghost riding what looked like a frisbee, made sense.

In the same way the guidebook did. As in, people actually believed in this stuff?

I suppose if I *were* going to jump aboard the crazy train, I'd choose bumping into Bigfoot over scavenging for berries on his behalf. A bit of googling also unearthed incidences of animal mutilations, cult activity, and a cursed swamp with a name that meant "where spirits dwell." In hindsight, I really should've researched the area more before diving headfirst.

You wanted a fresh start, away from all the memories that held you hostage, and this one is as alien as the little green men who allegedly carved those markings on Dighton Rock.

The strands that'd escaped my ponytail fell into my eyes, tinting everything brown— well, *cinnamon* brown according to the box I'd used to add some oomph to my color. It didn't help with the soupy humidity, though, so by the end of the day, my hair ended up half curly, half straight, and 100 percent frizzy.

It was a slow afternoon at the animal clinic that still donned the name of the veterinarian who'd sold me the place, so I hefted the survival guidebook and turned to chapter two. Even though the edible plants hardly looked appetizing, my stomach growled. It was a sad day in chilly ol' hell when a salad without dressing, bacon bits, or croutons caused tummy rumbling.

At this rate, I'll starve before I can afford a new sign, much less groceries.

I'd heard the stats. Half of new businesses failed within the first few years. But Dr. Vaughn had sweetened the deal with his roster of clients. Problem was, all but about five had immediately transferred to the only other vet in town, citing they were more comfortable going to a doctor they already knew.

Who was male.

Well, they didn't admit that part, but I saw it in their eyes after they gave me the once-over. Probably didn't help that I was twenty-six with the height and boobs of a thirteen-year-old. What I didn't have up top, I made up for in booty size, which also meant finding pants was akin to torture. Seriously, whoever made my body had just grabbed two random halves, stuck them together, and declared it *good enough*.

Determination flooded every inch of my five-foot-two-inch frame. No letting the outsider vibes bring me down. I'd earned a doctorate degree and weathered the internship from hell to get to where I was today.

As in purchasing a clinic so I could be my own boss, not so much the middle-of-nowhere locale.

After performing tasks like sorting through puppy poop for an antique ring, cupping my hands in time for a dog to puke into them, and conducting a private cremation ceremony for a cat's amputated tail, nothing much fazed me anymore.

"Bring on the challenges. I can take them," I said to the empty clinic, not appreciating the way the walls echoed them back at me. Surely the snarky tone was only my imagination, but considering not even the room respected me, I wasn't sure this was the upgrade to my career I thought it'd be.

I'll win the people over. I can be very charming.

When my lack of thinking before I speak doesn't get the best of me.

I could hear Mom's voice in my head, the phrase she repeated so often I automatically rolled my eyes. *Be sure to taste your words before you spit them out.*

Grams would then argue that if people didn't know their weaknesses, some fiery Tabasco sauce would inspire them to address it faster.

Grief rose, a string that bound my lungs. We'd lost Mom way too early to an automobile accident, leaving my maternal grandmother to raise me. It'd been just the two of us for nearly a decade, up until four months ago when Grams passed away. I'd wanted to stomp my foot over the unfairness of it all. I hardly had any family as it was, and now I'd been left without anyone.

My throat tightened, and tears burned my eyes.

No crying, in case someone comes in during the last—I glanced at the noisy clock ticking away on the opposite, slightly dingy wall—*twenty-eight minutes of the workday.*

Not that I was overly eager to return to my equally empty house. While the clinic I'd sunk my entire savings into looked exactly like the pictures I'd clicked through online, the cabin I'd rented sight unseen was unsightly, to say the least. The floorboards creaked as if I weighed as much as an African bush elephant—the heaviest land mammal tipped the scales at twice what the oft-used hippo did—and the heating unit squalled like a banshee that was way too excited about foretelling my death.

Which would likely be at the hands of the sparking oven.

I'd found out the hard way that using the microwave and stovetop at the same time overloaded the antique electrical system. I rubbed my thumb across the puckered red skin that marred the back of my wrist. On a good day, I was pale, but since I hadn't spent much time outside this summer, I was reaching Casper levels.

Guess I should pencil in tanning on my rotting front porch on my to-do list.

Exhaustion tugged at me, and I gave in, plunking myself on the nearby roller chair and enjoying the glide across the tile before bumping into the heavy duty, electrical lift exam table. When Dr. Vaughn handed over the keys, he'd muttered something about occasionally working on larger animals. I hadn't treated many horses and cows, but I'd studied the anatomy and knew my way around internal organs, regardless of the disposition.

"Guess I'll take another trip to the bookstore and find a manual on home repairs." The talking to myself thing wasn't new. I'd always been a bit of a lone wolf, which sometimes meant my inner thoughts were outer ones, too. And yeah, I could search up YouTube tutorials, but I was a highlight and tab kinda gal.

"Wait. Dung fires?" I pulled the guidebook closer, suspecting the author was messing with me. I'd rather eat forest roots raw than catch a cute squirrel or bunny and roast them with eau de pew.

Speaking of burning, my eyes were telling me they were done for the day, so I went ahead and let my lids drift closed. Only for a minute or two, and then I'd close up shop and head back to my stark, malevolent cabin.

A strange scraping noise jerked me awake, and I jumped as the heavy book in my lap crashed to the floor. I rubbed the sleep out of my eyes and worked to recover my bearings. The clock showed seven fifteen, so forty-five minutes past closing time.

Scratching. At the back door. Followed by a whimper and a loud *thud*.

That jolted me into motion, my heart racing as I rushed across the room. I flung open the door and gaped at the giant gray and brown...wolf? Its chocolate-colored eyes lifted, the light in them weak enough my stomach bottomed out, and what I originally thought were patches of wet fur dripped crimson onto the cement step.

"Shit, shit, shit. Hold on, buddy." I sprinted over to the cabinets, glass vials rattling together as I sorted through them, and snagged the dexmedetomidine and butorphanol. Only someone with a death wish handled wild animals without sedation. Especially one the size of a compact car.

That's probably the adrenaline talking. Wolves of that size only live in Alaska and Canada. Right?

After filling a syringe, I cautiously approached the beast. "I'm going to help you, okay? Please, *please* don't bite me." With the hind leg in my sights, I quickly jabbed the needle into the gluteal region, depressed the syringe, and retreated a few steps.

Within five minutes, the wolf would be putty in my hands, but the gaping hole that exposed several ribs made me pray the animal would last that long. Its enormous head sagged and then fell into the burgeoning pool of blood, and I decided to risk it.

A grunt escaped as I tugged the wolf toward the exam table. "I should've done all that weightlifting I vowed to do to get in shape, because *unnn*, you're heavy." Between the creature's weight and size, I figured it'd be safe to refer to the creature as male, although I'd have to confirm later.

Sweat beaded my forehead, and my hammering heart relocated to my throat, doing a bang-up job of restricting my air supply. "Deadweight takes on a new meaning with you, dude. Just...don't die, okay?"

Well on his way to sleepy land, he responded with a lolled tongue. After managing to get the animal halfway onto the table, I circled him and gasped at his torn-open cheek. Heavy breaths caused the flayed skin to flap, which drew my gaze to the row of long, razor-sharp teeth.

The wounds weren't consistent with teeth or claws, like I expected them to be. My blood ran cold as I took a closer look. Bullet holes. At least four of them that'd entered through his backside and exited the front. Despite all the blood, pus, and exposed organs I'd seen during countless procedures, I'd never once vomited, but bile rose now.

Who would shoot such a magnificent creature? Rage and resolve counteracted my nausea, and I shoved the wolf the rest of the way onto the table, which appeared Barbie-sized compared to the injured canine.

The gears loudly ground together and complained as I hit the button to raise the table, but within a handful of seconds, the wolf rested at counter height. Telling myself not to fixate on the oozing streams of blood, I grabbed my tools and got to work.

CHAPTER TWO
Kerrigan

THE WOLF'S muscles twitched as I used the forceps to retrieve the last bullet, something uncommon with this level of sedation. Then again, the projectile was lodged deep in the center of the chest, where it'd missed the heart and lungs by a mere inch. "We're so close to done, buddy. I promise."

If the bastard who shot the wolf hadn't used hollow points, the process would be a hell of a lot easier. They'd mushroomed on impact, causing severe organ damage and turning the tips into garish silver flowers drenched in scarlet.

At long last, I maneuvered the warped shell free and dropped it into the tray, where it clinked against the five others I'd removed. I swiped my forearm across my forehead, undoubtedly leaving a trail of blood, but there wasn't much of me left unsmeared anyway. Red splatters covered my formerly white lab coat, and my cushy shoes with the cartoon cats and dogs would never be the same again. But if Mr. Wolfie survived, none of that mattered.

Not that I was any expert, but the bullets seemed strange.

A snore echoed through the exam room, and the wolf's hind leg twitched. Perhaps Mr. Wolfie was chasing a bunny in his dreams.

WELCOME TO
BRIDGEWATER

The idea made me happy for all of two seconds before I experienced a pinch of sadness for the bunny, who didn't stand a chance. Since my beastly patient still wasn't out of the woods—metaphorically, anyway—I shook away that thought so I could focus on flushing and stitching the wounds.

His other leg twitched, enough to rattle the table.

"Whoa. Down, boy." After a quick internal debate, I decided I'd rather be safe than maimed and turned to grab more anesthetic. No matter how good of a job I'd done treating the wounds, most animals instinctively lashed out once they came to and felt the aftereffects of the pain. I didn't want the wolf to injure himself further, just like I didn't want to end up shredded by his claws for my efforts.

"Let's see. I don't want to give him too much. Then again, he's huge." Numbers tumbled through my brain, dosage versus guesstimated weight as I calculated how much to administer.

The tip of the needle gleamed in the overhead operating light as I spun around, elbow cocked at the ready. My heart lurched, and I stumbled backward, slamming my butt into the counter and dropping the syringe in the process.

The sight in front of me didn't make sense. My mind whirred, trying to force it to, even as pain throbbed through my backside.

Had I accidentally stabbed myself in the leg?

That was the only logical explanation for the naked man on my operating table.

Then again, I'd seen him before dropping the needle so... A steady throb formed behind my temples, and I squeezed my eyes shut and then opened them, hoping that'd be enough to correct my vision.

The man's ghastly pale skin gaped open in gruesome, ragged holes, the macabre scene straight out of a horror movie.

Holy shit, are the wounds knitting themselves together? Too afraid to look away, I merely blinked, blinked, blinked. With every flutter of my eyelashes, more invisible stitches tugged muscles and sinew closed, until all of his outside business returned to being inside.

The man who'd materialized in place of the giant wolf groaned, and I backpedaled in the direction of the door. Halfway there, my foot slipped in one of the many puddles of gore, and then I was free falling, my arms flailing like a baby bird's untested wings as I attempted to find purchase.

A jolt wrenched my spine as my butt hit the floor, and as if that didn't hurt badly enough, my head smacked the cabinet behind me as I slid into a crumpled marionette position. I gasped for air as sparks of light superimposed themselves over the impossible scene. "This can't be happening. I'm still asleep." I pinched my leg. "Wake up, wake up, *wake up*."

"I'm working on it," came a deep, husky voice, and I froze. What a spectacular time to discover my instincts leaned toward prey rather than predator.

Thick, muscular legs swung off the table, and it didn't speak well to my mental state that instead of leaping to my feet and fleeing, heat flooded me. Defined calf muscles led to ropy, hairy thighs, rippling abs, and pec muscles so large I suddenly understood motorboating.

Large, non-lupine feet hit the blood-smeared floor, and then the guy who'd inexplicably showed up on my operating table slowly stood, looming over me. His eyes gleamed gold, and with fear holding me hostage, I figured I might as well look my fill.

As someone with a healthy appreciation of anatomy, I could list off every muscle, all those dips and curves showcasing where each one ended and another began. Mr. Wolfie was put together like a Russian boxer, which was a thing I knew about because I'd seen a lot of *Rocky* movies in my day. Those flicks were legit romances disguised as dude movies. And as a gal who often slept alone, they'd served for inspiration on many an occasion.

Which was probably why a rush of anticipation streaked through my core. *Wow, I must be hard up if I can go from horrified to horny in two seconds flat.*

He took a step in my direction but wobbled and braced a hand on the counter. His forehead crinkled, and he dazedly shook his head.

"Please," I said, the two chapters of survival tricks I'd read doing jack and shit. "I don't know who you are, or why you're here, but—"

"Don't bite you?" he finished for me, and the fucker had the audacity to flash me a crooked, smug smile. My belly got in on the mutiny my dirty thoughts had started, heat pooling low and spreading throughout my entire body as the biggest cock I'd ever seen dangled a few inches above my head.

How could I be thinking about how hung he was right now?

How could I not?

"Don't worry. I don't bite the hand that saves me." He extended his open palm, and I simply stared, unable to budge from my prone position. Why was this happening to me? A question suited for one of those damsel-in-distress types, and believe me, I wasn't happy about it, but was I seriously supposed to be cool and composed right now?

For the past hour, I'd been treating an injured wolf. Now there was this sexy beast of a man in its place, and why couldn't I have gone insane *before* I'd spent all those hours cramming in med school?

In an attempt to reconciliate the ludicrousness of the situation, I searched his body for bullet wounds. Instead of finding the correlating puckered scars comforting, dizziness set in. I wasn't sure if I was going to pass out or puke. Knowing my luck, I'd puke and then pass out in the regurgitated mess. As long as I came to anywhere but here—or say, some torture dungeon— I'd take it.

"There weren't werewolves," I said. On the bright side, my tongue was functioning, even if the result was subpar at best.

"Don't you mean that there aren't supposed to be werewolves?" Again with that quirk at the corner of his mouth, as if I were amusing instead of losing my mind.

I adamantly shook my head. "On the sign welcoming people to town. There were aliens, ghosts, and Bigfoot. And yeah, you have big feet, but you're not actual Bigfoot."

The other corner of his mouth got in on his smile, and under about any other circumstances, my panties might've melted right off me. Okay, maybe they were melting the tiniest bit, regardless. "Let me get this straight. You're not upset that werewolves exist, but that the town sign didn't warn you?"

Exasperation pitched my voice higher. "Yes. No. I mean..." My shoulders sagged, and since I couldn't keep my eyes from fixating on his junk, I held up a hand and twisted it sideways to block as much of it as I could from my view. "Honestly, I don't know. But if you'll give me two shakes of a lamb's tail to recover from my shock, I'll get off my ass and check your vitals."

CHAPTER THREE
Conall

SINCE THE WOMAN *had* saved my life, I was doing my damnedest not to mock that *two shakes of a lamb's tail* comment.

Or the fact that every time I moved the slightest bit, her hand followed along with me, as if she were trying to preserve my sense of modesty. Hard to preserve something that didn't exist. Constantly shifting meant you got used to ruining clothes and people seeing you naked. Some of my friends gave me shit about being an exhibitionist, but they were just jealous they didn't have as much to display— enough that her small hand wasn't up to the task, that was for sure.

Finally, she seemed to register my outstretched arm as a friendly gesture and slipped her palm into mine. Wooziness set in, and for a mortifying second, I worried I wouldn't be able to lift this slip of a woman off the floor. I dug down deep, summoned my drowsy strength, and tugged her to her feet.

I swayed from the expended effort, and then she was the one attempting to prop me up.

"You should get out of the way," I said, "because if I fall,

I'll crush you. And believe it or not, I'm gentleman enough to at least get a name before I smash and dash."

Her brow crinkled as if she couldn't tell whether or not that was a joke, and not even I was entirely sure. The fuzziness came in waves.

I scratched the side of my head. "Did you drug me?"

Offense pinched her features. "You say it like I'm some sexual deviant who roofied your drink. A feral wolf showed up at the back door of my clinic, and I figured it'd be easier to save him if he couldn't bite off my arm, so yeah, I drugged him. Er, you. I'm not insane." Her nose crinkled, drawing my attention to eyes the color of the lake after a storm. Tumultuous and gray with a hint of blue. "Anyway, I'm fairly sure. Now, I'm gonna walk you back to the table."

I opened my mouth to tell her there was no need, but she nudged me, and despite not having much weight behind it, my body obeyed.

Well, most of my body. There was a certain part that twitched, headed in the opposite direction as the rest of me, and that wouldn't do. I fixed my gaze on her face. Narrow nose, slightly hooked at the end, and with the added gleam of the overhead lights, I caught a tinge of red in her soft-brown locks.

My thighs hit the cool metal table. The veterinarian lifted onto the tips of her toes, bringing her body close enough to mine that the fabric of her bloodstained lab coat brushed my bare skin. She placed her hands on my shoulders and pressed downward, guiding me to a seated position.

Strange how comforting it felt, having someone take care of me instead of awaiting orders to immediately obey. Not something I could indulge in often, and I'd have to cut it off soon. The doctor opened a nearby drawer, pulled out a stethoscope, and stuck it in her ears. The cool, circular end hit the center of my chest, and I got lost in the column of the woman's neck and the way her pulse fluttered at the base of it, keeping time with the beating of my heart.

She removed the stethoscope from her ears and draped it around her neck, the movements practiced and precise. "How do you feel?"

Surprisingly turned on for someone who was shot several times in the fucking back. "I'm fine. That's the thing about werewolves." I extended my arms, as if that were the best way to determine one's health. Moving hurt like a bitch, every inch of my torso radiating wave after wave of pain, but between the doc's pale pallor and her undercurrent of shock, I figured she could use some reassurance I was alive and well instead of an apparition on his way to the afterlife. "We heal fast."

"But you weren't healing before. Not until..." She glanced at the metal tray beside the table, and I followed suit. "Until I removed the bullets."

I picked up one of the shells so I could study it under the light. It sizzled against my skin, causing me to hiss and drop it right back in the tray. I popped the end of my finger in my mouth and sucked to soothe the burn. "Silver. That explains why my body couldn't reject the bullets, no matter how hard I tried to push them out."

Straight white teeth worried her plump lower lip. "I'm no bullet expert, but I've removed a couple in my day, and those struck me as strange. Although considering the wolf I was performing surgery on turned into...well, *you*, strange is taking on a whole new meaning." She lifted one shoulder higher than the other. "I guess I should just be glad you came to me instead of going to the vet everyone else in this town prefers."

"I didn't think I'd make it that far, honestly," I said without thinking, and she jerked my arm out straight and prodded at my fractured ribs. Under normal circumstances, my skin healed within a handful of minutes, internal organs around an hour or two, but broken bones— especially ones shattered by silver bullets—took a day or two. Judging from how quickly she'd gone from tender to sadistic, I'd offended her. "What I meant to say is that I heard you were the best in town and thought what better time to find out how true that is than when I'm circling the drain?"

Obviously, she wasn't buying it, but the torturous pressure stopped. Since the concern in her expression remained, I snagged her hand and folded it mine. The widening of her eyes suggested she'd felt the same current that'd coursed up my arm. "Let's try this again. Hello. I'm Conall Shaw. Pleased to meet you."

She slipped her thumb over mine in more of a classic-greeting grip and shook my hand. "Dr. Ryan. But not the Dr. Ryan dude who goes around doing all that CIA spy shit, lest you were confused."

Sunshine spread through my chest, softening the pain. Dr. Ryan was witty. She also seemed determined to keep me at a distance now that I'd turned from wolf to human, even though I could tell by her pointed efforts to avoid ogling me she was attracted. "Thank you, Dr. Ryan. If it makes you feel any better, you're definitely easier on the eyes than Doc Morris."

"Yes, that's my main goal in life." She hitched her chin higher. "I went to medical school in hopes that one day some cocky creature who shouldn't exist would tell me I'm pretty."

"I didn't say pretty."

Her gaze jerked to mine, embers igniting within those blue-gray irises. She yanked her hand out of my grasp, hell-bent on showing me how very little she cared about my opinion. Which, of course, only proved the opposite. It'd been a long time since I felt such a strong flare of awareness, that crackling connection that demanded I let my primitive side off the leash.

Carpe diem, carpe the dame. One in the same, really. When it came to humans, it was never a good idea to get too close, but it'd been a while since I'd been bad.

"I'm starting to see why someone would want to shoot you," Dr. Ryan said, and I clamped my lips so I wouldn't laugh and piss her off further. Then again, I wouldn't mind seeing more of her unexpected fiery side—more of her in general, honestly. "Any idea who pulled the trigger and why?"

Right. The reason I couldn't give in to my whims. I cracked my knuckles. "Figuring that out is next on my to-do list. Given the silver bullets, it's safe to say they meant to kill me. Hopefully, they think they did so they won't be prepared for what's about to happen next."

"What happens next is I call the cops to report this so that *they* can investigate, and justice will be served."

At that, I couldn't help snicker. "Don't bother. The sheriff and I have an understanding. He leaves my pack alone, and we keep the town safe. Justice means something else 'round these parts." Someone attempted to take me out, and that someone was going to pay in pints of blood. Anger infused my voice, leaving it rough and low. "Here in Guadalupe Falls, we go more of the animalistic vengeance route."

My priorities sharpened along with my thoughts—finally, the last of the medication was leaving my system. *Time to go.* I scooted off the table and stood.

"Wait." Dr. Ryan placed her hand on the center of my chest, and I peered down at her. She was so tiny, with full hips and an even fuller ass, and the parting of her lips made me want to plunder the pillowy pink softness. If I had more time and less responsibility, I'd sweep the sexy doctor who wouldn't even give me her first name off her feet and carry her into the woods with me.

But I had a pack to warn and protect, and that'd always be priority numero uno. "Afraid I can't. Don't get me wrong, Doc, I'd love to stay so we could get to know one another better. Unfortunately, my hectic schedule just got even busier." I patted my thighs and then my ass, where I'd keep my money if I had on jeans. "I guess I'll have to settle the bill later. I left my money in my other prison wallet."

She scrunched up her forehead. "Prison wallet? What's that?"

"It's where people in prison store and smuggle stuff they don't want the guards to find." Her confusion remained, so I guess I was spelling this out for her. "In their assholes."

Her jaw dropped as her eyebrows shot up. "Oh. I..." Pink crept across her cheeks, and her eyes moved around the room, willing to land anywhere but on me. "Wish I'd never asked."

Man, it'd be fun to stay and mess with her, but duty called, so I strode on past.

One last glance at her, standing in the center of the empty operating room covered in my blood, and then I shifted and darted out the door, sprinting as fast as I could toward the compound.

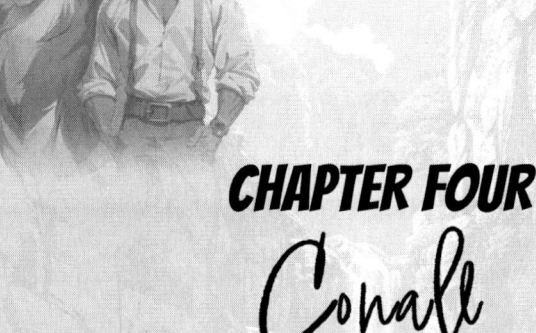

CHAPTER FOUR

Conall

"WHO WAS ON WATCH?" I growled at the men and women who made up my first line. My voice echoed through the chamber where we met to discuss pack business.

The fact that they all looked at each other didn't inspire a lot of confidence. We hadn't had a threat in long enough that I'd considered relaxing security measures, chalking it up to my paranoia that I never pulled the trigger.

Then I'd been shot in the fucking back. It'd taken every ounce of my strength to dig my claws into the dirt and drag my swiss cheese carcass to the clinic. If the spitfire vet hadn't been there...

Well, I wouldn't be here anymore, either. Dr. Ryan would've found a dead wolf at the back door tomorrow morning, and that would be that. The thought of those bullets hitting any of the Bridgewater Pack members, especially the younger wolves who wouldn't have survived the shooting, cranked my rage from a low simmer to a frenzied boil.

Scenes from my past punched their way through, images of carnage and blood. Memories of hiding and holding my breath as others gasped their last.

Since burning the entire forest to the ground to enact

vengeance fell into the cutting off my nose to spite my face territory, I'd had to keep a lid on the violent retribution I'd craved for the past two decades.

As the lack of answers grew longer, I turned up the heat on my alpha stare. "Someone better start talking, and I. Mean. *Now*."

Elias skidded into the room, and I rescanned the gathered shifters, annoyed at myself for failing to notice his absence. A hint of gangliness remained, but he was a long way from the scrawny fourteen-year-old I found in the forest seven years ago. "I was on watch, sir."

The rest of the troops' shoulders sagged with relief. Meanwhile, tension crept across the line of mine, tugging at the fresh wound there. The circle of life didn't include a section where kindness did anyone any favors. It was kill or be killed. Predator or prey, and survival of the most ruthless. As hard as I tried to shove away any mushy emotions that could weaken me as well as my pack, I had a soft spot for the kid. Finding a malnourished boy who'd been beaten within an inch of his life did that to a person.

Showing leniency endangered my position, and I was meant to lead. It was in my blood, the very marrow of my bones, and thanks to my past, I'd become an unabashed control freak. Never would I ever feel so helpless again.

Yeah, yeah, I know. The burden of being top dog, and heavy is the head that wears the crown. Ninety percent of the time I loved being the boss. But that other ten was a bitch. "Care to explain why I only found out about the enemies in our territory *after* being shot full of silver bullets?"

I strode toward the kid, clinging to my steel facade as his eyes flew wide. "What if they'd hit one of the pups? Or the elderly? Anyone but me? The reason I assign watch shifts is to ensure that sort of thing never fucking happens."

Elias's lower lip quivered, but he lifted his jaw, similar to the way Dr. Ryan had done earlier, although his had a hell of a lot more respect to it. "I take full responsibility. There was smoke in the east I thought might be a threat, but I didn't want to call for backup if it ended up being just a hiker or something else innocuous." I opened my mouth, but Elias rushed on. "Not that that's a good excuse. I messed up. I should've followed protocol."

"Did you see any strange activity on the south side? Hear any shots?"

The kid's throat worked a swallow. "No."

They'd hit so fast. I'd been running and then tumbling. I knew I was in trouble once my body refused to eject them, and town had been closer than the compound.

Dr. Ryan was so upset when I admitted I didn't think I'd make it to Doc Mullens on the far side of Guadalupe Falls. Very few were privy to our secret, and I hadn't been eager to add him to the short list. In a place where legends about mythical creatures abounded, it made it easy to grow a bit lax. The locals and visitors were used to exaggerated stories and imaginations running wild, so any slips got chalked up to that.

Still, I probably shouldn't have shifted in front of Dr. Ryan —had I not been disoriented and focused on healing, I wouldn't have. Too late now, and while her predecessor obviously hadn't mentioned the reality of the creatures inhabiting the woods, the fact that she'd gone from shock to offering to check my vitals suggested she remained cool under pressure.

My gut said Dr. Ryan would prove to be a good ally, the same way Dr. Vaughn had been when I'd taken Elias to him that first time. The kid nearly died from an infection that'd run rampant too long to simply heal it himself.

You say it like I'm some sexual deviant... Dr. Ryan's face flashed in my mind, and I idly wondered what it'd take to lure out her sexual deviant side so it could come and play with mine.

Seriously, what was wrong with me that I kept thinking about the pretty vet when there was a threat that needed to be taken out?

Must be some anesthesia left in my system, messing with my head. First, I'd deal with the current threat, and then I'd circle back and have a conversation with the vet about keeping our secret.

"Were there hunters in the forest today?" The season didn't start till fall for almost every type of game, but we were in a protected area, and wolves were never on the menu. Didn't mean we hadn't had to teach poachers a lesson before.

"No," Elias said. "I would've noticed, I'm sure of it. I'm sorry I didn't hear the shots or see you go down, but the smoke... It didn't look right. Didn't smell right. So I took Gideon with me to check it out. Like I said, I should've had someone fill my post while I was gone, but—"

"But nothing. The tower doesn't go unmanned." If he'd been with Gideon, he'd also been distracted. Due to the leftover landmines from his past, I'd let most anything involving his personal life slide. Far too much, it seemed, and now we both were going to have to face the consequences.

Elias dropped his chin so low it tapped his chest. "Yes, sir."

"Did you find the source of the smoke?"

He fiddled with the strings of his hoodie. "It was gone by the time we got there. Not just the smoke, but there wasn't any trace of a fire. The spot gave me the heebie-jeebies." Great. He hadn't a clue who shot me, but he got weird vibes from a stamped-out campfire.

"You four," I said, spinning toward my front line and pointing at Sasquatch, Diego, Tyrese, and my beta, Nissa. I hesitated as the last member's round belly caught my eye. Both noticing her baby bump and considering not sending her because she was pregnant would piss her off. She insisted she could do all the same tasks until she reached the tail end of her pregnancy, and while my small-but-there gentleman side wanted to argue, I also didn't want to be the misogynistic asshole she'd accused me of being when I first suggested she take time off from infantry.

Nissa arched a dark eyebrow, the gleam in her brown eyes practically daring me to dismiss her from the mission. Must be looking for a fight, and after being riddled with silver bullets, I wasn't in a pacifist mood myself. I'd rather she use her fists on our enemies than me, though, so I charged on, pretending I'd never considered anything else.

She and I had been friends since our teenage years, when we'd come across one another in the woods. After exchanging tragic backstories, we'd vowed to create a safe community for our kind.

A dimple flashed in her ebony skin as I rattled off orders, punctuating her self-satisfied smile. It was the same expression she gave Diego and me during those first few years together, whenever we attempted to explain she should be careful since she didn't have the same physical abilities as a male werewolf—right before she proceeded to show us up.

Despite knowing she could handle herself, the protective, sibling-type relationship had been hard for both Diego and me to shake. Once Nissa started dating Tyrese, Diego and I had issued multiple threats, and we'd had another big talk the night before their wedding. It took the guy a couple of years, but he won our trust eventually.

"Follow the trail of blood from the vet clinic to the south end of the forest. Cast a large perimeter and see what you can find." The sun had set, but wolf-form or human-form, our senses were heightened, so it shouldn't be a problem. We had an unknown enemy out there, and they needed to be interrogated and torn limb from limb ASAP. "Sasquatch, check every cave, nook, and cranny."

Sasquatch dipped his chin, which was the giant dude's response to most anything. A bow or a slight shake of the head. Maybe a short sentence or two. His long red hair and beard emphasized his old-school Viking warrior vibe, and while he rarely mingled with people, they instinctively shrank away from crossing his path.

"Elias," I said, and he flattened his arms to his sides as his spine went stick straight. He was beating himself up enough as it was, so I figured I'd give him a chance to redeem himself. "Take me to the site that freaks you out."

"I didn't say freaks me o—" My glare cut him short. "Yes, sir."

A knock echoed through the room, and I sighed. "Whatever it is, tell them it'll have to wait."

Diego went to deliver the news but returned with Monica, the elementary school principal. "She says it's an emergency."

If this was about the pups gnawing on the desks when their second set of teeth came in, I was going to lose my cool. What did she want me to do? Fit the kids with shock collars? The council had vehemently argued against it, so my hands were tied.

"It's one of the first graders," Monica said. "He fell off the rope bridge during recess." Normal playgrounds didn't stimulate werewolf children, so we'd installed an obstacle course akin to those found in basic military training. The rope bridge spanned a mile, weaving between treetops about three stories high.

This paper-pushing political stuff was the other sucky part of my position. Not to mention boring as fuck, and I'd assigned a task force so I wouldn't have to waste my time on it. "I fail to see how that's an emergency. Tell him to be more careful, but it's good for pups to get some bumps and bruises from time to time. Teaches them to be tough."

Monica shook her head. "You don't understand. The bone broke the skin and..." Worry flooded her features.

"Spit it out. We're in a hurry."

"He's not healing."

Not sure who gasped like a Nancy, only that it wasn't Nissa.

"As in it's taking a while?" I asked because that didn't make any sense. Monica shook her head again. "As in he's not healing at all."

CHAPTER FIVE
Conall

BEFORE HEADING INTO THE FOREST, I'd taken Elias along with me to the small room that doubled as our infirmary to check on the pup.

During the first five years of a werewolf's life, extra strength was the main perk, as well as the biggest issue, depending on whether you were the rambunctious wolf or their caretaker. By the time most pups enrolled in kindergarten, they'd shifted a time or two, but only with the aid of the full moon. Those first few transformations were rough, too, akin to breaking all your bones and being flipped inside out.

But with each passing year, our bodies adapted. Faster than our self-control, that was for sure. Losing one's temper often meant accidental shifting or that something as simple as a butterfly fluttering into a classroom would result in werewolves perched on desktops and running wild through the hallways. Basically, the younger lot were destructive, temperamental shits, so it was a good thing they were cute.

Sabine, our resident nurse, handled minor injuries that needed tending to. They didn't happen a lot, but luckily she had enough supplies to treat the injured first-grader. She'd reset the leg, wrapped it in a splint, and administered pain reliever.

I'd considered calling the vet, but Sabine thought getting the bone in proper alignment would be enough to stimulate healing. She assured me he was fine and that she'd continue to take good care of him with some "tricks of the trade," so I decided against calling Dr. Ryan just because I wanted to see her again. Especially since I had business to attend to.

Instead of taking the Jeep, I figured a run through the forest would do Elias and me both good. If only my damn ribs didn't ache like a bitch, my attempts to suck in more oxygen futile.

I rubbed at my side, regretting the climb up the hill and wishing I would've asked Sabine for a large dose of pain reliever myself.

"Do you need to rest?" Elias asked.

I shot him a murderous expression, indicating I'd turn him into my own wolfskin rug if he dared to ask one more time. This was the third, and it definitely wasn't a charm. "As I said before, I'm fine. The bones will finish healing in no time, and even injured, I could easily take out any threat that calls for it. Just take me to the site. Then we'll discuss the punishment for leaving your post."

Elias winced, and the sappy organ that pumped blood through my body gave an obnoxious, unnecessary tug. I'd slacked off in sternness as much as my troops had eased up on safety measures. No wonder someone saw us as a target.

"I just wanted to be the hero for once," Elias said in an admonished tone.

"It's not necessarily a bad thing to be, but sometimes it's a selfish thing to be, especially if you get yourself in over your head. Every member who follows my orders and works together in the ways that've proven the safest and most successful for the *entire pack* is a hero. What you wanted is glory, and that's less heroic."

He hung his head. "I know."

I batted away the urge to clap him on the back and assure him we all made mistakes. While true, he'd endangered the pack in an attempt to look brave in front of the guy he liked, and *that* wasn't okay. Softening the admonition wouldn't result in him learning a valuable lesson, so despite the incessant stabbing sensation in my chest and side, I clamped my lips and lengthened my stride, forcing him to have to work to keep up with me.

"It's just over the hill, in the center of the clearing." Even though we'd remained in our human forms for the hike, the meekness in his voice and the dragging of his limbs managed to convey that his tail was firmly tucked between his legs.

That was the way it should be, and Elias would learn that in time. At one point, I'd balked at being ordered around and following safety procedures, I deemed unnecessary. As frustrating as it was for the generations on both sides of the fence, it was part of growing up. Truth be told, I'd rather the youth in our pack not have to learn they and their families weren't invincible the hard way.

The instant I stepped into the meadow, every hair on my arms and neck pricked up, and the strange darkness hovering in the air permeated my skin and formed a tight knot in my gut. Looked like I owed the kid an apology for mocking his use of heebie-jeebies, as there wasn't a better word for it.

"See what I mean?" Elias asked in a quiet voice. "It doesn't feel right."

"It feels very, very wrong," I agreed. Since I'd lost enough clothes today, I shed mine before morphing into wolf form and putting my nose to the ground. Sulphur. Batshit. An overly sickly sweet flower I'd caught whiffs of here and there in the spring. The stringent scent grew stronger as I padded to the center of the area. At my next deep sniff, fire shot up my nose.

My eyes burned as though I'd inhaled an entire shaker of

pepper, and I backpedaled as quickly as my four legs could take me.

No matter how hard I shook my head, the searing sensation remained, so I pivoted around and raced to the nearby brook to rinse my snout.

It'd been a while since I'd literally stuck my nose in it. Used to happen all the time when I was a pup. I'd tasted insects that were never meant to be eaten and ended up swarmed by a hive of wasps that stung me so badly my mom shaved me bald in order to treat them with a thick, smelly salve.

There were lessons, and then there were lessons involving clippers. I'd always been proud of my thick gray and brown coat, and being shorn to the pink taught me a big lesson. One, don't be stupid, and two, don't go to Mom after stupidity occurred.

Mom's image formed, watery, as though seeing it at the bottom of a lake. At the glimpse of my brothers and sisters, I slammed the door on that memory, banishing it back to where it'd come from.

Never again had become my workout mantra from that day on. I flipped tractor tires, carried boulders back and forth across the community, and owned a few vehicles without working engines to pull around for fun. Lately, Diego had taken to training with me, the spark of competition pushing us both that much harder.

Whenever he got too cocky about how close he was to beating me, I pulled out my half- form. Not many werewolves could maintain the amalgamation of wolf and human, but it came in handy whenever I required use of my full lupine strength and senses while retaining the ability to speak.

After two decades of shifting, commanding my body to morph into human form was second nature. So why did pain explode in my chest? I braced my hands on my knees and wheezed out a few breaths. If anything, I should've healed faster on four legs, not reinjured myself during the transition. *"Fuck, that hurt."*

Good thing Elias wasn't in view, or he'd ask if I was all right again, and I'd get pissed I wasn't as healed as I should be.

I stepped into my clothes, grunting like an old man the entire time, and then returned to the meadow. Elias sat at the tree line in his hoodie and jeans, blinking red irritated eyes and rubbing at his nose.

"You ever smell wolfsbane?" I pointed to the spot that'd offended my inner wolf. Even human, it rankled, a handful of sharp nails slowly scratching the chalkboard as the acerbic air invaded my nose and lungs. And that was from ten yards away. "Don't get too close, but commit it to memory. If you ever smell that, note the location and then get out of there. Leave any further discovery to the experienced soldiers."

No matter how many times I paced the perimeter, I couldn't catch a single foreign scent. It was the equivalent of walking into a room that'd been cleaned so well you'd never suspect it'd ever been dirty. I hadn't encountered people capable of that sort of thing in over a decade, and if I had my way, I'd hunt them down and exterminate every last one.

But between my paranoia and the crushing sense of responsibility I felt for my pack, I'd let go of that desire to build a safe community. To the point that I also kept tabs on everything that happened in town. I hadn't been lying to the new vet about the deal the sheriff and I'd made. When it came to my enemies, he allowed me to handle them my way, as long as I kept him up to speed. In turn, he granted me full access to the goings-on in town so that we could ensure the safety of the people in both of our worlds.

While I hadn't gotten around to finding out more about the newest resident in Guadalupe Falls, like full name, address, and where she'd come from, only one person had recently moved in.

My brain struggled to believe it could be the veterinarian who'd gone wide-eyed over my existence. She'd even mentioned calling the cops.

Then again, she'd also said she could see why someone would shoot me.

People often wanted to dig deeper, forming preposterous ideas like frame jobs and conspiracy theories to explain away what they didn't want to be true. In my experience, the obvious choice was obvious for a reason, and it came down to that person being guilty as sin.

Why wouldn't she have just finished the job and killed me on the operating table? Or was that part of her plan? Gain my trust so she could later exploit it? It didn't make sense, yet it was the only possibility that did.

Shit. I'd flirted with her. I'd taken that damn shock electricity to mean we had chemistry, falling for her magic trick without a second thought. I'd be lying if I said I hadn't come up with a dozen reasons to pay her a visit in the near future, and hardly any of them would be considered noble.

Interrogation certainly hadn't been on the menu, and I figured bondage would be further down the road in our relationship, after we got to know each other better. Hours ago, the idea of acquainting myself with every inch of the woman's body had sparked. Even now, the memory of our interaction caused my blood to pump hotter.

It's just a spell. Who knows what else she did to me while I was out of it?

Come to think of it, *that's* probably why I wasn't healing. She must've done something to hinder the process while claiming to have fixed me up. It was smart, I'd give her that. But I'd give her a whole lot more, and none of it would be pleasant on her end.

"Boss? Are you...?" Elias flung up his hands, as if he might need to block an impending blow. "I mean, clearly you're fine and in top physical shape, but you seem...a little shaken? Is it okay to call you that?"

Disbelief and outrage trembled through my limbs at how easily I'd fallen for "Dr. Ryan's" act. A future of fun had just been wrecked, and it grated at me worse than it should, considering our interaction had been so brief.

But I'd get over it and do what I had to do, ugly and unpleasant or not, just like I always did. "Nah, that's glee. On the way here, all I could focus on was my vengeful mood, and now I'm going to get to unleash it on someone—it appears we have ourselves a witch problem."

CHAPTER SIX

Kerrigan

AS I SAT atop one of the stools and waited for the purple-haired bartender, I felt that same odd sensation that'd pestered me all day long.

It's nothing. If you keep checking over your shoulder, all that's going to happen is you'll look as paranoid as you feel.

The itch grew stronger, until my neck burned, and I scratched at the spot to see if it'd help. Too bad I kept my fingernails super short—less disgusting bodily fluids to scrub out later.

I tapped out a rhythm on the countertop with my fingertips until the one other guy seated at the bar lowered his bushy brows at me. The people at the tables and booths seemed to be having a blast as they wined and dined, the laughing and jibing stirring up longing. Going to bars with Grams and her friends had been one of the most frustrating yet hilarious highlights of my week. We'd hit the town on the weekend, a bunch of golden girls and a single gal in her twenties, and in between their matchmaking attempts, Grams would get more and more rambunctious. One night while dancing on the bar, she'd even yelled out, "I need to get my granddaughter laid already. Any takers?"

Residual embarrassment had me shaking my head and smothering a laugh, and then sorrow joined the anxiety corkscrewing through me. Since my earlier finger-drum solo hadn't been appreciated, I bounced my foot on the bottom rung of my stool. The clinic had been so quiet and slow today that part of me felt like I'd imagined yesterday's bizarre encounter.

How did one go about asking after werewolves without getting a rep as the kooky lady? I highly doubted that would land me many clients. I'd considered heading to the diner, but the waitress hadn't struck me as the most...let's go with "down to earth." When she'd spoken about the satanic cults, she sounded more jealous she wasn't a member than horrified.

I needed a credible source, so I went to where the most credible sources in any town were found: the local bar. Guadalupe Falls only had one, a place named Lou's.

Once the bartender came over, I just had to gather my courage and force words from my mouth. A tactic I also planned to deploy as I worked to fit into town and drum up some clients. Be brave, speak up, and hope for the best.

Here she comes... "Hi," I blurted out. "I'm new in town. Just moved in last week."

The woman leaned across the bar, a welcoming smile on her face. "I figured. I usually know most everyone who wanders into my bar. Name's Gina."

Score. She was familiar with all of the townsfolk and was a business owner like me, so yay for girl power bonding. "Kerrigan. I bought Dr. Vaughn's animal clinic."

"Ah, that rings a bell now that you mention it. I take my pets there, so I received your welcome letter. Nice to officially meet you."

We nodded and exchanged another smile, and this was going better than expected. I reached for a worn coaster and fiddled with it. "I haven't met many people yet. Dr. Vaughn before he left, of course, along with the few clients who didn't immediately jump ship. I'm a really good vet, I swear. Top of my class in school, and I landed a highly competitive internship where I learned a lot but also got fed up with constant mansplaining, which prompted me to open my own clinic."

"I believe you. On all counts, especially the mansplaining," Gina said with a laugh that alleviated my apprehension and tempted me to park my ass on this stool for the rest of the night. Was there anything better than a bartender who made it safe to pour out your thoughts and feelings? "When it comes to shots or anything else for my fur babies, I'll be sure to bring them to you."

"Thank you so much. I appreciate it."

"How do you feel about people who bring in random animals they've found hurt in the woods? Say, possums or raccoons or other creatures most vets might hesitate to treat?"

Okay, so no mention of wolves, but we were creeping closer to the right direction. "That they're saints," I answered honestly. "The people. Although I'm not saying the animals don't qualify for sainthood as well. I can't handle watching any type of critter suffer and would do everything I could to save them."

Gina beamed. "In that case, say hello to the client who'll bring you the weirdest cases ever."

"Can't wait," I said with a laugh, although I was fairly certain I'd already experienced the weirdest case ever. I glanced at the man down the bar and scooted closer to Gina, forming a more intimate bubble so we wouldn't be overheard. Sure, I could wait until after I ordered to get the scoop, but I might chicken out, and the bar would likely get busier during the dinner rush, so I needed to ovary up and spit it out. "I, uh, actually met this interesting guy yesterday. Do you happen to know Conall Shaw?"

Gina's open, friendly posture changed, her features shuttering as she straightened. "I do." I waited.

So did she. Just blinked her long lashes before lifting a strand of her brightly colored hair to study the ends.

"Oh," I said, unsure where to go from here. "I was just wondering about him."

Nothing at first, as if Gina had been paused. Then the corner of her mouth quirked up in a way that made me think I was the butt of a joke. I was well aware Conall was way out of my league, so if she was laughing at my odds, fair.

That same sense of foreboding that refused to leave me alone grew stronger, until the nape of my neck blazed with it.

"Is that right?" a deep voice asked from behind me.

"Fucksicord!" I jumped so high I nearly toppled off my stool. A large hand pressed against my lower back, the only thing that kept me from crashing to the floor, and my heart thundered so loud I was sure he could hear it, too.

Good thing that's impossible.

Oh, shit, maybe not. According to most mythology, werewolves have supersonic hearing.

The smug smile that spread across his face suggested that he could, in fact, hear the panic flooding my body.

Once again, I thought of a poor little bunny, hopping as fast as it could. Like me, it'd be no match for the man with the anaconda-size arms. With me seated on the stool, the cocky bastard dwarfed me to an almost humorous degree. I craned my neck, straining to take in his full height, and my oh my, were there a whole lot of inches. The heat of his hand soaked into my skin, stirring up a tornado of clashing emotions.

The guy undoubtedly had a domineering streak about a mile wide.

At that thought, desire quickly took the lead, taking my legs from flesh and bone to jelly, and I was pretty sure this was my libido's way of punishing me for ignoring it so long.

Conall's expression reeked of getting one over on me, but

the humor quickly drained from his features as his brow turned stern and his eyes narrowed to irritated slits.

Okay, so I'd been prying. But did he have to look at me like he might eat me?

And did I have to enjoy it so much?

My tongue stuck to the roof of my mouth as my gaze fixated on the pursed lips he'd use to devour me. His scruffy beard showcased them nicely, and another surge of heat flared as I studied his ruggedly handsome face. Had it been that freaking fine yesterday?

In my defense, it'd been difficult to catalogue everything, given so much of his body had been on display. Plus, I was short and he was tall, and didn't I get points for saying it was a nice face now?

Or that it went well with his extremely jacked body?

The way he blew air out of his nostrils like a bull about to charge brought me back to my senses, although I was starting to worry I'd permanently lost a few.

I peered past his sharpened features, noting his irregular breathing and the sweat beading his brow.

Conall's voice came out along with a growl that confirmed I wasn't off base about him being upset. "What exactly do you wanna know?"

CHAPTER SEVEN
Conall

GINA RETREATED A FEW PACES, allowing me to take it from here—not because she had any reason to fear me. The pint-size woman seated on the stool in front of me, on the other hand...

Having my palm fitted flat against Dr. Ryan's lower back made it harder to think, a sure sign I should remove it, but I couldn't convince myself to follow through. If this was going to be my last chance, I might as well indulge in as many touches as I could.

What a shame it'd be to rip out that pretty throat of hers. I hadn't even gotten to taste it yet. Hadn't pressed my lips to the fluttering pulse point at the base to see what it took to make it beat faster.

And that's enough of that.

Any spell that used wolfsbane involved hurting my people, and there was a kid with a broken bone in the pack infirmary.

"Well, first of all..." Dr. Ryan stood on the bottom rung of the stool, and my arm fell to my side as she placed a hand against the side of my face. She drifted her thumb over the part of my cheek that'd been a ragged mess yesterday, and my boiling rage slowed to a simmer, even though I didn't tell it to. "Are you okay? You look..."

Her pink tongue came out to wet her lips, and *shiiit*. Before I got swept away in those probing gray-blue eyes, I should drag her out into the woods—far enough no one would hear her scream—and take care of her already.

"Hot. As in pale and clammy." She moved her palm to my forehead. "Not that the lumberjack-sexual thing you've got going on doesn't work for you..." Her cheeks flushed, the same way they'd done when I'd snuck up and called her out for prying into my personal business.

She's a spy, she's a spy, she's a spy.

She glanced at our audience, who'd gone from scooting away to staring with interest, and thanks to the added height of the stool, her chest knocked against mine as she moved her mouth close to my ear.

I gripped her waist so she wouldn't fall.

Because if she landed in the ER, it'd be harder to extract information. *Yeah, let's go with that.* It's also why I hadn't called the sheriff to get her first name. That'd definitely implicate my involvement when she disappeared shortly after.

"But you're definitely running a fever. You sound kinda wheezy, too," she said, and did the fact that I wheezed harder mean I'd already fallen under one of her spells? "How do you feel? Any injuries you need me to take a look at?"

I closed my eyes and attempted to regain control. How did she make that question sound more like a sexy request?

Because she's playing you, you fool. And worse, you're falling for it.

Before I completely lost my head, I pushed her down onto the stool, my hand remaining firm on her shoulder to keep her there. *She's a witch, she's a witch, she's a witch.*

"Let's take dinner to your place." I lifted my finger to snag Gina's attention. "Have you ordered already?"

Minor consolation: Dr. Ryan was at least as flustered as I'd been a second ago. She glanced behind the bar, toward the shelf of alcohol and the window to the kitchen, as if she'd forgotten where she was—casting around for information like the dirty witch she was. "Oh. Yeah. But we can just stay here at the bar to ea—"

"Gina, can you grab me two double burgers and two orders of fries? To go."

Dr. Ryan gulped, and I decided I'd better soften for long enough to get her to her house where we'd be alone.

"Does that work for you? Trust me, you can't go wrong with the burgers and fries."

She nodded, and I sat on the stool next to hers, turning so my legs caged her in, her knees against my inner thighs.

"Before I answer any questions, you at least owe me your first name." I possessed a better built-in lie detector than most. I cast my senses outward, focused on picking up the beating of her heart.

She fidgeted, taking up the foot bouncing from earlier, when I'd been watching her through the window with the help of a nearby bush to camouflage me. "I suppose that's fair. And I didn't mean to pry. I mean, I did, but I wasn't trying to dig up dirt or anything. Not that there's dirt to dig up."

Seriously? *This* was the woman who'd pulled one over on me? She rambled so much I wasn't even sure *she* knew what she was saying. Her pulse sped up, but in a way that suggested I made her nervous rather than she wasn't telling the truth. Or was that what she wanted me to think? "Still haven't heard that name."

"It's Kerrigan. Speaking of names, did you know that your name means"—she lowered her voice to a whisper—"wolf wolf? A little redundant, don't you think?"

I rubbed my fingers over my jaw, never taking my eyes off hers. "I haven't the faintest clue what you're talking about."

It should be illegal for a nose crinkle to be so adorable. "Nothing. Forget it." Kerrigan spun toward the counter but met the resistance of my knee.

I scooted closer, using my massive frame to its full advantage. "Explain."

"It's probably going to sound a little bit crazy. Possibly even stalkerish. But you should know that I get bored easily. See, there's nothing for me to really do around here in the evenings. I've been reading this survival guidebook, but too long of trying to cram the info into my brain and I go cross-eyed. My TV's not hooked up yet, either, so I get bored."

"Explain more succinctly."

She fired a dirty look at me that only made me smile, and that served to piss her off further. But I continued to stare, sure she'd give in as most people did underneath my steady glower.

"While I was doing some googling about the town, I..." Kerrigan fiddled with the ring on her finger, spinning it round and round. "I've always been fascinated by the meaning behind names..."

"This is succinct?"

"You're succinctly being a pain in the butt. Long story short, Mr. Impatient, Conall's an Irish name that means 'strong wolf.' Shaw is derived from the Gaelic word *Sitheach* meaning wolf. I'm guessing your family were all...*you know.* Thus the name."

First I'd heard of it. Checking the meaning behind names was such a girly thing to do, which made me wonder if my mom had purposely gone so on the nose as she'd been searching out baby names. Unfortunately, she wasn't around to ask.

There was a reason I'd spent the last half of my life training, fighting, building a compound, and doing whatever it took to protect my people at all costs. It was the result of being helpless against preventing a coven of witches from murdering my entire family, along with the majority of my original pack.

I hadn't crossed paths with a witch since, but my hatred hadn't faded through the years. Which was why I couldn't let myself be amused by the way Kerrigan had called me Mr. Impatient or delude myself it was casual interest that led to her googling me late at night.

"So?" She batted her eyes at me, and it was going to suck ass to extinguish that light inside of them. "Am I right?"

"I'll neither confirm nor deny."

"But you said you'd answer my questions." Exasperation wafted off her, and how many times was I going to ruminate on how hard it was going to be to kill her? She was so fun to mess with, and under literally any other circumstances, I might be able to forgive and forget. But the only good witch was a dead witch.

"I asked what you wanted to know," I said. "I never said I was going to give it to you."

Her gaze dipped to my crotch, and she casually twisted a strand of hair around her finger. "You sure you don't wanna give it to me? I can handle it, I swear."

If I wasn't mistaken, she was attempting to flirt information out of me by turning that last line into an innuendo. While my brain understood, my body didn't get the memo about not falling for it, and I shifted in my seat, cursing the wooden stool for being so ungiving.

Gina placed the bag of food in front of me, and with a grunt that couldn't be helped, I stood, thanked her, and gestured for Kerrigan to come along.

Kerrigan leaped off her stool and gave Gina a huge farewell wave. "It was nice meeting you. Too bad somebody" —she jerked a thumb at me—"interrupted. I'm sure I'll see you around, though."

Gina glanced between Kerrigan and me, silently asking after the situation. Her face made it clear she'd already formed a soft spot for the doc, because that was what Gina did. Our only vegetarian wolf, her home housed a variety of pets—a few of which she'd personally rescued— and she was silently asking forgiveness on Kerrigan's behalf, even though she didn't know what she'd done besides ask about me.

At the tiny shake of my head, Gina's shoulders slumped, so she clearly understood the outcome wasn't going to be good.

And it wouldn't be. This was just a waiting game now. One I'd win. If my damn right side wouldn't insist on constantly throbbing and robbing me of breath, that'd be great. It'd never taken so long for me to heal, and I spent an irrational hour earlier today wondering if the spell preventing that pup from healing was affecting me, too.

Upon further investigation, I found out that a group of pups had been near the meadow around the time the smoke started. The scratch test we conducted confirmed they'd all been affected.

My skin, on the other hand, healed up as usual. Now no one was allowed on the obstacle courses until we sorted out the situation, which caused a lot of unhappy children and parents, as that pent-up energy needed somewhere to go.

Once we get to Kerrigan's house, I'll eat and do some prying of my own, and the pain will fade. Retribution is nice like that. It makes you forget anything else exists for a while.

The world momentarily tilted on its axis, leaving me panting and seeking out the countertop for purchase. I braced my palm flat on the dinged wood surface and worked to catch my breath.

Kerrigan scrunched up her eyebrows, the worry in her face so genuine I had to remind myself yet again she was playing me for a fool. "Something's clearly wrong. Go ahead and ignore my other questions if you want, but as your doctor, you should at least answer a few of my health questions."

I shushed her, reminding her we weren't alone. Most people instinctively gave me and my people space, but having a veterinarian loudly proclaim herself as my doctor was going to raise questions.

"I walked here, so we're taking your car to your place," I said, gripping the bag in my fist tighter and sweeping my arm in front of me. "After you, Dr. Ryan."

CHAPTER EIGHT
Kerrigan

CONALL SHAW TOOK up the entire passenger seat of my Mini Cooper and then some, not to mention the way his hulking presence soaked up all the air, leaving me struggling to catch my breath as much as he was. It felt like I'd been running a marathon ever since he called me out for asking Gina about him. No finish line in sight, just all gasping and burning muscles.

I was acutely aware of every shift of his body, every glance, every everything.

My mouth kept watering over the scent of greasy food, but it wasn't the only thing getting my appetite going. It'd be nice if the hottest guy I'd ever laid eyes on wasn't a bit of an asshole, but a zip of excitement still coursed through me at the idea of having dinner together. I didn't think my flirting tactics had worked on him, but maybe I wasn't as rusty as I thought.

Take that, two-year relationship with my vibrator. It wouldn't be so bad if it weren't an exclusive relationship that wasn't really doing it for me anymore. Last week I'd attempted to relive some stress, only to tell my battery-operated boyfriend, "It's not you, it's me. I'm afraid I need more."

The man currently doing the silent, stoic thing beside me was definitely more.

Don't get ahead of yourself. Just because he insisted on having dinner at your place doesn't mean you should jump into bed with him, even if he'd be into it.

Honestly, I could use a friend, and since Conall didn't strike me as the commitment type, I should probably stick to friendship. Crossing lines always complicated everything, and I'd inevitably screw it up because that was what I did in relationships. Whether from awkwardness, cluelessness, or sabotage, it didn't really matter when the end result was the same.

Me, alone once again.

It'd be nice if I could get a guy like Conall, who clearly had his pulse on the people in town—as the incident in the bar with Gina proved—to endorse my services, even if he couldn't admit to using them.

I glanced at him huffing away in the passenger seat, holding his right side. Once the silence stretched past my comfort zone, I decided to start the ball rolling with some small talk. "Work was super slow again today. Same as it's been since I arrived."

"Mmm."

Really? That was all he was going to give me? I hoped he'd take charge like he had in the bar, but evidently it was up to me. Too bad for him, because I steered conversations in one direction, and my comfort topics all involved nerdery.

"Here's the thing, research is my specialty." His frowning at my statement made me want to stuff the words back inside, but in for a nickel, in for a dime. "I like knowing how things work. Science and anatomy are my jam. And you, well, you're an anomaly. It's not like I could exactly google 'werewolves' and get accurate information, so I searched up your name. While I'm more of a science and facts gal, there's something about astronomy and words with power. Not that they have power if you don't let them, but it can also be motivating and inspiring, you know?"

The line of his mouth grew tighter, suggesting no, he didn't know.

"In case you're wondering, 'Kerrigan' means dark or dusky. I was so disappointed when I first found out. But Ryan means king, so when I put them together, my name means dark king. Which makes me sound super badass, if I do say so myself."

The slight arch of his eyebrow spoke to a certain amount of skepticism.

"What? You don't think I'm a badass? Because while you were asleep for most of your surgery, I wielded that scalpel like a total boss."

Another noncommittal "mmm" and I'd be tempted to slam on my brakes and tell him he could walk if he wasn't going to contribute. I guess I wasn't as tough as I liked to pretend to be, since I'd never follow through, especially with the way he kept favoring his side.

"Anyway, that's the long way of saying I thought the wolf-wolf thing was sort of funny. I'm sorry if I offended you by mentioning it."

"I don't offend easily."

Apparently, he didn't elaborate or cough up information easily, either.

I hit my blinker and took the sideroad that led to my cabin. "You seemed pretty offended that I asked Gina about you."

Nothing but steely silence and the slight narrowing of his espresso-colored eyes. The golden glowing thing must only happen in tense situations.

"She's the first person I've clicked with in a while, even before I moved to Guadalupe Falls, so that's why I asked her about you. I was just curious is all." "Why?"

"Um, because of that whole anomaly thing I mentioned.

You're not supposed to exist." I eased my car down the bumpy driveway, wincing as the fender scraped bottom a few times, and then pulled up in front of my rental cabin.

"Home Dilapidated Home." I killed the engine and reached for the bag of food. Not that it was heavy, but I wanted to lend any assistance that allowed him to rest his side until I convinced him to let me examine it. "This is why I suggested we might want to stay at the diner. The cabin is more of a deathtrap."

As we climbed up the rickety porch steps, Conall studied me like I was the one who morphed from a human to a wolf at a moment's notice. "What do you mean by that?"

"The doors don't hang quite right, the floor creaks, and the electricity is persnickety. And possibly out to get me, but that's not a thing, right?"

Why was he being so difficult? I'd only talked to him for all of five minutes yesterday, but he hadn't been this hostile—and he'd been severely injured at the time. He made that joke about his prison wallet, and I deluded myself into believing he'd also been flirting.

Suddenly I was thinking about how the closest house was over a half mile away.

Then again, if he wanted to hurt me, he could've done so yesterday. Besides, it'd be easier to convince him to let me take a peek at his ribs after settling in and eating. Then surely he'd see that I only wanted to help.

At the sound of the key in the door, Sir Pounce came streaking toward me with a loud meow, as if I wouldn't notice him otherwise. I bent to pat his black kitty head and give him some love. He arched his spine, his ears flattening and his hair going full poof as he hissed at Conall.

"A black cat," Conall muttered. "Wow, she's not even *trying* to hide it."

I scooped Sir Pounce into my arms, doing my best to assure him there was nothing to fear.

"Sir Pounce is a he, actually, but cats aren't well-known for sparing feelings." I scratched between his ears. "He's hesitant around strangers and..." Was it rude to compare werewolves to dogs? No one covered that in etiquette lessons.

Sir Pounce climbed onto my shoulder, his claws digging into my shirt as he sniffed and hissed. Conall's nostrils flared, and I quasi-expected him to snarl. I placed a hand against my kitty's furry chest so he didn't go biting off more than he could chew. "Is this gonna be a problem?"

"Not for me," Conall said, and at the dropping of my jaw, he shook his head. "What I meant to say is that I can deal with a cat. *He's* safe."

I pressed my lips together to stifle the laughter bubbling up in my throat and patted Conall's arm. "Don't worry, big guy. I'll make sure to keep you safe as well."

His stony expression remained.

Come on. That was funny. Maybe a smidge condescending, but funny all the same.

"Make yourself at home," I said, although evidently, I didn't have to.

Conall stood in front of my bookshelf, pushing books to and fro and studying the spines as though he were searching for something in particular.

Sir Pounce would complain if I didn't feed him first—regardless of the state of his food bowl, which was plenty full—so I added more treats to his dish. After washing my hands, I opened the fridge that hummed like a carburetor on its last leg. "Would you like something to drink?" Unfortunately, peering at the barren shelves didn't make better options appear. "I've got water, Coke, milk, and half a bottle of wine."

"Coke's fine," Conall said, right next to my ear, and he chuckled at my resulting jolt.

It was the first time today that I'd seen a flash of the guy I met last night. "Jeez, way to sneak up on me. How don't you make more noise?"

"The noisy go hungry."

"Not in my house." I handed him one of the cold cans of Coke. "I can storm to my fridge, and the ingredients don't dare move, they're *that scared* of my power."

He gave me a smile that danced along my nerve endings and then, as if he remembered he'd resolved to be grumpy tonight, quickly stifled it.

A little too eager to keep things going, I lifted the bottle of wine. "Can you get drunk?" "Not on that," he said, turning up his nose.

"I do have a bottle of Jack Daniels tucked away if you'd rather."

Was I imagining things, or did he seem impressed? Like with the smile, it was fleeting.

"It takes quite a bit to get me drunk, and it burns off fast."

"Do you want to get a tad buzzed, then?" It'd make it so much easier if I didn't have to wrestle him to the ground to examine his ribs—not that I believed that was possible. And I could use some liquid courage to calm my somersaulting nerves and prevent me from overanalyzing every move and word.

"Better not," Conall said, his tone resolute. "I've still got a lot to take care of tonight."

In spite of him not being the friendliest companion so far, the idea of cutting our hangout short dug at me, a pang of rejection coming along for the ride. I did my best to remind my deluded brain this was a casual, impromptu hangout and not a date. Since it didn't take me much to get drunk and his ribs needed tended to, I probably shouldn't imbibe, either. With a sigh, I grabbed a Coke for myself, and we headed back to the living room and sat on the couch.

Conall closely shadowed my moves. Like all up in my grill as I pulled out the food, no personal bubble room. If he were anyone else, I'd insist on more space, but the scent of his cologne invaded my senses, and the smoking-hot thing definitely helped.

Either food would fix his sour mood, or we'd eat in tense silence. The sad thing was that after a week and a half of only myself as my own company, I'd take it.

As we dug into our burgers and fries, his gaze continued to roam the room, cataloging everything I owned. It felt a pinch invasive, giving me enough of a taste of my own medicine that I understood why he'd been so upset at the bar.

But surely this put us on level ground, and my inquisitive side bobbed to the surface once again. "So, what exactly would it take to get you to answer a few of my questions?"

CHAPTER NINE
Kerrigan

CONALL SWALLOWED the last bite of his double burger and reached for his Coke. His eyes never left mine as he downed the sugary liquid, big gulps that made his Adam's apple bob up and down.

Was it possible to be hypnotized by that tiny movement? Because I was damn close.

Yeah, after he left, I'd definitely need to cue up *Creed II* and take care of business. If watching a guy drink was turning me on, it'd obviously been too long. The *clink* of the empty can hitting the coffee table echoed through the quiet. "How about you answer a couple of my questions first?"

His tone bordered on threatening, and my heart thumped faster. More with desire than fear, so clearly my common sense had gone on vacation. I sucked salt off the end of my fingertips, and at his hard swallow, adrenaline coursed through my body. No idea why he was fighting it, but there was definitely attraction on his end, too.

I twisted so that my knee knocked into his. "Let's go the *quid pro quo* route. I'll answer one question for every question you answer."

"You have yourself a deal, Dr. Ryan." Conall extended his hand, and I slipped my palm into his. Instead of shaking, he held on, the tip of his pointer finger resting directly over the pulse point on the underside of my wrist.

"What was your real reason for moving to Guadalupe Falls?"

Real reason? I lowered my eyebrows, wondering if I'd ever told him *any* reason. "There was a vet clinic for sale that I could actually afford."

The muscles along his jaw flexed, leading me to believe I'd somehow given the wrong answer. Too bad it was the only one I had. "Have you lived here all your life?"

"No."

"Where else have you liv—?"

"Ah, ah, ah," Conall said with a click of his tongue. "You already asked your question." His fingertip pressed harder against my wrist, and every ounce of my blood rushed toward that spot at once. He paled in front of my eyes, a rasp coming out along with his words. "Where do you keep your potions?"

Why was he speaking as though I were some snake oil salesman who'd gone to college in a saloon during the Wild West Era? "Are you talking about the meds I gave you? They're at the clinic."

Bile churned in my gut, his interest in me suddenly making sense. So much for being good at reading social cues. "Are you some kind of tweaker?"

One corner of his mouth turned up, that cocky lilt that was perpetually quirked over something I'd said or done. "Nah, I ran all the meth dealers out of town years ago."

I wanted to ask about his family, but sweat beaded his forehead and his chest heaved, so I switched into doctor mode. "Does it feel like you can't get any oxygen when you inhale? Or that your lungs won't expand?"

"You already had your question. You chose to ask me if I was a tweaker."

My jaw dropped. "Not to sound like a little kid, but that's unfair and you know it." "I'll tell you what's unfair..." He dipped his head so that his eyes bored into mine. A shiver tiptoed down my spine, my amygdala finally producing the fear it should've last night when I'd discovered the existence of werewolves; earlier at the bar when Conall caught me asking about him; and a moment ago, when we started this interrogation game. "I thought about you several times last night, and it was harder than it should've been to conjure up the hatred I've always felt for you and your kind."

Whoa. What?

Hysteria surged, turning my blood to ice, and Conall gripped my hand tighter, that fingertip pressing so hard the bones in my wrist groaned. I grappled against his grip, tugging and tearing at his fingers when I couldn't break free, and this was the perfect example of why you weren't supposed to invite strange werewolves over for dinner.

"Conall." My voice trembled, and his pupils dilatated, robbing me of breath. "I have no idea what you're talking about, but this isn't funny. You're hurting me."

"Tell me about"—*wheeze*—"the spell, and maybe I'll show you mercy."

What little color remained in his features drained until his lips were as pale as his skin, and I wanted him to leave, but my instincts screamed there was something physically wrong with him. Not that it excused his assholish behavior, but I also recognized a wounded animal in distress. "I think you're going into shock. Let me go, and I'll grab my medical bag and fix you up, okay?"

He shook his head. "You're a witch. You've put...some sort of...spell on me." His eyes rolled back in his head, only the whites showing.

But before I could react, he jerked himself straight, and the haziness faded from his features.

Since I could tell how much effort it'd taken, I did my best to wedge my way inside that tiny opening. "I'm gonna go ahead and ignore the fact that you called me a witch. Now, be reasonable and let me help you. Or release me and hit the road. Those are your options."

"So that you can summon your coven and tell them everything you've discovered? Not a chance. That's why I have to take care of you now. Before you have a chance to call for backup."

All right. He'd passed the point of delirium, so time for a new plan. If he broke my wrist, I'd never be able to perform the surgery he obviously needed, and my efforts to calm him had gone nowhere. If I managed to snag my phone off the coffee table, I could sprint out of my house, call 9-1-1, and hopefully get the help both of us needed.

I glanced around the room, calculating the distance between me and my phone. The front door. The patio door. Which gave me a better chance?

"I'm faster," Conall growled, and the organ in the center of my chest pumped so hard and fast I worried I'd have a heart attack before I ventured an escape. "As the alpha, I'm obligated to take care of you. Do you think I *want* to torture information out of you? That I'm happy about it?"

His gaze raked down me, hungry and invasive, yet I craved the passion swimming in his eyes as they flashed gold. Scared and turned on. Well, that was a new combo for me.

"I'm furious at you for turning out to be the one thing I despise more than anything else in the world. Your kind brutally murdered practically everyone I cared about. You took away my home, my family." Using his grip on my wrist, he yanked me closer, and his other hand wrapped around my neck. "And in spite of all that, here I am trying to justify fucking you out of my system."

My breath lodged in my throat, not because he was squeezing my neck, but because I knew I was in trouble and so shouldn't entertain thoughts of seducing my way out of this. Then again, it might buy me some time...

Conall's lids fluttered, and his fingers slipped from my neck. His enormous body swayed, and he caught himself on the coffee table, his reflexes ridiculously fast for someone whose lips were turning blue.

This was my chance to run.

I stood, planning to do just that. Then I internally screamed at myself for dropping to my knees to check his pulse. This was the part in the horror movie when I called the heroine too stupid to live. Guess I owed her an apology.

"Don't move," he barked, the muscles in his arms straining as he attempted to push himself to his feet. Instead, he crashed into the coffee table, sending my phone flying onto the floor, so there went my backup plan. "No offense, but I think you should take your own advice. Your heart rate is dropping, and you're in hypoxic-ischemic shock. I'm gonna go grab my bag and—"

His low growl sent goosebumps across my skin, and yep, I was an idiot for not fleeing. Conall let loose a howl, the haunted sound traveling deep down into my bones.

Perhaps I just needed to appeal to his human side, although if I were being honest, I preferred the wolf. "Remember how you came to my vet clinic all shot to hell? How I helped you? I didn't call the cops, either, because you asked me not to."

"Not that it would've done you any good. Like I told you, Sheriff Martin and I have an understanding. I'm not sure why you saved me, but that spell you did hurt a member of my pack, so that's not going to be enough to save you."

Another idea popped into my head. "Is it possible you have rabies? Is that why you went from calm to insane in a matter of minutes?"

Judging from the fact that he roared in my face, it was the wrong thing to ask.

A ring of sweat formed around the collar of his T-shirt, and my hand trembled as I stretched it toward the side he kept holding. He flinched as I placed my palm flat over his ribs, but he didn't snarl or snap his teeth, so I rubbed it lightly over his muscles. Sure enough, I heard a crackle. That crumpling newspaper sound meant one thing, and it didn't bode well for him. "Listen, you've got a leak in your chest, and I need to get you to the clinic so I can fix it. I'm not sure how magical your healing abilities are, but I'm guessing they won't bring you back from the dead."

If only one lung had collapsed, death wasn't imminent, although it might feel preferable, considering the rapid deterioration of his oxygen supply.

Dazedly, he shook his head. "No. You're trying to...rid of me."

The man in front of me transformed, not into a wolf, but every inch a predator. His fight or flight instinct was kicking in, and naturally he'd be the kind of guy who preferred to fight.

I suppressed my panic the best I could and affected a casual expression. "Fine. I'll just wait till you pass out and then do what I need to, you stubborn ass."

Pretty sure he wanted to reply with another threatening growl, but the knock at the door drew both of our attention.

Conall barked an order to come on in, and two people burst into my house. An early twenties white male with shaggy brown hair who could pass for a member of a boy band, and a woman with deep bronze skin and ebony dreads adorned with golden cuffs. In spite of the tense situation, she was so strikingly beautiful that all I could do for a couple of seconds was gape.

"What did you do to him?" she barked, and that woke me from my stupor and dampened my hopes for assistance.

"I didn't *do* anything to him. Besides dig the silver bullets out of him and save his life. But he took off last night before I could finish up, and he's suffering from a punctured lung."

Doubt crept into her expression. "He would've healed from it by now."

"Not if shards of his rib cage keep poking holes in his lungs. He's out of alignment, and my theory is that any time the bones try to mend together, they jab another hole. He's leaking air, and it's getting worse every minute we sit here doing nothing, so it'd be great if one of you can talk some sense into him."

"Is that why he keeps holding his side?" the guy asked, concern swimming through his eyes as Conall writhed and wheezed. "I knew something was off, but he got mad when I asked if he was okay."

The woman sighed. "Sounds like him." She crossed the room, placing her hand on Conall's shoulder as she squatted next to him. "Conall, come—" A gasp escaped, and then she frowned at me as if I'd caused the destruction. She appeared to be having an internal debate, her disappointment palpable as she said, "We'd better let the doctor fix you up."

Conall gargled a ragged, oddly wet response I couldn't make it out, and considering his associates looked to me to translate, they hadn't understood it, either.

I latched on to one of his arms and heaved—dang guy didn't budge. "We need to get him to the clinic ASAP."

"No," Conall said, so at least he had that word down pat. But then his eyes rolled into his head again, and with all his effort going into that last word, he lost his struggle to remain conscious.

Relief and worry clashed inside of me, contrary emotions I'd have to sort out later.

Without his interference, the two people I suspected were also werewolves loaded Conall into the bed of a shiny black pickup truck that followed me and my Mini Cooper to the clinic.

And when the woman brought in the chains she kept in her truck "just in case" and suggested we use them so Conall wouldn't come to and do more damage fighting us off—or you know, kill me before I could fix his lungs—I didn't object.

CHAPTER TEN
Conall

I CAME TO WITH A GASP, but when I tried to sit up, I met the resistance of heavy chains. A loop around my shirtless torso secured me to the cold exam table, and both my wrists had been cuffed.

Chains? She chained me down like some kind of rabid animal! The good doctor had asked if I had rabies, too.

At the sound of metal clanking against metal, the woman who'd somehow bested me turned, looking every bit the sexy mad scientist in her lab coat and goggles. "Oh good. You're awake."

"What's this?" I asked, yanking against my shackles. Blood pumped through my veins in feverish bursts, but a distant part of me recognized I could take a full breath again. After going twenty-four hours without enough oxygen, I inhaled enough to leave me dizzy, basking in the way it coated my throat and inflated my lungs.

"Drastic measures and all." Kerrigan removed her goggles, set them aside, and then came a step closer. "I dug out the bone shards that kept puncturing your chest wall and right lung and reset your ribs. You should've seen the scar tissue—so thick I'm not sure your bones could've broken through many more times. Don't you feel better now that everything's in the proper alignment? With that done, you'll be able to fully heal."

I didn't say anything, just glared.

"Glad you asked," Kerrigan deadpanned. "I reestablished negative pressure by sucking out the air with a needle and syringe. It'd take a dog about a month to recuperate, but I'm guessing it'll be much faster for you." She lowered the stethoscope to my chest, and I debated snagging her arm and tugging her close enough to put the fear of God in her. "Your heart rate is steady, if a bit high."

"That's because I'm chained to a fucking table."

"Well, if you hadn't been so unreasonable, I wouldn't have had to resort to such aggressive measures."

"If you don't undo these restraints—and I'm talking *right fucking now*—you're going to see just how unreasonable I can be."

"The incision site is already mending itself nicely," she prattled on as if I hadn't spoken. "That whole skin meld thing isn't quite as neat as my stitches, but I wish all my patients had that ability. It'd save oodles of treating and healing time."

I lifted my head, straining to scan the room. "Where are Nissa and Elias?" I'd texted them as a failsafe once I'd arrived at the doctor's cabin. It was also supposed to serve as motivation to follow through, my reasoning that I wouldn't be able to face either of them if I failed to take care of Kerrigan. Plus, I'd considered that I might need help disposing of the body since mine had been on the fritz.

"They got called away for an emergency."

"I can't believe they left me in the hands of a witch."

Kerrigan peeled off her gloves and tossed them in the nearby trash can. "I'm really trying not to let that hurt my feelings, but I gotta tell you, I'm not a fan of you calling me that. And what the hell's wrong with you that you take advantage of the lonely new woman in town, pretending like you want to have dinner together only to accuse me of being a witch and attack me?"

Better question: what the hell was wrong with her that she lectured a man who could snap her in half so easily? Did she have no sense of self-preservation?

Kerrigan pointed a finger my way. "*This* is why I asked around about you. If someone would've told me you were a raging psychopath, I would've refused your dinner request. Maybe it's sad to eat alone every night, but if the alternative is dealing with a moody werewolf, I'll take sad and boring any day."

With every word, I became less and less sure of the conclusion I'd drawn about the woman at my bedside. Without my chest and side screaming so loudly, and oxygen finally flowing to my brain, thoughts came easier. Clearer. I'd used my senses to scour her living room and kitchen, and there hadn't been any objects or scents that suggested she dabbled in the occult, much less was immersed in it. Even the best of spies couldn't hide scents from noses like mine. "You're saying you're not a witch."

Kerrigan crossed her arms, every inch of her petite posture on the defensive side. "Are you saying there is such a thing? And if so, would they be as shocked as I was to discover werewolves exist?"

Doubt flickered, mostly because I'd been so sure when I'd followed her throughout the day. I'd also wrapped my hand around her neck, and if I'd done that without her deserving it...? "You could be acting."

Kerrigan rolled her eyes. For a spy, she sure wore her feelings on her sleeve. "Why don't I give you the number to my drama teacher? My acting was so poor during my high school production of *A Midsummer Night's Dream*, I was demoted from a woodland creature with three lines to a tree that constantly got in trouble for waving its branches too much."

A snort came out—I couldn't help it. I sat up as much as I could and wiggled the cuffs around my wrists. It was Nissa's work for sure, and she was in for an earful. But first things first. "Are you going to unshackle me?"

Kerrigan's chin tipped up in that same defiant way it had yesterday. "Depends. Are you going to try to break my wrist again?"

"If I'd meant to break it, it'd be broken, Doc."

An offended noise sounded in the back of her throat. Okay, so I probably could've given a better, more tactful answer. With the truth crystalizing, shining a spotlight on Kerrigan and how she hadn't lost any of her sass even after I'd been a scary raging asshole, the contempt I'd clung to faded.

Thank God I hadn't hurt her.

Lead filled my lungs, leaving them too heavy mere minutes after they'd returned to normal. I'd almost killed an innocent civilian. A beautiful, fiery one that hadn't freaked out and left me to die. She'd saved my ass twice now. Not great for my pride, but I appreciated it. This needed to be the last time, though.

Kerrigan removed her bloodied lab coat and snagged the jacket she'd been wearing earlier off a hook near the door. She slipped one arm inside, the fabric of her shirt growing tighter across her breasts as she wrestled with the other sleeve.

I attempted to readjust my dick without the use of my hands, but big surprise, it didn't work. The chains grew heavier and more irritating, and I hated being tied down more than about anything else in the world—hated anything that prevented me from being completely and totally in control. "Kerrigan."

She abandoned her battle with the other sleeve of her jacket, her lips parting on an exhale that didn't help the mashed-junk situation. Then she blinked at me, as if she couldn't figure out why I'd possibly called her name like that.

"My patience is growing real fucking thin," I gritted out. "Time to undo these restraints." "Are you going to say please?"

Really? After my interrogation tactics, she hadn't gotten through her skull she should fear me? I thought she was smarter than that. "I don't say please."

"If you're going to continue being unreasonable, you can just lie there until your friends return to pick you up. A nap might do you good. Try to wake up on the other side of the bed, m'kay?"

So it was gonna be the hard way, then. Having had to expend too much energy already, I'd hoped to avoid it, but evidently Kerrigan needed a display to knock some sense into her. Not only did creatures like me exist, but there was also a witch on the loose, and that meant my life was about to involve more danger than usual.

Like it or not, I needed to cut ties with the ridiculously stubborn doctor.

Drawing upon all my strength, I braced myself as the heavy links dug into my wrists and lower abdomen. Inch by inch, I wriggled the chain secured around my middle down to my waist, liberating me enough to sit up the rest of the way. Then I yanked, clenching my jaw against the pain in my right arm as I pushed my muscles to the limit.

The metal groaned, and that certainly got Kerrigan's attention. She backpedaled and blindly reached toward the medicine cabinet, assumedly in search of something that'd knock me out.

No way was I going to let her give me another dose of that groggy shit. Especially since my error in judgment meant I still had a witch to hunt down.

The cuff on my right wrist creaked and complained and then finally snapped, and she let out a yelp.

"You-you broke it," Kerrigan breathed more than said.

I slid free of the coil that'd secured me to the table and swung my legs around until my feet hit the floor.

Kerrigan snagged a vial and a syringe from the open cabinet. She jabbed the needle into the top.

"These restraints might've held while I was sedated. But awake, there's not a whole lot that can stop me." With a roar, I wrenched my left arm with all my might, and the chain securing my other wrist to the exam table snapped. The peeled-apart links fell to the floor, hitting the tile with an echoing *clang*, and the vial Kerrigan had been holding slipped through her hands.

The little glass bottle rolled across the floor and bumped my toes. Since I'd broken the links on my left wrist instead of the cuff, the few still connected to my fat silver bracelet rattled against the tile as I scooped up the vial. I tossed it aside, satisfied by the shatter of glass against the wall. "No more drugs. I suppose I do owe you an apology, though."

Kerrigan gaped at me, her mouth hanging open. After several seconds of silence, she asked, "Is that supposed to be one? Usually apologies involve words about being sorry and promises to never do it again."

"I'm sorry I thought you were a witch."

"And?" she prompted.

"And I'll never do it again, since I know that you're not one."

"That was the worst apology ever," she huffed.

True. But too soft and she'd go thinking I was some overgrown puppy she could tame.

Not only was it miles from the truth, my world would chew her up and spit her out. "Tell you what. I still owe you information, right?"

The hesitance in her features disclosed she suspected this was a setup, but she finally nodded.

I took a step toward her, and my pulse beat a savage rhythm at the sharp rise and fall of her chest. I closed the distance between us, bending until our noses nearly touched. While her eyes widened, the fact that she didn't step back— didn't even attempt to reach for another vial of medicine or anything else she could use as a weapon—proved this was as necessary as I worried it'd be.

Her fragrance invaded my senses, a feminine mixture of blackberry, vanilla, and some exotic flower that didn't grow around here beckoning me closer. My focus waned as the line of her collarbone seized my attention. I traced it with my eyes, and my fingers itched to traverse the same course until I managed to coax out a hum of pleasure. That quickening throb at the base of her throat called to me like a siren song, her delicate neck so achingly close it might be worth it to crash against the rocks and take a quick taste before I drowned.

Damn it. It'd be nice if my gutter-diving thoughts wouldn't work against me. I curled my hands into fists, fortifying my self-control so I wouldn't reach for her, and infused my words with a warning I hoped she would heed as much as I prayed she didn't. "There's only one thing you should know about me...

"I'm not quite a man, and I'm not quite a wolf." I let out a low growl, putting an exclamation point on a truth intended to strike fear. "I'm the primitive amplification of them both. The feral in between. There's no taming, no reasoning, no humanity or mercy, and I came damn close to ripping out your throat tonight. If it weren't for the punctured lung, I would've done it, too."

The words echoed in the space between us, which was too much and not enough at the same time. As I backed toward the exit, I ground out one last sentence. "From now on, you stay out of my business, and I'll stay out of yours."

CHAPTER ELEVEN
Kerrigan

IT'D BEEN NEARLY a week since my last encounter with Conall, and yet any time the door to the vet clinic swung open, I half expected it to be him.

With each passing day, I also changed my mind as to how I'd react if he dared to darken my door, injured or not.

Call the cops?

Give him the silent treatment?

Chew him out some more?

Once I'd fixed his punctured lung, he'd made it pretty clear he didn't want anything to do with me, so why did my brain keep fixating on the thrilling portion of our encounter instead of the terrifying ending, when he admitted he'd considered ripping out my throat?

"Man, I must be hard up," I said to the bunny roaming the front desk as we awaited her owner's arrival. On Monday, I'd treated her for a case of the snuffles that required antibiotics, and today I'd trimmed her teeth to prevent future health problems.

Since BunBun didn't seem to mind lending me one of her extra-long ears, I prattled on. "It's not easy out there in the human dating world. My last relationship was three years ago, and the entire time, Grams kept telling me I was settling, choosing boring and safe when I deserved fireworks and adventure. In the end, *he* dumped *me*. Not great for the self-esteem, you know?"

BunBun settled into a furry loaf position, encouraging me to continue spilling my woes.

"Part of the reason I bought this clinic in the middle of the nowhere was because I heard Grams in my head, telling me to be bold, brave, and take life by the balls already." Using a couple fingertips, I petted BunBun's furry face and stroked her ears. "But look at where it's landed me."

BunBun lifted her head, her nose twitching like crazy.

"Don't look at me like that. *Of course*, I'm glad you and I met, but the truth is, I'm short on patients, and my one other frequent flyer is short on patience." I chuckled at my own joke and then sighed. It wasn't much fun without anyone else joining in. "Maybe I should just go back to being an introvert who never talks to people. Animals who always remain animals are where it's at."

Business continued to trickle in, like a leaky sink that outputs about a cup of water a day. I'd administered a couple of vaccinations this week, and when someone called and asked about grooming, I told them to go ahead and bring in their poodle. Beggars couldn't be choosers and all that.

"I suppose I should force myself to get back out there. Stroll around Guadalupe Falls, meet more of the townsfolk, and see if there are any events going on. As for dating, there are other fish in the sea. No reason to go prowling for wolves in the woods, right?"

BunBun and I *both* needed to avoid wolves, and the way she bumped her nose against my hand meant she agreed with me. Well, that and she wanted more lettuce, so I extended another leaf her way.

"And the thing with fireworks is they're a good way to get burned." That line Conall had delivered in my living room, about fucking me out of his system, played in my head rent free, scrambling my thoughts and unfurling heat in my gut. The unbridled desire in his voice haunted me, not because it'd scared me, but because I feared it was the most passion I'd ever experience.

And that was without him following through.

He'd been delirious. Short on oxygen. Calling me a witch.

Revealing the murder of his family and destruction of his former home. My heart knotted, and my insides turned to mush. If I let those sappy emotions linger, my absurd impulse to soothe his inner beast would land me in trouble. Again.

The chime over the door sounded, causing me to jerk upright.

In walked a werewolf, and my ability to swallow became compromised. It wasn't *the* werewolf I'd been obsessing over, but one of his lackeys—Mr. Boy Band from the other night.

He glanced around while rubbing at the side of his neck. "Hey. We, uh, didn't get a chance to officially meet." He strode closer and extended his arm. "I'm Elias."

Hesitantly, I took his hand and gave it a quick shake. "Dr. Kerrigan Ryan." I pulled free, glad for the sturdy counter between me and BunBun and Elias. I tiptoed my fingers toward my phone, just in case.

"Anyway, Conall asked me to com—"

The door opened, and a man in black slacks, shiny shoes, and a white button-up with a silky green tie strolled in. A German shorthaired pointer with a beautiful white-and-brown-speckled coat obediently stood at his side, the leash in the man's hand slack.

The newcomer's gaze sharpened as it landed on Elias, who bobbed his head in a greeting but addressed the spot over the man's shoulder instead of the man. "Mayor."

"Elias." The businessman—the mayor, apparently—then turned a wide, toothpaste-commercial-worthy smile on me. "And this must be our newest resident, Dr. Kerrigan Ryan."

For some reason I almost curtsied, my awkwardness rising faster with two dudes to juggle. Er, interact with. I couldn't stop stewing over how Elias had been going to finish that last sentence, and meeting new people never failed to overwhelm my circuits, and why was the freaking mayor in my vet clinic?

He extended a hand. "Please excuse me for taking so long to welcome you to our lovely little town. It's been a busy couple of weeks. Mayor Craig Sullivan, at your service." He reeled in the leash wound around his fist and gestured to his dog. "And this is Jasper."

I rounded the counter halfway, squatting to greet the dog, since at least that came naturally. I let him sniff my hand and then patted his head. "You're a good doggie, aren't you?"

"He's up-to-date on his shots, but I figured I might as well bring him along to meet our new veterinarian." Mayor Sullivan leaned an elbow on my countertop, and I straightened and double-checked that BunBun was still safe and secure on the desk. "By the way, have you heard about the carnival this weekend? You should come."

"Oh. That sounds fun. I was wondering if there were any events going on. I haven't met many people yet, so I'm trying to gather my courage to get out there and let them know there's another vet in town."

"Perfect. In fact, I'll meet you there. Introduce you around." Mayor Sullivan glanced over his shoulder, at where Elias stood—poor guy looked about as awkward as I'd felt moments ago, and my heart went out to him. "Unless...I'm sorry, Elias. Am I stepping on your toes? Were you about to ask the doctor to go to the carnival with you?"

Elias made a sour face, his lip curling along with his nose. "Nah, she's not really my type." He craned his neck and aimed an apologetic smile around the mayor's head. "No offense."

If my ego took any more blows, there'd be nothing but crumbs left. But Elias wasn't my type, either, not to mention too young for me. The guy who shouldn't be my type, however...

No more thinking about Conall. Even if that's damn near impossible with his lackey here for some inexplicable reason I'm dying to find out.

"Well, then." Seriously, if Mayor Sullivan turned up the wattage on his smile anymore, I'd need sunglasses. "What do you say? Will you meet me there?"

An excuse sprang to the tip of my tongue, a vague reply about having to check my calendar, in case I chickened out. But he'd offered to introduce me around, which could be good for business. He'd also asked, not demanded, unlike another cocksure man who barked orders and jumped to wrong conclusions without bothering to ask a simple question like: are you, or are you not, a witch?

I also heard Grams in my head, encouraging me to push my limits and obnoxiously clucking at me when I hesitated. As if all that wasn't enough, BunBun hopped closer, her cocked head and big chocolate-brown eyes seeming to say, "We talked about this, remember?"

Once you dove in, you had to find a way to keep on swimming. "I'd love to."

"Perfect." Mayor Sullivan slipped me his business card and told me to just shoot him a text when I arrived at the carnival grounds. "I'll let you get back to it, but I'll see you then." He tugged Jasper's leash, and the two of them exited the clinic, leaving me and Elias the werewolf alone in the office once again.

A thought hit me, one that should've struck earlier. "Sorry for the interruption. I should've asked if you were injured or having trouble healing. I hope you'd tell me instead of just standing there, bleeding out while the mayor and I talked."

Elias's attention remained out the window, on the mayor as he climbed into his vehicle with Jasper. Slowly, he turned to me. "No. Nothing like that." He reached into his back pocket and withdrew a wad of cash. "Conall told me to come settle his account."

Wow, he *so* did not want to see me. Not a newsflash or anything I should experience disappointment over, but the pinch in my gut didn't care. "I didn't even send him a bill."

"He said this should cover it." Elias placed the bills on the countertop and then lowered his voice, even though we were alone save BunBun. "Thanks for fixing him up. I'm sure he didn't say it, so I'll do it for him."

"Yeah, I'm guessing the guy's never apologized or expressed gratitude in his life. There's pride, and then there's being a pigheaded ass who refuses to say please, sorry, or thank you, even when someone is trying to save your freaking life." It felt good to rattle off a few of the grievances I should've kept inside my head, and since I was on a roll, I kept on unleashing. "And you can tell Conall I said all that if you want to. I don't care." Okay, I did, but I was trying not to, and wouldn't relaying the message make it my choice to stay away from him instead of the other way around?

Elias's gulp echoed through the room. "I'd, uh, rather not give him that message. He's already..." He retreated a step and rubbed at his neck again as if I'd tackle him and demand he deliver my insults to Conall if he didn't escape fast enough. "Anyway, goodbye or whatever."

With that cryptic nonsense, Elias charged out the door, right as Mrs. Stewart arrived to pick up her bunny.

And I did my best to convince myself it didn't matter if I never encountered another werewolf again.

CHAPTER TWELVE
Conall

I DROVE the Jeep up a rocky side trail, the windshield wipers swiftly clearing the rain that'd slowed to a drizzle. Once I couldn't go any farther without scratching up the paint and dinging the sides, I launched myself out of the vehicle and raced toward the green beam of light that cast the entire area in a slime-hued glow. There'd be claims of another UFO sighting buzzing around town tomorrow.

Hell, I wished that was all it was. Aliens would be easier to handle.

Earlier this evening, three of my people had been at the lake and spotted a large plume of smoke. They radioed for backup as they headed to check it out, hoping they could catch the culprit in the act.

Now they were stuck inside a witch's version of a booby trap. The instant they'd crossed the border of the sigil trap, it ensnared them within its circle, zapping anyone who tried to get in or out.

Irritation raked at my insides, and I wanted to rip off my shirt and howl at the moon. Not that it'd do any good, but how could a witch—or several as the case may be—be eluding us so easily?

This was the second time this week our enemy had evaded us. Yesterday, another member of my pack had been hunting, spotted an unfamiliar figure, and sprinted after them. During the pursuit, Claudia undershot a jump to the other side of a ravine and slammed face-first into the sheer cliffside. She'd made the leap countless times, so I didn't buy that she merely miscalculated—especially since she also wasn't healing. Luckily, she'd managed to claw her way up to safety, or she would have suffered broken bones on top of the busted nose and scrapes running the length of her shins and forearms.

I crested the hill in time to see Diego charge the column of light. Sparks erupted, and a zap accompanied the acrid odor of sizzling flesh. Diego yelped and swore, the charge enough to send him flying back on his ass.

I strode over to where Nissa and Tyrese stood. "Anything new?"

"I picked up a strange scent on the west end," Tyrese said. "Me and a couple of men followed it to the creek. We spotted tracks but lost them in the rain. Before returning here to help Diego and Nissa try to free Betty, Cara, and David, I instructed them to keep poking around for clues and to report if they found anything more."

"What kind of tracks?"

"Human and wolf." Tyrese peeled his gaze off the column encapsulating our people and turned to fully face me. "The footprints could belong to someone in town, but it's unlikely, as they don't normally wander this deep into the woods without us sighting them in advance. As for the pawprints, I can't say for sure they weren't one of ours, but I asked around, and no one admitted to being out and about. Plus, I would've noticed if the scent were familiar."

Kerrigan lived on the east side, a fact that had nothing to do with anything, and why did she keep coming to mind time and time again? Lately, my senses and instincts were cranked to high, screaming that something was fishy, and that was clearly throwing me off.

"Betty's not doing so well." Nissa jerked her chin toward the circle, where Betty had just crumpled to the ground. Her daughter, Kara, and son-in-law, David, huddled around her, doing their best to assure Betty even though their features spoke of suffering and desperation. "We can't hear anything they say, but David tried hitting the forcefield from the inside, and the skin on his fist isn't healing."

Shit. That meant they might die while attempting to break out.

Nissa rested a hand over her swollen belly. "The little guy doesn't like it, either. He's kicking like crazy, as if he wants to get away."

Both she and Tyrese had taken to calling the baby *the little guy*, even though they hadn't had an ultrasound to discover the baby's sex. Before I'd burned the bridge with the new vet in town, I'd contemplated asking if she would perform one for my beta. If I could talk Nissa into it, that was, which was a big if. A few months before she ran into Diego and me, she'd escaped from a medical facility where they'd experimented on her, lots of testing her pain tolerance and healing, so she was wary of anyone in the medical field.

Not even her husband could convince her to see a doctor, local or in another city. I wasn't sure Nissa would take kindly to me suggesting a veterinarian instead, but my main concern was the health of her and her baby.

Which also meant getting her as far away from the witchy vibes, in a way that wouldn't cause an argument. We didn't have long before curious humans would seek out the odd light, but at least it'd require a hell of a hike. "You two secure the perimeter. I'm gonna take a closer look and figure out what exactly we're up against."

I strode toward the illuminated column, raising my

shoulders against the snapping electricity that nipped at my skin.

Scorch marks crisscrossed Diego's fists, forearms, and his face. While the red, puckered flesh undoubtedly hurt, his hide had knitted itself together, so at least there was that. I placed my hand on his shoulder and told him to rest while I took a spin at it.

I met David and Cara's eyes through the trap, keeping steady contact despite the burning it caused. Then, even though they probably couldn't hear me, I raised my voice, adding assurance to my words. "Just hold tight. We're gonna get you out of there."

I squatted and studied the ground. I couldn't see the lines of the magical sigil, which made it next to impossible to attempt to break the circuit. Based on the high current coursing through my body from merely being near the trap, it wasn't weak enough to break by simply smearing the line of the circle anyway. A spell this powerful often came equipped with a failsafe.

Throughout history, there'd been plenty of strife between the different supernatural species as they battled for the diminishing amount of land where they could live without fear of discovery. But witches usually attacked as a coven. They hit hard, without warning, so this didn't fit their usual M.O.

Footprints and *pawprints*. Coincidental? My gut said no.

The Crescent Pack resided up north in one of Maine's national parks, around four hundred miles away. A good three days' travel in wolf-form, or one full day by car. If any of their wolves had wandered through, they would've checked in. Those rules and boundaries were in place for a reason, and wars had been started over less. Earlier this year, the alpha of their pack and I had a major disagreement about my obligations and the future in general. I'd shown him that if it came down to a brawl, I'd win, and our packs had given one another a wide berth since.

"No weak spots," Sasquatch's deep voice said next to my ear, so low it was like hearing only the bass line of a song. "This is high-level sorcery."

The guy had seen a lot of things in his day. Although I joked it was due to him being a good foot taller than everyone, it was more that he'd wandered the forests for so long, with nothing but the company of a hawk he got defensive over whenever anyone dared to ask. He used to remain on the sidelines, never joining a pack until he and I met up. Sometimes I experienced a twinge of guilt for pulling him into the fold, even though I also believed he was better for it.

A muffled scream filtered through the wall of light. Cara had shifted—well, partway. Claws tipped the ends of gnarled, furry fingers, and wolfen ears and an incomplete snout had formed. Her body quivered as she raked her hand down her face, leaving cuts that welled with blood.

We were out of time. I shucked my jacket and kicked off my shoes. I demanded everyone give me space and then backed up several yards so I could gain extra speed. Summoning all my strength, I propelled myself forward and slammed into the high-voltage beam, shoulder first.

A bolt fired through me, bouncing me off the wall with an explosion of light, and I caught myself in a low crouch.

A sizzling noise popped in my ears, steam rising off my body as the drizzle of rain hit the angry red skin of my arm.

With a roar, I charged again. Searing pain exploded behind my temples, and I was afraid to check and see if my skin was being flayed from my bones or if it just felt like it.

No matter.

I dug in my feet, my claws shooting out to help me stand my ground. My snout elongated and my muscles roiled under my skin until I'd become the crude fusion of both beast and man. I tore at the surface with my teeth and claws, biting back the yelp that wanted to come out as blisters erupted and burst across my hide.

The revolting odors of charred hair and hide invaded my nostrils, and I steeled myself, gritting my teeth and forcing myself forward.

One inch. Another.

A howl of agony ripped from my throat. My body turned from flesh, fur, and bones to a vessel of torturous pain as I threw the last of my strength behind my momentum.

The outlines of my pack members took shape. Then light burst, so bright the world went completely white.

In the next instant, I was on all fours on the ground, Cara, Betty, and David in front of me. No more green light. Just voltage and crispified skin and the faint glow of the moon.

I pushed to my feet, gathered them in my arms, and walked out of the charred circle.

People rushed forward to check on Cara, Betty, and David, and distantly I heard them thanking me.

I lumbered over to a nearby stump and parked myself there. No reason to ever move again. I shook my head, sure the voltage in my teeth and bones could recharge a battery. Ugh, my ears rang, too, the high-pitched squeal leaving me twitchy.

"Conall," a garbled voice said, and I searched for the source.

Whoa. When had Nissa, Tyrese, and Elias shown up?

"Are you okay?" Nissa asked, dropping to her knees in front of me.

Depressing a finger to my ear, I wiggled the fleshy triangle part around, experimenting whether or not that stopped the buzzing—it didn't. "I'm fine."

"Phew, he's healing," said Elias. "I was worried he'd need to see the vet, and that would not go well at all."

The vet. The sexy, pillow-lipped vet with the fierce

attitude and a distressing lack of fear regarding werewolves. I definitely wanted to see her.

I couldn't, though. The reason eluded me right now, and then I was glancing at the blackened area conspiracy theorists would call a crop circle.

"I hate things that don't fit." How could we exploit our enemies' weaknesses if we couldn't pinpoint the source? If we couldn't predict the attacks. It'd take that much longer to get under control, and too many of my people had been hurt already.

"Well, if that isn't the understatement of the year." Relief flooded Nissa's features as Tyrese used her outstretched hand to pull her to her feet.

"How are Cara, David, and Betty?"

"Shaken up," Tyrese said. "But they'll be fine."

"Are they healing?"

Tyrese and Nissa glanced at each other, which meant no.

"Damn it." I stood. "We'd better clear out and get them to the compound."

We started toward the tree line, and I bent and scooped up my shoes and jacket, not bothering to put them on.

Elias walked beside me, and with my mind clearing, I pondered the meaning of his comment regarding the vet. "Did you settle up with Dr. Ryan like I asked?" "Yeah. I went by and gave Kerrigan the money this afternoon."

My spine jolted straight, the name like a ramrod of lightning. Kerrigan. Not Dr. Ryan. I frowned, not liking that one bit, regardless of the fact that it was her name and I'd been the one to tell Elias to go to the clinic.

Just leave it alone. Put her out of your head and focus on your own business. "How'd she seem?"

"Um, okay."

Of all the times the kid chose not to expound, he picked now. The longer the phrase rang through the air without further explanation, the more I wanted to act like a scavenger, begging for scraps of the picked-apart meat. "*Um*? What's with the *um*? Is she okay or not?" Elias slowed to gape at me, which prompted Nissa and Tyrese to pause and study me as well.

I scowled at my audience, letting them know I didn't appreciate their shock and awe. "What? I nearly ripped out her throat for moving to the wrong place at the wrong time. I can't ask if she's okay?"

"You can," Nissa said, the corners of her mouth quivering. "You just normally don't follow up with the people you threaten, falsely accused or not."

I glared, and Tyrese's posture tensed, his loyalty to his wife and his fealty to me grating against each other. If he thought I'd hurt his wife, he wouldn't hesitate to tussle with me, but we both knew that wasn't necessary. Not only because we had other shit to focus on, but also because Nissa would put us in our places.

My beta hooked her hand in the crook of her husband's elbow. "Let's go see if we can pick up anything on the east end, babe, and leave Conall to seethe at the forest instead of us."

"What about me?" Elias squeaked, his unspoken silent plea to take him with them loud and clear.

"Go ahead," I said so they'd leave me be. This wasn't about Dr. Ryan. It was about an intruder coming into my territory and fucking shit up.

Elias bounded toward Nissa and Tyrese like an overgrown puppy, but then he abruptly spun around. "The 'um' was because Kerrigan's still pretty upset at you. That's why I was glad you didn't need a doctor—I'm not sure she'd treat you. But she really is all right. The mayor came into the clinic while I was there, and the two of them got friendly fast. He invited her to the carnival, and she seemed excited about it."

Nissa winced and pinched the bridge of her nose.

"Seriously, Elias? Have you ever heard the expression 'less is more?'"

The kid appeared utterly confused. "What? I held back the part about her calling him a pigheaded ass with too much pride. Something like that, anyway. Although she did say I could tell him she said so."

"Just go to the truck, Elias." Nissa nudged him on down the hill, in the direction of the road. "We'll meet you there."

Nissa lifted that haughty eyebrow she always spoke volumes with. "Are you in control?"

"Of course, I am," I snarled, contrary to my claim. Tensions were high, so sue me. If the good doctor wanted to be wined and dined by the illustrious, highbrow mayor, she was free to do so.

It'd be good for her to meet and mingle with the townsfolk. Then she could forget about me and my pack and get on with her life. No looming danger, at least not from or because of me.

"You'll let me know if that changes?" Nissa asked.

"No," I automatically retorted, and then we both laughed. I scrubbed a hand over my face. "It's fine. The mayor's a..." I meant to say *decent guy* but couldn't quite force out the words now that I was picturing Kerrigan on his arm. "I'm just worried about all the injuries that are stacking up. The faster I hunt down the culprit, the sooner I can assure the safety of the entire pack, and we can get back to normal life."

"And could that normal life possibly include a certain veterinarian?"

"Not in this lifetime." Better to get it through my head. Entanglements with humans were frowned upon—to say the least—and with Kerrigan out of the equation, there'd be less complications, no matter what threat we faced. From the outside, Guadalupe Falls seemed like a sleepy town, but because of the sacred ground and that other thing involving protected forested areas where we could roam as far and wide as we craved, it would always attract a certain supernatural element.

Which wouldn't be a big deal if we all could live together in peace. Centuries-worth of wars resulting in dwindling numbers left me cautiously pessimistic.

"We'll get 'em." Nissa's voice dipped with the growled threat. "Whoever they are."

"We always do." I gestured for her to go on, watching as she, Tyrese, and Elias melted into the darkness of the trees. Neither of us had lost a fight since we were teenagers who'd been caught off guard. Never again, we'd vowed on countless occasions, and together, we'd taken down plenty of enemies.

But between the sinking sensation in my gut and that annoying, insistent voice in the back of my head, I couldn't shake the feeling we were on the brink of facing our biggest threat yet.

CHAPTER THIRTEEN

Kerrigan

"WHAT DOES one wear to her first town fair? Or carnival-thing. Whatever it's called."

Sir Pounce lifted his head. When I didn't drop the off-the-shoulder navy-and-white shirt I'd held up over my strapless bra as he rubbed himself against the thighs of my jeans, he gave a chirrup that meant I was neglecting my duties. I quickly threw on the top and petted between his ears. He twisted his head and presented his chin, so I scratched until he rattled a contented purr.

Helpful fashion advisor, he was not. But his purr alleviated stress, upped oxytocin, dopamine, and serotonin, so I let it slide. While my furry companion was much appreciated, it didn't mean I wasn't looking for human companionship, too, and the idea of going without sex for the rest of my life made me want to cry.

And in spite of all that, here I am trying to justify fucking you out of my system. Last night I'd taken the edge off by indulging in a steamy session with my vibrator that'd included that line, the memory of Conall's large hand around my neck, and a daydream that involved him peeling off my clothes in the living room and fucking me in front of the window, where anyone could drive by and see.

But no one ever drove by, and that wasn't an option, and that was precisely why I was headed to the carnival to meet up with the mayor. Not that I thought this was a date or I'd decided if I would be interested in one with him, but I did need clients in order to continue providing for Sir Pounce and myself.

Besides, while that sort of volatile passion worked great for fantasy sessions between the sheets, in real life, I wanted a reliable guy I could be myself around. One who made me feel safe and didn't tell me to stay out of his business and avoid me to the point that he sent another person to pay his bills.

I turned toward the mirror and twisted a red, white, and navy scarf into a headband, wishing my stomach would stop twisting itself into complicated pretzel shapes.

I'd given a presentation on a new surgical procedure in front of an auditorium of first-year students. How silly to be so nervous over a small-town event. The summer dress I'd originally slipped on made me feel like I was trying too hard, and the checkered red and white shirt and ripped jeans ended up tipping too far toward the hoedown side of the scale.

"This ho's not going down like that," I'd told Sir Pounce before selecting this top from my closet.

To finish off my outfit, I slipped into some simple white Keds. Paired with the ripped jeans, I hoped I appeared casual and approachable.

And like the type of person you'd entrust your pets to.

"Wish me good skill." I kissed Sir Pounce goodbye, climbed into my car, and drove the handful of miles to the heart of town. Even if Guadalupe Falls wasn't so teeny tiny, it would've been hard to miss the whirring carnival rides peeking over the tops of trees, the cloudless blue-sky backdrop painting the picture-perfect image of summer fun.

After I parked my car, I sent a text to the mayor as

promised, and then entered the melee and searched for friendly faces among the crowd. The aromas of fried foods, grass, gas from the machines, and cotton candy mingled with the excited screams and laughter of the people soaring through the air, delighting over or regretting their decision to climb aboard.

Grams's gravelly, affectionate voice drifted through my mind, from the one other carnival I'd attended during my senior year of high school. It'd been a fundraiser, with the help of the student body's parents, so naturally Grams had not only attended but ridden every ride. "Don't spoil my fun with your logical brain," she'd replied to my quip about not trusting machines that were put together and taken down within hours. "Either you learn to take a risk, or the risk takes you."

"That doesn't even make sense, Grams," I'd countered.

"Neither does your face, yet I love it like crazy."

I snickered aloud at the memory, drawing a few stares. Hopefully, the townsfolk found muttering and giggling to themselves endearing. Throughout the years, several medical professionals had declared Grams's lifestyle problematic. She smoked, drank, and raked men half her age over the coals during poker games. Whenever a doctor told her she needed to slow down, eat better, exercise more, and act her age, Grams would simply find a new one.

During her final year on earth, after she was diagnosed with lung cancer and I expressed my concerns over her health, she hadn't kicked me to the curb. Instead, she declared that life was to be lived, and while we hadn't always agreed about how, she'd lived a full, happy life, with no regrets.

"You made it," a male voice said at my side, and I turned, a smile already spreading across my face. Mayor Sullivan had cotton candy in one hand and a book of tickets in the other.

"Yeah, I heard it was the place to be today." I racked my brain for something else to say, preferably a clever joke or anything that would make my attendance seem more natural. Nothing like that came to me, so I resorted to my default. "How's Jasper?"

"Good. He's very well-behaved, but not so much so that I dared to bring him along. He'd be sneaking off toward the hot dog stand in no time."

"I don't blame him. I'm about to attack it myself, they smell so good."

Mayor Sullivan chuckled, and my heart rate returned to a nice steady pace. This was fine. I could do this.

It wasn't until after he'd insisted I call him Craig and bought me a hot dog that I contemplated whether a steady pulse went in the pro or con column. Why did we women always associate tachycardia with passion?

Mayor—er, Craig—didn't incite a riot of emotions like a certain werewolf, but sometimes evolution required an accelerating push. Perhaps big and brawny helped our ancestors survive, but these days, sensible and reliable equaled less inconsistent and easier to maintain and sustain.

"That's not how you buy a car," Grams had said when I'd described a sedan I was considering buying in a similar manner. "Fast, fun, and unforgettable. That's how you want your ride, whether it's a man or a car. Well, maybe more like fast to notice you, not too fast in the bedr—"

"Okay, we get it," I had cut in, since the salesman mentioned he'd had a heart attack the previous month and I hadn't wanted him to have his second there in the car lot.

"Ah, here's the row of tents where local vendors sell their goods," Craig said. "Why don't I introduce you around?" See? He was intelligent and reliable, and a pragmatic option I promised myself I'd be open to if it turned out he was interested in more than showing around the town's newest resident.

We headed down the line, and I complimented the townsfolk's merchandise and skills before mentioning my line of work. The couple who owned the local grocery store had six kids and joked they had their hands too full to add pets to the mix. That offended the three-year-old, who wanted a hamster and began wailing about it. Considering I'd triggered the meltdown, I was fairly certain that if they ever did get said pet, the mother wouldn't be bringing business my way.

Oops.

Right as I was about to call off the mini-introduction parade, I met a couple of farmers and assured them I could handle big animals. Evidently, the other vet in town made a big ordeal about it, so with any luck, I'd just secured a new client.

My luck ran out about two seconds later, when I spotted a face I wouldn't exactly call friendly but was familiar, and stumbled over my own feet. *Conall.*

The mere sight of him lit a sparkler within me, one that burned fast and hot. My breath hitched, and there went my heart, beating as fast as a woodpecker on a mission.

My brain searched for a distraction, and the looming Ferris wheel caught my eye. Heights weren't my thing, and I maintained my opinion on not trusting rides that were set up and taken down an outlandish number of times. But it was the slower of the tall rides, and honestly, I regretted not climbing into the rickety metal deathtrap with Grams while I'd had the option.

I can try new things.

I can be brave.

I'll do it for Grams.

"Let's ride the Ferris wheel," I said to Craig, pointing as if he might miss the enormous contraption otherwise.

"Oh, rides aren't really my thing." Craig put his hand on his stomach. "All that whirring and spinning after greasy food."

"It doesn't go very fast." A shaky argument at best, but it

did the job. He hesitantly picked up his pace as I rushed toward the giant flashing wheel and attached buckets. The closer we got, the taller it became, and it was a good thing I was pushing past my fear of heights. My trembling hands just needed to get onboard.

As we stepped into line behind the rest of the people awaiting their turn, I did my best to ignore the heat blossoming at the back of my neck.

I almost managed to convince myself it was the sun turning my skin scarlet, and not a certain werewolf paying attention to me. But then cheers erupted. I automatically glanced in the direction of the noise, smiling at the excitement over a young girl winning a large stuffed teddy bear, and caught a glimpse of Conall in my peripheral. Along with two other hulking dudes that looked like they ate jocks for breakfast.

No, more like deer and elk. Surely not bear, but it wouldn't surprise me. In a pack, wolves could take out virtually any animal they set their sights on. Which led me to wonder if there were bears in the woods around here, another thing I should've researched before relocating. Not that the town website mentioned the werewolves—I'd checked. Totally after the fact, but still.

My breath caught as Conall's head swiveled in my direction, and I failed to turn away, rendering all delusional pretenses null and void.

Then the world ground to an abrupt halt as Conall Shaw's gaze latched onto mine.

CHAPTER FOURTEEN

Conall

A LOW NOISE emanated from my throat, and my men immediately went on alert.

"You sense the witch?" Diego's eyes tracked side to side, keeping his movements small the same way I'd do to avoid rousing suspicion.

If I answered affirmatively to explain my rising hackles, Kerrigan would probably overhear somehow and yell at me again for assuming she was a witch in the first place. If I didn't dispel the tension, my men would snap into attack mode in the middle of a town carnival with civilians and kids everywhere, and that wouldn't do. "No. It's something else."

Thank God Nissa wasn't here to rat me out—she would've discerned the reason for my growl in two seconds flat. If it weren't for that, I'd rather have my beta at my side. But since she, Tyrese, and Sasquatch were the best trackers, they were scouring our borders in search of clues and had been since Friday morning.

In addition to checking if there were any other newcomers or visitors in town, the carnival provided one other benefit: the Ferris wheel. It would take me to the highest point in town, even taller than our watch tower.

Only Kerrigan and the mayor were standing in line for the ride. Together, so Elias hadn't exaggerated them hitting it off. The kid was around here somewhere. Granted, he counted as another person I experienced gladness over not currently being at my side. Subtlety wasn't in his skill set.

Dr. Ryan had tried to hide her reaction as our eyes met, but I'd heard her sharp inhale, along with the steady rise of her pulse. Watched as she worked to return air to her lungs. Craig Sullivan and I had clashed in a few town meetings, mostly over luring in tourists and any events taking place in my territory, although he wasn't privy to why we required privacy out at the compound. Sheriff Martin was and therefore never failed to take my side. I didn't delude myself that the mayor didn't hold some resentment over that, but he would never cross me—he didn't have the balls.

My logical side also knew he was a nice, respectable guy.

That feral side I warned Kerrigan about, however? It screamed *mine*. The mayor was standing way too close to *my woman*, and despite having no right to refer to her as such, my primal disposition didn't give a damn.

"You two flank the edges," I said to Diego and Mikal. "I'm going to hop on the Ferris wheel and take advantage of the view."

Mikal lifted his sunglasses, settling them atop his head as he peered up at the ride. "Sure you don't need an extra pair of eyes?"

Maniacal likely described my smile right now, but I let it loose anyway. "Already taken care of," I said, charging toward the end of the line before my men asked more questions.

Honestly, this was as much for Mayor Sullivan's safety as anything. Not only did the thought of Kerrigan being around any male who might put his hands on her gnaw at me more than expected, but he also wouldn't be able to protect her if the need arose.

The people standing in line parted, gesturing for me to go on ahead, instinctively recognizing a man on a mission. One they'd best avoid interrupting. Then riders began filing out of and into the buckets, the queue becoming shorter as people moved forward in unison.

Finally, I stepped into position behind Kerrigan and the mayor. I tapped Craig on the shoulder and gave him an exceedingly agreeable—or perhaps threatening, it's not like I had a mirror—smile. "Mind if I cut in?"

Craig immediately retreated a couple of paces and said, "Go ahead," while at the same time, Kerrigan replied with a firm, "Nope."

A hint of betrayal showed on the doctor's pretty features as she frowned at the mayor.

Too bad, so sad. Hit the road, Jack.

"Like I said, I'm not a fan of carnival rides, anyway." Craig pulled in his chin and slid his hands in his pockets, classic signals of surrendering that fed my already inflated ego. Yeah, I was a dick sometimes. I owned that.

Perfect timing, we were next to load. I moved my mouth next to her ear, folding her hand into mine as I did so. "Trust me, it's for the best. You need a real man to hold your hand on the Ferris wheel."

A storm brewed in the eyes that'd previously held more tenderness than I deserved, lightning flashing and thunder rumbling under the surface. She jerked her hand out of my grasp and crossed her arms. "That wasn't very nice."

Between the exposed shoulders and that adorable-as-fuck bow she'd tied in the scarf around her hair, I couldn't decide what to soak in first. Vanilla, blackberry, and floral notes hit me, and I stifled a groan as her pheromones compelled me closer. "Who ever said I was nice?"

She opened her mouth, presumably to light into me. But then the conductor ushered us toward the bucket. She glanced at the people growing anxious behind us, and I could practically see her calculating how it'd look if she stamped away.

With a resigned sigh, she climbed into the bucket. I paused to slip the conductor a twenty and asked for a favor that'd likely get me into even more trouble with my riding buddy.

Judging from the scowl she fired at me as I settled into place, causing the bucket to sway, *buddy* was the wrong word. It wasn't the word I wanted anyway, but I wasn't quite sure what to settle on. None of the options fit, and I didn't have time for entanglements, so I hadn't a clue what I meant to gain by this.

Besides being near her for a while. There was that swirl of amusement, too, as she pointedly studied everything but me. Our bucket lifted higher into the air, and Kerrigan gripped the handlebar tightly, the snail-pace speed notwithstanding.

I leaned back in my seat, casually draping my arm over the metal back as the last cluster of people loaded into the final empty bucket. "Don't you want to ask me how I'm feeling, Doc?"

Hands still clenched around the metal rod, Kerrigan swiveled her knees and face in the direction opposite me. "That's not my business, remember?"

We weren't quite high enough to see the compound yet but would be as soon as the ride whirred into motion. "Funny. I thought your business was fixing up animals. Because of that, I feel much better this weekend than I did the last one."

Again with that haughty lift of her chin. "Oh, I'm well aware of what my job entails, and you've settled your bill, so I'm done with you. I don't want to know anything about you or *your business* ever again, so don't bother telling me. Fickle guys are such a turnoff."

My jaw about hit my knee. Evidently, her kitty wasn't the

only one with claws. The engine whined as the ride soared into motion, and my stomach lifted along with the bucket.

Kerrigan's knuckles whitened, the blood draining from her face as well as her fingers. If I didn't think she'd rip my arm off and beat me with it, I'd extend it her way so she would have something better to hold onto.

A tiny, regretful noise emanated from her when we soared toward the sky. She cracked open an eye, then frowned when she found me peering at her. "I'm sort of afraid of heights. It's not a big..." She let out a tiny scream and, keeping her iron grip on the handle, eyed the door as if she were contemplating bailing. "Shit, I've made a huge mistake, and I want out. Like, right now."

"Hate to break it to you, and I'd like for you to remember that saying about not shooting the messenger, but we've passed the point of no return."

"I didn't shoot Elias when he came in, but you were in charge of that message—one I got loud and clear, so your request is denied. As I said before, more and more I see why someone would want to shoot you."

Since she was obviously distressed, I let that slide right off me. "Oh, you think the mayor would've handled this better?"

If looks could kill, I'd be dead, and I was fairly certain she'd celebrate. *Elias was right about it not going so well if I needed another trip to the vet.*

Kerrigan lowered her face to the fingers encircling the bar, mumbling about how she didn't care if she was bold or brave anymore.

A string in the center of my chest tugged. I tried to remind myself I was on a mission, but the urge to blow it off gathered steam. *She's gonna be pissed as hell in a moment, so I might as well do some preventative maintenance.*

I stretched out my legs and scanned the treetops. "Wow, you can really see the entire town from up here. Take a look while you can; it's beautiful."

"No, thank you," she muttered.

"Here I thought *I* was the caged animal." I risked placing a hand on her knee, and when she didn't push it away, I swiped my thumb over the denim, hoping it made her feel more safe and secure, whether or not she'd admit it. "Relax. If we fell—even from the tippy top—I'd survive it."

"How comforting for me, the human who doesn't regenerate."

Balking at how little faith she had in me wouldn't help the situation, but seriously? She thought I'd let any harm come to her? "I meant that I'd curl you into my body and let you use me as a shield. I owe you one. More like two."

"You don't, because you already paid me. Overpaid me, honestly. You don't have to bribe me, you know. I'm not going to expose you or your pack."

"It was fair compensation. Nothing more."

Kerrigan twisted her head my way, leaving her cheek resting against her knuckles. She inhaled a deep breath and then lunged in my direction, both of her arms winding around my left one. Happiness spread through my chest, and I internally pumped my fist. Her breasts pressed tighter to my biceps as she exhaled a shaky breath. "I'm still mad. You just also made a good point about using you as a shield, and I trust your healing abilities more than I trust this deathtrap machine."

I clamped my lips to keep my laughter from slipping out and ruining the moment. "If it makes you feel any better, it only seems so high because of how short you are." No surprise, that earned me a glare, but if she was focused on me instead of her fears, I could handle her ire. In fact, I might as well stoke it a bit, because apparently it was how I got my kicks these days. "And you're the one who was already in line for the tallest ride."

"I was trying to prove to myself that I can be bold and brave. But I'm not, and I want to get off. Right now."

I debated for a beat and then tiptoed my fingers a couple of inches higher on her thigh. "If that'll help you, I'd be happy to oblige."

It took her a second to put the words together, but then she smacked my arm before immediately clinging on to it again.

A crinkle bisected her forehead, and holy shit, the wheels were spinning in that incredible brain of hers.

"You're considering it."

"No," she said. Then she sank her teeth into her lower lip. "Well, maybe. More in a hypothetical way, as in would that truly be enough to distract me?"

"You wound me," I teased, shifting my hand to her inner thigh and sliding it up until I reached the spot where it met her torso. At the slight lift of her hips, I rested my thumb right on the very center of her, over the seam of her jeans. Her eyelashes fluttered and her nipples puckered beneath the thin cotton of her shirt. "And yet, I'm happy to play test subject." I stroked her through the too-thick fabric, hardening at her soft mewl. "Full disclosure: I'm going to be better at it than most anyone else you'd experiment with."

Her lips parted, and I halfway expected her to tell me our distraction game had gone far enough. But then she said, "As someone who's very serious about the scientific method, I'm afraid I'm going to need you to prove it."

CHAPTER FIFTEEN

Kerrigan

WHAT WAS I DOING?

Not thinking, that's what. I also figured that while I was being brave and bold, I might as well go all out. Already this brash decision was working out better than pushing past my fear of rickety machines and heights.

At the sound of my zipper going down, my thoughts split into two categories: *you should stop this* and *yes,* please God *get more of your large hand on more of me.*

Conall palmed me over my panties, eliciting a moan, and I quickly clenched my jaw shut, working on stifling any other sounds from spilling out. The tantalizing combo of soft lips and scruff brushed the shell of my ear. "Don't worry," he whispered, and my sense of euphoria heightened at the circling of his fingertips and the corresponding twitch of the muscles in his forearm. "The bucket comes up high enough no one can see what I'm doing to you but me. And fuck if I'm not enjoying the hell out of the show."

My head fell back against the metal seat, the sun bright enough to turn my whole world orange, even with my eyes closed.

Conall hooked the silky triangle of fabric covering me,

shifting it aside and then dragging a callused fingertip over my clit. Liquid pooled, and he spread it over me, and *holy shit*, I'd never been so turned on in my life.

My hips bucked as he increased the tempo, and I whipped up my head, panicked at the idea of getting off on a carnival ride and even more panicked at having to walk around unsatisfied.

A whimper came out as my legs quivered, pressure gathering into a tight ball deep within my core. I clamped onto his arm and peered into eyes so dark and intense that it drove me that much faster toward the edge. "I... I'm not good at being quiet."

"I'm afraid I'm going to need you to prove it," he said, echoing my words from earlier, and the dip of the wheel sent my stomach up to meet my rib cage. The rise and fall of the machine and whir of the scenery no longer concerned me; if anything, it amplified my pleasure.

It hit me that others were shouting as well, in enjoyment or fear as they rode along, hopefully unaware that I was getting an entirely different kind of ride.

Every muscle in my body coiled, ready to unleash in a rapturous blur, and then Conall plunged a finger inside me. His thumb hit my clit, and he crashed his mouth over mine as I screamed his name.

The languid strokes of his tongue matched the pumping of his finger. I teetered on the brink of gratification, and then I was flying apart, faster than the whirling of scenery, so high in the air that I gave into the free-fall, sure Conall would catch me.

As soon as mobility returned to my body, I kissed him back, moving my mouth and tongue against his as he brought me all the way down from my quick trip to paradise.

Vaguely, I noticed the ride slowing to a stop, with our bucket at the very top.

Conall readjusted my panties to cover me as he withdrew his finger, and then he sucked it into his mouth and groaned.

I didn't know what to say or do. I waited for the embarrassment to hit, but it was lost in the sea of rapture, no sight of it as far as the eye could see.

"I think I owed you that," he said, his voice extra gruff.

For a couple of seconds, all I could do was stare at the giant beast of a man—no, literally beast of a beast. "Does that make me or you the hooker?"

His laugh filled the air, the deep and devious sound vibrating across my nerve endings and intensifying the residual throb between my thighs. "If you ever want a repeat, call me. No payment required."

I dared a glance over the side of our bucket, and while my pulse skittered, the hysterical edge from earlier was gone. "The experiment definitely worked."

"That's real good news," Conall said. "Try to keep that in mind when I break the bad news. The reason we're stopped at the tippy top is because I paid the guy running the ride to give me a few minutes to look around. My pack is in danger, and since we both know you're not the witch, I need to take advantage of this eagle-eye view. But I won't let you fall, I promise."

Apprehension rose, but I did my best to appear calm and collected anyway. It wasn't like I could say, *Well, too bad for your pack.* "Okay. Just...be careful."

"I'd blush over the fact that you're worried about me, Doc, but I think that's just the orgasm talking."

The seat rocked as I slapped a hand over his mouth. Immediately, I regretted the movement. Still, did he have to say it so loud? "Maybe I'm just sick of patching you up. But fine. Don't be careful. Just hurry it up already. I'm anxious to return to solid ground."

Conall took my hand from his mouth, placed it on the bar, and instructed me to hold on tight. Then he stood—not just on the rust-speckled floor, either. The daredevil placed one foot on the seat and one on the front of the bucket.

At least I got to have an amazing orgasm before plummeting to my death.

Now do I owe him one? I'm not sure we'd have time for me to give him a hand job, as they've never been my specialty, but I don't want him to think I used him. Even if I kind of did.

"I don't see any unfamiliar faces," Conall muttered, and I wasn't sure if he was talking to me but decided talking would keep me from obsessing on how far down the ground was.

"You know everyone in town, then?"

"I make it my business to know," he said, as though he were a superhero protecting his city. Which was probably close to the truth, come to think of it.

After a couple more seconds, Conall extended his hand to me. I eyed it the same way I would a live wire. "Just take my hand," he said. "I want to show you how beautiful my forest is."

His forest? That was neither here nor there, so I lifted my head enough to glance at the treetops. "Yep. Super pretty."

Conall didn't budge. Damn guy just continued to hold out his hand. "The faster you let me show you, the faster we return to the ground."

Grumbling and glaring to show how little I appreciated his coerced high-rise tour, I slapped my palm in his. My knees wobbled as I stood, and he at least placed both feet on the seat as he wrapped an arm around my middle, drawing my back to his front. Then he pointed over my shoulder while I clung to his other arm. "FYI, if I die, I'm going to kill you. Even if it takes coming back as a ghost. And don't even try to tell me those don't exist, because I'm not taking the word of a mythical creature."

He laughed, relaying how scary he found my threat. "See that out there? That's Watuppa Pond. The moss-covered chunk of granite next to it is Solitude Stone. Some folks call it the 'suicide stone.' Supposedly, when a person stands atop of it, they suddenly have the urge to jump. Possibly due to the creepy transcription: *All ye, who in future days, Walk by Nunckatessett Stream, the Beauty that he wooed, In this quiet solitude."*

I peeped over my shoulder at him, unable to help my smile. Okay, so I enjoyed having his arm around me and the vibration of his voice as he gave the arial tour of Guadalupe Falls.

Below us, several of the people on the ride murmured questions, but they all seemed to be too caught up wondering what was happening while casting their gazes downward to notice there was a freaking werewolf standing on the top bucket.

"And if you follow the ridge, there's the werewolf compound. Hmm. I don't see anything out of the ordinary." Frustration pervaded the statement.

"I'd make a joke about casting a spell to help," I said, "but I'm not sure if it's too soon or if you'd realize I'm only kidding."

It certainly didn't get a laugh out of him, although he did finally step us down. Immediately I plunked myself into a safer, seated position and renewed my firm grip on the bar. "Okay, so how do you tell the guy to get us going again?"

Conall cocked his head, and my skin prickled under his scrutiny. "About Mayor Sullivan... Did I interrupt a date?"

"We can talk about that as soon as we're on the ground."

"Why?"

"Because our experiment is starting to wear off, and I'm going to use every advantage I have to ensure we get off *this ride* ASAP." I'd never use the word *regret*, but I was starting to feel weak for not holding him more accountable for everything that'd happened last week. The guy was volatile, and I didn't want to be the foolish girl who ignored red flags.

Or say or do anything that might leave us at this revolting height longer than necessary.

Not to mention that I wasn't sure myself whether my outing with the mayor counted as a date. Guilt arose, regardless—I'd skipped out on our whatever-it-was to climb into a bucket with Conall and do a whole lot more than flirt.

"Either way," Conall said, "you'll be sticking by my side for the rest of the carnival. It's as much for the mayor's safety as it is for yours."

Before I could shoot him an appropriate scowl, he banged the metal door of the bucket. The ride jolted into motion, and I crossed my arms. "You can't demand I stay by you." "Fine. I'll stay by *your* side."

I heaved a sigh. This was the perfect example of why I didn't ordinarily make impulsive decisions. Throwing caution to the wind was for people who didn't care about the consequences.

My mission today was to make a good impression, and if the townsfolk thought I flitted from man to man, that wouldn't help the outsider vibes I was already fighting against. Ugh.

Sorry, Grams. It was fun while it lasted, but I'm no good at it.

As soon as we were unloaded and back on solid ground, I turned to Conall, ready to explain that I had a few demands of my own if we were going to continue doing...whatever this was.

But then a man with umber skin and shorn dark hair rushed toward us. If it weren't for the stern expression, he'd be at home on the cover of *GQ* magazine. Guadalupe Falls wasn't only a hotbed for paranormal activity, it appeared to be the hub for outrageously ripped and sexy dudes.

"There's been another..." The guy eyed me. "Incident. We need to go." He took a step toward the parking lot, and Conall caught his shoulder and then jerked his head to indicate the tiny alley between two booths.

Then he placed his hand on my lower back and propelled me toward the narrow space as well. Apparently, I was going along for another ride—although from the sounds of it, this wouldn't be nearly as fun. "Mikal, Kerrigan is the vet who dug out the bullets after I was shot. You can speak freely in front of her."

Mikal nodded and said, "It's Justin. While he was out in wolf form, someone shot him with a bow and arrow. Silver tipped. Barely missed his heart and lungs. But he's not healing, which means—"

"We could use a doctor," Conall finished for him, his gaze moving to me. "My emergency medical bag's in the trunk of my car."

CHAPTER SIXTEEN

Kerrigan

MY GORE-COVERED clothes were definitely ruined, leaving me looking like I belonged on the set of a horror movie, but my main concern was the amount of blood the wolf I'd operated on had lost. Whoever yanked out the arrow hadn't been careful about it. Hazards of accelerated healing, I supposed. Evidently, minimizing muscle and tissue damage weren't a priority for anyone who healed in a day or two.

The woman who'd assisted me washed up alongside me, the soap bubbles forming an oddly beautiful, pink foam cloud in the sink. Sabine had been holding a bloodied rag against the wound when I first arrived on the scene. She made an excellent vet technician, quick to follow directions and perform the tasks with precision, but I could tell I'd stepped on her toes by taking charge.

I got it. My operating room, my rules. Although this tiny medical office didn't allow much space to move around—it was more like an operating cubicle.

After drying her hands, Sabine walked over to the wolf and ran a hand along the matted russet fur. "Now that you're all stitched up, you'll be okay. Why don't you shift and see if that kickstarts the healing?"

The wolf whimpered, his back paw raising to itch at his injury site, and I nudged his leg back down, same as last time. "Should I fashion him a cone?"

Good thing Sabine didn't have laser vision, or I would've been reduced to a smoldering heap of ash. "Put a cone on my brother, and you'll need a doctor of your own."

Ah, it's her brother. The ferocity with which she protected him with suddenly made more sense. Although I got the feeling the werewolves were a tight-knit group, which also why I hadn't asked how they were sure it was Justin and not, say, an actual wolf.

"Come on, Justin," Sabine nudged him. "Shift already."

A high-pitched whine accompanied his twitchy movements, and Sabine patted his side and asked, "Do the drugs make it harder for him to shift? Or is it the injury that's blocking his abilities?"

Being brand spanking new to the whole werewolf thing, I hadn't honed my Dr. Doolittle skills. I mean, I chatted with my clients on the regular, but they'd never spoken in return. At least not in English, anyway. "He sounds more frustrated than pained."

The door opened, and Conall strode into the room. While the guy always emanated a menacing vibe, his smirk and smart-assness usually softened it. Without either of those things present and accounted for, I understood why someone's first instinct might involve avoiding him at all costs. Judging from the stress on his features and the dirt streaking his arms and face, his past hour had been as hectic as mine. "How is he?"

I licked my lips, in dire need of a glass of water. "I managed to—"

"We stopped the—" Sabine grimaced and then gestured to me. "Sorry. You go ahead."

I explained how I'd repaired the organs and muscles and

gave my assessment: everything went as smoothly as possible, but he'd lost a lot of blood and needed rest.

Worry radiated off Sabine as she continued to fuss over her brother. "I don't think he can shift."

At the questioning look Conall aimed my way, I shrugged. "Um, I have no idea how to tell something like that. This *is* my first rodeo."

More tension crept into the line of his shoulders as he ran a hand over his hair, and I reached out and squeezed his other hand. Sabine frowned at the contact, so I let my arm drop to my side.

"Guess there's one way to find out." Conall crouched next to the hospital bed and locked eyes with the wolf. "As your alpha, I command you to shift. Right. Now."

The creature trembled, and I watched, transfixed, so I wouldn't miss a second of the transformation. Since Conall had gone human while my back was turned, I hadn't seen the in-between, and my medical curiosity got the best of me.

But then blood dripped from the wolf's nose and his limbs gave out.

"Fuck." Conall turned, punched a hole in the wall, and then charged out of the room. Sabine dragged a chair next to the bed to console her brother, but not before casting me a dirty look, I was fairly sure I didn't deserve.

I darted into the hallway and checked right, toward the entrance of the big building that sat in the middle of the community. Nothing, so I checked to the left and barely caught sight of Conall's backside as he rounded the corner.

I raced after him, cursing his longer legs and speediness.

I took the turn too fast and nearly collided with the mountain of a man posted in the center of the hallway. I thought Conall was tall, but this guy had to be close to seven feet. His red hair cascaded to about the middle of his back, and even with the top half pulled into a bun, it was thick enough for two additional braids that nicely framed his bearded face. A helix bar threaded through the top of his ear and large black gauges stretched out the lobes.

Hot damn. The whole emo rock star Viking thing really worked for him. If I hadn't already set my poor misguided sights on Conall, I wouldn't put up much resistance to this guy doing some plundering.

"Sorry," I said, shifting my weight to my other leg so I could step around him.

But the man blocked my way again.

"Conall," I yelled after him, a curl of genuine fear unfurling within me. "Wait up. Can you call off your guard?"

He glanced over his shoulder, seemingly surprised to find me in the hallway. "I have a meeting to get to."

"I can sit through a meeting. I'm happy to help however I can, even if it's just holding your hand." I couldn't help it. I was a healer. A hand-holder. A make-it-righter.

Conall's large shoulders slumped, his deflated posture so at odds with the guy I'd initially met that my heart panged. "I appreciate that, but you've already helped enough. Not to mention I can't let you attend a meeting involving werewolf matters."

The pang sharpened. Was that his way of telling me to mind my own business again? "Sasquatch, take Dr. Ryan home for me."

"I don't need an escort."

Finally, Conall fully turned around. Three long strides was all it took for him to cross the space. "Listen, the whole back-and-forth thing we do? I'm a fan of all the sexual tension that builds until you realize my way is better—"

"I don't remember a single case where that's happened," I said, but he continued on as if I hadn't interrupted.

"Unfortunately, I have too much on my plate right now to argue with you." The damn werewolf cupped my cheek and swiped a tingly trail across the top, scrambling the case I'd planned to make. "As I mentioned the other night, I don't say 'please.' If that makes me a pigheaded ass, so be it."

I winced and dared a quick peek at the stoic gentleman watching over our interaction, wondering how much waving or hollering it'd take to get a reaction, and then decided I'd rather take my chances with Conall. "Elias mentioned that, did he?"

Conall nodded.

"Would it honestly be so hard for you to say 'please?'" I asked and got another nod.

"It's not who I am, and I don't bend or break for anyone. My pride simply won't allow it.

"I don't compromise much, either." The conviction behind his words rang through my chest, wiggling loose so many emotions I struggled to sort one from the other. "But I will ask you one more time to go with Sasquatch before I turn the request into an order."

A snarky comment about how that hardly counted as a question sprang to the tip of my tongue, but I read the room and judged it to be the wrong time to push this. Ditto when it came to asking if a mother had really named her son Sasquatch, or if it was a nickname.

Conall wound his fingers through my hair. "I need to know you're safe so I can focus on all the other shit I have to do tonight. It looks like we need to enlist your services while I sort out who's attacking my pack, hunt them down, and make them pay. Which means I have to go convince a room full of werewolves who don't trust outsiders that it's the right move. And then, when several of them inevitably cause a fuss about it, tell them too damn bad because it's happening."

"They don't trust me?" Not sure why that stung. Most of them hadn't even met me.

"It's not personal. They don't trust anyone. Now, before I go throw myself to the wolves"—Conall cracked a smile at his own joke, only with the stress weighing him down, it didn't contain its usual wattage—"I suppose I'd better make sure you're up to the task. I know you've been super slammed at the clinic…"

I pursed my lips, warning the smart-ass he was treading on thin ice.

"What?" All false innocence and the way he traced my jawline with his fingertips proved just how dirty he played. My skin hummed and begged for more, and my body leaned toward his as if it couldn't help itself. "You've had two emergency surgeries since you've arrived in town— I'd know."

"Well, you do require the attention of about five fractious animals—fractious means they require sedation, or they'll bite the hell out of you. Or in your case, break chains and punch a hole through the wall." I lifted his hand and studied his bloodied knuckles. "I can clean and wrap these for you."

"No need. They'll be fine in a matter of minutes, and minor scrapes are the least of my worries."

"Are you sure you don't want me to stick around? You helped me from freaking out on the Ferris wheel earlier, and I feel like the least I could do is…" Out of my peripheral, I confirmed the giant redheaded dude hadn't given us so much as an inch of extra space. "Help relieve you of some of that tension you're carrying around."

Conall groaned and lowered his forehead to mine. "You're not making this easy." "I'd claim I'm not easy, but…" Flirting was hard enough without an audience.

"Oh, you made me work plenty hard before—"

I slapped a hand over his mouth, the same way I'd done in that rickety bucket, and his Viking bodyguard shifted toward us—no, make that toward *me*. At his terrifying glower, I squeaked and wound my arms around Conall's waist.

The jerk chuckled as he held up a hand to Sasquatch. "It's okay. As for you…" Conall planted a hand on my ass. "I was going to say you made me work plenty hard before you stopped hurling insults at me." The twinkle in his eye claimed opposite, and at the thought of his large hand and long fingers on me, my body automatically took his side.

A door opened at the end of the hall, and a woman with bright purple hair stuck her head out of it. "Boss. Everyone's ready and waitin—Kerrigan! Hi!" Gina waved as if we'd crossed paths in the grocery store, just two local gals out for a casual stroll down the food aisles. "Sorry about the other night, by the way."

"You're a werewolf?" A question that didn't need to be asked, yet I'd blurted it out anyway.

"Last I checked. It's why, even though I was totally enjoying our chat, your question threw me for a loop. I wasn't sure *why* you were asking about Conall. Then he showed up, and girl, I wanted to warn you so bad, but—"

"What's the holdup?" Another female voice eclipsed Gina's words. "We don't have all night." The woman who'd shown up at my house with Elias stepped into the hallway and tapped an impatient foot, saying a lot without saying anything at all.

Conall's eyes returned to mine, a question swimming in the brown, although it was more of a request. Not an actual please, but likely as much as he gave.

"Okay, I'll go with Sasquatch." Yeah, that was a sentence I'd just uttered. What even was my life right now? "But he'll need to escort me to the carnival grounds, since that's where I left my car."

"Drop her off and follow her home," Conall told Sasquatch, his words clipped, no wiggle room. "Clear the perimeter before she goes inside, and if you notice anything fishy, report it right away."

"Yes, sir." Sasquatch bowed his head, and I gaped at the dynamic between them. Power radiated from Conall, so strongly I almost saluted. Not that I'd admit it, but I could see his point the tiniest bit about having to be unyielding to earn the respect of his people.

His people, who were under attack from supernatural beings. The realization summoned the fear Conall tried to instill in me last week. Every member of his pack was in danger.

He was in danger.

"Give me your phone," I said, gesturing for it with a finger wiggle.

Sasquatch broke character, frowning at me as if I'd been raised in a barn. Had I wandered into some weird wolfie version of a royalty movie, where I constantly broke protocol and his loyal constituents declared me crass?

Did I care? I should, but anticipation over being able to call to check in or hear his voice overtook my sense of decorum. "That way," I explained, "if Justin takes a turn, or if anyone else gets injured, you can call my direct line instead of the emergency number at the clinic."

Light taps filled the air as we plugged our information into each other's contacts. Then Conall reached around me and slid my phone in the back pocket of my jeans. My body misfired, zaps of energy renewing my low stores. He moved his lips next to my ear and sank his teeth into the shell. "I can't stop thinking about how good you taste, and how next time, I'm going to lap you up with my tongue."

His nose grazed my cheek as he straightened, and judging from the smug slant of his lips as he gave me a once-over, he'd noticed my nipples straining against the fabric of my shirt. After one quick smack on the ass, Conall rushed off to his meeting.

As soon as he disappeared into the room where I wasn't allowed to follow, I looked up, up, up at the werewolf who'd been assigned to babysit me.

CHAPTER SEVENTEEN

Conall

FOR THE SAFETY of the pack, I forced myself to remain close to home instead of making excuses to head to the east side of town, to a certain cabin where a certain sexy veterinarian lived.

By the time I lumbered into my bedroom, my limbs were made up of more exhaustion than flesh and bone. I shed my clothes, stepped into a pair of boxers, and crashed to the bed, sure I'd fall asleep seconds after my head hit the pillow.

Blip, went my dirty mind reel, replaying the image of Kerrigan seated in that metal carnival bucket, writhing against the hand I had down her pants. I relived her walls clamping around my finger as she came, and the residual taste of her danced across my tongue, too weak to leave me satisfied but enough to awaken my libido.

I'd never get to sleep now, my balls already launching a complaint at being painfully blue and engorged for the second time today.

The least I could do is help relieve you of some of that tension you're carrying around.

The woman must've wanted me to conduct the pack meeting with a raging erection. I was tempted to push her

121

into a room and take her right then and there, but I didn't want the first time I fucked her to be rushed.

An idea clicked into place, one that gave free rein to the feral side I'd kept on a leash for far too long.

I reached for the phone I'd placed on the nightstand. If Kerrigan didn't answer, I'd take a steamy shower and use the images I'd immediately stowed away of her in my spank bank. Nothing compared to the real thing, though, and my body screamed it wouldn't settle for anything less.

With every ring, my disappointment and sexual frustration rose, and then Kerrigan's sleep-roughened voice filled my ear. "Hello? Conall? Is someone hurt?"

"Not anyone new," I said. Shit. I'd been too horny to realize she might jump to that conclusion. "The council agreed on allowing you to handle our medical needs while we figure out how to break the spell. You'll be heavily compensated, of course."

"And you didn't think that news could wait till tomorrow?" she teased. I imagined her stretched out in bed, in nothing but those tiny polka-dot panties she'd been wearing earlier today. My erection pushed against the confines of my boxers, bobbing in anticipation.

"Not when it's your fault that I can't sleep. I'm exhausted from scouring every inch of the forest, but as soon as I climbed into bed, I replayed you coming around my finger, and now I'm hard as a fucking rock."

"Ah. I'm pretty sure this is what the *Backwoods Survival Guide* meant when it listed 'Be prepared for anything' as the number one survival rule. It sounds like you weren't prepared for me niggling my way into your mind. It's all part of my charm—it sneaks up on you."

"Oh, I'm prepared. I'm about to wrap my hand around my cock and release some of that tension you mentioned today in the hallway. For my own survival, of course."

"Of course," Kerrigan said in a breathy tone that only

served to turn me on that much more. At the rustling of sheets and light squeak of bedsprings, I was about to cum in my underwear like a teenager with no control.

Not happening. "What I need is your voice in my ear as I get off. I'm thinking about you down on your knees, begging for mercy. Feel free to run with the scenario."

"So, you're saying you want me to pretend I'm afraid of the big bad wolf?"

Pure unadulterated need flared, radiating outward until my body pulsed with it. I kicked off my boxers and sat up. "I'd never ask you to fake it with me, baby. And trust me, you wouldn't have to."

"My, my, what sexy promises you make."

"The better to seduce you with," I growled as I fisted my protruding arousal.

"Now I'm getting all hot and bothered, too."

"You'd better be alone. You never did answer my question about Craig Sullivan." "You're right, I didn't," she said, and I growled again. She had the audacity to giggle, and I was going to have to punish her for that the next time I plundered her sassy mouth. A red handprint on her ass to remember me by should do the trick.

"You're not going to think it's very funny if I rip off his arms. He's a decent guy, so I'd experience a pinch of remorse, but the fact of the matter is that once I've got you in my sights, it's a done deal."

"Is that right? And how many done deals are you balancing right now? I bet you make a woman feel incredible by delivering all the right lines and showering her with affection, but after you sleep with her, you forget to call."

If she only knew how long it'd been—too much pressure came along with dating shifters. Everyone wanted to declare them my mate before the two of us even went on a couple of dates, and I'd heard several speeches about how it was my duty and other such nonsense. "Not my style. I'm more of a possessive asshole who sees what he wants and goes after it. And right now, what I want is the smart, funny, sexy doctor who talks circles around me. So, unless you tell me you're not interested, I'm letting you know that I'm going to pursue this thing between us."

Silence stretched over the line until the air vibrated with it.

My cock literally wept when I let it go. I'd thought she'd been onboard, but if she wasn't, this had just gone from phone sex to a phone call. "Kerrigan. That giant space is your opening. I laid out all my cards and told you where I stand. Now it's your turn."

"Wow, you really can't help your bossiness, can you?" she shot back.

"No," I answered, not an ounce of hesitation. "Patience isn't my forte, either. But I am trying to be respectful here."

"That sounds...surprisingly reasonable for you. Being respectful while jacking off."

"*Reasonable.*" I spat out the awful word. "I pride myself on being unreasonable. Do I need to wake up half the compound by shifting, howling at the moon, and then racing to your house to either devour you or maim whoever's with you to prove it?"

"You want to hear that I've thought about you, your ripped body, and your notable, uh, asset far too often since the night we met?" she purred, and my heart beat out an erratic rhythm. "About how even after you were a total asshole, I spent the following days hoping to run into you? That I've replayed you fingering me on the Ferris wheel on an endless loop?"

A groan slipped out, and I returned my fist to my steely length for a long, languid stroke.

"That I can't consider Mayor Sullivan or any other man as an option, because thoughts of you crowd out the possibility of anyone else," she added, and the shakiness in her voice led me to believe our conversation had spurred her to touch herself as well.

"That's *exactly* what I want to hear." I stood and propped my phone against the wall, so it'd show me from mid-thigh up. Then I tapped the request to add video to the call. "And now I need to see you."

A second passed, and then another, and then a mussed-haired Kerrigan finally filled the screen. Black spots danced across my vision, the sensual overload almost too much to handle, and I grunted, annoyed at anything that'd obscure my view of her.

Just as I expected, she had her hand down her panties. Two peaked nipples showed through her thin cotton tank top, and greedy bastard that I was, I wanted more. "Pull down that skimpy tank top so I can see those tits."

"They're more impressive in my bra. If you'll just give me a sec—"

"Now, Kerrigan."

My hips jerked in time to the thrusts into my fists as she tugged down the shirt, revealing glorious pert breasts with pink nipples. "I'd like to be all agreeable since we're getting along so well, but I have to tell you that you're wrong."

Kerrigan wrinkled her nose. "They're just so small. Couldn't some of my ass have gone to them? I have enough to spare there."

"That's enough nonsense," I barked, unable to allow her to speak like that about one of my favorite assets of hers. "Your ass is perfect as it is." The thought of seeing it without fabric in the way in the near future drove me closer to the edge. I gritted my teeth, holding on to that last unbroken thread of my control. "As for your breasts, all I need is a mouthful. Once I get the chance, I'll show you how well yours fit in my hot mouth."

Every muscle in my body tensed, and the world turned hazy on the edges.

As if our steamy session couldn't get any more perfect, Kerrigan pouted her lips and affected a tiny voice. "Please, show me mercy, Mr. Big Bad Wolf. I'll do anything."

My chest heaved with rapid breaths, and I peered into her eyes, the rapture inside of them expounding mine as well. "Turn to face the camera so I can show you how much I love those tits by coming on them."

She pivoted as instructed, and I snagged a couple of tissues, sure I was about to shoot every load that'd built up during all my time going without. Her fingers continued to delve into her panties as she gyrated and moaned, faster and faster, and I matched her tempo.

Then she shattered apart, igniting my orgasm as well.

We both tumbled over the edge with a cacophony of grunts, moans, cries, and groans, apart but together.

Considering I'd just come harder than I'd ever come with anyone else, I knew I was going to resent every single thing that got in the way of me getting my hands and mouth on her again.

CHAPTER EIGHTEEN

Kerrigan

AROUND NOON ON SUNDAY, two visitors showed up at my door.

"Elias is going to fix your electrical issues," Gina said, looping her elbow through mine, "and you and I are going to work on our tans. Or just read magazines and drink. It's my first day off from the bar in eons, so I'm not picky."

I glanced back at Elias as Gina towed me toward the sliding patio door, her eyes fixed on the deck and weathered lounge chairs. "I feel bad making Elias work on something that could get him electrocuted," I said. "I should just call in a professional to handle it." Although I worried I couldn't afford the consultation, much less the repairs.

"This is my punishment for leaving my post." With ease, Elias scooted out the oven I'd tried and failed to budge and used the flashlight on his cell to peer behind the appliance. "Taking care of outdated wires is far better than any other chores Conall could assign me, and something I'm completely qualified for, so I should actually be thanking you."

That seemed like a stretch but placated me enough to give in to Gina's pull. Before long, she and I were chatting and gossiping over a pitcher of sangria.

I learned all about how Gina came to live in Guadalupe Falls—she'd been born and raised in the woods southeast of here, her family hiding in plain sight until Conall showed up and invited them to join his pack. Then we discussed our hobbies. I had my fascination with the medical world, and she derived pleasure from playing the guitar, singing, and even dabbled in writing, which I told her was super cool.

By the time we covered our interests, I'd also drunk enough to drop Conall's name. "Not to risk a repeat of the night we met, and I asked about Conall, but woman to woman..." Whenever I was around him, it was like some nympho had possessed my body, and I couldn't decide whether to tell her to take a hike or beg her to stay forever. Asking about his past dating life wasn't bravery, though; it was me being a chicken and needing reassurance I wasn't playing the fool, getting way too close to falling for him so quickly. "Never mind."

Gina sat up and leaned in conspiratorially. "Now that I know you know about us, my lips might be a little looser. Within reason."

Within reason. I doubted I was the best judge of that, but here I went anyway. "Does he... Has he...? Have there been a lot of women who...?" I upended the last of the fruity contents from my glass, giving the bottom a tap to dislodge a stubborn chunk of orange. "Is he a player?"

Gina snorted her drink, coughing and blinking her watery eyes. "Sorry. I wasn't expecting that."

"He claimed he wasn't a womanizer," I continued, my words slurring together, "and it's not that I don't believe him, it's just that I've..."

"Met too many douchebags in your day?"

I tipped my glass at her. "Yes, that."

"Well, he's never struggled to land a date, and plenty of women have attempted to catch his eye and hold his attention, but he's very committed to his position as alpha.

I've known him for over a decade, and I can at least assure you the interest he's taken in you isn't anything I've witnessed before. Wouldn't you agree, Elias?"

At my frozen posture and widening eyes, Gina shrugged a shoulder. "With our superior hearing, any pretenses of whispering or secrets around werewolves are just that."

Elias emerged from the house, rested a hip against the frame of the open patio door, and tapped the pair of pliers in his hand against his palm. "For sure. Not to mention, providing shelter and safety are big gestures in the animal kingdom, and well, I'm here to ensure you don't get electrocuted, so..."

Gina pointed at Elias. "Bingo. There's the general helping out our community, but this, with you, is on another level."

"It's just that I called him an asshole, and he didn't dispute he was one. In fact, he admitted it. Same with being unreasonable and not nice. I keep worrying those are red flags, ones that'd be reckless to ignore."

"Hmmm." Gina tapped a finger to her lip. "Conall can be harsh, unyielding, and about as cuddly as a honey badger. Since becoming the Alpha of the Bridgewater Pack, he's won every brawl and battle he's gotten into, and there's been quite a few. I wouldn't want to be his enemy, that's for sure..."

That had Elias nodding.

"But he's also fair, honest, and genuinely cares about his people," Gina finished. "Our family no longer has to live in constant fear of discovery, and he listens to our input on issues. If he makes a stand, no one doubts he's got his reasons, which is why we'll all fight beside him without question."

"I used to belong to another pack," Elias said, his expression turning grim. "They discovered I was gay and kicked me out, but not before beating the shit out of me and leaving me out in the middle of nowhere to die."

An ache radiated through the center of my chest on his

behalf. At one point, I'd naively assumed places like that didn't exist anymore, only to be shocked and appalled by some of the homophobia and hatred I'd seen online.

It called to mind that moment between him and the mayor in the lobby of the vet clinic. Elias had acted slightly cagey. Although that didn't add up, as the mayor suggested Elias might've come in to hit on me. Perhaps Elias was hesitant to tell people, or distrustful in general, and regardless of the why, no one should have to live in fear of being who they truly were.

"If Conall hadn't found me..." Elias's voice wavered, and he cleared his throat and scuffed his shoe against the peeling paint of the deck. "I don't want to think about where I'd be."

Affection coursed through my body, for Elias, Gina, and Conall. I wanted to throw my arms around the two werewolves and swear to keep them safe, despite it being a promise I might be unable to follow through with, no matter how hard I tried. But I'd do my best, and the thought of anymore werewolf injuries tore me up inside.

While I'd ventured into this line of conversation in an attempt to protect my heart, all it did was fill another piece of it with Conall and his pack.

———

That night, once Sir Pounce and I were alone again in the house, my lights, oven, and microwave working remarkably well, I sent Conall a thank-you text. I did my best not to stare at my phone screen, anxiously awaiting a response.

I failed.

It was like seeing a piece of a triple-layer fudge cake behind glass and, after drooling over it and watching it be placed on a beautiful plate, getting told you couldn't eat it.

This gal wanted to sink her teeth into her cake.

Since I couldn't seem to release my hold on my phone, I

decided to multitask. I pulled up Google and out of mere curiosity searched up werewolves.

I found an article on hypertrichosis, a genetic mutation that led to excessive hair growth that had been nicknamed "werewolf syndrome." No cure, and nothing helpful, as I didn't think lasering off hair would endear me to the pack.

Striving to find answers with more validity, I typed: *what to do if you can't shift into a werewolf anymore.*

Big surprise, the results were far from helpful. Two pages worth of videogame tricks that I read just in case there was a hidden gem. Which there was in one game, but it was a literal sapphire.

I was relatively sure I hadn't done any internet searches that'd earn me an FBI agent watchdog, but I covered my tracks by playing the videogame anyhow, as if that was my only experience with lycanthropy. I then spent hours trying to kill the Frost Giant and steal the gemstone, to no avail.

As an hour of waiting turned into two, I rubbed at my tired eyes. My thank-you text hadn't exactly warranted a provocative response, but the insecure side of me fretted I'd given in to a booty call and turned myself into the woman Conall used for that and nothing more.

But that was silly. He'd sent Elias to fix my electricity. I debated typing out a follow-up text. A question about his day or Justin or anything else that could possibly inspire a conversation.

A high-pitched squeal alerted me that my kettle of water was ready, and I abandoned my laptop and phone to make myself a cup of tea. As I poured a healthy amount of honey into my mug, I heard Sir Pounce hiss and growl.

"Kitty? What's going on?"

I gripped my mug of tea in both hands and cautiously entered the living room. If it was a spider or bug, I figured I could go with the stomping method, or perhaps even throw hot tea on it—any creature with more than four legs deserved what they got for breaking into my house.

What if it's an intruder? A totally unfounded, errant thought, but tea could burn them, too, so yay for options?

Sir Pounce stood at the front door, paws up on the screen. It'd been a stifling hot day, so I'd flung open all the windows, as my cabin didn't have the luxury of A/C.

"What do you see?" I squinted into the darkness, but what with it being pitch black, I couldn't see a damn thing. Since I hadn't engaged the locks after Gina and Elias left, I clicked them into place, even as I assured myself it was likely a mouse or bunny or moth.

Sir Pounce loved chasing and eating moths.

Although usually that involved more of a chirrup than a growl.

A loud scraping noise sounded at the patio door, like sharp nails on glass, and I whirled around. Tea sloshed over the rim of my mug, burning my hand as it splattered the thigh of my jeans. "Ouch, ouch, ouch."

I set down my mug and danced around, needing the fabric off—it held the heat against my leg as if it'd decided on blister territory or bust. But if someone was out there, they'd see, and what a weird thing to care about. Obviously, I needed to dig deeper into my survival guide, as I doubted it said to prioritize pantslessness over catching a burglar.

Like I could actually catch a burglar—and joke was on them. I didn't have anything of value to steal besides my car, and it was out there.

Logically, I knew that was unlikely in this tiny town, with its nearly non-existent crime rate. I considered dialing 9-1 so all it'd take was one last digit if it turned into an emergency situation, then thought Conall would likely be the faster and scarier of my options. I pulled up his contact and hovered my thumb over the call button.

"I'm a strong, independent woman," I said aloud, wishing

my voice wouldn't waver so much. On the way through the kitchen, I found the biggest knife I had and wielded it in my left, so that I could call Conall, yell for help, and then get to stabbing.

Sir Pounce walked alongside me, to the point he nearly tripped me. With my luck, I'd stab myself and end up using my last breath to tell Conall that I regretted we hadn't gotten to have sex before I left this world.

Jeez, overdramatic much?

The screech sounded again, louder this time, and I flung open the door. A raccoon sat in the middle of the contents that'd spilled from my overturned trash can, scraping the leftover lasagna out of the disposable foil pan.

Sir Pounce growled, and the raccoon just stared at us like he didn't mind our presence, but could we please not interrupt his dinner?

Since I didn't want my furball to get rabies, I picked him up, tightening my grip on him when he tried to lunge at the masked bandit.

"I almost called Conall over a raccoon. Could you imagine how much he'd mock me for that?"

Still, as I backed into the cabin, flickers of light and dark danced through the swaying branches of trees that suddenly seemed to be everywhere. So many hiding places for a wannabe predator. The forest had eyes, and while I was sure it was my city girl side insisting on shutting out nature instead of basking in it, new blinds just got bumped up on my to-do list.

CHAPTER NINETEEN

Kerrigan

WHY HAD this Monday been a billion years long already?

Don't get me wrong, I was grateful for the whopping three appointments with new clients, but as soon as the clock struck four, I locked up the clinic and barely resisted sprinting to my car.

My Mini Cooper bounced along the dirt road to the Bridgewater Bluff Community—aka, the werewolf compound, but only to people in the know. I rather liked being in the know.

When Conall had driven me there, we'd been in a rush and I'd been hyper aware of every one of his movements. From how the line in his forearms stood out as he shifted to the sunshine pouring through the window and highlighting his strong jawline to the way the long fingers that'd stroked me into oblivion wrapped around the steering wheel.

While I'd noted the plethora of trees before, the deeper into the forest I went, the more it felt like nothing else existed. Just dirt, pines, and a sliver of ultra-blue sky. Left me experiencing a pinch of claustrophobia, to be honest, so I cranked up the radio and psyched myself up to see Conall.

My lips and body tingled in anticipation, the dirty dream

I'd had last night coming along for the ride, and then I was shifting in my seat and cracking a window.

Right as I began to worry I'd forgotten a turn, the trees thinned and I spotted the compound. The first time Conall used that word, I'd pictured cement fences with twisted barbed wire along the top and square homes that lacked personality. In realty, the place looked like a woodsy suburbia that'd been dropped in the middle of nowhere. The stone and wrought iron fence showcased various cabins ranging from cottage style, modern, and rustic.

I slowed next to the call box, identified myself, and waited for the gate to swing open. I drove through the entryway and headed toward the only building I'd been inside. A mixture of wood and stone, the community center housed the school, the medical room, and the space where they had meetings.

Big meetings to discuss werewolf matters, and oh, to be a fly on the wall. Conall's family was another subject I'd speculated about. Had I wanted to pry deeper into what happened to them? I was only human, so of course.

But I hadn't delved into my personal losses yet, either, and he'd tell me when he was ready. Fingers crossed, anyway.

After parking near the entrance, I hesitated for a moment, unsure if I should charge on in or if someone would greet me. *It's not like it's a military facility, and you're* supposed *to be here. Go do your job so you can get to the part with the embracing and kissing.*

Sasquatch, the mountain of a man who escorted me home the other night, opened the front door to the community center as I approached. Then he started down the hallway toward the medical office, and I was obviously expected to follow.

I picked up my pace, taking about three steps for every one of his. "How's it going?" He'd hardly said a thing during the ride to get my car the other night, but then again, neither had I, so I decided to take the lead today.

"Fine." Such a unique, low timbre that I'd bet he could make a fortune as a voice actor. Although that'd require speaking multiple words at once, so I doubted he'd do it.

"What about Justin? Any change?"

"Nope," Sasquatch said.

"Any new leads on the bad guys?"

"I'm not allowed to discuss werewolf matters with outsiders."

Ouch. So glad his longest sentence involved insulting me. But I was nothing if not persistent. "Well then, how's your day, Mr. Sasquatch? Or is it just Sasquatch? Do anything fun?"

His brow furrowed, as if he couldn't figure me out. *Right back at you, big guy.*

"Is making polite conversation a faux pas in werewolf land or something? Does no one here chat for the sake of chatting?"

"I don't," he said

"Noted." Same way I noted he didn't tell me whether to add the Mr. in front of his name. Evidently, it was dealer's choice, and I entertained the idea of adding another prefix to see if I could garner a reaction.

Major? Admiral? Captain? Chief? Plenty of fun options.

Sasquatch walked past a line of chairs occupied by three people, slowing as we reached the door to the medical office. He posted himself in the center of the hallway, and I took that to mean I hadn't been cleared to go anywhere else in the building.

I wanted to ask if Conall was around—and if he could tell my security detail, who acted more like a prison warden than a bodyguard, to lighten up—but since Sasquatch had already expressed he didn't discuss werewolf matters, I suspected I'd get iced out. Choosing the higher route, I flashed him my most winning smile. "Thank you, Lieutenant Sasquatch. Couldn't have made it here without you."

Not even a flicker of amusement.

No disdain, either. So, win?

"I'll let Sabine know you're here, and she'll bring Justin," he said, withdrawing a phone from his pocket. Then he gestured to the people seated against the wall. "Go ahead and get started on the others."

I saw the boy with the broken leg first. Sabine had fashioned a splint for him. I'd have to tell her what a good job she'd done, both because it was true, and also with the intention of preventing hurt feelings over my insistence we upgrade him to a cast. While the mom and son were annoyed at the slow healing, I informed them he was on track as far as the human timeline went, which they balked at.

I doubted relaying the dog timeline would've earned me a different reaction, so I sent them off and called in a woman named Claudia, who'd faceplanted on a rocky cliffside. She claimed to have jumped the ravine countless times before, which I believed while marveling that was a regular activity for her.

After treating Claudia's scrapes and ensuring she hadn't broken anything, I opened the door so she could head to wherever, right in time for Sabine to wheel Justin inside the room.

In a wheelbarrow. A first for me, and a laugh bubbled up at the sight, but I managed to swallow it down. Good thing, too, because once I got a better look at the wolf, I could tell something was wrong, even before I registered his weak whimper.

Sabine launched into an update, detailing his eating, bathroom habits, and how he yelped and whined whenever he moved. "He walked around for about an hour yesterday, which doesn't strike me as enough time, but I couldn't get him to do anything this afternoon besides sit in the sun. Do you think that's enough fresh air and exercise? I didn't want to overtire him, either."

Not having seen the guy in human form, I had no idea. And once again, I was hesitant to make dog comparisons.

Unshed tears glistened in Sabine's eyes, along with the exhaustion and stress of caring for her brother the past couple of days. "I get that he doesn't have his accelerated healing abilities, even though I don't understand why, but I'm afraid something is horribly wrong."

I agreed, but saying so would only upset her more, and it'd be harder to do my job if I needed to comfort both of them. "I'll give him a thorough examination and see what's going on. Would you like to have a seat in the hal—"

"I've been the medical expert at this compound for years, and while I'm willing to admit you may be more qualified in certain areas, I'm not leaving him alone."

"Okay." I reached for her shoulder to deliver a consoling squeeze, but she sidestepped me, rolled Justin over to the exam table, and hefted him onto it.

The injured wolf trembled before flopping to the table in an exhausted pile of fur and bones, a high-pitched whine of pain accompanying the movement. Sabine's gaze darted to me, begging me to fix her brother, and as I slipped on a pair of gloves, I hoped like hell that I could.

Usually this would be the point in the examination where I asked a pet owner how long their furry companion had been acting strange. But one, this situation was already odd; and two, I feared I'd end up with two patients, Sabine was already strung so tight.

All I had with me was a rectal thermometer, as most dogs chewed up anything I put into their mouths, so thank goodness Justin had remained in wolf form. Still, Sabine lurched forward and caught my wrist when I lifted his tail.

"What do you think you're doing?" she asked.

"I assumed the thermometer would clue you in. I realize you're concerned, but if you're going to remain in the room, you need to let me do my job."

Sabine bared her human teeth at me, the effect not any less disturbing than had she used the lupine version. But she took a whole step back, her bated breath warming my neck as I confirmed her brother was running a fever, coming in at a toasty 105 degrees.

Which led me to run my hand over his tan coat.

At his loud yelp, Sabine eradicated the already minimal space between us. "What's wrong?" she asked. "I knew I should've called you yesterday when he hadn't improved. I thought I was overreacting, and it's so frustrating that he can't tell me what's going on. Now if he dies, it'll be all my fault."

I turned to face her, summoning my patience and injecting my words with as much reassurance as I could. "My guess is he has a secondary infection. It's not uncommon in animals after a surgery or large wound. But again, if you don't give me room, it'll be that much harder for me to diagnose and take care of."

My heart twanged as Sabine backed up against the wall, a stream of tears escaping as she put her hand over her mouth. As if that wasn't enough pressure, she whispered, "He's the only family I have."

I expelled a long breath and returned to examining the wolf. Carefully, I felt around the spot that'd caused the pained cry, and sure enough, the site radiated heat. The skin around his wound was also purplish red and inflamed.

I snagged a scalpel out of my kit and made a small incision. At my gentle push, yellowish discharge exploded from the wound with an oozing gush. "Jackpot."

"What did you win?" a familiar deep voice asked.

The sight of Conall in the doorway caused my heart to go all fluttery. A hint of embarrassment over how brazen I'd been over the phone whorled into the mix, and all the words I wanted to say crashed onto the tip of my tongue, forcing out the worst possible option. "A whole lot of pus."

Yep. My first words to Conall after our steamy phone sex session involved pus. Talk about a smooth operator.

Before I could recoup my revolting greeting, I spotted the swirl of silver discharge that'd come out with the mess. A knot formed in my gut, and my unsexy greeting to Conall didn't seem to be such a big deal anymore.

Not if I had to follow it up with the news that one of his pack members was about to die.

CHAPTER TWENTY

Kerrigan

I COMBED through Justin's wolf hair with my fingers and studied his skin, alarm surging at the bluish tint.

The tempo of my heart increased as I reached for his snout. "I'm going to check out your gums. No biting."

The wolf nodded its head, the move so oddly human it threw me for a second. Then, using the gloved hand that hadn't been hit with any of the pus, I peeled up his lip. As I suspected, his gums held the same off-colored hue. "Did his skin appear blue-gray before he was shot?"

"No," Sabine said. "Is he short on oxygen?"

I shook my head. "His vitals, save the fever, are solid." Further inspection revealed a similar pigmentation issue with his claws. "Did he get worse after playing in the sun today?"

"Um, I'm not sure. Like I said, he just seemed so tired. Was I not supposed to let him go outside? I thought it'd be good for him." With that statement, Sabine burst into tears, no more silently wiping them from her cheeks.

I glanced over her head at Conall, imploring him for help. This was why family wasn't normally permitted in the exam room.

He nudged her toward the chair in the corner. "Go ahead and have a seat. Don't worry. Justin's in good hands."

I appreciated the vote of confidence, but my stomach sank as I processed the diagnosis. The secondary infection would take flushing, diluted iodine, and antibiotics. If my suspicions about the blue skin proved true, well, argyria—or the discoloration that occurred when the body came into contact with excessive amounts of silver—didn't have a cure. It wasn't common in animals, but since I studied bizarre cases in my spare time like the nerd I was, I'd poured over a story about a guy who consumed enough colloidal silver to make him look like a life-size version of Papa Smurf.

My phone vibrated in my pocket, and I was all set to ignore it until Conall lifted his cell to signal the text had come from him.

> Conall: What is it? Your face says it's not good.

I did my best to shutter my expression so Sabine wouldn't panic. A lightbulb pinged on in my brain, and I turned toward her. "Did you happen to keep the arrow you removed before I arrived?"

Utter bafflement crinkled her features, and then she gestured to the trash can. "I'm sure it's still in there."

"Mind playing fetch for me?" I asked Conall, and his imperious expression conveyed he'd make me pay for that later. "Oh, and use gloves."

That shook Sabine out of her stupor. Her bewilderment morphed into anger, and I replayed my words in an attempt to figure out why. Was she offended on Conall's behalf? "The gloves are for his own protection. The arrowhead might not be the only part that contains silver, and I don't want him to get hurt."

"It's the casual way you speak to the alpha. Show some respect."

I wanted to argue I had more pressing matters to attend to, but Sabine was distraught, and I didn't have the time to discuss werewolf hierarchy.

Conall was either focused or playing Switzerland, so I began treating Justin's abscess while "the alpha" dug the arrow from the trash. He tossed it on the counter, as if he couldn't wait to get it away from him. Then he scowled at it, as if that'd teach it a lesson. "What else do you need?"

"If you could please grab an IV bag out of my kit, that'd be much appreciated." His smirk as he fulfilled my request was less appreciated, but I let it slide because he appeared to be as concerned about Justin as Sabine.

Once I placed the IV, I turned to the woman who refused to leave, intending to convince her to do so anyway. "Would you be a dear and get me a mug filled with hot water so I can make a cup of tea?"

She muttered something about my priorities and me being a diva but exited the office.

As soon as the door had clicked into place behind her, Conall asked, "What is it?" At my pointed glance at the door, he added, "All the walls and doors in this building are reinforced. Keeps people from overhearing things they're not supposed to."

Good to know. "My theory is colloidal silver. Poisons work quickly, so if it were straight silver or wolfsbane, I doubt he would've survived this long. It takes quite a buildup of colloidal silver to turn the skin blue, but it's more of a human condition, so I can't be sure. It makes sense, though, since you also couldn't shift when you had silver in your system. The IV will flush out as much—"

The door opened, and Sabine extended a mug my way. "For your tea, Doctor."

Talk about supernaturally fast.

I dropped a teabag into the water and nudged the steaming mug toward her. "It's for you, actually. You appear to be a little dehydrated." Small fib. She was as high strung as a cat after an impromptu baptism. Thanks to my special valerian and chamomile tea, she should be much calmer in a few minutes, especially since I'd made it a two-bag special. Which sounded dirty, but I digress. "Drink it all down, as quick as you can without scalding your tongue."

Sabine reluctantly followed my instructions, and I stepped around Conall to study the arrow he'd dug out of the trash. Sure enough, the shaft was hollow, and when I shook it, liquid splatted the counter in tiny droplets.

Conall raised an eyebrow.

I gathered my hair in a makeshift ponytail so it wouldn't drag through the mystery substance, leaned over, and sniffed. "Um, I'm not exactly sure what it smells like or how to test my theory. Like I said, it was a random case study I saw online, so..."

With a shrug, Conall pressed a fingertip to one of shimmery globules. He jerked back his hand with a hiss, and I snagged his wrist and studied the tip of his index finger. Bile rose at the scent of charred flesh, and I guided his hand under the faucet and turned the water full blast.

Then I studied it again, sticking out my lower lip at the large blister that'd formed.

"I appreciate that you worry about me, Doc, but I'm fine." Conall's eyes met mine, leaving my head pleasantly swimmy.

Movement caught my eye—Sabine rubbing at her eyes. She yawned. "Sorry. My sleepless nights are catching up to me. It sorta hit all at once." She blinked watery eyes, her lids and chin drooping before she jerked herself upright.

She could say what she wanted about my priorities, but my two-fold plan was falling into place. She'd left Conall and me for long enough to discuss the possibility of silver poisoning, and I needed her out of the room as I thought up experimental treatments that might counteract its effects.

"Why don't you go rest?" I suggested in a low, singsong voice. "This will take a while, but I'll stay by Justin's side the entire time. It'll make it easier to move around in this small room anyway."

"That's o—"

"I'll have Sasquatch escort you home." Conall flung open the door, and suddenly I was grateful for the whole alpha thing she'd scolded me for not considering. Since she *was* respectful, she literally couldn't refuse.

As soon as the door closed, Conall spun to face me. "What can we do?"

"Nitric acid dissolves silver. Problem is, it's also poisonous."

"What if we gave him just enough to flush it out?"

I leaned a hip on the counter and racked my brain. "It's like giving someone a battery acid cocktail. Even inhaling it is enough to cause acute respiratory distress, which doesn't bode well for his organs. It's also not the easiest to get a hold of, although the chemistry teacher at the local high school would likely have some in stock."

"If Justin can rid his body of the silver, he might be able to heal his lungs."

"But if he stops breathing before he can do enough healing..." I exhaled and paced the room, which was only about five steps one way and five back with Conall taking up the space near the door. "We'd better consider that the nuclear option."

Justin snagged both of our attention with a hacking, liquid cough. His body convulsed, and he dry heaved until he puked a puddle of blood.

Desperation besieged Conall's expression. "Is there anything else we can do?"

My mind raced through several scenarios, and only one survived the pros versus cons test. "Blood transfusion."

Conall yanked up his sleeve and sat on the chair, the vein in the inside of his elbow presented and ready to go.

"Do you know if you're the same blood type?"

"Yeah. We're both werewolf positive."

Time was of the essence, and with Justin's convulsions growing worse by the second, there wasn't time to test blood and go through the usual protocols. Not that there were any for *werewolf poisoned by witch magic and liquid silver arrows.*

Originally, I worried I'd overpacked, but now I was glad I'd decided it was the better option, as opposed to constantly having to retrieve supplies from the office and vice versa. I added a sedative to the IV to help Justin cope and fished my car keys out of my pocket. "I'll be right back. I'm not sure if Sasquatch is as quick at his tasks as Sabine was to get hot water, but perhaps you should mention that he shouldn't bother stopping me this time."

CHAPTER TWENTY-ONE
Conall

THE PAST TWO times Kerrigan had been standing over me performing surgery, everything had been hazy, and I hadn't particularly appreciated it. Coming to in strange places did that to a guy. Especially one who craved control and dominance over every situation.

As she drew my blood, her movements deft and precise, all in the name of saving a werewolf she'd only met in animal form, I marveled at her adeptness and intelligence. At how strongly she cared. At everything I'd learned about her, and I couldn't wait to discover more. "Thank you. I know this is above and beyond."

She paused, her cleavage inches from my face, and I totally deserved extra points for maintaining eye contact. I could use them after the points I'd already lost drinking in the sight of her while she jabbed a needle into my vein. It'd been a legitimate distraction tactic, but I'd milked the opportunity for all it was worth.

"Just doing my job," Kerrigan said, shrugging off the compliment as if it were no big deal.

I snagged her hand and slipped my fingers between hers. "No, you're not. I asked the impossible of you, and you took it on anyway. That head of yours contains one of the sexiest brains I've ever seen. Or I guess I haven't technically seen it, but you get what I'm saying."

A smile spread across her face, lighting her gray eyes and adding a glow to her features. "Well, I had to jump on in, since if I waited for you to add a 'please,' I'd be waiting all day."

"Likely all year," I teased back, and if one of my pack members wasn't next to me fighting for his life, I'd pull Kerrigan into my arms, inhale her skin, and kiss the lips I was becoming obsessed with.

"I only hope you'll remember all that when your people want to string me up for not bowing and gobbling up every word you say, like some starving, doe-eyed groupie."

"You can be my groupie any day."

"Nah. You can be mine."

I chuckled, desire mingling with the swell of admiration. "That can be arranged. In private, anyway. Can't lose my forest cred."

Kerrigan snorted a laugh. "Forest cred. Good one, Alpha."

Heat surged, a low rattle of satisfaction rumbling through my chest. As much as I enjoyed all the ways she challenged me, hearing that from her lips was a hell of a turn-on.

The tips of her hair brushed my arm as she finished securing the tape to the needle and tube. "You'd better behave. If you keep growling, I'll fit you with a cone of shame."

"I'd like to see you try." Using my grip on her hand, I tugged her onto my lap. If we were going to have to sit here for a few minutes waiting for the bag to fill, we might as well make the most of it.

I inhaled as I dragged my nose across her cheek. Then I buried my head in the crook of her neck and sucked in more of her scent.

A tiny squeal came out as she squirmed, and thanks to the

added friction, my pants were growing too tight in record time. "Are you...sniffing me?"

"Yes, yes, I am. You smell really fucking good, too." With her unique aroma invading my senses, the rest of the world took a backseat. The tip of my tongue darted out for a tiny taste, and as she melted against me, the sweet tang of her arousal swirled into the mix.

Kerrigan tilted her head, allowing me better access. "You realize it's a little odd to *start* with sniffing, right?"

"*Mmm.*" I licked up the column of her neck and nipped at her jaw. "It's how we do things in the animal kingdom, and you definitely bring out my inner beast."

"Carry on, then," she uttered throatily. She lifted her feet from either side of the chair, tucking up her legs in a way that shifted her weight forward. Her moan filled the space between us as she slid into place—might as well go ahead and dub it Kerrigan's spot, from this moment forward.

I lavished attention on the other side of her neck, licking, kissing, and sucking, and then lifted my head so that our faces aligned. I slid my hands into her back pockets, groping and bringing her tighter against me, as I angled my mouth over hers.

A loud knock echoed through the room, and Kerrigan sprang away as if we were teenagers who'd been caught by her parents. The movement yanked at the needle in my arm and caused a sharp twinge to shoot through my elbow, but thanks to her taping job, it didn't slide free.

As she hastened to greet whoever I might have to kill for the interruption, she tripped over the leg of the chair. My free arm darted out, snagging her around the waist to steady her. I imagined we made quite the sight as I stood, half in and half out of the chair, straining to prevent her from falling without yanking the tube out of my other arm.

"Sorry, sir," Sasquatch said, his voice as expressionless as his face. "Nissa and Tyrese have returned and request an audience with you."

"Send them in." I quickly readjusted my crotch, sighing my regret at the deflating despite it being necessary. Two seconds around Kerrigan, and my dick acted as though it'd gone without for years.

Nissa and Tyrese kept a couple of feet between them as they stepped inside the room, uber professional to the point had I not been privy to the fact the two were married, I never would've guessed. As much as I bragged about my self-control, I wasn't sure I'd be able to pass by my woman without a reaction.

Hell, I'd only been in the room with Kerrigan for a half hour or so, with all of five whole minutes to ourselves, and *that*'d been too long to go without reaching for her.

"Boss." Nissa dipped her head, her mouth pressing into a tight, disapproving line as she glanced from me to Kerrigan. Obviously, she could sense they'd interrupted something, and if we'd done that shitty of a job of hiding the evidence, Kerrigan might as well return to my lap.

I cleared my throat. "I believe you two met the night Dr. Ryan performed surgery to repair my broken ribs and punctured lung, but allow me to properly introduce you. Kerrigan, meet my beta, Nissa Jones. Nissa, Dr. Kerrigan Ryan."

Kerrigan extended her hand, switching to an awkward wave after the move wasn't reciprocated. "Nice to meet you. Again. Or officially or whatever." The cheery tone meant she was trying her best, while my number two didn't soften even after I gave her serious stink-eye. I could turn on the alpha glare, but Nissa would despise me for forcing her hand, and Kerrigan would see that I'd had to. In female matters such as these, I'd learned it was better not to intrude.

"I didn't notice the other night that you're expecting," Kerrigan said. "Congratulations! Boy or girl?"

Nissa's hands went protectively to her stomach. "I don't know."

A crinkle of concern formed between Kerrigan's eyebrows. "How far along are you? No ultrasound yet? Or do you want it to be a surprise? There's also the gender-neutral route, of course, which more and more people are choosing nowadays, as scientific studies show—"

"I came to talk to Conall, not to be interrogated. And no offense, but it's none of your business."

No offense. A phrase that rarely failed to negate the sting of the words, and the way Kerrigan's hand rubbed at her chest meant she'd taken plenty of offense. Later, I'd have to explain the reason behind the contempt. If I did so now, it'd only land Kerrigan *and* me in hot water. Nissa detested being spoken about as though she couldn't speak for herself.

I'd know. At least she reamed me out in private when I'd made the mistake of doing it in the past, but I didn't want a repeat performance.

At the sniveling noise Justin made, Kerrigan whirred around. The sedative she'd added to his IV had put him to sleep, but it hadn't completely stopped the spasming or the foaming at the mouth. She used the stethoscope around her neck to listen to his heart and then eyed the bag of blood.

"That should be enough." She dropped to her knees, a sight I'd happily indulge in if we didn't have company. She removed the needle from my arm and placed a bandage over the spot before I could tell her not to bother. "You feel okay? Any faintness?"

Come to think of it, I was a pinch woozy. Then again, that might be on account of the angel at my feet fussing over me. I detoured my thoughts to safer territory in an effort to avoid dealing with blue balls for the next few hours. "What did you need to talk to me about, Nissa?"

Instead of answering, Nissa pointedly looked at Kerrigan. When I stood and stared right back, showing I was well aware of her presence, Nissa said, "I haven't eaten since breakfast, and the baby's as hungry as I am. How about we head to the kitchen so I can brief you there?"

Clever, finding a viable excuse to not talk in front of our guest. Using the baby was a nice touch, too, since I was a total sucker for my unborn nephew or niece, and she knew it.

"I have to get this transfusion going anyway," Kerrigan said. "Too many bodies in here will only make it more difficult. There's hardly enough room as it is."

Both Nissa and Tyrese tracked the hand I placed on Kerrigan's back. They might as well see that my opinion on Kerrigan was as set as theirs. And fair or not, mine overruled theirs. "I'll try to swing by later, but the night might get away from me again."

"It's highly likely," Nissa ever so helpfully added, and I sighed.

"I'll leave Sasquatch posted at the door. If it's an emergency and you need me, say the word and he'll track me down."

Kerrigan nodded, and I lowered my forehead to hers, inhaling her scent to help get me through the rest of the night. Then, since I refused to treat the incredible woman like my dirty little secret, I fused my mouth to hers to finish our cut-short kiss.

As I ran my tongue over the seam of her mouth, everything inside of me scrambled to find reasons to linger. But we'd pressed our luck enough as it was with the experimental treatment, and given the amount of silver coursing through Justin's system, there was no guarantee he'd make it through the night.

Duty called. We'd track down our enemies eventually, and once we did, I'd ensure they rued the day they ever messed with me and my pack.

CHAPTER TWENTY-TWO

Kerrigan

A TWITCH. Bones shifting beneath the surface of Justin's furry face. A human foot formed on the end of a lupine leg, and as the fur receded in a ghastly wave, stretching too tight over raw, pink skin, I fought a wave of nausea. I wasn't a puker, and in my short time working on werewolves, I'd come damn close to retching twice now.

The creature on the table mutated again, until he had a human face, the body of a wolf, and one overly long male leg. Not on the leg with the human foot, either, so I didn't feel too bad about my queasy reaction.

Cautiously, I approached the hospital table. "I'm not sure how much you've heard or understood the past few days, but my name is Dr. Ryan, and—"

Justin's woeful yelp rasped across my skin and provoked a pang of empathy. He vomited blood, along with something that looked suspiciously like a chicken skeleton, bones, beak and all.

I rushed to the window, flung it open, and inhaled a breath of fresh mountain air before sprinting back to assist however I could. The door swung open, and relief surged— Conall would be able to help.

Instead, Sasquatch charged inside. "What's going on?"

I gestured toward Justin, as if that would help. "He's stuck between human and wolf. His body seems to be resisting the shift, but I think the blood transfusion is working."

"You *think*? Shouldn't you know by now?"

I clenched my jaw, fighting the urge to aim my frustrations at him. "Well, Dr. Sasquatch, who's evidently attended medical school without telling anyone, this was our best bet, but science isn't an exact science." Okay, so a pinch of sarcasm had slipped out.

The giant ginger werewolf frowned. Under other circumstances, I might consider evoking that much emotion a win, but too much was going on to stop and celebrate.

"I said what I said. Experiments come along with failures and successes. I'm doing the best that I can, okay?"

His severe features softened, and he gave one sharp nod. "Okay."

Another tremor seized control of Justin's body. An arm exploded from his naked mole- rat-esque torso, one that appeared to be inside out.

At the sight of the gory mess of muscles and veins, Sasquatch turned ashen and swayed on his feet. He braced a hand against the wall and brought a massive hand to his mouth.

Keeping one hand on the quivering wolf, I snagged a syringe and bit off the cap. "Either get yourself together or get out of my operating room."

Sasquatch blew the air from his nostrils and swallowed. "What do you need me to do?"

"Hold him down. I'm going to give him a shot of Diazepam to try to stop the seizures." After filling the syringe with the medication, I hesitated, afraid the medication might hinder his transformation. I hovered the sharp tip over a vein, debating what would be worse in the long run. Brain damage versus being stuck in half-animal and half-human form.

Sometimes, you had to roll the dice.

Right as I was about to jam in the needle, Justin lunged at me, jaws open wide. I automatically dropped the syringe and flung my arms in front of my face for protection, wincing and bracing for the moment his fangs tore into my flesh.

One second, two, and then three ticked by.

I cracked open an eye to see Sasquatch holding the disfigured wolf by his underbelly and hind leg. Justin's rancid breath wafted over me, the decaying scent of death so strong my eyes watered.

Before I could fully process being alive and whole, Justin convulsed again.

Sasquatch readjusted his grip as a human arm replaced one of the front wolf legs. Then he wrangled Justin onto the table and flung his body over the top of him, effectively pinning him in place.

Bones shifted once again, skin and fur stretching in a nightmarish blur. I watched in horror, halfway crouched in search of my syringe, as the creature on the table morphed into a naked male covered in a sheen of sweat.

Sasquatch straightened and gaped, showing the most emotion I'd seen from him thus far.

A forlorn moan pierced the tension-laced silence as Justin curled himself into the fetal position. Then a pair of weak, hazel-colored eyes lifted in my direction. "Thank you," he wheezed. "Thank you for saving me."

An unexpected lump rose in my throat. "You're welcome." Since the tussle had ripped out his IV, I gently tugged on his arm and secured the needle with new pieces of tape. Then I placed my hand on his shoulder. "Talk to me. What hurts?"

"Everything," Justin said. "But I can feel myself healing."

I glanced at Sasquatch, who was already moving toward the door. "I'll call Conall and go wake up Sabine."

———

Day number three at the compound was coming to a close, and I hadn't seen Conall since drawing his blood and our kiss goodbye.

Monday evening, after all the excitement, Sasquatch had returned with Sabine, who'd burst into tears at the sight of her brother. She hadn't totally abandoned the chip on her shoulder—after all, I'd "drugged her and forced her to sleep," as she put it—but I had received a begrudging, "Thank you."

Around ten p.m. that night, Sasquatch escorted me to my car, as stoic and laconic as ever. It was hard not to take the don't-let-the-door-hit-you-on-the-way-out vibe personally. Particularly since it felt like most of the werewolves *wanted* the door to hit me.

On Tuesday, I woke up to see Conall had sent me a text in the wee hours of the morning, thanking me for saving Justin's life and caring for his injured pack members. Then he promised to make up for his absence as soon as he could.

That afternoon, after a long day at my clinic, I'd headed to the compound to check the other injured wolves for silver poisoning. None of them showed signs, and their vitals were stellar, which made it that much harder to pinpoint why they'd lost their accelerated healing abilities.

With Conall still MIA on Wednesday—my last couple of texts had gone unanswered as well—I broke down and asked where he'd gone, and if everything was okay.

"He's out of range, pursuing a lead," was all I was told. When I'd asked after Elias, I got a vague, "He's currently unavailable."

Fortunately, I managed to catch Gina before her shift at the bar. She didn't know where Conall was, but she did chat with me for an hour and help distract me from his absence and lack of communication.

By Thursday evening's checkup appointment, Justin had returned to full strength, so I told my disappointment over not seeing Conall to take a hike. We'd saved a life, and that was what mattered most. Moreover, we could use the newfound knowledge if anyone else got hit with an arrow.

After sending Justin off with a clean bill of health, I debated performing blood transfusions on the other injured werewolves.

See? I thought as I calculated needed liters of blood. *I can make myself useful and keep busy, missing werewolf boyfriend or not.*

Not that we'd had an official discussion about titles. But considering our whirlwind of intense interactions and experiments that ranged from medical to sexual, calling him the guy I was sorta seeing fell short.

The sound of the door opening interrupted my conversation, party of one, and I automatically turned to greet my incoming patient.

At the sight of Conall, happiness and relief crashed over me. I didn't think about decorum or the fact that Nissa was by his side; I took a running start and flung my arms around his neck. "Thank God. I was starting to worry you'd been hurt."

Conall squeezed me so tightly my feet left the ground and my breath puffed out over his shoulder. "You'd be the first to know if that was the case."

"Wow, so reassuring."

Conall's chuckle drifted across my nerve endings, giving my waning energy a much-needed boost. "I think you're just disappointed you haven't gotten to chain me up in a while."

I pulled back enough to place a hand on his cheek. "Don't act like you wouldn't be into it."

Nissa loudly cleared her throat, and oh yeah, she was here. The first night we crossed paths, she'd given me the chains and demanded I do whatever it took to save Conall, so I wasn't sure what I'd done to deserve her ire. Didn't help that she was as scary as she was beautiful.

Conall slowly lowered me to the ground, snaked his arm around my waist, and hooked a hand on my hip. His fingers dug into my skin as he pivoted the both of us to face Nissa. Judging by how snugly he tucked me against his side, he'd missed me almost as much as I'd missed him.

Affection careened through me until my mood floated above me in a hazy, lust-lined cloud.

"Shouldn't we go brief everyone?" Nissa asked, and my mood deflated along with my heart. I'd finally gotten my hands on Conall after too many days apart, and now I was going to have to let him go?

"You go ahead. You're the information expert." Conall slipped his thumb under the hem of my shirt and drew a tingly arc across my hip bone, back and forth, back and forth. "I promised Kerrigan I'd make up for leaving her in the lurch. It would appear that I need to make up for worrying her as well." He arched an eyebrow, and I bobbed my head.

"So, *so* much making up to do. I'm not sure you'll even be able to fit it all into one evening."

"Probably not. But I'll give it my all." He dipped his head and nipped at the shell of my ear. "Give you my all."

"Conall," Nissa snapped, and he whipped his head toward her so quickly that had he not been holding me in place, *I* would've taken a step back.

A low, threatening sound emanated from the back of Conall's throat.

Shit, they were going to get into a fight, and I was the cause. Now I'd end up having to play peacemaker instead of getting my promised alone time with Conall.

A totally selfish thought, but there it was anyway.

"You're the one who always tells me you can do more and that I should learn to delegate," Conall said, their glare-off reaching a whole new terrifying level. "I have full faith in you. You're dismissed."

The scowl Nissa fired at us lowered the temperature of the room to arctic levels far more suited for polar bears than wolves. She clamped her jaw so hard her teeth clattered together, and then she bowed her head a fraction of an inch. "Yes, sir. Whatever you say, sir."

As soon as the door shut behind her, Conall turned to me, his smile a pinch forced and his shoulders too tight. "Let's get out of here. There's a place I've been wanting to show you."

I barely refrained from telling him that anywhere he went, I'd follow.

CHAPTER TWENTY-THREE

Conall

MY FAVORITE ACTIVITIES alternated between running uninhibited in the forest in wolf form and riding my motorcycle to spots mostly untouched by man. With Kerrigan behind me, the scales tipped in the bike's favor.

I'd instructed her to hold on tight, and as I maneuvered around the rocks and knotted roots along the steep trail, her grip on me reached boa-constrictor levels. Not that I was complaining over having a beautiful woman clinging to me; I just hoped I hadn't scared her before we reached the more adventurous portion of our outing.

Stolen moments were few and far between, and I planned to take advantage of the brief window we had before any more shit hit the fan.

Yep, I was a selfish bastard who'd left my pregnant beta to handle a debriefing, and with the heat of Kerrigan's body soaking into me, I didn't even care. As for the impending blowout between Nissa and me?

It was going to be a bitch. Nissa had probed me about my interest in the woman riding behind me a handful of times as we'd been scouring miles and miles of forest, and each time, I'd replied that my dating life was none of her business. Truth was, I knew if I'd answered Nissa's questions, she and Tyrese would see how deeply Kerrigan had already burrowed beneath my skin.

What'd started out as fun was turning into something akin to obsession. I should care more—or at least take preventative measures to avoid a future disaster—but whenever I tried to summon up the will, there wasn't any to be found.

Since I'd already made my choice, I refused to spend my limited time with Kerrigan agonizing over my failed duties.

As the roaring waterfall that fed into a crystal blue lake came into view, I slowed and steered us to level ground. Once I engaged the kickstand, Kerrigan removed the helmet I'd provided her with, a spellbound glow to her features as she surveyed one of nature's masterpieces. "It's beautiful."

"Just wait. It gets even better." I climbed off the motorcycle, helped Kerrigan to the ground, and snagged the small cooler I'd brought along. Then I laced my fingers through hers and led her to the water's edge. The stream snaked down the side of the mountain until it leveled out and widened near town. This location provided a picturesque view of the endless ocean of trees, rocks, and blue, blue sky.

Kerrigan leaned her head on my shoulder. "I guess I have to take back what I said about Guadalupe Falls not having any falls."

"Just lupes?"

She cast me a curious side glance.

"Guadalupe means the valley of wolves. Nissa, Diego, and I got a kick out of it when we decided to make it our home."

"Wait. That means... You're Wolf Wolf, living in the valley of wolves?" Kerrigan shook her head. "Now I feel so foolish for not *expecting* to meet a werewolf when I moved to town."

"That's precisely why Sheriff Martin and I voted against putting werewolves on the town sign."

Kerrigan's eyes went wide. "Seriously?"

I chuckled and tapped her nose. "No, that was a joke.

Although, when it comes to Bigfoot, that's actually how Sasquatch got his nickname."

One of her eyes squinted closed, and was she trying to give me the evil eye? "I can't tell if you're telling me the truth or pulling my leg again."

Using my grip on her hand, I drew her closer and kissed the crinkle between her eyebrows. "One hundred percent serious. We often joke that all the Bigfoot sightings are just a result of him living in the forest by himself for decades. He's so much taller and bigger than most people, and sometimes he rustles the bushes to play it up for the tourists."

"*No*," she said, her utter disbelief clear. "You can't be talking about the same dude who escorts me home in deafening silence, never cracks a smile, and hardly speaks."

"One and the same."

"See, now I really don't believe you. I've tried to coax out a smile, and all I get is a whole lot of nothing in return. And I'm freaking funny, damn it."

"I wholeheartedly agree," I said, and why did that cause the humor to drain from her features?

"It's the outsider thing, isn't it? No matter what I say or do, it's not enough to change their minds."

Well, shit. This wasn't where this conversation was supposed to go. We'd have to deal plenty with that later, so I sidestepped. "Sasquatch is extremely serious when it comes to his duties. Now, no more frowning. We've got a couple hours before we have to head back, and I plan on enjoying it to the fullest."

I released her hand and spread out the food for our picnic. Nothing fancy. Sub sandwiches, extra heavy on the meat, cheese, and mayo. We sat on a rock that'd been warmed by the sun and chatted as we ate.

Kerrigan declined her second sandwich, so I ate it before packing up the mess. Then I stood and kicked off my boots. I reached behind my neck, snagged the collar of my T-shirt, and peeled it off over my head.

"Um, not that I mind you adding eye candy to the view," Kerrigan said, "but if this is your idea of a first date, I feel obligated to inform you that the social norm is to discuss stripping beforehand."

I chuckled—like she'd said, she was funny. "I'm sure you can imagine how much I care about social norms. It also sounds like you're quite the expert on stripping, and I'm all for a demonstration..."

She daggered a glare at me but lost the battle to suppress her smile.

"I want to show you my favorite place in the entire world. The climb there is steep enough that it's easier for me to get there in wolf form."

"How handy for you. You recall I'm not a werewolf, right?"

"I'm aware." Too aware due to the fuss Nissa and the rest of the pack kept making. Elias had greeted us upon our return, and when I pulled the kid aside and inquired how everyone had treated Kerrigan—and told him this was his chance to be brutally detailed and honest—he relayed most disregarded her and griped over her presence.

Even Sabine, whose brother was alive *because of her*.

"Conall? Did someone press pause on you? Is it your belly button?" Kerrigan reached for it, and I caught her hand.

"I'm all for you pushing my buttons, but not that one."

She stuck out her lips in a dramatic pout, so I tugged her to me and kissed them until they and her body both became pliant.

I used that to my advantage, twisting her around so that her back hit my chest. Then I pointed over her shoulder, to the gushing stream of water. "See that ridge along the top? You can't tell from this angle, but there's a cave behind the waterfall. It's the prettiest spot you ever did see, completely hidden from the rest of the world. That's where we're headed."

Her eyes widened as she studied the sheer rock face. "That's the kind of climb that requires rope and those metal thingies that you"—she fisted her hand and brought it down in a hammer motion—"into the rock."

"I don't need those. My center of gravity is lower in wolf form, my footing extra sure. That's why you're going to ride me."

"Another thing that's usually discussed beforehand," she said, and I huffed a laugh. "I get that you have special wolf skills, but I'd require a whole bag of gear to make that climb safely. Plus, like, a shit-ton of bubble wrap and some football pads."

I wound my arms around her waist and lowered my mouth to her neck. "Have I mentioned how sexy your sense of humor is?"

"Now I *know* you're buttering me up—most people find it obnoxious."

"Sounds like you've been hanging out with all the wrong people, sweetheart."

"Maybe it's just people, period. Werewolves are where it's at. Then again, as I mentioned earlier, Sasquatch is definitely of the opinion it's obnox—"

I spun her around and plundered her mouth with my tongue. Distraction was the name of the game when it came to Kerrigan's anxieties. As long as I kept her focused on the here and now, she'd forget why she'd hesitated in the first place.

She cupped the back of my neck, drawing me closer as her mouth moved against mine, and I willingly gave into her gravitational pull, my body becoming a pleasure-seeking missile. As I stroked my tongue over hers, desire detonated and spread, the rapturous debris raining down around us until it was the only thing that existed.

Her lips. The heat of her body. Her hands drifting over my bare torso. My hands on her ass, squeezing and kneading as I notched her tighter against me. Our tongues tangled in a dance that spoke of anticipation, obsession, and surrendering to temptation.

Pure unadulterated need streaked through me as she gripped the waistband of my pants over the button that I internally begged her to undo. If I didn't reinforce my willpower, I'd forget that my show and tell plan consisted of more than our bodies.

I reluctantly broke the kiss, pride roaring to the surface as I took in her half-lidded expression. If she ensnared me again, I wasn't sure I'd ever find my way out. "Holy shit, woman."

The siren beamed at me, innocently batting her eyes, and I took a large step back so I wouldn't reach for her again. "I was gonna accuse you of using your humor as a delay tactic, but then you upped the ante with all"—I encompassed her, head to toe, with the circling of my finger—"that. Trust me, once we're inside the cave, it'll be worth the wait."

Kerrigan hugged her arms around herself. "Don't you remember my fear of heights?" Before I could reply that I certainly recalled the way I'd helped her get over them on the Ferris wheel, she added, "Grams was the brave one in the family. She's the reason I've been taking more risks. It's what I do in her memory, because weird or not, she was one of my best friends and I miss her. But this time, the stakes are too high. We're in the middle of nowhere, with no equipment or rails, and if we fall..."

I closed the distance between us and captured her quivering chin in my fist. "I understand your hesitance, and if you decide not to go, I'll respect your decision. But I haven't shared this spot with anyone else in the whole world, and I want to share it with you. I promise I'll get you into that cave without so much as a scratch. You might get a little wet, but that's the extent of the danger, and you could always

minimize soggy clothes by shedding a layer or two—
something I highly recommend, by the way."

"Seems mighty convenient," she said, glancing from me to
the waterfall to me again. With a comingled grumble and
sigh, she removed one shoe and then the other. "Fine. We all
know you're gonna win in the end anyway."

"I prefer to think of it as us both winning," I said with a
triumphant smile.

Kerrigan shook her head and peeled off her shirt,
revealing a lacy purple bra that reminded me of the tiny
flowers that grew in the meadows during spring. "The things
I do for you."

My mouth watered as I watched her unzip her jeans and
shimmy out of the denim as though she'd learned how to
undress in a porno. Hip pop, hip pop, perky tits bouncing
with each movement.

As she bent to pick up her discarded clothes, dizziness set
in. The lacy thong showcased her supple, heart-shaped ass,
and one particular part of my body stood at attention.
Anyway, it tried. The too-thick denim got in the way,
prompting me to shed my jeans. I rarely bothered with
underwear, as it was one more layer to discard before
shifting.

The blood in my veins turned molten. With her standing
in front of me in matching underwear, my hedonistic side
grappled with my self-control. If I didn't get her to the cave
within the next few minutes, she'd likely change her mind, so
I reminded myself I'd have time for more ogling once we
reached our destination.

I let my inner wolf loose, shifting as I strode—and then
padded—over to Kerrigan.

She squatted to eye level, which worked out nicely as it
gave me the perfect view of her cleavage. "I probably
shouldn't pet you, but since you can't tell me any
differently..." She rubbed her hand along my pepper-colored

coat, and I tipped my head into her touch, inhaling her familiar, intoxicating scent as she scratched her way down my side.

Then I licked her cheek, basking in her giggle.

"Okay, I'm gonna climb on you now. Which we did at least discuss first, so... Here I go." Kerrigan boosted herself onto my back and wound her arms around my neck.

I darted toward the rocky cliff, the surge of adrenaline the type of natural high that came from running in wolf form. Instead of turning my senses fuzzy, it sharpened them, every tree, rock, and blade of grass standing out. The roar of the waterfall sounded louder; I could feel Kerrigan's chest moving with rapid breaths.

Within minutes, we were near the cave. With my sights set on the rock outcropping behind the steady spray of water, I picked up speed.

"Wait. We're not—" Kerrigan's scream echoed through the air as I leaped through the waterfall.

CHAPTER TWENTY-FOUR

Kerrigan

COOL WATER RUSHED OVER ME, several buckets worth, all at once. Conall skidded to a stop, and I made a mental note to inform him that having my underwear plastered to my skin by several gallons of water hardly qualified as getting "a little wet."

But we'd made it safely through the waterfall and into the cave. I didn't want to think about the fact that we'd have to somehow make it back out. As I sat up from my spot astride my lupine steed, I gasped at the beauty of the hidden world we'd crashed our way into. Moss covered the sides in a display that boasted every shade of green. Leafy vines hung over the mouth, and with the sun nearing the horizon, the beads clinging to them glowed, turning the waterfall into a glittery curtain that spit flecks onto my skin.

Ever so carefully, I climbed off Conall. A handful of years ago, I'd ridden a pony of similar size, only the werewolf at my side was much stockier, with slightly shorter legs. He certainly shook his coat out like a dog, sending droplets over me once again.

I brought my arms up and laughed, and by the time I

dropped them, Conall had returned to his human form. He straightened to his full height, as naked as the day he'd materialized on my exam table.

My hair sent rivulets of water down my body, and a quick glance confirmed that yep, my nipples were as hard as they felt, not to mention visible through the thinly lined cups of my bra. It wasn't like he hadn't seen them before, however via phone screen and real life felt a lot different.

I ran my gaze over his sculpted torso, taking my time admiring each line and divot carved from flesh. My teeth sank into my lower lip of their own accord as I followed the trail of dark hair and arrived at the particular body part I couldn't wait to get my hands on. *Damn*.

"Eyes are up here, sweetheart." His mouth lifted in the smirk that'd infuriated me more than once.

Not today, though. Today it solicited desire-laced heat and overpowering palpitations. The sunlit waterfall created a disco-ball effect that highlighted Conall in intervals, playing off the planes of his face, his muscles, and his skin.

Grasping hold of the boldness that'd landed me in this town, on that Ferris wheel, and in this cave with this man, I lifted my chin and locked eyes with him. Then I strode closer, experiencing a surge of power as his Adam's apple bobbed in his brawny throat.

I trailed my fingers over his shoulders and across his collarbone, similar to the way he'd once done to me, and now I got the allure. I pressed my palm to the center of his chest, feeling the thump of his heart, beating away as fast as mine. "What's it like? Shifting from a human to a wolf? Does it hurt?"

"Not anymore," he said, his voice raspy. "As pups we can only shift during the week of the full moon. Around adolescence come the more intense, painful shifts as we gain the ability to change at will, but our bodies quickly adapt and get better and faster."

"That's interesting that the moon only factors into it when you're young."

"Actually," he said, "the pull of the moon is always there. The fuller it gets, the more amplified it becomes. Just like our emotions. Joy, sorrow, irritation, elation." Conall slid his arm around my lower back, yanking me to him and wedging one of his massive thighs between both of mine. His growing erection pressed against my lower abdomen, and he licked a heated trail along my jaw, to the spot just beneath my ear. "Desire."

A delicious, hazy sensation overtook me, and I decided to go all in on the delirium and taunt the beast at the same time.

I rubbed myself against his hard length, the needy spot between my thighs instantly demanding more. "Isn't there a full moon tomorrow?" I rolled my hips, pushing harder, and he groaned, his warm breath hitting my neck and eliciting a shiver.

"There is." Conall lowered his lips to mine, resting but not kissing, his tongue flicking out as he asked, "Do you trust me?"

Not what I was expecting. I blinked up at him, and while a dozen sarcastic responses flitted through my brain, this wasn't a joking moment. I could see the sincerity swimming in the depths of his eyes, a raw honesty he didn't usually show. "Implicitly."

He walked us closer to the edge of the rock outcropping and pivoted me outward— the opposite of the direction I'd expected and yearned for. But he'd asked me to trust him, and I did. "This is the best way I can describe what shifting's like for me now. It's more of a show and tell. I'm going to swing you outward, and I want you to extend your fingers and touch the waterfall. I've got you, I swear."

You're gonna do what now?

My protest faded into oblivion as Conall's cock nudged the crease of my ass. He palmed one of my breasts and squeezed. "It's like being aware of every sensation, every cell in your body, every nerve ending."

Rapture replaced my misgivings about his plan when he pinched my nipple through the lace.

"And suddenly..." He sent me soaring through the air, spinning me as though we were in the middle of a complicated ballroom dance.

My body turned weightless, and I stretched out my fingers. My stomach drifted up, high fiving my heart as I plunged my hand into the cold water.

In the next instant, I was back in Conall's arms, my chest mashed up against his. As I came down from the free-fall, my center of gravity tethered myself to his body, his breaths, his rapid pulse.

"Whoa," I said.

Satisfaction merged with the passion written across his face. "Yeah, that's exactly what it feels like. A pinch of fear before exhilaration takes over and you find yourself clicking into place, as if it were always what you were meant to be." Vaguely I realized I was being propelled backward. "It's the same type of thrill I get whenever I'm with you."

My back hit the wall, and I'd never been so happy to be between a rock and a hard man. His lips recaptured mine, his kiss brutal and life-giving. He boosted me in his arms, groaning as my center hit his thickness. The light scrape of stone resulted in a potent combination of pleasure and pain that drove me that much higher.

I wrapped my legs around his waist, securing us tighter together.

At his low growl of pleasure, I arched against him. God, he felt as good as he looked, the friction enough to leave me panting. I couldn't believe how close I already was to the edge, a testament to just how good Conall was with his mouth and tongue.

He slipped his hand between us and hooked a finger in the tiny string that held up my underwear. "Tell me you wore these for me. That you wanted me to see you in your matching bra and panties."

"Who's giving away my secrets?"

"The internet," he said, moving to suck on my neck. "I saw a meme that said if a woman's wearing matching underwear, then *she's* the one who decided to have sex."

"I did," I whispered, sliding one of my bra straps down my shoulder. "I wore them just for you. I've been wearing lacy underwear every day, hoping it'd be the day you returned, and that we'd end up like this."

He thrust his tongue into my mouth, and his fingers inched lower, a mere whisper away from the pulsating bundle of nerves that craved his touch.

I braced my hands on his shoulders and dragged my nose across his whiskered cheek. "You warned me I might get a little wet, but my panties are soaked completely through, and it's all your fault."

Silence descended, so heavy that even with the roar of the waterfall, it spoke louder. Had I accidentally crossed from sexy territory into TMI?

Gold rolled over his irises. "That's something I definitely need to verify for myself."

Time crawled to a stop, the only thing continuing to move the rapid breaths sawing in and out of our mouths and mingling in the air between us.

At long last, two of his fingertips hit my clit. He delved his fingers into my pussy, leaving me no choice but to dig my fingernails into his skin. "Why, Doctor Ryan, you're absolutely soaked."

A complaint escaped without my permission as he withdrew his hand, leaving it flat against my abdomen, tantalizing close and yet way too far away.

"Patience," Conall said, far too smugly, so I reached between us, gripped his shaft, and gave it a firm squeeze.

"*Fuck*," he grunted, his hips bucking and knocking into mine.

"Yeah, that's what I'm saying. We've already established you're not nice or reasonable. As for me, I'm not patient."

Elation and awe spread across his features, and he lowered his forehead to mine and exhaled. "Me, neither. Which is why I need to taste you again. I want that wetness coating my throat as I fuck you with my tongue."

Every ounce of oxygen whooshed from my lungs at once, leaving me unable to breathe or talk or do anything as he lowered my feet to the ground.

"First things first, this has to go." Conall unhooked my bra, yanked it off, and tossed it aside. A low, appreciative noise rumbled through him. The hum continued as he bent to peel off my panties. "Now, put your legs over my shoulders."

I did so in a trance, my system still too busy short circuiting to do anything but obey.

Once my knees were on either side of my neck, he straightened to his full height, placing a hand between the rock and moss wall to keep my back from scraping. Then he gave a quick jerk of his chin, indicating the area above my head. "Grab onto those vines. They're strong enough for me to hang on, so they'll hold. I've got you, too. I won't let you fall. Same way I didn't on the climb up."

I reached a few inches above and to the side of my head, wound one of the vines around my fist, and did the same with my other hand.

"Good girl," Conall said, his lips brushing my sex. Then he put his entire mouth on me. My moan echoed back at me, the sound so erotic that I drifted on a sea of bliss, not a care to whether or not I'd ever be found again.

My hips rocked of their own accord as he lapped at me, his groan of pleasure reverberating through my core. His course whiskers abraded my wet, swollen flesh seconds before he thrust his tongue inside of me, fucking me with it as promised.

Each stroke and pump tightened more and more muscles, until I was a panting, wanton mess. The pressure built and built, and my head *thunked* against the wall of the cave. Right when I thought I'd reached the rapturous peak, he sucked my clit into his mouth and showed me how much higher I could climb. "Conall. *Holy shit, holy shit, holy shit.*"

I closed my eyes, giving myself over to the euphoric sensations. Then came the tumble into nirvana, soaring and shattering and bursting in a hundred different directions at once.

Slowly, Conall brought me back down, ekeing out every last ounce of pleasure.

I unhooked my ankles and slid down his body. After taking a quick second to regain my bearings, I peered up at him through the sublime haze only a mind-blowing orgasm could bring. "That...was amazing."

"Watching you come apart as you rode my face—that was amazing. Whatever we do next is up to you. One of the bonuses of accelerated healing means there's no possibility of STDs, but obviously neither of us is ready for a baby. I tossed a few condoms in my saddlebag, so once we return to the picnic blanket, we can—"

"Did you not hear the part about me being impatient? I'm not leaving this cave until there's been mutual satisfaction." I seized hold of his arousal, releasing a hum of pleasure over finding him so hard and ready.

"Really, Kerrigan. It's—" His grunt ricocheted through the cave, urging me on.

"You're right. It's been hard to find time together, and if we're being honest, I've wanted my hands on your cock since it dangled over my head that night we met, even as I was processing the impossibility of what'd happened."

I swiped the pre-cum leaking from the head of his penis and ran it down his length for lubrication.

Gold glimmered in the brown depths of his irises, and I squeezed him tighter. "And now I want to watch as *I* make *you* lose control."

CHAPTER TWENTY-FIVE

Conall

LOSE CONTROL? I was about to transform into a feral beast right before her eyes. My plan had been to give Kerrigan an orgasm and return to the lake. I didn't want her thinking she owed me anything, especially not in a damp, semi-dark cave where there wasn't anywhere to get comfortable.

But once she'd wrapped her hand around my cock, she *owned* me.

"I don't lose control," I gritted out. My inner wolf insisted I shut my mouth and wave the white flag already. Kerrigan had only seen a glimpse of that guy. Due to the approaching full moon, my baser desires were near the surface, and with her bared to me, it'd already been difficult enough not to bury myself between her thighs.

"Is that right?" Kerrigan asked, a defiant gleam in her eye. I fixated on her purple fingernails as she stroked, my jaw dropping, every muscle flexing. My self-restraint thrashed in the deluge of heady sensations, and I stopped fighting and fully surrendered.

After all, I was only human.

Well, half human. Every side of me wanted this, though.

"This ass, by the way..." I smacked it, watching for her reaction as the illicit sound echoed around us. Glee lit her eyes, and she pressed tighter against me, wiggling her hips side to side as my swollen head swiped across her upper stomach.

Oh, she wanted to play? I filled my hands with her bounteous cheeks, the tips of my claws jutting out and pricking the skin. "It's incredible, and it's all mine."

"There's my big bad wolf. Let him loose to play. I don't want to tame the beast. I just want him all to myself." Kerrigan hooked a knee over my hip, spreading herself wider for me as she dragged her silken heat from the bottom of my balls to the tippy top of my cock.

I braced my hands on the wall on either side of her head as she alternated between undulating and stroking. The tip of her pink tongue darted out to wet her lips, and greedy bastard that I was, I craved more control and more devouring. I seized her mouth with mine, digging my fingers so hard into the stone wall that it began to crumble beneath my palms.

Tiny rocks rained down on Kerrigan's head and shoulders, and instead of flinching, she squeezed my shaft that much tighter, creating more friction as she increased the tempo. My entire body shuddered; my inhibitions ran wild.

Black dots danced across my vision as I all-out fucked her hand.

"That's it," she murmured as my balls constricted and my entire body quaked. "Now cum on my stomach. I want to smell like you when I crawl under my covers tonight."

The statement was so unexpectedly indecent that I nearly lost it. I clung to that last thread tethering me to my control, to the ground, and to Kerrigan. I wound one of my hands in her damp hair and jerked back her head, allowing me deeper access. I plunged my tongue inside her mouth, tasting, devouring, and marking every inch as mine.

The pressure within me swelled to the unbearable point, and I roared as my orgasm rocketed through me. I emptied myself onto her stomach as requested, the sight so erotic I was already craving the next time, when I'd be nestled deep within her pussy.

As soon as I'd expelled the last drop, I drew Kerrigan to my heaving chest. Then I buried my head in her hair and inhaled the scents clinging to her skin. Dewy-fresh mountain, lake water, and her perfume, as well as her arousal and the result of mine.

"That thing you said earlier about crawling into your bed?" I growled, unleashing my full alpha stare. "Fuck that. You'll be crawling under my covers with me tonight."

———

By the time Kerrigan and I hiked down from the cave, rain clouds had covered the sun, resulting in a significant drop in temperature.

She shed her underwear, and both of us pulled on our dry clothes. Since she continued to shiver, I unearthed the leather jacket from my bike's saddlebag. I rarely got cold, the jacket more about protecting my human skin than keeping me toasty. It looked way better on Kerrigan than it did on me anyway.

Her hair was drying in slightly frizzy waves that brought out the hint of red within the brown, and already I yearned for later tonight, when those silky strands would be splayed across the pillow as I took her in my bed.

I planned on avoiding Nissa until tomorrow morning if possible, so I'd check in with Diego to see what I'd missed and if there was anything that required my attention.

Kerrigan tucked her bra into the jacket pocket, and I quickly snatched her thong off the ground. "These are mine now," I informed her, fiddling with the string for a moment before stuffing them into the pocket of my jeans.

She affected an offended expression, but the gorgeous smile spreading across her face immediately undermined it. "No fair. Since you go commando, I don't get a souvenir." She lifted a hand to her stomach, her skin flushing pink. "Never mind, I'm good."

Evidently, she was hellbent on getting me to completely abandon my duties and take her right here and now.

"This place is as amazing as you claimed and was totally worth putting my life in your hands. Or paws." Kerrigan wound her arms around my waist. "Thank you for showing it to me."

"I've always felt a bit selfish not sharing it. But as soon as I became the official alpha of the pack, I was glad I'd kept one place where I could disappear to for snippets of time."

"Somewhere you could also be alone to think of your family, I assume." Kerrigan winced slightly, as though she weren't sure if she'd crossed into forbidden territory. She'd hit the nail on the head, though. I didn't like being vulnerable in front of anyone, and more, it was dangerous to allow myself to be.

"I'm sure you put pieces of the puzzle together after the night I thought you were a witch." I cupped her neck and brushed my thumb over the thin skin I'd come frightening close to marring. Regret welled, along with bitterness and grief over what'd happened all those years ago. "My parents, siblings, and everyone from my pack except for Diego, were killed by a coven witches when I was twelve years old. I wanted to save them, but—"

Please. Please spare our lives. At least the lives of our children... The words spouted from the muck I'd buried so deep I pretended it didn't exist. My parents told me to run and hide mere minutes before our assailants caught up to them.

My sisters and two brothers were too young to flee, no

chance of escape. Begging hadn't changed the witch's mind; she'd cackled as she executed my whole family, not a second's consideration to their appeal.

If either my mom or dad had used their last moments to launch an attack, maybe I wouldn't be the only survivor from my family. Maybe I wouldn't have had to restrain my screams behind my hand as I'd cowardly raced away.

That was why I'd never allow my mouth to form a word meant for feeble people who begged instead of demanded.

"I wasn't strong enough." I swallowed in an attempt to dislodge the lump in my throat— it didn't work. "It was over before I even knew what happened. Diego and I were the only two who survived. We wandered on our own for a few years, met Nissa, and formed our own pack four years after that attack. I've spent years lifting weights, reading books on military strategies, and learning to fight so I'd never be put in that helpless position ever again."

"You can't beat yourself up for the past, Conall. You did what was necessary to survive."

"Enough sob stories," I said, refusing to continue down this path. I strode over to the motorcycle and handed her the helmet without looking back.

Kerrigan skirted my extended arm and squeezed herself between me and the bike. She bracketed my face with her hands, steady and unmovable as I usually was, until I dropped my gaze to hers. "I'm sorry," she said. "For what happened, and for pushing. I can't imagine how hard it must've been to lose so many people you loved."

"Sounds like you've experienced loss yourself."

Kerrigan shrugged a shoulder, fidgeting now that the spotlight had been turned on her. "It wasn't nearly as traumatic." She told me about her mother and grandmother, giving me a brief snapshot of her background. "Like I said, I miss my grandma, but she lived a long, full life."

"It doesn't make it any easier."

A sad smile ghosted her lips. "You're right. That's why you should grant yourself more grace. I've seen the way you take care of your pack. You're a good guy, Conall Shaw."

I grunted, disliking that as much as when she'd called me reasonable. "You're getting the wrong idea about me, sweetheart, and that's only gonna lead to disappointment. As you've pointed out yourself, I'm an unreasonable asshole. I'm possessive, volatile, and downright ruthless if a situation calls for it. Plus, I'm about as stubborn as you are, and that's saying a lot."

Kerrigan canted her head. "You're wrong. Well, maybe not about all of it, but you're wrong about me not seeing you for who you are. Yes, you're cocky and moody and one of the most frustrating people I've ever met."

"You forgot sexy," I said, doing my best to lighten the mood and distract her from the fact that I had valid reasons to warn her away. How'd we go from the incredible session in the cave to this?

One corner of her mouth quirked up, and she tipped onto her toes and softly kissed my lips. "Super sexy. You're hung like a werewolf, too." The other side of her mouth got in on the smile. "You're fiercely protective, plus you're funny and smart. You're tough but kind. Occasionally harsh but fair. You see me for me and make me feel safe, physically and emotionally. I'm not scared to be me around you, either. Which is why—"

The trill of my cell cut her off, and I dug into the saddlebag to silence it. But then I saw Nissa had called three times, as well as left a voicemail, and Sasquatch had also tried to reach me. "Fuck. I'm so sorry, Kerrigan. There must be some kind of emergency."

"Go ahead. I understand."

Since I couldn't rewind time and take the call, I scanned through the messages, praying Nissa was overreacting.

Ignoring the fact that Sasquatch hardly reacted, so a call meant...

Another sigil trap. Nissa's voice cut in and out, the crackle of electricity obviously messing with her signal. While I missed who'd been ensnared, the swearwords she peppered throughout the message came through crystal clear.

Location was the most important detail, and I had that much, so I instructed Kerrigan to climb onto the motorcycle and then plunked the helmet on her head. I fired up the engine and sped down the trail. I called Nissa back, but between the roar of the engine and the static still interfering with her phone, the conversation was spotty at best. Finally, I just yelled that I'd be there as soon as possible.

My gut knotted as I debated my two super-shitty options.

Did I risk Kerrigan's safety by heading directly to where Nissa and a handful of my soldiers were struggling to break the sigil trap? Or did I drop her off at the compound and further endanger the life—or lives—of one of my pack members?

CHAPTER TWENTY-SIX

Conall

THE INSTANT the sigil trap burst, I didn't let myself slow or drop to the ground despite the searing pain and ringing in my ears. I ignored the burns on my arms and legs and scooped up Elias.

"I got my post covered like you told me to..." *Wheeze.* "Almost caught the witch, but..." Elias's eyes drooped, and his chest heaved. "Saw the trap. Couldn't let Gideon..."

The amount of self-loathing flowing through my veins hurt worse than my injuries, and with each second that Elias didn't gasp for another gulp of air, more of it pumped through my body.

Later I'd question Gideon about what exactly happened. All that mattered now was getting Elias to the compound, so I tightened my grip on Elias and raced toward the Jeep. Several people tried to keep pace, but even with the kid in my arms, few could keep up.

"Need me to drive?" Tyrese asked as I carefully maneuvered Elias into the backset, where Diego was ready and waiting. He tugged as I heaved, and as soon as Elias's feet were clear, I slammed the door closed.

"Nah, I got it." No one drove as fast or as well as I did, and the kid was my responsibility. His injuries, my fault.

If I'd only gotten there sooner...

In order to shave a mile off the trip, I cut across the meadow, asking mother nature to forgive me this one time and vowing to reseed it myself.

As long as Elias survived, I'd do anything.

The shocks complained as we bumped along the knotted path through the trees meant for hikers, the screech of tree branches so loud they drowned out everything but the panic screaming through me.

As we neared the dirt road that'd take us to the compound, the trail widened, and I cranked the wheel, taking the sharp right turn at a frowned-upon speed.

A harsh curse punctuated the air as Diego's head slammed against the backseat window. He'd held onto Elias instead of bracing himself, and I appreciated the hell out of him for it.

"How's he doing?" I asked, my voice coming out with the hysterical edge that'd carved up my lungs the instant I'd crested the hill and spotted Elias inside the eerie green beam of light of the sigil trap. Blood had oozed from every inch of his peeling flesh, and the cracking of his lips accelerated each time he inhaled more of the thick silver mist that hung within the incandescent snare.

The image superimposed itself over the familiar path in front of me, causing bile to rise up and coat the inside of my throat, and I desperately hoped it wouldn't be one that haunted me for the rest of my days.

"He's still losing a lot of blood," Diego said, "and I can't hear him breathing anymore, but I think that's a result of all the noise interference."

Dust clouded the air behind us as I pushed the speedometer to its limit.

If I'd brought Kerrigan along... I white-knuckled the steering wheel, turning into the tail end of the Jeep as it swerved and fishtailed. I'd reasoned that if she ended up injured, she couldn't patch up anyone else, and assured myself it was the best way to choose everyone.

But Elias needed those minutes back. The sigil trap had been rigged with a flash bomb loaded with silver, and the kid had been exposed to both for way too long.

If he didn't make it, his death was on me.

"Goddammit." I slammed my fist into the dash, unable to keep the lid on my temper. The outburst was also supposed to stifle the blurring of my vision.

It fucking didn't.

If anyone asked, I'd insist the leaking was due to them nearly being scorched from my skull.

Of all the people, why him? A dangerous route to go down, and shame rose. Every member of my pack was important, but Elias had already been through enough.

The tires squealed as I turned into the compound, and I slammed on the brakes hard enough for my seat belt to leave a mark.

Diego started out of the Jeep with Elias, and I hefted the kid in my arms. I sprinted toward the infirmary, calling Kerrigan's name the entire time.

She was already in the room, supplies laid out and ready to go. She paled when she saw the two of us, horror widening her eyes. She stretched her fingertips toward my jaw, stopping just short of touching me. "Oh my God, Conall, your skin."

"I'll be fine. Just fix Elias." I lowered him onto the table.

"That's...? Elias? Can you hear me?" She rapidly blinked her eyelashes, visibly choking back her emotions. Determination overtook her features as she cracked her knuckles and got to work.

The next several minutes were a blur as she yelled out instructions to Sabine. She intubated Elias and handed Sabine the bag to pump, muttering to herself about next steps as she continued chest compressions.

People gathered near the doorway, gasping at the injuries and crying out Elias's name.

"Get your hands off him," a shrill voice yelled. Linda, a woman in her fifties who formed committees with too many rules to occupy her time, breached the entrance of the room and shook an accusatory finger at Kerrigan. "She's the witch. None of this happened before she arrived."

Sasquatch blocked her path, preventing her from coming any closer. While his interference would typically be enough, Linda lunged to get around him. He snagged her around the middle, using necessary force to remove her from the room.

"Close the door and tell them to go home," I told Sasquatch. "No one else gets in, got it?" "Yes, sir," he replied.

As door swung closed, Linda shouted, "Conall, can't you see that she's got you under a spell? How can you forsake your people like this?"

A twinge wrenched my chest, the surplus of regret and sorrow too thick for me to find my go-to anger. What a mess I'd made.

I placed my hand on Kerrigan's shoulder, the rigidity of her posture the only sign the tirade had affected her. Nothing I said would make it better, so I simply squeezed, assuring her I had the utmost faith in her.

"Reaching two minutes," Sabine said, and Kerrigan requested I grab the stored bag of leftover blood from the tiny medical fridge in the corner.

After applying gel onto the shock paddles, Kerrigan told everyone to stand back. The *beep, beep, beep* counted down, she hollered, "Clear," and then the kid's entire body convulsed.

At the banging on the door window, I turned, ready to light into whoever it was, along with Sasquatch for allowing it.

Gideon's dirt and tear-streaked face stirred up compassion I hadn't realized I possessed. I couldn't hear him, but the word he mouthed was plain enough to read. "Please."

I didn't have it in me to refuse and signaled for Sasquatch to let him in.

The door hadn't even completely swung open when Gideon rushed inside. He skidded a foot from the exam table, a hand flying to cover his mouth as he caught sight of Elias.

I cleared my throat, not that it removed the lump that'd made a home there. "Kerrigan, this is Gideon. One of Elias's—"

"I'm his boyfriend." Gideon snagged Elias's limp hand and curled it to his chest. Evidently, they'd become official in the past week or so. Happiness flickered for a whole second before a swell of remorse extinguished it. "I'm not sure how he sensed the sigil trap, but he shoved me out of the way seconds before it snapped with him inside. Why'd you do that, babe?"

A muscle ticked in his jaw, his chin quivering as he turned to Kerrigan. "I love him, and he saved my life today, and I really need him to be okay. Please tell me he's going to be okay."

Damn. Not only had I let down Elias, Gideon, and several of my soldiers, I'd unintentionally piled more pressure on Kerrigan.

I stepped forward to draw his attention to me right as Kerrigan placed a hand on Gideon's shoulder. "I promise to do everything in my power to ensure he will be."

———

After making the rounds and taking care of a handful of tasks, I rubbed at my tired eyes and headed toward the infirmary.

It'd been days since I'd slept well. My previous plans of

taking Kerrigan in my bed had been shot to hell. I didn't deserve to have sex, anyway—didn't even deserve our picnic and time in the cave.

The scent of charred flesh clung to my body, an ever-present reminder of the hellish evening, and I desperately needed a shower to wash away the dirt and gore. Unfortunately, it wouldn't do the same for my guilt.

Sasquatch stood posted outside the door, and I nodded at him before stepping inside the room that smelled like antiseptic. I opened my mouth to ask Kerrigan for a status update, the words dying on my tongue as she came into view. She'd pulled up a chair next to the exam table and had fallen asleep with her head inches from Elias's, her arm curled protectively around his upper chest.

Gideon was slumped over in the chair at her side, also dozing away, his fingers twined with Elias's.

Clashing emotions rioted within me. Since my feelings hadn't sorted themselves out in the past hour, it was unlikely I'd solve anything in my beyond-exhausted state.

Noise alerted me to Sabine's presence—she sat in a folding chair in the corner, poised and alert.

"Will you be okay if I take Kerrigan to my place for a few hours of sleep?" I asked. "Yes, sir. I can handle everything here."

"Call me if anything changes." I bent and scooped Kerrigan into my arms. Her eyelashes fluttered, and she placed a hand on my cheek.

"You have eyebrows again," she said, and I huffed a laugh. Her eyelids drooped for a fleeting moment before she pried them open again. "Wait, where are we going? I should stay." "My place. We both need some rest. Sabine will call if anything changes."

Kerrigan yawned. "'kay. Just for a few hours."

As we passed by Sasquatch, she waved. "Night, Professor Sasquatch."

Professor? Did she know something I didn't? Honestly, it wouldn't surprise me if he'd earned a fancy degree and hadn't thought to tell us.

Cool night air drifted over us as I pushed out of the building. "I could totally walk," Kerrigan said, even as she snuggled closer. "I'm heavy, and you're still healing."

"I'm all healed up, and you're not even a little bit heavy. Obviously, you have no idea how strong I am. Remind me to give you a demonstration later."

"Could you roll me up like a dumbbell?"

Somehow, even after one of the worst days I'd ever had, she'd effortlessly lifted my spirits. I did a couple of bicep curls, rolling her up and down.

Kerrigan squeezed the muscles I'd just worked, adding a low hum of appreciation. "Now you don't have to spend time at the gym maintaining these guns. You're welcome."

"Always taking one for the team, aren't you?" I teased. "For the record, you're not a dumbbell. You're a smart bell."

Kerrigan laughed, but within a few more strides, she'd drifted back to sleep. I had to do some juggling and rearranging but managed to open my front door without waking her. I headed straight for the bedroom, gently placed her on my bed, and tugged the covers up to her chin. "You sleep," I whispered, pressing a light kiss to her forehead. "I'm going to take a shower."

"Mmm. You in the shower. I'm picturing it."

If it hadn't been such an awful day, I'd tell her she could join me and get an eyeful of the real thing. But more than anything—even sex—I needed her to rest up, so she'd have the strength to heal Elias.

The blood transfusion hadn't done for him what it'd done for Justin—at least not yet. The memory of finding him as a teenager, battered to the point he couldn't heal his injuries or the resulting infection, kept drifting to mind. His old pack had just dumped him in the woods like he was garbage, and I'd vowed to protect him right then and there.

My hand curled into a fist, and I let my claws jut out into my palm to redirect the sting radiating through my chest to my palm.

Kerrigan covered another yawn with her hand. "A quick nap, and then I'll head home to shower and grab a change of clothes, so I can get back to the clinic." She stretched. "How many guards would stop me if I snuck out of the compound before dawn?"

"Three," I said, kicking off my shoes.

"*Pfft*. Only three. I could take out that many, no problem." Kerrigan sure talked a tough game while semi-delirious.

I peeled off my shirt and tossed it in the direction of the hamper. "You'd only see them if they were attacking, and by then it'd be too late."

Her eyes remained closed, but her forehead crinkled. "Wait. Are we still joking?" "*Still*? When did we start?"

One eye cracked open. "You're serious about the guards?"

"Deadly. Which is the force I'll apply if anyone messes with you or any of my pack members." Too many people had been hurt, and the lack of clues was infuriating. Tonight I'd rest up, because tomorrow, I was going to double the patrols and do whatever it took to hunt down the coven of witches and slaughter every. Last. One.

CHAPTER TWENTY-SEVEN

Conall

THE DIN in the large dining room died the instant Kerrigan stepped inside. The soldiers eating breakfast with me gawked as though they'd never seen a human before.

They certainly didn't greet her with the respect she deserved after countless hours spent saving our wounded comrades. She'd awoken around dawn, not to care for her own needs, but to check on Elias.

Last night I'd crashed out curled around her, so she'd wiggled out of my grasp, kissed my cheek, and urged me to get more sleep. At the doorway of my bedroom, she'd double-checked checked no one would tackle her if she headed to the infirmary and went on her way.

This cold-shoulder bullshit had gone on long enough. I gestured her over and filled a plate with eggs, bacon, biscuits, and sausage gravy. Not only because she was probably famished, but also to show everyone at the table that *I'd* prepared her food.

In other words, I was providing for her, so get onboard.

After a quick update on Elias—still unconscious, pulse rate low but steady, and since he still required oxygen, she'd administered a steroid shot to help his lungs—I introduced her to Mikal, Diego, and Chandra, rattling off their specialties along with their names. "Tyrese is our tracker, so he took off bright and early. Nissa's our expert in military tactics and in gathering intelligence."

Kerrigan swallowed her bite of eggs. "Wow, what an impressive team. It's so nice to meet everyone."

Did they say the same back? Nope. Assholes, and I glared to convey as much.

Kerrigan swung her fork between Nissa and me. "If she's your beta, did you two have to fight for the top-dog spot?"

"The alpha position is about much more than being the 'top dog,'" Nissa spat.

I draped my arm around Kerrigan's shoulders and aimed a smile at my number two, hoping to return the mood to casual territory. "Nissa and I would never fight."

"Because she's female?" Kerrigan appeared slightly offended by her own question; meanwhile, Nissa lobbed a death-ray glare.

"Nah. Because she'd kick my ass." I nudged Nissa's foot beneath the table. "She and I have been friends since we were teenagers. She, Diego, and I forged relationships with like-minded shifters and formed the Bridgewater Pack. She's married to Tyrese, in case you didn't catch that—they're absurdly formal about it."

"Personal details," Nissa gritted out.

"That I'm choosing to share so Kerrigan can get to know us and better do her job." "With all due respect, I don't understand how that'll help her do her job."

"With all due respect, you don't need to." While I didn't relish reminding Nissa I was in charge, that didn't mean I wouldn't.

My beta's spine went stick straight, and the fuming smart-ass saluted me.

This time the room fell silent for a different reason, the other wolves afraid to move, blink, or breathe, for fear it'd ignite the fight that'd been brewing for days. Nissa had scared off females who'd shown interest before, but I'd never cared much—it prevented power-hungry women from other packs from getting too close. It also meant I didn't come off like a jerk when I informed the women I wasn't looking for anything serious.

But something serious had come along when I'd least expected it, and I wanted Kerrigan and Nissa to get along. Not just for my sake, but for the good of the pack.

"Kerrigan, would you mind taking your food to the lobby and waiting for me there? There's a pack matter that evidently can't wait any longer." Guilt emerged at her sagging posture, her dislike of being dismissed loud and clear. Or perhaps it was the glaring lack of acceptance. Either way, it was for her own protection; this conversation was about to get ugly.

Once the door closed behind Kerrigan, I turned my full attention on Nissa. "When you started dating Tyrese, you demanded I give him a chance. Don't I deserve the same courtesy?"

Nissa sat back in her chair and crossed her arms. "Sorry, sir. I'm not sure if I'm allowed to speak freely after being reprimanded."

Everyone else at the table studied their plates as if they'd discovered the likeness of the Virgin Mary in their scraps.

"Really?" I tilted my head. "This is how you wanna play it?"

"She's a doctor, Conall!" Nissa's sentence resonated through the room and reverberated in my ears. "I can't just ignore that fact."

"Then I guess I'll tell you the same thing you told me after I warned Tyrese that I could make him disappear with the snap of my fingers." I met her gaze. "Back off, or I'll make you back off."

"It's different, and you know it. She's *human*," Nissa spat, with more hatred than she'd used during our discussions about witches.

It felt as though she'd gouged a dull sword through the center of my chest. I'd expected that to be thrown in my face eventually, but not from one of my closest friends. "A damn good one, at that. I suspected a handful of the pack elders would object, but I never dreamed you'd be so narrow-minded."

Lightning flashed in her brown eyes. "Narrow-minded? How dare you, after everything we've been through."

"Right back at you, Niss. We could fight about this all day long, but it won't fucking change anything. When it comes to who I choose to be with, you don't get a say."

"The Council does."

Talk about a punch to the gut. The Grand Werewolf Counsel oversaw all shifters, affiliated or not. They were powerful, their resources vast, and they considered themselves supernatural royalty. They only meddled in pack business when it suited them. Or if they had something to gain.

They hadn't intervened when a coven slaughtered my family and former pack, or when Nissa was being used as a guinea pig. Going to them would bring extra scrutiny to every one of our members, as well as put a giant target on my back. Worse, Nissa was well aware how much I blamed and despised them.

"Wow. Bitter insults, blind judgments, and planning a coup, all before noon. Here I thought you, Diego, and I formed this pack to be different—that we formed it without the help of the Council because we couldn't rely on them."

Nissa set her jaw. "Yeah, well, I thought you always had my back, but then you brought a doctor into our inner circle. As if that weren't bad enough, at the height of the greatest danger we've ever faced, you went out gallivanting with her instead of ensuring the protection of your people."

My temper flared, and I stood, palms braced on the table as I forced Nissa to absorb every extra inch. All the strength, muscles, and power. I barely withheld letting my eyes flash gold, unwilling to go there, even though she sure as shit hadn't held back. "Kerrigan saved Justin's life, and she's doing her damnedest to save Elias as well.

"Elias wouldn't *need* her to if you'd been here." Nissa hurled that insult like a javelin to my chest.

I'd beaten myself up plenty but was working to come to terms with the harsh truth that I couldn't be everywhere always.

"If having the doctor here is going to endanger our people further," Nissa continued, "chasing her out of town is a sacrifice I'd be willing to make."

A destructive tornado of emotions whirred within me. Sorrow. Betrayal. Panic. Doubt. Anger. I clung to that last one, allowing it to conceal and overtake the rest. "What about me? Am I expendable? How about Tyrese? Should we appoint someone to decide who in the pack lives and who dies?"

"Don't be ridiculous," Nissa said.

"Why? Because you've already got carte blanche on the subject?"

"That's rich coming from someone who's willing to risk tearing the pack apart for a woman he barely met. Do you honestly think I'm the only one who feels this way?" For the first time since we started arguing, Nissa glanced at the other three people at the table. "Tell him, guys. Tell him I'm not the only one."

———

Undoubtedly, Kerrigan could sense the meeting hadn't gone well. A simple matter had progressed to my front line relaying the multitude of reasons my relationship concerned them. I'd wanted to argue, but several of them hit too close to home.

As I walked her outside of the main complex, my body weighed a thousand pounds. Fucking birds chirped in the branches over our heads, way too happy. Must be nice to only worry about where to fly next and catching the occasional worm.

Once we reached Kerrigan's car, she dug the toe of her shoe into the dirt. "What is it? I can tell something's wrong."

I raked my hand through my hair, wishing I could pause this moment before everything went to shit. Strike that—I'd rewind to our time in the cave, when nothing else existed besides Kerrigan and me.

But that wasn't a fantasy I could indulge in.

It wasn't even a reality I got to indulge in.

"This thing between us was just supposed to be a fun escape," I said, my words scraping my throat and coming out raw. "But now everything's getting so complicated."

Immediately, Kerrigan withdrew into herself, hugging her arms around her middle, same way she'd done yesterday. Only difference was, yesterday I'd been able to make it right. "I can see how you'd assume it'd be easy after I let you finger me on a carnival ride."

Out of the corner of my eye, I noticed the slack jaws of a couple out for a stroll. At my warning glower, they rushed on. Sasquatch had likely heard it from his position near the door as well, although his expression remained as impassive as ever.

I snagged Kerrigan's hand, but she pulled it free and shook her head. "No. Don't, Conall. Just don't."

Despite her plea, I couldn't leave it be. "It's not like that, Kerrigan. I *want* complicated— I want you. But the timing's off. Maybe after this threat—"

"I'm seriously supposed to come here every day, take care of people who despise me, occasionally cross your path, and what?" Tears bordered her eyes as she shrugged a shoulder. "Act like nothing happened between us?"

"You're right—that'd be unfair. Sabine insists she can handle it, so I guess we'll see. I'll call in Doc Morris if need be."

Pain flooded Kerrigan's features. "Oh, so suddenly I'm expendable? That guy will never take as good a care of Elias as I will, and I can't accept that—I *won't*."

"I'm not firing you. I'd love for you to stay on. I'm trying to give you an out if it's too much."

"Do me a favor, and don't do me any favors." Kerrigan whipped around, leaving me to puzzle out that statement. She yanked open the door to her car, and I pushed it closed.

"Wait. Just give me a goddamn minute to think."

"You don't need a minute; you already decided. You want this to be easy, so I'll make it easy. Anyone requiring medical care is welcome at my clinic. I should be there growing my practice anyway." She opened the car door again, and I slammed it shut again.

Not sure why. Guess I was the pigheaded ass she'd accused me of being. "Fine. I'll escort you home."

"No, thank you."

"With our enemies hiding in the surrounding woods, you need an escort," I said.

"Deputy Sasquatch?" Kerrigan called over my shoulder, and I did a double take, wondering when he'd left his post. "Will you take me home? I'm assuming that'd be preferable to me strangling the alpha of your pack?"

Sasquatch dipped his head, following her orders as promptly as he filled mine, and what the hell?

Kerrigan started around the hood of her car, and I caught her wrist, alarm screeching through me. The idea that this could be our last interaction gnawed at me, propelling me to the brink of desperation.

Sasquatch wedged himself between us and planted a firm hand on my chest.

A growl emanated from the back of my throat. "Trust me, you don't want to fight me right now."

"You need to cool off before you say or so anything you'll later regret." His gaze drifted to the hawk circling the air above us. "Trust *me*. There are certain things you can't take back."

CHAPTER TWENTY-EIGHT

Kerrigan

OVER THE PAST five lonely and rather depressing days, I'd continued to brainstorm treatments that might help Elias between examinations of my other furry patients.

The snap of my blue gloves into place filled the exam room, and I moved to examine the chihuahua who'd eaten the beak off a rubber duckie. His owner brought him in right away, conveying that his breath seemed more labored than usual and asking about the odds of the puppy passing it without help.

I placed the stethoscope on Rex's furry, white and tan chest. His heart rate was normal, but his breaths did sound labored. He wasn't choking, though, and he obviously was getting oxygen.

Elias was still on oxygen, too. Thanks to exchanging numbers with both Gideon and Gina—or the Double G's as I'd taken to calling them—I'd received a couple of updates. Gideon was worried about Elias's temperature, although Sabine kept insisting werewolves simply ran hot. But was it normal for someone in his condition to sweat through three hospital gowns a day, Gideon had asked.

Short answer: no.

Long answer: factoring in the combination of lupine and homo sapiens genes, I had no earthly idea what temperature was ideal. Only that canines did run slightly higher and if I could take enough temperatures from enough werewolves, I could compare and contrast.

As far as Conall went, there'd been no keeping me in the loop, no communication, no nothing. Or I guess that would make it something, and in this case, it was a whole heap of sadness over being suddenly secluded from Conall, as well as any werewolf ongoings.

The chihuahua on the table gave a yip and bit at the end of my stethoscope, apparently unhappy I'd dared to think of another canine while it was his time to shine. "Sorry, Rex. But did you seriously not learn your lesson about eating things you shouldn't?"

And had I not learned my own lesson about daydreaming about the loss of a man I had no business tackling a relationship with anyway? It was pointless and painful, with a side of stinging rejection. Still, Elias deserved my all, regardless of what'd transpired—or was no longer transpiring—between the alpha of his pack and me.

While I took comfort that Elias wasn't any worse, the fact that his health wasn't improving gnawed at me, a wound I couldn't stop worrying over and picking at.

Say he did have a change in heart rate or oxygen levels, and his temperature shot too high. Sabine wouldn't know what to do as well as I would if I were there watching over him. Hands on my hips, I peered down at my furry patient. "I'd rather not cut you open if I don't have to. I'm thinking you'll spend the day with me so I can continue to observe you and see if you don't force that rubber beak out the other side. As for the duckie..." I glanced at where it sat on the shiny countertop, far enough from Rex he couldn't finish the job. "I'm afraid there's nothing I can do."

Rex responded to my joke with a hacking cough, and then he vomited the contents of his stomach onto the exam table.

I crinkled my nose as I studied the mess. "Uh-oh. You ate more than part of that bath toy, didn't you? Is that...?" The scent of chocolate hit me at the same time as I lifted the red foil wrapper from the mess, extra glad for the invention of gloves as I squinted at the symbol of a bird—more accurately, a dove.

Rex regurgitated another heap of sparkly foil and dark brown onto the exam table paper I'd laid down. No time to read the inspirational messages scribbled inside the Dove wrappers— the darker the chocolate, the higher the risk, and now that I knew what Rex had eaten, I sprang into action so I could flush it from his system as quickly as possible.

Just like that, the idea that'd been skirting the depths of my mind crystalized. First things first, I'd stabilize Rex, and then I'd hop in my car and race to the compound as fast as the four wheels could take me.

———

The first time I'd come into the bar seemed like a lifetime ago, my mind too busy to fully take it in. A hint rustic, with twinkle lights and a string of green shamrocks, the place felt alive and cozy at the same time.

I sidled up to the wooden countertop, plunking myself on the stool opposite Gina. "Silly question: are you Irish, or do you believe in lucky charms?"

"Italian, actually, but I ate some Lucky Charms just last week, so not only do they exist, they're delicious to boot." Gina stacked the glass she'd finished drying on top of the others. Then she leaned a forearm on the bar and whispered, "If you're asking about leprechauns, however, while I've never seen one, I tend not to assume when it comes to things that shouldn't exist."

The joke deserved a laugh, but a weak smile was the best I could do. I pointed at the string of shamrock lights. "I meant the decor. But I'll keep an open mind about the elusive leprechauns and their pots of gold."

Gina patted my hand, sensing without me having to tell her that I was as melancholy as I'd been at the compound earlier that afternoon. Conall hadn't been there, and I'd assured myself that was for the best.

I changed my mind during my power struggle with Sabine, wishing he were there to pull rank, even though it'd hurt like hell to see him. To be around him, breathing the same air and sharing the same space, knowing we'd never share more again.

Sabine wanted to continue the treatments she was currently using, and I argued my idea was the way to go, and Sasquatch had watched over our interaction like it was a tennis match.

After a couple of minutes that were growing extra heated by the second, Sasquatch had finally cut in. "Let her do it, Sabine," he'd said, and when she'd balked, he'd added, "You know Conall would say the same."

And so I'd flushed his system, administered some meds, and waited around an hour before I'd decided to head home so I wouldn't drive myself insane waiting, watching, and hoping with so much of my efforts it'd left me exhausted.

On my way out of the community building, I crossed paths with Gina, and she'd told me I should swing by the bar later. It was officially later, and so here I was.

"What can I get you?" she asked.

Food should be the priority, but it wasn't what I wanted. "I'll have one of whatever'll get me nice and buzzed, the faster the better."

"I think I've got something that'll help what ails you. Hold tight."

A minute or so later, a mason jar filled to the brim with

sunset-colored liquid landed on the bar in front of me. "One Bacardi Party. Or as I like to call it..." Gina beamed at me. "Just what the doctor ordered."

I snorted at her joke, which felt especially good after so many long, humorless days. Then I took a healthy glug of my drink. "Mmm." I licked my upper lip, savoring the burst of flavors. "I can hardly even taste the alcohol."

"Fair warning, that's how it sneaks up on you."

Another generous swig down the hatch, and already the numbing effects were setting in. Halfway through my drink, I spilled my guts to Gina about everything that'd gone down with Conall last weekend, from the tense breakfast, being kicked out so they could have a meeting about me, and then Conall telling me that there were too many complications to being with me right now.

"I'm so sorry, hon. I can tell he's completely miserable, on top of all the stress he's under." Gina shook her head and sighed. "Timing's such a bitch."

"Maybe it's for the best. How long could we have lasted if everyone around him hated me?" Ugh, what a bunch of unsatisfying reasons, partially true or not. "I can't help but think that if he truly wanted to be with me, he'd fight for us."

"One, he's crazy about you. We've established that, remember? And two, it's not everyone at the compound. I adore you, and have since day one."

I lunged over the bar and hugged her as an "aww" escaped. I declared her the absolute best, and she went to take more orders as I continued to nurse my drink.

"Kerrigan, hello." At the familiar male timbre, I swiveled around on my stool top, acutely aware it wasn't *the voice* I longed to hear.

"Hey, Mayor Sullivan."

"It's nice to see you again. And please, call me Craig."

"Right. Craig." I smacked my forehead before forcing my arm down. "Long time no see.

How's Jasper?"

A soft laugh came out, one I couldn't quite decipher. "He's all right. Just catching sticks and balls and hamming it up for attention."

"Sounds like an ideal night to me," I said with a snort, my mind drifting to a different place entirely.

Craig's smile widened, and then he jerked a thumb over his shoulder, indicating the other side of the room. "Say, I was about to play a game of pool. Care to join me?"

"Sure, but I should warn you in advance..." I polished off the last of my drink, braced my palm on the bar, and stood. *Whoa. Is the floor slanted? Or am I more think than I drunk I am?* After taking a second to regain my bearings, I put one foot in front of the other, sights set on the felt-covered table. "I'm not very good."

Craig chuckled again. "I thought you were about to fess up to being a pool shark who hustled people out of their money."

"Nope, but if someone brought in a pet shark, I could perform surgery on it. If it wasn't bitey, you know?"

More laughter. Either I was killing it with the jokes tonight, or I'd grown so used to Sasquatch's stoic presence that any laughter seemed like a lot. There were a few benefits to no longer heading to the compound every day, I supposed.

In fact, tossing back a drink at the local bar with the friendly mayor and proving to myself there was a whole world out there that existed without werewolf drama might just be what this doctor needed, if not ordered.

CHAPTER TWENTY-NINE

Kerrigan

GIVE me a scalpel and I could slice and dice with precision. Throw sports into the mix, and my accuracy flew right out the window. To be fair, I would never operate drunk, and I was as buzzed as Gina promised I'd be.

Enough so that the clatter of the balls slamming into one another as Craig broke caused me to jump and then giggle at myself, to the point tears formed in my eyes.

An excuse I could totally use if—or let's face it when—I inevitably missed or scratched.

"Looks like I'm solids," he said, sinking two more balls before he missed and it was my turn.

Blue coated the tip of my pool stick as I chalked it for the second time since I'd lifted it off the wall, as if that would make any difference in my accuracy. Sure enough, the now-blue dotted ball rolled across the green felt, missing the striped thirteen I'd been aiming for.

Over the next fifteen or so minutes, the mayor and I played out our game until only two solid-colored balls remained, plus the eight ball. So far, I'd only sunk three. Time to make my comeback.

Another swipe of chalk and then I leaned over the table,

squinted an eye, and waited for the white cue ball to stop splitting into two blurry versions so I could take my shot.

I jerked back my elbow so I could gain enough momentum to really hit the ball, but the end of my stick bumped into something solid. Not a wall, though. I'd already ensured I'd have enough room.

I turned to see what'd impeded my hit, my entire body lighting up like a firework when I found Conall standing directly behind me. "Hey!" A moment too late, I realized I wasn't supposed to care he was here, or why he looked so grumpy, and I quickly doused the sparking in my gut. "I mean. Oh, it's you. If you'll excuse me, I'm in the middle of a game."

I pivoted toward the table, but Conall gripped my hip, hindering me from completing the full one-eighty spin I'd intended.

His fingers dug deeper, igniting a whorl of heat as memories of him having them on me—and inside of me— rose, unbidden.

Don't go there. It's just gonna make the aftereffects of bumping into him worse.

Conall's gaze drifted to the mayor on the other side of the table before slowly returning to me. "I tried to call and even swung by your place. When you didn't answer your phone after my third try, I started to worry."

With a frown, I patted my empty pockets. "Hmm. I had my phone earlier. I must have left it at the bar. Like the wooden bar where you get drinks, not the whole..." I gestured around to encompass the entire room and tipped sideways. If not for Conall's hand, I likely would've fallen, which left me as glad as I was irritated he'd so casually put his hands on me, as if the incident last weekend had never happened.

Grumpiness spread across his face like an angry sunrise,

even though that wasn't a thing, and was there such a thing as a stormrise? A storm roll? "You're drunk," he said.

I held up my fingers and pinched them together until only the tiniest bit of light shone through. "Little bit."

"Tell me, Kerrigan. Before you and the mayor started this here pool game, did you tell him about me?"

Surely, he didn't mean... I braced a hand on Conall's chest, tipped onto my toes, and whispered, "I'd never tell anyone your secret about being a you-know-what."

Conall pinched the bridge of his nose and exhaled. "I meant who I am to you."

"Who are you to me? Are you speaking in riddles?"

Goose bumps spread across my skin as his expression turned deadly, even though it was aimed over my shoulder. "I'm asking if the mayor knew about us when he was trying to look down your shirt."

Yikes. Finally, my fuzzy brain put together more pieces of the puzzle. "I'm sure he was merely awaiting the epic shot I was about to take. Besides"—I cupped myself over my bra— "it's not like I have much to look at."

Oh shit, I got the low growl. Conall slid his hand to my lower back, sprawling his fingers as he pressed me tighter against him. "What matters is they're mine."

If I'd been sober, I might've been able to stifle the ovary implosion. I was pissed at myself for the reaction, but my indignation was better aimed at him. "They're not yours." I shoved him away, and since he didn't budge, it sent my other hip into the pool table. *Ouch. That's gonna leave a mark.* "You can't have it both ways, Conall."

"I told you I couldn't get serious *right now.*"

I thwacked him in the arm, the move immature yet satisfying. "Then stop acting so serious in the bar."

"It sounds to me like the lady's asking you to back off," Craig said, starting toward us, and I threw up a *stop-right-there* hand.

"While I appreciate that, Craig, please just let me handle—"

"If you don't keep your eyes and hands off her," Conall said, jabbing a finger over my shoulder, "I'll remove them for you."

Gina burst on to the scene, launching herself over the pool table and placing herself in the middle of the melee. "All right, boys, that's enough dick measuring for the night. None of us have the time or energy to deal with a brawl. Not me, not the two of you, and certainly not the sheriff." The glare she fired at Conall expressed that in *her bar*, she was the alpha. "I remained nearby the entire time, watching to ensure lines didn't get crossed and that Kerrigan remained safe."

"Safe? She's wasted."

"If you want someone to blame for that, blame yourself," Gina retorted. "You're the one who's yanking her around. Telling her one thing one day and then changing your mind when you see her doing her best to move on. Figure it out."

My thoughts and emotions whirled like a Merry-Go-Round set on destruction. Gina had come in clutch for me several times, and I wasn't going to let her take heat for *my* decisions.

"Okay, that's enough," I said in my most authoritarian voice, which yes, would've worked better if my words didn't slur together. "I'm a big girl, and I wanted a strong drink, something I can decide to have all by myself. Same way I can play pool with whomever I want. Mayor Sullivan..."

This time he didn't insist I call him Craig, so at least he understood the direness of the situation.

"I'm sorry that you got caught in the middle. Conall and I... Honestly, I'm not exactly sure what we are anymore. Suffice it to say, he and I have a few issues to resolve. If I gave you the wrong impression, and you thought this was more than a friendly game of pool, that wasn't my intention."

"Well, you did ask after my dog instead of me, so I can't

say I'm surprised. Conall also always gets what he wants, so again, not a total shock," Craig said, and did he think he was helping the situation? I took back what I thought about him understanding. He was stoking the fire rather than putting it out.

On cue, Conall bellowed, "What the fuck's that supposed to mean?"

"Hello, didn't you hear Gina? No fighting. Now, if y'all will excuse me, I'm going to take my shot, since it's the first one that's lined up semi-decently for me. Prepare for the comeback of the century. Or, you know, day." I pivoted toward the table, and Conall caught the end of the pool stick an instant before it would've smacked him in the face. I winced. "Oops. Sorry about that."

"And I'm sorry about how mad you're going to be about this." Conall yanked the wooden stick from my grasp and slammed it on the table. "Kerrigan and I are leaving, so she and I can have ourselves a discussion about those issues that need resolving."

With that declaration still ringing in the air, he scooped me up and tossed me over his shoulder.

Between having his hard clavicle bone digging into my gut, and how quickly he whirled around and charged toward the door, I couldn't tell which way was up or down anymore. But one thing was for sure: this fight was far from over.

CHAPTER THIRTY

Conall

KERRIGAN CROSSED her arms tighter as I sped her tiny tin can of a car away from Lou's Bar. "You didn't have to make a big spectacle, you know."

"Oh, I know," I said since sarcasm was safer than letting my anger get the best of me. "It's not like I didn't warn you how possessive I am. I was crystal fucking clear on that point." "That doesn't mean you can show up, bark orders, and then carry me out of the bar like some kind of Neanderthal."

"Funny, based on what happened back there, it's exactly what it means."

"*Argh.*" Frustration radiated off her, to the point I wouldn't be surprised if her ears started steaming. "So, what? Even though you dumped me, you think you maintain the right to storm in wherever and whenever and use your brute force to punish me for trying to move on with my life?" Her voice broke on the end, and regret twinged.

Instead of admitting she had a valid point—and I hated that she did—I sidestepped. "I didn't dump you. You left before we could finish our conversation."

Kerrigan whipped toward me, fire in her eyes. "Are you

serious right now? You hurt me, Conall. And then you didn't call, didn't update on me on Elias or bring him by the clinic— didn't *anything*."

"Not sure if this'll help my case or not, but I did come to find you to tell you that Elias woke up this evening."

The fight leaked out of her in a rush, hope and happiness rushing up to take its place. "He did?"

"Not for very long, but yeah. His wounds seem to be healing, slower than our usual regeneration, but still a vast improvement." I reached across the cab, lifted her knuckles to my mouth, and kissed them. "Whatever you did, it's definitely helping."

"Thank God. I feel like an idiot for not considering wolfsbane poisoning before. A mixture of apomorphine and extra flushing of IV fluids, plus switching to humidified oxygen to help clear the lungs of anything he inhaled while within the trap, and..." Her smile faded, a crestfallen expression replacing it far too quickly. "That's why you came to find me. For medical reasons."

I shook my head, tightening my hold on her hand as she started to withdraw. "What you witnessed in the bar is the result of the empty void I've felt ever since you left. When I couldn't find you, I began imagining worst-case scenarios. I almost lost Elias, and that nearly destroyed me.

"Then I thought I'd lost you, and..." Residual panic rose. "I was ready to tear the town apart to find you. Then I saw the mayor leering at you, got jealous, and lost my shit."

I pulled into the driveway of her cabin, cut the engine, and glanced across the dim interior at her beautiful face. "Even before that, when I'd returned to the compound after a long day spent tracking and found out that you'd worked so hard to save Elias, despite everything I've put you through, it hit me how foolish I'd been to let you go. Honestly, I don't think I'm capable of letting you go."

Her chest fell as she exhaled, more of her scent filling my head as I waited.

"My original plan was to sweep you off your feet with my charm and ask you for another chance." I ran my palms down the thighs of my jeans. "Did it work?"

A startled laugh burst out of her, immediately followed by a sob.

"Fuck, Kerrigan." I unclicked her seat belt and yanked her to me, holding her against my chest. "I screwed up. I let my doubts get the best of me, and worst of all, I hurt you. Does it matter that I hurt me, too?"

She shrugged one shoulder, and a tight band formed around my chest.

It wasn't enough, and that meant I was going to have to spill more, to be vulnerable in a way that scraped at my insides worse than any spell or wolfsbane, and far more dangerous than either as well. "More than that, Kerrigan, I haven't experienced that type of darkness since the aftermath of my family members' deaths. It not only scared the shit out of me and left me a miserable sap this past week, it also made me realize how much I need you."

I cupped her cheek and used my thumb to brush away her tears. "I don't deserve your forgiveness—I know that. But here I am, asking for it anyway."

"I appreciate the apology, especially knowing it's not easy for you. I've been miserable without you, too," she said, and I didn't dare let that rising sliver of hope lodge too deeply in my chest, afraid it might be left to fester instead of heal. "It's bigger than you and me, though, isn't it? Most of your pack hates me. No matter how hard I try, they seem immune to my winning personality."

"What? That's preposterous." My joke didn't soften the seriousness in her features. "What happens if they never accept me, Conall?"

"First of all, they don't hate you. They're reluctant to let any outsiders into our sanctum. Don't worry. No one would dare hurt you, and they'll be respectful because I demand it." Kerrigan frowned, sadly underwhelmed by my promise. "You only addressed half of what I mentioned. This is also where you're supposed to assure me that once they get to know me better, they'll warm up."

"Werewolves tend to be set in their ways and slow to evolve, but I'm sure they'll come around. Just get up and do some of your adorable medical rambling, and they'll see you're obviously not a witch, but a vet who's there to help."

"Like you did? Are we talking before or after you attempted to rip out my throat?"

"Again, if I'd attempted, you wouldn't be here anymore. What's important is that I didn't follow through."

Kerrigan groaned, the ends of her hair tickling my collarbone as she shook her head. "FYI, you suck at the reassuring thing." She scrunched up her eyebrows. "Wait. How many people think I'm a witch? More than the lady who yelled at me while I was treating Elias?"

I flinched and directed my gaze out the window, debating how brutally honest to be. "Conall." Kerrigan gripped my chin, turning my face back to hers.

"A significant number of them think you cured Justin with a spell so you could infiltrate the pack. It's one of the other reasons that meeting went so long the day that I..." I couldn't finish. Not when everything in me wanted to take it back. That day I'd been trying to put my pack first and had failed Kerrigan. By choosing to ignore their fears and advice and choosing to be with her, my pack was going to determine that I'd failed them. I couldn't win, but after five days of going without the woman in my arms, I also knew I couldn't let her go—I *wouldn't*. Selfish or not, she was mine.

"There's nothing about this that's going to be easy," she said, smoothing her hands over my shoulders. "It's going to be complicated. You and me will always be complicated."

"Preaching to the choir, Doc." I dipped my head and brushed my mouth over hers. "I'm willing to do complicated if you are—make that until I convince you to get onboard." There. No wiggle room. "Then I'll convince the rest of the pack. Whatever it takes."

Her sigh stirred a dash of worry, and if her posture hadn't slackened, I might've lost my shit for the second time today. "Do we need to head to the compound to check on Elias?"

I shook my head. "Sabine administered enough pain meds he'll likely be out for hours, and she'll call if anything changes."

"Okay." Kerrigan craned her neck, peering at her dark house through the windshield. "You wanna come in and continue to work out our issues where we'll have more room?"

That was all it took for the erection I'd been fighting since pulling her onto my lap to stand at attention. I moved my lips to her neck, inhaled her scent, and whispered, "It's actually vampires that have to be invited in. Werewolves are better known for barging on in, regardless."

Kerrigan canted her head, granting me better access as one corner of her mouth lifted in a smile. "Oh, believe me, I know."

———

Claws scrabbled against the wood floor as Kerrigan's black cat darted under the couch.

She bent over, heart-shaped ass in the air, and assured him that I wouldn't be a bad dog and hurt him.

I growled and, when she cast a dirty look over her shoulder, said, "Don't worry. I won't hurt your kitty. But you, *woman*, are asking for it. Calling me a bad dog. Bending over like that, practically begging me to attack you."

Kerrigan straightened and batted her eyes at me. "Begging. That's a good idea, making you beg."

"Not gonna happen."

One eyebrow shot up. "We'll see. Which, come to think of it, I should've used my chance to make you say 'please' with that whole speech in the car. Maybe I won't forgive you."

I strode toward her. "Too late."

"You hungry? I don't have much, but—"

I crashed my mouth over hers, sweeping my tongue in for a taste. "Not for food. There's only one thing I want right now." A thought hit me, one I wanted to bat away because I couldn't imagine going a minute longer without burying myself in her wet pussy. However, there were certain lines I never crossed. "Are you still drunk? If you're not sober enough to consent—"

"I'm sober enough, and I totally consent. I wouldn't go for a joy ride behind the wheel of a car, but I'm going to enjoy riding you." Kerrigan dragged her finger across my pecs, down the center of my abdomen, and then swiped her finger back and forth along the waistband of my jeans until I was rock hard.

A grunt came out as she cupped me over the denim, and I caught her hand and peered into her eyes for my own assessment.

"Watch." Kerrigan stood on one foot and placed her finger on the tip of her nose. "Want me to recite the alphabet backward? Rattle off the veterinarian hypocritic oath?" She put her hand up in the square. "I solemnly swear to use my scientific knowledge and skills for the—"

"Good enough," I said, planting my hands on her ass and hauling her against me to finish the devouring kiss I'd started. As I rolled my tongue over hers, she hooked my shirt in her thumbs and peeled it off me. While she went up, I went down, unbuttoning her jeans and shoving them down around her knees.

She bent to remove them, so I shucked my pants, kicking at the fabric until it fell to the floor. Kerrigan didn't have as much luck, her ankles getting entangled in the denim. She stumbled into me, and I caught her around the waist and propelled us backward until I fell to the couch with her in my arms.

She sank further onto me as she reached for her bound ankles, still working at removing her pants. With her silk-covered pussy so exquisitely notched against my hard-on, I forewent offering to help so I could bask in the divine friction. At the feel of her damp heat, I groaned and arched my hips, too impatient to wait to get more of her on more of me.

After she freed her legs, she explored my neck with her tongue, tracing my Adam's apple and then sucking the spot where my throat met my jaw.

Once my fingers found their way to the clasp of her bra, I quickly undid it and ridded her of the last scrap of fabric between me and her breasts. With one hand, I kneaded her, plucking my thumb over her hardened nipple and groaning as she rocked against me.

I dipped my head, flicking the other pink nub with my tongue before drawing a lazy circle around it. Her shallow breaths spurred me on, and I dragged my scruffy chin across the sensitive underside of her curves, grinning at her whimper. "Remember the promise I made you that night over the phone, when I jerked off to the image of you touching yourself?"

"Yes," she whispered, her eyes fluttering closed.

"I intend to keep it. Now, open your eyes and watch so you can see just how perfectly your tits fit in my mouth."

CHAPTER THIRTY-ONE

Kerrigan

I SHUDDERED as Conall sucked my breast into his mouth.

His eyes remained on mine as he lightly dug his teeth into the skin. "The first night we met, you asked me not to bite you. How would you feel about me biting you now?"

A whimper came out, and I tipped back my head, willing him to do it—evidently, I was more masochistic than I realized. Last second, I hesitated. "Wait. If you bite me, will I...? Turn into a werewolf?"

Conall flicked my hardened nipple with the tip of his tongue, and my eyes rolled back in my head. "It's more complicated than that. It'd require a bite from an alpha, sinking the teeth into a vein, and injecting quite a bit of toxin. In other words, I'd never do it accidentally."

"Okay, then. Yeah, I want you to bite me. Bite me *hard*."

His teeth broke the skin, tiny pinpricks of pleasure and pain he prolonged by raking stinging lines across the swell of my breast, all the way to my nipple.

He moved to give the other side the same treatment, his groan vibrating all the way down to my sex. My body turned into a ravenous, hazy mess, and I rubbed myself over his hardness, cursing the fact that my panties were still in the way. "I need you inside of me, Conall. Remember how I don't have any patience? And what little I have is all used up."

"There's nowhere I'd rather be," he said, scooting us to the end of the couch. He stood with me in his arms, and while I wondered how he moved so smoothly, at the moment, I didn't really care. Questions might delay gratification, and I wasn't willing to risk it.

As he carried me down the hall, I fused our mouths together, taking charge of the devouring while he did the propelling.

"Bedroom?" he asked in a husky voice that scored a searing to the tips of my toes. "Second door on the left."

In three long strides, Conall reached it and kicked it open. Once we reached the bed, he lowered me to my feet, both of us groaning as my body slid down the length of him, his hard length purgatory and paradise.

I gaped down at the cock that was moments away from being buried deep inside of me. It felt an eternity away, yet the anticipation left me in a state of perpetual fervor.

"Eyes are up here, sweetheart," Conall said, same way he had in the cave, and I let loose a contented sigh as I continued to gape.

"I'm aware. But you're not the only one I missed."

He lunged for me, cupping my neck and yanking me closer so that our chests collided. He dragged his tongue across my lower lip, each swipe intensifying the lust overtaking my system.

Another emotion filtered through, one that scared me too much to name. I so desperately wanted to let go of my doubts and free-fall into the intoxicating sensations, but I was hardly in any state to logically consider the aftereffects.

The last time I dived in without thinking, it'd brought me to this town, to this place, to this man. At first, that might've been an argument to slow things down. But as I considered how much I was enjoying the here and now, I understood being brave and taking risks more than I ever had before. Playing safe didn't lead to regrets. Missed opportunities did.

With that in mind, I wound my arms around Conall's neck, savoring his bare skin against mine and having my heart beating hard and fast enough to remind me that I was fully alive.

"I'm all in, babe," Conall said with a low rumble. "I want to be with you, and as long as you're onboard, I'll never let anything rip us apart ever again."

"Me, too. I mean, I'm onboard and yes to being with you —that's what I want as well."

Of all the grins he'd given me, this one was softer and more sincere, yet unyielding and filled with wicked intentions. "Then you should know that once I fuck you all out, the way I'm about to, we'll pass the point of return. My ability to remain calm if any guy so much as looks at you will go from reasonable to remorseless. We're talking barbaric."

"Just to clarify, you're implying that threatening to maim someone is reasonable?"

"As I keep telling you, I've never claimed to be reasonable. But that's more or less it, yes. We're not talking jealousy—that involves wanting something that's not yours. I'm a territorial asshole, and I'll fight tooth and nail to protect what's already mine.

"And you, Kerrigan Ryan..." Using the iron grip he had on my neck, he guided my face to his. He nipped at my lower lip. "You're mine."

In a lust-filled trance, I nodded.

"Say it," he demanded, all growly and possessive, and if my mind went any hazier, I'd never find my way out of the fog. Then again, clarity was overrated.

"I'm yours."

He gave me a pleased expression that left me like a star student—only one in, like, BDSM class. "Good girl."

His fingers encircled my hips, and suddenly I was airborne, for all of two seconds before I fell to the soft mattress. My werewolf knelt between my legs, hooked his fingers in the tiny string of elastic that held up my panties, and slid them off me.

Then he placed his hands on my inner thighs and spread them farther apart. He wrapped his fist around the base of his shaft and stroked himself as he studied me, completely bared to him and wetter than I'd ever been. "Now that's a view I could stare at for the rest of my life."

Using his teeth, he ripped open a foil wrapper. I watched, transfixed, as he rolled on the condom. At long last, he poised himself at my entrance. Anticipation swelled and swelled— and finally crested when he pushed inside.

"So wet, so perfect," Conall muttered, and I brought up my knees, keeping them spread wide to accommodate his size. The shift caused the head of his penis to ram against the perfect spot, a keening noise erupting of its own accord.

With each thrust, each grunt, my muscles tightened, the pressure building and building to the point my body rocked with it. I clenched fistfuls of my sheets as I linked my ankles behind his lower back, eradicating the minimal space between our bodies. The stretch and the pressure as the head of his dick trailed across the most sensitive part of me elicited a charge so strong it left me a shuddering, panting puddle of bliss.

Tighter I gripped the sheets, "faster and harder" I encouraged his thrusts, and dizziness set in as I lost myself to the exquisite barrage of sensations.

Conall swiped the hair from my eyes and ran his thumb along my jaw. "Tell me again that you're mine."

"I'm yours," I gasped through the whorl of ecstasy. "I'll always be yours."

My body arched off the bed, too impatient and needy to wait for his body to return, and the world around us spun as I circled higher and higher. I dug my nails into his biceps and lifted my head for a kiss.

One he freely gave, and then the tension burst. I cried out his name, allowing the sensations to envelop me. Floating and grounded, weightless and pinned down, taut yet pliant, famished yet sated.

Conall pumped into me, harder, faster, deeper. In awe I watched, relishing the moment he gave himself over to me, to us, to this profound moment...

Then he came with a roar, filling me and fulfilling me as he finished fully claiming me as his.

———

Immediately upon waking up, I sensed Conall's absence.

Vaguely, I remembered him whispering a goodbye in my ear, something about having to get back to the compound before softly kissing my lips and telling me he'd see me tomorrow.

Was that hours ago or mere minutes? I felt his side of the bed. Cold. The guy was basically a space heater, so he must've left a while ago.

So, what'd woken me up? It was pitch black outside, save the light of the waxing gibbous moon, which lit up a feline form.

A hiss and a growl emanated from my kitty, and I clenched my phone and scooted to the other side of the bed. I thought I saw a flash of light, but my mind might be playing tricks on me.

"What is it?" I asked Sir Pounce. "Is the raccoon back?"

I hoped it was nothing more than the masked trash bandit, although it'd be easier to convince myself of if my instincts weren't sounding a three-alarm alert. Now the question became whether or not to turn on the lights, alerting the possible intruder I was awake and hoping it'd scare them off, or to creep around like Nancy Drew.

My heart thundered as I dropped to my hands and knees and crawled over to the window, feeling ridiculous yet scared enough to follow through with the move. Crouching so that I was balanced on the balls of my feet, I lifted myself enough to peek through the panes, into the blackness, no idea what I'd do if I found eyes starting back at me.

Remembering what Gina had said about shifter hearing, I whispered Conall's name. "Conall?" After what'd happened at the bar, maybe my closest werewolf friend had come to check on me. "Gina?"

Nothing.

"Sasquatch?" That last one was a literal shot in the dark, although considering Conall's overprotective side, not totally absurd.

The same sense of being watched that plagued me after my first encounter with Conall settled over me.

Only this felt different.

Darker.

My phone chirmed, and I jumped, nearly dropping it. I spun to a seated position on the floor to read the message on my screen.

> Gina: Hey, crazy night at the bar. Hopefully, you're tucked into your bed after ironing out things with Conall, but I'm locking up now, so if you need me, let me know. XOXO

I told myself there could be a simple explanation for the creepy-crawly sensation pricking my skin, much like the night a critter had tipped over my trash can. After taking a couple of seconds to gather my courage, I flicked on the lights. I stood, flattening myself to the wall beside the window frame and squinting into the inky night. *Man, I could really use some supernatural senses right now.*

I nibbled on my thumbnail and then pulled up Conall's contact information.

> Me: Hey. Just woke up missing my cuddle buddy and checking to see if you made it home safely.

> Conall: Cuddle Buddy? Am I being friendzoned?

I quickly tapped out another text, doing my best to remain calm and collected while feeling anything but.

> Me: Sorry, I forgot how much I have to stroke your fragile ego. I meant to say I'm missing my big, bad, SEXY werewolf. Are you at the compound already, then?

> Conall: I got home about an hour ago and was about to crawl into bed. Why? Wanna come join me for round two?

> Conall: Because if we're being honest, there's something else I'd much rather you stroke...

My stretched-thin nerves unraveled in a pile at my feet. Whatever was going bump in the night outside of my cabin, it definitely hadn't been him.

If I asked him to, I had no doubt he'd rush right over. But he was clearly tired after a day spent being Super Alpha, and if he came to check out the cause of my "weird feeling," only to find nothing, I'd feel awful. The other werewolves would irrefutably resent me for it, too.

Everything felt more ominous at night—that was probably it. I padded into the living room to check if Conall locked up on his way out. Sure enough, the front door was secured, and a quick glance at the patio door showed the bar was still down.

I headed to the window at the front of the house, beating myself up for not getting new blinds like I'd sworn I was going to do. I hadn't realized it'd take driving to another town at the time, and then life got unexpectedly busy, and, and, and...

This time, I remained in the corner of the room as I did another sweep of the yard. Trees, rocks, dirt. Basically, a whole lot of nothing.

Guadalupe Falls was a tiny town with a low crime rate, and I refused to be the city girl who cried wolf.

Well, something besides wolf, considering.

I quickly typed out a message telling Conall good night and that I'd head to the compound after my last appointment at two so I could check on Elias. I hit send and climbed into bed with the lights blaring, assuring myself that my paranoia that someone—or some*thing*—was out there watching me was nothing more than a case of my imagination getting carried away with me.

CHAPTER THIRTY-TWO

Conall

SASQUATCH SENT a text informing me Kerrigan had arrived at the compound, and I practically skipped to the infirmary.

I peeked through the tiny rectangle window on the door, grinning at the sight of Elias sitting up on his own, talking animatedly as the sexy doctor checked his vitals. Gideon played sentinel, same way he'd done since his boyfriend's arrival. While they had to be exhausted, the three of them were outputting the type of energy reserved for keggers.

"You waiting for an invitation?" Sasquatch teased, nudging me with a bony elbow.

I flipped him off and reached for the doorknob. His low laugh followed after me—pretty sure that was his version of calling me whipped, and I didn't even care.

"...did not," Elias said, a dry cough coming out along with the words. His pallor was still off, the clear tube fitted into his nose a reminder of the beating his lungs had taken.

"Did, too," Gideon argued. "Even without a layer of skin, you're fine as hell."

Kerrigan laughed. "That's how you know you're a goner.

Like when I saw Conall without eyebrows and was like 'still hot.'"

I cleared my throat, and Kerrigan whipped toward me. Two spots of pink rose to her cheeks. "Pretend you didn't hear that."

"Not a chance, babe." I wound an arm around her waist and gave her a hello kiss with extra tongue.

The two twenty-year-old werewolves beamed at us. So much for my badass rep. Not that anyone in this cramped room would judge.

"How's the kid?" I asked, and Kerrigan turned in my embrace, one of her hands going to my forearm as she jerked her chin at the noisy monitor.

"His vitals are bouncing back, slowly but surely." Kerrigan's theory about the wolfsbane being laced in with the silver nitrate explained how Elias had sensed the trap last second. "If this were a full hospital, I'd request he stay, but in order to keep him as comfortable as possible, I'm going to send him home where he'll have access to a bigger bed—the oxygen stays on, though. At all times except for a quick trip to the bathroom or short shower."

"Thank God." Gideon slung his arm around Elias's shoulders. "I have no desire to sleep in that tiny chair one more night. Don't get me wrong, I'd do it. But I'd prefer to sleep in my own bed. I wouldn't mind company, either." He waggled his eyebrows at Elias, and what do you know? The kid had a bashful side.

My heart swelled—after everything he'd been through, he'd found someone who saw and understood him.

Gideon's brow furrowed as he glanced at Kerrigan. "Uh, do we need to wait to...? I wouldn't want to hurt him."

"Depends on how Elias feels," Kerrigan said. "The portable oxygen machine will beep if his levels go down, and if that happens, all activities cease. But as long as you're careful, you're cleared to go about your daily tasks—make that human-level-type daily tasks. And absolutely no more witch traps, you hear me?"

Elias covered his cough with his hand. "Yes, ma'am." With help from Gideon, he stood, and then he took one large step toward Kerrigan and wrapped her in a hug. "Thank you for saving me."

Since I'd already shown my mushy side, I went ahead and stretched my arms to envelop Elias as well, creating a group hug situation.

The thick emotion in his voice had my throat tightening, too.

Gideon relayed his appreciation as he joined in, and I glanced toward the window— Sasquatch would never let me hear the end of it. But the hall was clear, and he would've informed me if anyone lingered near the door.

The two of them left, eager to escape the tiny room they'd been stuck in all week, and I lowered my forehead to Kerrigan's and inhaled her addictive scent. "I'd like to add my gratitude to the mix. If you hadn't returned to the compound to perform that extra procedure, who knows if..." I couldn't finish.

"You're not the only one who'd never forgive themselves if he didn't make it," she said, proving she also understood me in ways most people didn't.

"How about me?" I slipped my hand in her back pocket and squeezed her ass. "Am I cleared to do all the things?"

Kerrigan looped her arms around my neck and grazed my jaw with her lips. "Depends on what's on the agenda. I wasn't sure if you'd be able to get away."

Right. The agenda. If I relayed the schedule for this evening, it might kill the mood. "We have about an hour before..." I exhaled. "I need to tell you something. Do me a favor and focus on my good qualities while I do."

She tensed, her arms automatically falling to her sides.

"Like that you yourself said that I'm hot with or without eyebrows—"

Already she was pursing her lips. As much as I hated it, I couldn't have it both ways. I couldn't keep Kerrigan sheltered from the pack and expect them to trust her.

I lifted her hand and kissed her knuckles, leaving my lips on the top of them as I spoke.

"Remember how you wanted to attend a pack meeting with me?"

"Yeah, the first night I came to the compound, before I realized that'd be like strolling into a tiger's cage with raw stakes strapped to my person." Dawning spread across her face, slow and steady like a sunrise. One that meant your last day on earth. "You're not saying..."

"I'll protect you. With the attacks steadily increasing, we need to formulate a better, proactive strategy."

In the name of preserving feelings, I considered softening the rest, but it'd be unfair to keep her in the dark. "A significant number of werewolves still believe you're a witch, and several claimed they'd rather die than allow you to treat them. Which is totally unacceptable. We can't give up before the battle's even begun. The best way to address it is for them to see you for who you truly are. A smart, kind, and incredible doctor who's helped our injured werewolves, saved Justin's and Elias's lives, and has my complete and utter faith and trust."

Unfortunately, Kerrigan didn't suddenly appear reassured and ready to be fed to the wolves. *Damn.* How did I expect her abandon her doubts when my own betrayed me?

Her safety was one thing I could guarantee, so I clung to that—I'd already pulled the pin on the grenade; no reason to wait till it blew up in my face. "You'll only have to speak for ten minutes. Fifteen tops." I laced our fingers and implored her with my eyes to please believe in me as much as I believed in her and do as I asked. Although my obstinate nature wouldn't permit my mouth to form a word meant for feeble people who begged instead of demanded.

Please spare our lives. At least the lives of our children... I batted away the memory that'd been rising far too often lately.

I brought our entwined hands to my chest, to where my heart hammered out a steady rhythm. "I'll take care of you, I swear."

Kerrigan put on a brave front that the wobble in her voice immediately betrayed. "What's fifteen minutes? I could survive most anything that long, save maybe a gunshot wound or the whole throat-ripping thing, right?"

My muscles coiled, ready to unleash death and damnation. Ironic, considering I should kick my own ass for causing her to fret over that second one. "No would dare defy me like that, I assure you. I'd rip them limb from limb and stick their head on a pike as a warning."

Unadulterated shock registered on Kerrigan's face. I wouldn't take it back, though. Weakness got you and the people you loved killed. "While I appreciate how safe I'll feel next to you, let's count to ten before going that far, m'kay? My medical skills are stellar enough I might be able to pull off a limb reattachment. The head, however, is a no-go."

"Budging on the subject of your safety is also a no-go," I said.

"Conall, be reasonable—er, less unreasonable."

"We've talked about this. It's not in my nature, and I'm afraid I can't be, especially when it comes to you."

She sighed. "I guess I'll just call it a draw, since there for a second, I thought you were going to dump me again."

"Take a break, you mea—"

Kerrigan cut off the rest of my words with a kiss. "Do you really want to spend the hour we have arguing?"

"Good point." On our way out of the office, I informed

Sasquatch that if anyone asked, he had no idea where I was, and rushed Kerrigan to my cabin.

The instant the door shut, we stripped as though we were in a race. Even better, no matter who was naked first, we both won.

As I had less layers, I technically came in first. Bonus, I got to stand and watch as she bent to remove her jeans, leaving her in nothing but her hot pink bra and a teeny-tiny thong that matched.

A squeak fell from her lips as I charged, the quick pace at which she backpedaled triggering my predatory instincts. Within seconds, I caught up to her and pushed her against the nearest wall.

The slip and slide of our skin awakened my carnal side, and I nipped at her neck, her jaw, her lower lip. I slanted my mouth over hers and swept my tongue inside, determined to taste every inch. I groped her over her bra, annoyed at the fabric for being in the way, so I yanked, hard enough to rip it right off her, grinning at the loud *rip*.

"Conall"—she smacked my arm—"that was one of my nicest bras."

"I'll buy you a new one." I bunched the triangle of her thong in my fist. "Might as well buy you a pair of panties, too." Her sharp intake of breath accompanied the extending of my claws. The fabric shredded so easily, the resulting pink ribbons falling to the floor.

"I swear. We've got that big meeting coming up, and now I'm not going to have underwear."

"Overrated, babe. I go commando all the time."

She shook her head and then reached for me, but I wasn't ready to give over control. I snagged her wrists, lifted her arms over her head, and manacled both of them in my fist. Slowly I raked my gaze over her, relishing the way her body arched as she fought against her restraints.

"Don't worry. I know what you want." My free hand went

to her pussy, and I groaned as loud as she did when my fingers travailed her sensitive flesh. "Look who's nice and wet for me."

Her hips bucked, chasing after my touch, and I paused with my thumb poised over her clit.

"Quick question—just something that's been on my mind since last night. Did you call up the mayor and clarify that we're together?"

The way her lips parted yet no words came out had me tsking. "Whatever am I going to do with you, Dr. Ryan?"

"I vote for giving me multiple orgasms," she said. "That'll really teach me a lesson." She tilted her hips, aiming to force my touch where she wanted it. Instead, I used it to pin her against the wall. She rubbed her thighs together, a whimper coming out as she did so. "Conall, I'm too horny for this. We're wasting precious time."

"It would've only taken you a few minutes to call. Seems you're the one who wasted time."

"Seriously? That'd be super weird. It's not like I call up random people to tell them my relationship status has changed. I don't start off conversations by saying, 'Hello, my name is Kerrigan, and I have a boyfriend; oh, you brought your dog in for a teeth cleaning? You should know I have a boyfriend; why yes, I'll take a burger and fries, and by the way, I have a boyfriend.'"

"I see nothing wrong with that. In fact, I'd prefer it."

"Fine. From now on, I'll tell everyone I meet that I have a boyfriend. Now, bury your cock inside me before someone interrupts us."

If we had more time, I would've drawn out the torment. Since she had a point, I glided my hand from her hip to her lower back and guided her closer, until that erection was nuzzled up against her slick center. I repeated the drag, over and over again, until both of us were panting.

Keeping her wrists pinned, I pulled a condom out of my

pocket, managing to get it on one handed. I gripped the base of my shaft and entered her. Then I released my hold on my cock, giving it on over to her.

As we moved together, I pressed my thumb to her lower lip. "You don't just have a boyfriend, by the way." My eyes burned gold, the passion and conviction inside of me igniting them with the fiery glow. "You have a *mate*."

CHAPTER THIRTY-THREE

Kerrigan

MURMURS and whispers erupted as I stepped into the chamber on Conall's arm. What remained of my tattered nerves frayed further as we walked to the front, and I thought of my royalty comparison once again. Wearing ripped jeans, a tank top, and Conall's leather jacket, I was closer to the raggedy version of Cinderella—sans fairy godmother—and if werewolves and witches were real, why couldn't I snag one of those?

At least I'd had a few orgasms to loosen me up and help me power through, although I'd forgone the chance at a shower in favor of that last one. *No regrets.*

A flash of purple caught my eye. Gina cut through the rows of chairs, shouted an exuberant hello, and flung her arms around me. The attack-hug felt so good, I decided I'd take it over mice henchmen, a pumpkin carriage, and glass slippers—honestly, those unyielding heels had to hurt like a bitch anyway.

"I'm especially glad my fairy godmother has access to booze," I muttered, and at Gina's confused crinkle, I swiped a hand through the air. "I'll explain later. I'm just glad you're here."

"Oh, well..." Gina glanced at Conall, a grimace on her face that I translated into *you- tell-her*.

"Gina and Sasquatch already appreciate what you bring to the team, so they're going to be on watch during the meeting, along with a handful of others."

My momentary relief popped in my face like a balloon I'd blown too full of hot air. In order to avoid freaking out, I did what I usually did in tense situations and made a joke. "Did Sasquatch say the thing about appreciating my special skills aloud? Or did you tell him his opinion and take his stony silence as agreement?"

Gina snorted and patted me on the arm. "You'll do great. I'm cheering for you."

I cast her a forlorn wave, and then Conall and I finished our walk to the front.

No thrones for the record. Given the raised platform and abundance of cherry wood, along with the rows of unfriendly faces, it felt more like a courtroom.

Lucky me, I'd be the one on trial.

Nissa, Tyrese, Diego, and Chandra occupied the other seats on the platform.

I thought I'd seen Conall's barbaric side the night he'd accused me of being a witch. Not only in my cabin, but when he'd broken his chains. He'd been dealing with a punctured lung, and I... Well, I'd made excuses on his behalf, guzzled up his apology, and pushed that evening to the far recess of my mind.

Since then, he'd shown me a kinder, softer side. There was also the man he became in the bedroom, when his hands were on me and when mine were on him.

Then man who gestured me into a chair and then sat at my side filled in another slice of the overall picture that made up Conall Shaw. His position as the alpha involved being responsible for the welfare of the entire pack, making hard decisions on its behalf, and doing what was best to protect its members. This version of Conall was the unyielding badass who'd annihilate anyone who challenged him, and having his overprotective nature aimed directly at me, like a laser beam of unharnessed power, sent my pulse on a dizzying rampage. The man was the uranium of defense, with enough unstable energy to fuel a nuclear bomb.

Was this just a normal day in the life of a pack alpha? Or had the attacks catapulted him into ruthless territory?

Had I witnessed this version of Conall before, I wasn't sure I would've provoked the beast in the cave.

A frisson of heat shivered through me, all the times he'd ravished my body flickering through my mind in a blur of satisfaction and debauchery. Without even one of his pieces, no matter how big or small, Conall wouldn't be who he was.

He'd lived in this brutal werewolf world his entire life. After losing his first pack, along with his entire family, I understood why he would do whatever it took to prevent it from happening again.

Conall reached over the arm of my chair and folded my hand in his. Regardless of the bumps along the way, the lack of acceptance from his pack members, and my looming concerns over an impending battle, I wouldn't take back any of our time together; I wouldn't trade it for another, less cruel world; and I absolutely wouldn't abandon him.

I was ready to do anything to save him and his pack from the same fate his last one suffered. Even if the other shifters always despised me, and not only because I'd sworn an oath to promote animal health and welfare and relieve their suffering.

Maybe let's not start our spiel with that in case some of them aren't flattered by the comparison.

More than that, I'd do it just to save Conall from experiencing any more pain and agony. I squeezed his hand, peered into his warm brown eyes, and said, "I realize this isn't the right time, but I love you, and I just wanted you to know that."

A slow, awestruck smile spread across his face. "That means a lot to me. Thank you." Okay, so he didn't say it back.

Everyone began whispering, and I heard snippets about myself and my confession. "Shit," I said, recognizing far too late that the supernatural crowd could hear me. The rest of the werewolves up front shifted nervously in their seats as a steady stream of negative attention got aimed my way.

The man at my side remained calm and collected, his smile morphing into the same cocky smirk he'd given me the night we'd met. "Don't worry. I was about to introduce you as my mate, anyway."

A uniform gasp reverberated through our audience.

Conall kissed my cheek before pushing to his feet, and a hush fell over the room. "If any of you are wondering if you heard that right, you did. I'd like to introduce everyone to Dr. Kerrigan Ryan. She's to be treated with the utmost respect. While she details what she's done and what she needs as she continues to help us, everyone will be dead fucking silent and listen to every word. Or they'll have to deal with me."

My stomach soared up, bypassing my rib cage and lodging in my throat. Was this seriously happening?

"Our pack is under attack. Most of you know a coven of witches exterminated all but one of my former pack members, and only because he and I fled. Leaving my family behind instead of fighting to my dying breath, regardless of how young and inexperienced I was at the time, still haunts me to this day."

Conall and Diego shared a glance, the sorrow within them so strong it echoed inside of me.

"I consider myself responsible for every single loss the Bridgewater Pack suffers," Conall continued, "which is why I'm unwilling to shrug off the loss of a single soul. We'll protect our territory and our people at all costs. But with the witches attacking our healing abilities, we won't be able to do it without Dr. Ryan's help."

Murmurs slithered around the audience, a snake that grew stronger and louder as it recruited members to its cause.

Sabine popped to her feet and bowed her head. "Sir, may I please speak?"

He nodded, and considering her eyes wouldn't go near me, I steeled myself for what would follow.

"While I appreciate everything Dr. Ryan has done here at the compound, I've worked by her side and can use her methods to combat the poisoned arrows and any exposure to wolfsbane or silver. I can take care of everyone, same as I always have."

It stung more than expected, the slice of pain lodging deep.

Another person stood, an older man with a stubbled white beard who looked like he wrestled grizzly bears for fun.

"I recognize our elder pack member would like the floor," Conall said, gesturing for him to speak.

"You said yourself that your pack was exterminated, and it was undoubtedly outsiders who provided the information that enabled the coven to find you. It's too risky to invite a stranger into the compound right now. Humans will only muddle things and cause a bigger mess with a larger fallout. We must only invite in people we can trust."

At that, more of the pack members stood, popping to their feet in their best impression of popcorn kernels in hot oil. Conall let out a growl, and everyone froze, all conversation dying in an instant.

The respect he generated from his members was truly impressive, and I hoped he wasn't about to lose any of it over me.

"Sabine, your statement omitted much of the truth. For instance, whether or not your brother would be alive if it wasn't for Dr. Ryan."

"She's definitely faster with the scalpel and neater with her stitches, but mine would've held. It also took her some time to get him to shift back, using an experimental, untested treatment."

"Yeah, and I couldn't get him to shift back, either, so careful what you go accusing her of." The sharp bite in Conall's words caused the entire audience to sit straighter in their seats.

"You're still avoiding the main question. Would Justin be here today, able to shift and heal, if it weren't for Dr. Ryan?"

Sabine's mouth opened and closed, and then Justin stood, his gaze swinging to me as he did so. "No. The answer is no." His gratitude helped soothe my hurt feelings and remind me why I'd vowed to help, no matter what. "I was on the verge of death, and she brought me back from the brink. I'd like to voice my support in bringing her into our pack."

Conall nodded at Justin, and he took his seat. More people stood, and Conall pinched the bridge of his nose, exhaled, and then raised his voice. "I do my best to invite input, listen, and weigh our choices fairly. But the majority of you haven't even met or heard Dr. Ryan speak yet, and in spite of that, you're jumping to unfounded conclusions."

Panic beat at my senses, my face heating as I awaited my introduction to an audience who didn't particularly want to hear from me, didn't trust me, and obviously didn't think I was worthy of someone like Conall.

Grams, I could really use some of that extra bravery and boldness you conjured up so easily.

Gold sparked in Conall's eyes, and the intensity within them resonated in his voice. "While she speaks, you will sit, and you will listen. You will give her the respect she deserves, or as I mentioned early, you'll have me to contend with. Everyone, I'd like you to meet my mate. Dr. Kerrigan Ryan."

CHAPTER THIRTY-FOUR
Conall

I EXTENDED A HAND, helped Kerrigan to her feet, and gestured for her to take the floor. While I wanted to stand at her side and glower, I also knew it was important for her to stand on her own. It'd been a while since I'd been nervous. I practically forgot how it felt for every cell in my body to revolt at once. I forced my knees to buckle and my ass to hit the seat of my chair. The crossed arms couldn't be helped.

Kerrigan reached up to twist her hair around her finger and then slowly dropped her arm by her side. "Here's the thing: I can't make any of you trust me. But if you end up with poison coursing through your veins, I'm the one with the power to save you. So maybe think about that. Not just for yourself, but for your parents, your siblings, your children, your best friend."

Well, shit. If she was gonna continue on like that, I might as well call it a day and go crack open a beer.

She took a few minutes to explain the treatments, peppering her words with various medical terms. Confidence infused her voice as she spoke of her surgical skills and how far they surpassed most veterinarians who'd been in the field for decades.

"Along with the odd tinge of Justin's skin, he had a secondary infection that'd gone unnoticed. Another hour, and it would've been too late." Kerrigan let that hang in the air for several seconds. "His sister loves him, no doubt about it, just like you all care for your family, your friends, and fellow pack members. But love isn't what's going to keep you alive if you get hit with silver or wolfsbane. *I am*."

I pressed my lips together to suppress the goofy-ass grin on my face. Damn, I loved her. I hadn't wanted to say it in front of everyone. *Mate* was strong enough for them. It'd burst out of me earlier, the unexpected declaration kicking me in the gut. I wasn't sure when the tables had turned, but I'd tear the world apart for Kerrigan Ryan.

My mate.

My beloved.

"Which leads me to what I need to keep everybody breathing and shifting." She asked for blood donations and then pivoted in my direction, the slight raise of her eyebrow asking if that was enough. At my slight nod, she straightened and leveled her gaze at the audience. "Yeah, that's all I have to say. For now."

I gripped the arms of my chair, about to stand, but Nissa was faster. My anxieties from earlier, when I'd given Kerrigan the floor returned, stronger and more destructive.

If Nissa mentions going to the council, and the pack members see that she and I don't agree, all Kerrigan just managed to accomplish will come undone.

If I had to, I'd pull rank again, no matter how much it'd hurt us both. But if the council got involved... How was I going to fight them, the witches, and my own people at once?

"When I was a young girl, a group of doctors and scientists turned me into their own special guinea pig," Nissa said, and a hollow pit formed in my stomach. "You've all seen the scars, the patches where hair doesn't grow on my coat when I transform. Of everyone in this room, I have more reasons than anyone to distrust Dr. Ryan..."

I held my breath, afraid of what would come next. I could hardly tackle her on the spot after what she'd said, though.

"But I'm bringing a baby into this world," Nissa continued, "and if any of you die because you were too stubborn and bigoted to listen to Dr. Ryan, my little guy will be less safe. Many of us have come from other communities where we've been picked off or virtually exterminated. How many of you sat in meetings exactly like this one, where they decided to refuse help from outsiders?"

The room fell silent, the downturned gazes, along with every slight shift and fidget portraying the answer loud and clear.

My beta looked at me and gave me a nod. *Take it home*, it said. There might be a pinch of *you owe me* in there as well.

I pushed to my feet, standing straight and tall. "Like Nissa, I don't want to later regret this moment. Neither do any of you when—as Kerrigan pointed out—it's your wife, husband, or child who's on the operating table. We all want our loved ones in the best hands, and without a doubt, that's Dr. Ryan. We're not only lucky to have her, we *need* her in order to win this battle."

One by one, people popped to their feet, but to voice their support of Kerrigan this time. We didn't get them all, but we got the majority, and victory sang through my veins as I adjourned the meeting.

Once everyone except those who remained on the podium with me had filtered out of the room, I pulled Nissa into a side hug. "Thank you," I said, my throat and lungs too tight. I hadn't realized how much I'd needed her support.

Then I turned toward Kerrigan, who'd hesitantly pushed to her feet, and planted a kiss on her luscious lips. "You did it, sweetheart. Just like I knew you could."

"Thank you, but that definitely wasn't all me." Kerrigan

peered around me and gave Nissa a cautious but grateful smile. "Thank you. I know it wasn't easy for you to speak up for me like that."

"Admittedly, it wasn't my plan at the beginning of this meeting." Nissa snagged Tyrese's hand and pulled him into the conversation as well, assumedly because she could use extra support. Neither of us were very good at apologizing nor admitting we might've been wrong. "My husband did his best to calm my fears and reassure me Conall's a good judge of character, but I was sure he was making the wrong move and hellbent on standing my ground.

"Seeing how much you care about the lug"—Nissa socked my shoulder with her free hand—"and hearing you speak so intelligently and passionately about your career and skills, well, you won me over." She scuffed her foot against the wooden floor. "It's been rough, having things so off between Conall and me. I've always considered him and Diego my annoying big brothers."

"Did somebody say my name?" Diego crashed his way into the center of the conversation, and happiness swelled within me. I'd missed them. Missed this.

"Don't make this about you, dude. I'm still mad at you for eating the last of *my* potato chips." After shooting him a deadly look, Nissa returned her gaze to Kerrigan and spoke quickly enough her words came out in a rushed blur. "I'm sorry that I judged you so harshly."

Kerrigan reached across me to squeeze Nissa's shoulder, and while I flinched on her behalf, my beta took it in stride. "And I'm sorry some asshole doctor gave you a reason to."

"Does this mean you'll let Dr. Ryan do an ultrasound?" Tyrese asked, bouncing on his heels like a little kid before Christmas. "Can we?"

Nissa placed a hand on her stomach. "Okay, baby. I'll take that as a yes." Her eyes brimmed with tenderness and adoration, and then she snagged my hand and guided my palm to one side of her belly.

Bam, bam. My niece or nephew kicked against the walls of his current home.

I was just about to suggest a toast when Sasquatch burst into the room.

"Sire Sasquatch, welcome-eth to the party," Kerrigan said. When he didn't smile or rush to join us, she pointed. "See. Not a jokester. I'm funny, and I never get so much as a glimmer of a reaction." She nudged my arm. "Conall, do that glowworm thing with your eyes and demand he appreciate how hilarious I am."

Sasquatch strode forward, all business, and bowed his head. "Sir, please tell your mate that while it's difficult not to be amused by her constant efforts to get me to crack a smile, I haven't found any of her jokes particularly funny."

Kerrigan's jaw dropped, and hers wasn't the only one. Gaping expressions went through the rest of us in a wave.

The giant ginger werewolf straightened and winked. "Only kidding, Duchess. You almost got me with some of the titles you've assigned me."

At Kerrigan's triumphant squeak, happiness pinged through me.

Losing my family and pack just about wrecked me, and I'd accepted the role of an orphan who fought to ensure others wouldn't have to experience the same tragedy.

Blood didn't necessarily make a family, though. Protecting one another, taking care of one another, overlooking flaws, and forming an unbreakable bond forged with mutual affection and love did. For a guy who'd never been the mushy type, I was damn close to making a sappy speech proclaiming how much I appreciated my second family.

"Unfortunately," Sasquatch said, his usual solemnity returning, "I must decline the party invitation and steal away a couple of the guests, as we have a situation."

My muscles tensed, my mood shifting from celebratory to preparing for battle.

"A member from the Crescent Pack just showed up at the compound. He claims a coven of witches attacked their community last night. He managed to flee, although he's beat up from the journey and isn't healing. Sabine's doing what she can, but I'm sure she could use help."

"Guess that's my cue," Kerrigan said, starting for the podium stairs.

I caught hold of her wrist, halting her progress one step into her descent. "Not so fast." The timing seemed suspicious. Or maybe I'd grown even more paranoid this past month. Either way, I wasn't letting Kerrigan out of my sight until I'd had a chance to talk to the guy. "I'll walk you. I have some questions for our unannounced guest. If he wants us to treat his wounds, he's going to have to convince me he's answering them truthfully."

CHAPTER THIRTY-FIVE

Conall

OUR FOOTSTEPS ECHOED through a hallway thick with tension and worried expressions. When it came to threats and pertinent information, I'd never believed in keeping my people in the dark. The news that the Crescent Pack had been attacked had obviously spread, and I could see their questions plain as day.

How long did we have until the coven reached our homes?

Were we going to be ready to fight them in time?

As soon as Kerrigan entered the infirmary, she shed my leather jacket and hung it on a hook in the corner. The evidence of her not wearing a bra showed through the thin fabric of her shirt.

Our visitor stared a second too long—which was a second, for the record—and I growled, drawing his attention to me.

Damn filthy animal finally yanked away his gaze—not that I could really talk, since it took Kerrigan buttoning her white lab coat for me to regain my focus.

"Dr. Ryan, this is Sam Wilson from the Crescent Pack," Sabine said. "He has a gash in his upper arm and shoulder, deep enough I thought you'd better take a look to see if any tendons have been severed." Was it my imagination, or was there a hint of genuine humility on the features of the woman who'd spoken out against Kerrigan not thirty minutes ago? "I didn't want him to lose the use of his arm because I stitched him up before you could assess the full extent of the damage."

Kerrigan nodded in Sabine's direction as she gathered supplies. "Thank you, Sabine. That was a good call."

As my mate went to work, Sam talked about the strange smoke, people trapped in sigil circles, and injuries that didn't heal. Like us, they suspected witches, but no one had been able to get eyes on them. Until their community was attacked with silver arrows last night. "I was coming back from a hunt when I heard the screams from the ambush," Sam said, his voice cracking. He cleared his throat twice before he could continue. "Most of our members are presumed to be seriously injured. Or worse."

Dread tightened my lungs, the story too familiar and one I didn't want to relive right now.

"I'm going to have to suture the two ends of the tendon together," Kerrigan said, wielding a needle. "I've numbed the cut the best I can, but this is still going to hurt a bit."

Sam gritted his teeth against the pain and then picked up his tale from where he'd left off. "Like I said, I was on my way back and heard the screams. Then Frank called..."

Frank Wallace was the alpha of the Crescent Pack. He was the one I'd tussled with earlier this year, after his adamant insistence I marry his daughter and further cement our alliance by providing our communities with "superior offspring bred to lead." I'd taken issue with anyone telling me what to do, especially since one of my goals was to get away from that close-minded thinking and allow my people true freedom. It'd turned ugly enough that I thought we'd end up taking each other out instead of joining forces. Evidently, an attack he couldn't counter meant Frank forgave and forgot. Or more accurately, he didn't have another choice.

"Almost done with the tendons," Kerrigan said. "Then I'll suture the gash."

"You were saying that Frank called," I prompted, anxious to hear the rest of the story. "He and every able-bodied pack member fled toward the mountains, into rocky terrain they hoped would slow or deter the witches. He told me to run as fast as I could, find Conall Shaw, and request the help of you and your pack."

Something rubbed me the wrong way as Sam spoke, but I couldn't put my finger on it.

"I guess I was close enough to whatever spell they cast to lose my ability to regenerate. At one point, I sensed someone behind me, so I started zigzagging and covering my tracks better to throw whoever it was off the scent. By the time I reached a gulch with a low-running river at the bottom and tried to leap it, I was so tired that I missed it and took quite a tumble. It left me with these injuries, but I didn't let it stop me. My people needed me, so I climbed up the other side and didn't stop until I reached your compound."

His emotions rang true, and his heart rate remained fairly steady through the telling. I tended to judge people harsher than necessary, so perhaps it was my skeptical side throwing me off. In my world, outsiders were guilty until proven innocent, and since it'd kept us safer, I didn't feel bad about it.

Except for with Kerrigan, although the fact that she'd saved my life the night we'd met immediately put her on my good side. Then again, the very next day I'd jumped to the wrong conclusion about her being a witch, so I wasn't sure I should pat myself too hard on the back. It did, however, provide a good reminder of why it'd taken longer for the rest of my pack to get onboard and why some of them remained skeptical.

All heads swiveled toward the knock on the door, and Diego and Mikal stepped into the room.

A wild gleam lit Mikal's features. "You'll never believe it. We finally found—"

"We need to speak with you about an urgent matter," Diego butted in, his eyes narrowing not on Kerrigan, but on Sam. "In private."

I placed my hand on Kerrigan's lower back. "You'll be okay?"

"Yep. This is something I've done more times than I can count, and Sabine is here if I need an extra hand."

I hated to leave her alone too long with a stranger I wasn't sure we could trust, but there were plenty of safeguards in place. With that thought to comfort me, I bent to give her a kiss goodbye, hoping our time apart would be brief, even though I had my doubts. It wasn't like my life ever slowed down, and things were only going to continue escalating until we took out the coven making our lives hell.

Between the meeting and the craziness of discovering another pack may very well be in need of her medical expertise, I wasn't sure all the orgasms in the world would be enough to offset the cons of being with me.

But there was no going back, and at this point, I wouldn't even entertain letting Kerrigan go. Luckily, she'd somehow fallen in love with me, and once we took care of the current threat and peace was restored, I'd spend every day I could making it up to her.

As we broke apart, I shot Sam another glare that had him sitting straighter. "I'll leave the door open a crack and post Sasquatch there. If anyone steps out of line or needs convincing to cooperate and make your job easier, he'll also help with that. Just say the word."

After Diego and Mikal told me who or what they'd "finally found," I'd try to get in touch with Frank and verify Sam's story. If it checked out, I'd put together a team to go bring the remaining members of the Crescent Pack here, where we could treat the injuries and combine forces.

"We'll give him the benefit of the doubt, along with a warm welcome and room and board," I told Sasquatch after latching the door for what would be a very brief second or two. "But keep eyes on him at all times."

He nodded and cracked the door to the medical office once again.

As soon as we were out of hearing range, I turned my attention to Diego and Elias. "What's up?"

"We found the werewolf," Mikal said, with so much excitement I wondered if I'd heard him wrong.

Luckily, Diego was there to clarify. "The one who's been helping the witches."

CHAPTER THIRTY-SIX

Kerrigan

SAM GAVE ME A PUNCTUATED SNIFF. "You smell human."

A weird thing to say, yet not untrue, so I continued to fill a syringe with antibiotics and replied with, "Um, thanks?"

"I can also smell him on you. He kissed you goodbye in front of witnesses, so you must be more than a side piece."

I jabbed the needle into Sam's shoulder a bit harder than necessary, so he'd get the message I didn't appreciate his choice of words, even as I protected his body from infection. Also, who used *side piece* these days?

"Ouch." He rubbed a hand over the spot. "I meant no offense to you. I'm just not sure what Conall is thinking. He could've wed the princess of our pack as our alpha bid him to do, and instead he's dallying with you."

I glanced in the direction Sabine had gone, this time to get water for tea for me. Not the sleepy kind, but the caffeinated kind to keep me going. The door was still cracked, and I wondered if Sasquatch was trying not to butt in or if he thought I should remain as stoic as he did whenever people rattled off their opinions, unappreciated or not.

"Oh. You don't know." Sam huffed a laugh, one that was

unquestionably at my offense, and a strange ringing filled my ears. "Alphas can't take human mates. Lovers, occasionally, but werewolves are a dying breed. If we mate with a human, there's only a fifty-fifty shot that the offspring will be lupine, and they definitely won't be strong enough to ensure the future of our race."

A pit opened in my stomach, my attempt to ignore Sam's comments crashing and burning. Had Conall been purposely keeping this from me? Had I thrown myself fully into our relationship only to discover it had an expiration date?

No way.

What would be Sam's purpose for spinning lies, though?

When I'd called Conall my boyfriend, he was the one who'd taken it to the next level by referring to himself as my mate. He'd also declared it in front of an entire room of werewolves earlier tonight.

They *had* all gasped in disbelief, come to think of it. Was that why?

Forget my tome on backwoods survival, which had been rather neglected as of late. Time to revisit the bookstore and find a manual on werewolf hierarchy.

Alphas can't take human mates.

Ugh, I wasn't going to let some stranger mess with my head. I trusted Conall. He hadn't given me a reason not to. I lifted my chin and faked my way into confidence, similar to the way I'd done the night I met my alpha werewolf. "Fortunately for us, your approval—or disapproval, as you've made crystal clear—doesn't matter. I'm his mate, and nothing you do or say will change that."

"Maybe not anything *I* do, but if the Council finds out, they'll intervene for sure—I'm surprised they haven't pushed Conall to pick an acceptable mate already. It's incredibly indulgent on both sides." Sam rubbed his fingers along his jaw, as though the wheels in his brain were spinning hard over how unsuitable I was. "Frank's gonna shit bricks when he finds out you're the reason Conall refuses to wed his daughter. How long have you been together?"

I peeled off my gloves, stepped on the trash can lever to open the lid, and tossed them inside. "Oh, it's been exactly..." I ticked off on my fingers, acting as though I was counting it down for him. "*None* of your business."

A wolfish grin spread across his face. "I'll find out anyway."

"Not from me. I don't discuss my private life with my patients." For some reason, I felt it was better if he assumed it'd been a while, but maybe that was more my urge to justify how quickly our relationship had progressed. Had Conall fully considered his choices? Was falling for me going to be a detriment to his people?

Don't go there. It's what this guy wants.

I leaned my hip against the counter and changed the subject. "How many of your people were hit with arrows leading up to the big attack?"

"Let me get this straight. You won't answer my questions, but I'm supposed to answer yours?"

I raised my voice. "Hey, Sasquatch, did you want to come in here and help me coax information out of our uncooperative visitor?"

Hinges creaked, and Sasquatch stepped into the open doorway, his large frame taking up every single inch. He crossed his massive arms and pinned the guy on the exam table in place with a heated glare. Panic rolled across Sam's features, and even though I probably should've been above it, a vindicated swirl went through me.

Take that, dude. That's what you get for telling me I'm a foolish dalliance after I saved your shoulder.

Sam held up his hands in classic surrender posture. "Okay, fine. I'll tell you. No reason to bring in that guy, *jeez*." He eyed Sasquatch as if he expected my bodyguard to leave, and it was all I could do not to hug the guy for his sober temperament as he remained firmly in place. Sam fidgeted in his seat and cleared his throat. "Let's see... There were two last week and five this week. One of the girls was barely fourteen."

"How many pulled through?"

Sam gaped at me as if I'd been dropped on my head. "No one survives having silver injected into their bloodstream. Not pups, not teens, and not even the strongest of our species. If one of those arrows hits you, it's a death sentence." He fixated on a spot on the wall. "If you're lucky, you've got two to three days to say goodbye to your loved ones, but it's time spent in pure agony. After seeing how much they suffered, I started to think they'd be better off if the arrows had killed them on impact."

The strings in my heart tugged, and I considered informing him I'd found a way. But for some reason, my instincts told me to play it close to my chest. What I needed to do was talk to Conall—about Sam and everything he'd said, and about us.

I quickly swapped my lab coat for Conall's leather jacket, a little too aware of my braless situation. Not that I really required the support, more like a thicker shirt to hide the evidence of not having any, especially with how nippy it'd likely be outside this time of day. Pun totally intended.

Although the memory of why I didn't have any underwear was enough to keep me nice and toasty.

On my way out of the office, I snagged Sasquatch's arm, tugged him into the hall—or more accurately, he indulged me by following—and closed the door behind us. "Did you hear what he told me? About alphas not being permitted to marry humans?" At Sasquatch's reluctant nod, I added, "Is it true?"

Was that pity on his face? If he finally showed me an emotion and it was fucking pity, I was gonna be so pissed. "It's true that's what the Council prefers," Sasquatch said. "Or, more accurately, demands. As long as I've known Conall, he's always proclaimed that anyone who stands on the sidelines while their kind are being slaughtered don't get a say in how we live our lives. He's already made his choice, and it's you."

"But what if that results in having a target on his back, all because of me?" The fissure that'd formed in my heart shuddered, unsure whether it was about to split deeper or get the chance to knit together. "No wonder everyone in the room gasped. I'm sure that choice affects them, too."

"Conall's already declared you his mate. He won't change his mind, and he sure as hell won't take it back. He loves you, and there's no force more powerful on earth than love." Sasquatch's statement came out with an undercurrent of sorrow and conviction borne of experience and grief. He placed his hand on my shoulder and gave it a reassuring squeeze, the light touch enough to eviscerate my resolve to keep my feelings all walled up until I could reach the confines of my car. "He'd battle to the ends of the earth for you. I'd be by his side the entire time, too, as would most of his pack members."

Tears stung my eyes, and I swallowed the rising lump in my throat. Meeting Conall had changed me inside and out. He'd given me wings, along with a sense of family I'd desperately needed. Not only did he feel like my family, but I'd grown close to Gina, Elias, and Sasquatch as well. Even Nissa, Tyrese, Gideon, and Diego factored into it. Surely, I could win over the rest of the pack eventually.

But could I handle being responsible for their being in danger?

I ran my hand through my hair, trying to sort through my merry-go-round of thoughts. So much had happened today that it seemed like a week of events and emotions packed into twenty- four hours. I needed to think. To figure out what all this meant for my future, the future of the pack, and the werewolf I'd fallen head-over-heels for. "Where's Conall?"

"I'm afraid he's unavailable at the moment." Sasquatch leaned closer and dropped his voice low. "We've captured a member from the party responsible for the attacks. Conall's with him now so we can glean more information. But I'll have him call you as soon as he's free."

"Okay. I could use some processing time anyway."

Sasquatch glanced through the soundproof glass to the werewolf inside. "I've got to stand watch, but—"

"Don't worry about me."

"It's part of my job. Give me two minutes, and I'll find someone to escort you home."

"That's okay. I think I'm going to head to Gina's house and chat things over with her, actually. Girl talk, you know?" Since I didn't want him to think our little chat hadn't also been appreciated and knew he wouldn't initiate a hug, I threw my arms around his middle—I'd never be able to reach his neck. "Thank you," I said. "For talking me down and letting me know what's going on and just...everything."

As soon as I let go of him and stepped back, Sasquatch dipped his head and graced me with the tiniest of smiles. "My pleasure, Consort."

CHAPTER THIRTY-SEVEN

Conall

I STEPPED into the dim basement, nothing more than a single bulb to illuminate the werewolf chained to the chair beneath it.

I took no pleasure in torture; it merely happened to be highly effective, and something I undertook as the alpha. Forcing the truth out of someone required a certain level of cruelty and brutality the majority of my pack members didn't possess, regardless of their fortitude and strength in other areas.

The traitor glanced up at my approach, his blackened eye standing out against his sallow skin. Mikal was the one who'd noticed an unfamiliar vehicle parked at a formerly abandoned cabin and called Diego for backup. They snuck up on the guy as he was gathering firewood and, thanks to the element of surprise, the fight had been fast and furious.

"Let's get right to the point, Mr."—I flipped open the wallet that'd been removed from his pocket to study the ID— "Tony Russo." Sure, it might be an alias, but truth be told, I didn't much care either way.

"As the alpha of this pack, it's my job to know everything that goes on in my territory. Which brings us to you." I stopped about a yard short of him and crossed my arms in a way that showcased he didn't want to mess with me. "What are you doing in *my* territory?"

"I'm just visiting the area, doing some sightseeing," he said, so much smarmy false innocence I cracked my knuckles. His stony facade remained in place as the sound echoed through the room, which meant he was very foolish or foolishly confident.

Wiry guys often turned out to be stronger than they looked, but I had the advantage of bulk and more pound-for-pound strength. No contest, I could take this guy if it came down to it—without the help of the chains that imprisoned him, too, although they made interrogations easier. "From where? Which pack do you belong to?"

"I'm unaffiliated, and I move around a lot."

"What pack were you born into, then?"

"I'm more of a lone wolf."

I rubbed my fingers along my jaw, relaying that I could be just as casual-cool as he could be while he lied through his teeth. "I don't believe you."

He shrugged his shoulder the best he could while yoked to the chair. "That's not my problem."

Oh, he wanted to be a smart-ass? I closed the distance and loomed over him, letting him get a better look of every solid inch of me under the light. "It's gonna be your fucking problem once I crack open my toolkit and torture the information out of you. Sure you don't want to pick the easy way?"

He at least had the good sense to glance around, so not a complete fool.

With a low growl, I let the gold roll over my eyes and shifted enough for claws to shoot from my fingertips. Gathering all my concentration, I transformed my face and torso into my half form, testing my own bounds. I didn't want to deal with kicking off my shoes, but this way I could terrify him with my control and carry on speaking through my mouthful of sharp, elongated teeth.

Our unwelcome guest's breath hitched, and the smug twist of his mouth faded.

"Now that you and I understand each other better, let's try again," I said. "No one enters my territory without my say-so. Why are you here?"

When he didn't answer, I curled my fingers around the spot where the chains crisscrossed his chest and lifted him off the floor, chair and all. Hot air billowed from my nostrils and hit his face. "One last chance before you relearn the meaning of pain. We found pawprints near traps that'd been set for my people. Were they yours?"

The traitor's chin quivered, and then he set it, his strong front not doing him any favors— I could hear his rapid heart rate. Scent his fear. A little more motivation and he'd spill his guts, possibly literally if I didn't like the information.

I lifted my free hand to the lower half of his belly and extended my claws until they punctured the skin.

At his continued silence, I drove my fingers deeper, gripped a fistful of his guts and squeezed until his entire body quaked with the agony.

A tormented cry burst from his lips, along with a spurt of blood. He fought against his restraints, drawing out his suffering, but he'd been crystal clear how he felt about other people's problems before, and this was all his.

"Stop, stop, stop," he rasped with a wet-sounding wheeze. "I'll talk." I retracted the claws but didn't release my hold on him.

"I'm a private investigator. I was hired by a coven of witches. I watched the Crescent Pack for about a week, and after reporting what I'd found, they sent me here to gain information on Conall Shaw and his Bridgewater Pack."

The scowl remained cemented on my face as I vacillated on whether or not to believe him. Tony had turned a one-eighty rather quickly. That was the goal, but he'd also made it a point to use my name and imply he knew all about me. I decided to tug on the thread and see what else I could unravel. "To what purpose?"

"They gave me a big enough pile of cash that I didn't ask, and they didn't tell. Now that I've been caught, it doesn't matter. Whatever you do to me, they'll do worse."

"It almost sounds like you're *daring me* to prove you wrong."

A creepy grin split his features, and he laughed. *Laughed!* "Honestly, I expected you to catch me sooner. Someone's been distracted with a certain female lately, hasn't he?" His laugh morphed into a cough, and my heart ceased beating as the words sank in. "I knew I was pressing my luck prowling around your woman's house last night, trying to dig up information to earn me a bonus. I think I scared her, considering she slept with the lights on. All the better to watch her sleep."

A roar ripped from my mouth as I let go of the chains and caught him around the throat. Blood trickled from where my claws punctured the skin beneath his jaw. "Did you tell them about her?" I shook him, hard enough the rattling of his teeth and bones filled the air. "Did you tell them about Kerrigan?"

I shouldn't have said her name, but this man would never see the light of day again, and too much panic flooded my system to focus on anything else.

Perspiration beaded his forehead, and the color drained from his face. "The failsafe spell the witches placed on me when we signed the contract is about to take effect. Once my heart rate drops low enough"—he attempted to snap his fingers, but his depleted strength failed to create the clicking noise—"*poof*, it'll be lights out for good."

A lie? Unlikely, although his vitals had dropped enough I couldn't be sure. "Why tell me anything, then?"

"If I'm gonna go out, I might as well take the famous

Conall Shaw's ego down a couple of notches. I informed the witches you were the tougher, superior of the two alphas, by far. It's more satisfying than I expected, seeing genuine fear in your eyes. Knowing that I'm the one who caused it, when so many others have tried and failed."

Tony's eyelids drooped, and I glanced back the way I'd come, deliberating the idea of rushing him to the medical office. If Kerrigan was still there, she might be able to revive his pulse and give me extra time to extract more information.

But then she'd see what I'd done. Who I truly was.

She stitched up injuries, and I inflicted them; she saved lives, and I took them.

She told me she loved me, and I knew she did, but a part of me still worried I'd go too far and scare her away. There was also a side of me that didn't believe I deserved the amount of happiness being with Kerrigan brought me.

Or that I couldn't fully sink into the comfort and joy without it getting yanked out from under me.

Fucking witches. They'd burn the entire world to the ground and still not have their fill of death and destruction. They couldn't wait to take my second family away from me, and I'd be damned if I'd let that happen. If it necessitated leading my people to war against them to eradicate every last one from off the face of the earth, so be it.

"Besides," Tony wheezed, his chin slumping against his chest as the light in his eyes dimmed, "if the coven's busy with you, it'll give my wife time to take the money I stashed and run. The witches weren't the only ones with the failsafe." His weak laugh evolved into a hacking cough that ended with a wheeze.

Magic licked at the underside of my palm, the air around us buzzing with it. The intruder's neck wrenched to the side with an awful pop, and then he went limp.

Not only had the witches killed him with their premeditated spell, they'd left me with the dead body to dispose of. Angry heat pumped through me as I lowered him and the chair to the floor.

I withdrew the cell he'd had on him from my back pocket. I'd destroy it so no one would track it to the compound, but not before combing it for information that might give us an advantage or lead us to the coven.

I dialed the last number he'd called and paced the room.

"Hello?" After a couple of seconds, the female voice said, "Tony? Is that you?"

"Yeah," I said, waiting and hoping the woman on the other side would spill information.

A shrill cackle filled my ear. "You think I didn't feel my spell taking effect? Please tell me I'm talking to the illustrious Conall Shaw."

That awful laugh dredged up memories of the day my family was executed. It might not be the same witch, but in a lot of ways, they were all the same. Ruthless, cruel, and in need of a lesson. "I'm going to rip you limb from fucking limb. You'll pay for what you've done to my family and to other werewolf packs."

"Now, now, now," she said with a cluck of her tongue. "Are you sure you want to start with threats?"

"I'm sure I want to enact them. I'm counting down the moments till we meet on the battlefield."

"Ah, here I was hoping we might come to an agreement. Guess I was right about you needing extra motivation. Just do me one tiny favor and hold onto my number. I have a feeling you'll want to give me a call here pretty quick. Until then..."

The line went dead, and I pulled the phone from my ear to frown at it. Why did she sound so confident? Did she think messing with my head would cause a moment's hesitation to ripping out her throat?

Thank God I'd hesitated with Kerrigan.

Why hadn't she told me some asshole had scared her? Lead filled my lungs at the realization he could've done worse, my chest twinging over the fact that I'd been the one to put her in harm's way, just like I worried I would.

Foreboding slithered through me, even as I told myself I was only being paranoid—it was my MO, after all. Kerrigan was safe and sound inside the medical office. Even if she'd finished up in there, she would've remained at the compound.

Shit, why didn't I tell someone besides Sasquatch to keep an eye on the werewolf from the Crescent Pack and instruct him to remain with Kerrigan, no matter what?

My pulse picked up speed, reaching the danger zone withing seconds. *He wouldn't have let her leave without an escort. He's well aware of how I'd feel about that, especially right now.*

"Damn it." I bolted up the stairs, panic pulverizing my internal organs as every thought, every beat of my heart, every *everything* turned to finding my mate.

CHAPTER THIRTY-EIGHT

Kerrigan

I PULLED my car up to my cabin, warmth spreading through me at the dark kitty outline in the window. For the first time since moving here, it felt like home. A bit shabby and still in need of repair, but still.

The lights had been off in Gina's house when I swung by her place, the front door locked. I discovered via text she'd headed to the bar to leave instructions for her staff, as the next week would probably be hectic. With nothing else to do at the compound, I decided to make use of my time by grabbing an overnight bag, along with a few changes of clothes. And extra underwear— a supply of those, both comfy and sexy, landed at the top of the list.

A thrill went through me at the memory of Conall shredding my panties before we had sex against the wall. Depending on how many members of the Crescent Pack were injured, I might be tied up for the next several days. But if Conall and I found pockets of time to kill, well, we definitely knew how to blow off steam in the sexiest of ways.

Shoot. What about the clinic?

Honestly, I wasn't sure when I'd be able to open my personal practice again for the more conventional animals of

Guadalupe Falls, but I'd stay at the compound as long as Conall and the two packs needed me. Which meant I should probably coax Sir Pounce into his carrier and bring him along as well. Instead of asking Conall for permission, I'd go with the asking forgiveness angle. If he and I were going to work, the two boys in my life were going to have to learn how to get along anyway.

If. It was what I wanted more than anything, but I still couldn't quite shake my concerns about the ominous werewolf hierarchy and their declaration against alphas daring to breed with humans. *O-M-G. Conall's Prince Harry and I'm totally Meghan Markle.*

I snorted at the comparison, wondering if Conall would get it. Most likely not.

After releasing an exhale, I pushed out of my car and did my best to ignore my whirring thoughts. "One day at a time," I whispered to myself as I unlocked the door and stepped into my living room.

It smelled kinda funky, like I'd had an Easter egg hunt four months ago and hadn't found all the eggs. "Remind me to crack a window before we go, Sir Pounce." My city gal instincts opined it was a good way to get robbed, but I'd learned here in Guadalupe Falls, I was more likely to be mauled by wild animals than experience a B-and-E.

"Real cheery thought, Kerrigan. Let's work on our silver linings." I shed Conall's jacket and tossed it on the couch. Then I crouched over and patted my thighs. "Come 'ere, kitty. Want some food?"

Sir Pounce leaped off the windowsill and padded over. I started toward the kitchen, expecting him to follow, but instead he sat his butt on the ground and gave an offended meow.

"I know, I left you alone all day and I'm sorry, but we're going on adventure." Well, that was more Hobbit-esque than

I'd meant it to be. "Come on. If you eat your treats now, you'll be happier for the car ride."

All I got from Sir Pounce was a slow blink using his entire face. No matter. Once the salmon-flavored Temptations hit his bowl, he'd come running.

As I strode across the living room, I frowned at the smudge of mud on the floor. I couldn't recall a time I'd even gotten muddy. My eyes must be playing tricks on me because I swore light flickered for a fraction of a second as I stepped over it.

Was this a dream? It *felt* like a dream.

Wait. The gears in my brain clicked into gear too late, the meaning caught in the continuing grind of them as a circle flashed around me, along with triangles, and funky lines I'd never seen before.

A loud buzz filled my ears as energy slammed into me, the resulting shock similar to diving underwater without plugging my nose. My foot hit the edge of the smeared mess, meeting resistance instead of air, and a chill racked my body as a sense of wrongness settled deep into my bones. My legs turned rubbery, lightheadedness took hold, and each labored gulp of oxygen caused my lungs to contract rather than inflate.

At the feel of trickling liquid, I swiped a finger under my nose, frowning as it came away covered in blood. My blurry finger separated into three as I studied the crimson stain. "What the hell?"

An eerie glow came from the front of the room, the rectangle imprinting itself on my retinas seconds before a creaking groaning noise filled the air. Then the door burst inward, pieces of the wood splintering and hitting my skin. I automatically lifted my arms to protect my face, freezing in horror as a hooded figure stepped through the large, blown-out hole.

I backpedaled a few steps, only to slam into something

solid. A jolt fired through me, strong enough to send me to my hands and knees. I blinked at the current encircling me, shimmery green, with an obnoxious, high-pitched hum that reverberated through my head and overtook my brain.

Blood dripped from my nose, thick splatters against the wood floor, and my flight instinct kicked into high gear. I pushed to my wobbly feet and took another run at the odd wall of light, only to be stunned into submission again.

Not a dream, a nightmare.

Ten long, fuchsia fingernails gripped the hood hiding the intruder's face. A shiver skated down my spine as she lowered the velvety hunter-green material, and lucky me, I'd just met my first witch. Curls the color of champagne framed her alabaster skin. She cocked her head and pursed her pearly-pink lips, the slight lines that formed around them hinting she was older than I originally assumed.

"Not what I expected the alpha's mate to look like, considering all the fuss. I'm actually impressed that beauty's not the only thing Conall cares about."

"What the hell is that supposed to mean?" Oh, good. I'd found my voice in time to insult the witch who'd obviously come to kill me. Stellar survival skills, I had them. "Never mind. It doesn't matter, because I'm afraid you've got the wrong girl."

There. Much better, and I prayed I sounded convincing. It was hard to tell with the loud droning coming from the sigil trap—and I had no doubt that was this.

With a cruel smile that sent shards of ice into the marrow of my bones, she stepped through the circle as if it were merely funky-colored air. I took a step back, and crackling electricity nipped at my skin and lifted the hair from my scalp. I wasn't sure I could take one more shock and get back up again. Maybe if I bided my time, I'd find the right opening.

The woman caught my chin in her hand, the sharp tips of

her nails piercing my skin. "Hmm. There's such a fine balance when it comes to proper motivation. Personally, I like to err on the side of more is more." She raked her razor-sharp talons across my throat, one quick slash that left me gasping for air.

Then she just stood there, looking disgusted by me as blood ran a trail from her fingers to her elbow. The warm liquid coated my neck, oozed down the front of my shirt, and dripped onto the floor.

The world swam, and I swayed and braced my hands on my knees.

Searing pain.

A sanguine puddle slowly spreading beneath me.

Sir Pounce's green eyes blinking at me from underneath the couch.

It should hurt more. Dying. I thought it'd be different somehow.

"Hurry," I heard, a voice in the distance. Female. A mix of agitation and alarm. "He's coming."

Conall.

Of course he'd come for me. If I could speak, I'd yell at him to stay away. To save himself and the pack—not that he'd listen. I loved that about him, even during the moments it also drove me crazy.

Picturing his rugged features filled me with serenity, despite my blurring vision and my body's spasming death throes. I wished I could run my fingers through his hair as he sniffed me. Wrap my arms around him and kiss him one last time. Remind him that I'd always be his family, regardless of our time getting cut short.

Conall had shown me what it was like to be loved by a powerful man who occasionally verged into beastly territory. He'd let me in to his heart with a ferocity I'd never experienced before, and I wished it wouldn't hurt for him to lose me.

It seemed almost lavish to have been loved so

unconditionally by three amazing people. I hated to let go of Conall, but at least I'd be reunited with Mom and Grams soon. *Sorry, my love. I promise to watch over you as you take on the coven.*

Kick witch ass for me...

Just don't let it make you bitter.

With that final thought, I crumpled to the floor like a marionette whose strings had been snipped, allowing the darkness that'd come for me to swallow me whole.

CHAPTER THIRTY-NINE

Conall

RAGE AND FURY replaced the blood in my veins.

As a guy who'd memorized Kerrigan's scent, smelling it along with the sharp copper tang of her blood left me on the brink of insanity and contemplating throwing myself on over. My stomach roiled, and the wave of hysteria that crashed over me just about sent me to my knees.

"I should've never let her out of my sight," Sasquatch said, and I turned, gripped him by the front of his shirt, and roared in his face.

His expression remained unchanged. Not because he was being his usual stoic self but because there was too much self-loathing in his features to allow for anything else. The same emotion whirled into the tornado currently wreaking havoc on my insides.

Seconds. I'd missed her by fucking seconds. My internal organs collapsed on themselves, my body threatening to shut down from the pain.

After that phone call, I'd asked around the compound, desperate to find Kerrigan. I'd followed her scent to Gina's place and from there to the parking lot, letting loose a howl at finding her car gone. I'd barked an order to Nissa to check in with Gina and then shifted and tore a trail to Kerrigan's cabin, Sasquatch and Tyrese hot on my heels.

At the circle of light near her cabin, I'd pushed my body to my limits. My lungs screamed for oxygen and still I'd pushed, relishing the sight of the wide eyes of one of the witches as I crested the hill.

I'd take a bounding leap, stretching out my fingertips and grazing the hem of a dark cloak's...

Only for the light to disappear and leave me tumbling into the nearest tree, so hard that I split a crack through the trunk with my skull.

My stupid, thick hardheaded skull.

I dropped my hands to my side, my shoulders sagging so low my knuckles about touched the floor. "I should've never put her in their sights in the first place. We weren't at war yet, but..." I exhaled past the misery coating my throat, so thick it left a bitter taste in my mouth. "I'd been shot in the back with silver bullets. What the fuck did I think was going to happen?"

That I'd sweep her off her feet and we'd live happily ever after?

How stupid, allowing myself to think that was a possibility. I'd assumed our biggest opposition would be the council, and frankly, I'd almost *wanted* them to try and tell me what I could and couldn't do. That way, I'd be justified in punishing them for all the times they'd stood idly by, specifically when it came to the death of my family. I'd show them and every other pack, werewolf, and possible enemy that no one was capable of beating me.

I was the alpha and omega, and I'd fight to maintain that position to my dying breath.

"It's a lot of blood," Nissa said softly, extending a hand so Tyrese could help her to her feet.

A few seconds sooner and it'd be the witch's blood splattered across the room and puddled on the floor. If I could go back, and skip tracing Kerrigan's scent to the house. If I'd never left her side in the first place. If, if, if...

"But I doubt they would've bothered carrying her through the portal if they didn't plan on keeping her alive," Nissa continued. "They wanted you to see she'd bled before her abduction, hoping to incite your anger and use it against you. Likely so they can control when and where the battle takes place."

"Well, it fucking worked, and on their day of reckoning, I'll be sure to use my wrath to dole out vengeance with a heavy hand." For every injury, every hurt they inflicted on Kerrigan...

The vise that'd clamped onto my heart the instant I'd seen her go through that portal compressed the organ that much tighter. *Just stay alive, sweetheart*—I refused to consider any other possibility, or I'd become completely untethered and cause more damage to myself and those around me.

But make no mistake, I was going to hunt down the coven responsible and slaughter each and every one of them. Slowly and painfully, until they knew what it was like to long for death.

———

Restraint had never been one of my strong suits.

After charging into the woods, I lifted a boulder and hurled it as hard as I could. It ping- ponged off tree branches and trunks, burrowing a wide trail until landing a football field away. Birds flew from branches, other critters ran and hid, and my insides tore at me, going in too many directions at once.

I scrubbed a hand over my face and withdrew the phone I'd taken off the dead P.I.

I have a feeling you'll want to give me a call here pretty quick... I'd wanted to frisbee the damn thing into the cement wall of the basement, and now it was my only lifeline to Kerrigan. With my constraint as shaky as my hands, I needed a moment to think. If I delayed the call in order to allow my pack more time to track down the coven's headquarters, the witches might take it out on my mate. If I discovered their location and marched my people against them, they might kill Kerrigan before I reached her. If I lost my temper during the call and pissed off her captors, I ran those same risks.

Somewhere along the way, Kerrigan had become intrinsic to my survival, and just the thought of losing her...

I howled, a mournful noise that caused every wolf and werewolf in the nearby vicinity to add cries of solidarity. Tyrese, Nissa, and Sasquatch appeared in front of me.

"Just tell us what to do, and we'll make it happen," Nissa said, and Tyrese and Sasquatch nodded.

"Head to the compound and ready everyone for war. Arm and prepare anyone who's over the age of eighteen and physically able to fight."

More nods. Nissa whispered something to Tyrese, and then he and Sasquatch took off into the trees. I opened my mouth to tell Nissa to go with her husband, but the words wouldn't form. "I should be here for the call," she said. "That way, you can focus on how to respond, and I can listen to background noises and note anything else that might help."

Both of us knew it was more about keeping me from unraveling, but I clung to the reason to have her by my side all the same.

I sucked in a breath, steeled my nerves, and dialed the same number I'd called less than an hour ago.

"Conall, hello. How unexpected to hear from you again so soon. To what do I owe the pleasure?"

I half expected plumes of smoke to billow from ears. "You know why I'm calling. There's no reason to drag a human into this. Release Dr. Ryan, and you and I can work this out."

Naturally, the brazen bitch cackled. I'd never felt so angry and vulnerable and out-of- fucking-control in my life. "*You* dragged her into this."

Of that, I was painfully aware, and the animosity I'd aimed at the witches reflected right back at me. "If your coven hadn't attacked my pack and hindered our healing abilities, we wouldn't have had to recruit a doctor."

"Don't talk to me like I'm stupid, or we might as well end this discussion without further ado," she snapped. "We both know she's more than your doctor."

"Okay, you've got me." If it wouldn't give them more fuel to set me on fire, I'd abandon my refusal to say the word *please* and beg them not to hurt Kerrigan. "Let her go, and I'll let you set the terms of our upcoming battle. That's more than generous."

"Careful, Alpha. You're making too many presumptions. I don't want a fight—I never did. It was your kind who turned this into a war."

"We've left you alone for decades, and I'd be happy to continue doing so if you'll call off your attacks and return what's mine." It'd eat at me day and night, letting them go unpunished for everything they'd done, but if that was what it took to get Kerrigan back, I'd do it in a heartbeat.

"You might want to talk to your buddies in the Crescent Pack about that."

"Return Kerrigan to me, unharmed, and I will, I assure you. They'll never mess with you again or they'll have me to deal with."

"It's too late for that."

Needing to expend some restless energy, I paced, remaining close enough that Nissa would still be able to overhear the conversation. "What is it you want from me, then?"

"A meeting. I'll send you the details tomorrow evening, shortly before the meetup time, so be ready. You're to come alone and unarmed, and we'll take additional preventative measures that I'll also reveal tomorrow. Those are my terms."

"Let me speak with Kerrigan, and I'll come alone right now so we can get this over and done with."

"Don't push your luck, wolf. I wanted to show you how serious I was with the display in the living room, but no further harm will come to her as long as you comply."

Further. She'd *been* harmed, a fact I already knew because of all the blood, and they wouldn't hesitate to do more damage. My blood boiled, and I wanted to scream threats and follow through with them and tell her that by tomorrow night, she'd be six feet in the ground.

But none of that would result in the safety of my mate, so what else could I do but agree?

CHAPTER FORTY

Conall

"I'VE DONE SEVERAL TRANSFUSIONS," Sabine told me as she swiped at the sweat-dampened strands of hair plastered to her face. "But there are so many of them, and our blood supply is already running low again..."

Her shuddered breaths suggested she was working hard to prevent herself from bursting into tears. In order to accommodate the staggering number of injured Crescent Pack wolves, we'd converted the large community room where we held special events into a triage center.

"Not all of them are responding well, and I..." Sabine lost the fight to hold back her frustrations and began to cry. "Some of them have died. I'm not sure why—I think the poison's already done too much damage. Several are barely hanging on, and I'm out of my league here."

"What about Sheriff Martin? He said he'd gather up a team of nurses and bring in Dr. Mullens, too." I hated to expose our secret to more townsfolk, as the last thing we needed were additional chinks in our armor, but it was better than having shifter blood on my hands.

Sabine glanced toward the corner of the room occupied by the Crescent Pack Hierarchy. No surprise, King Alpha

Asshole himself stood in the center. "Frank met them out front and turned them away. He said he'd never allow an outsider to treat his people."

As if I didn't have enough shit to deal with today. Every couple of minutes, I checked the phone in my pocket, ensuring the ringer was on, the volume turned up, and that the maximum bars of service filled the top right corner.

"I'll take care of it," I grumbled, and I'd already taken a step in their direction when Sabine tapped my elbow.

"Sir?"

I expected her to ask me not to interfere, baffled by people's inability to let go of their prejudices. "Seeing Frank act like that made me realize how foolishly my behavior has been this past month. I was out of line in last night's meeting. You've always protected us. I know I don't have any right to say this, but I really wish Dr. Ryan was here."

You and me both. If the wounded shifters strewn across tables and lying on the unforgiving floor with only the support of sleeping bags, linens, and towels ever met Kerrigan or witnessed her surgical skills, they'd undoubtedly wish for the same.

"I'll get her back," I said. Hope was a dangerous and cruel mistress, one that lifted you higher so the subsequent drop could do greater damage. I refused to succumb to the despair that'd infested my spirits since Kerrigan's abduction.

I strode across the room, posted up behind Frank, and cleared my throat.

The thorn in my side slowly turned around, the grim set of his features belying his tough display. His gaze darted around, his shrewd eyes broadcasting he cared more about how his people viewed him than whether or not they pulled through.

"You dare to show up here, after failing to keep your pack safe, and go against my orders?"

His mouth opened and closed, like a fish gasping for air,

and it'd be so satisfying to enact my outrage on him. He deserved it. His wounded pack members, however, did not. Particularly the ones who'd landed in their current predicament due to following orders. *Frank's* orders.

He shrugged a shoulder. "They knew the risks."

"What about me? We're now suffering because of decisions you made." Before I'd realized it, my fists were in his shirt and I'd lifted him off the ground. I unleashed the alpha glare. "My mate is paying the price for those same shitty decisions, and I'm sick and tired of cleaning up your messes."

"If you would've married my daughter, none of this would've happened."

Snap went the last thread on my control, and I tossed the asshole into his group of men, satisfaction zinging as they went down like bowling pins. Did I need to pick up a spare?

Nope. Got 'em all. Mark it with an X.

I stepped through the mess of bodies and renewed my fury-filled hold on Frank. "Ready to try again?"

He glanced around, clearly seeking help, so I shook him hard enough he focused on me and my wrath. Over the next few minutes, out the full story came. After discovering several witches were hiding out in a town on the outskirts of Bangor, Maine, they'd proceeded to pick them off one by one.

One when she closed up shop for the night; another as they walked home from work; and a few more as they were sleeping in their fucking beds. Finally, Frank and his dogs managed to torture the location of their coven out of one of their captives.

The one semi-admirable thing about witches was that they rarely cracked, so I couldn't imagine how far they'd taken it—didn't want to. And that was coming from a guy who loathed the creatures.

"So I sent my top soldiers to ambush the coven. They sensed them coming, and we lost a dozen men during the bloody skirmish that followed," Frank finished. "But since we'd slaughtered thirty-two of their kind, we considered it a win. Don't tell me you're upset there are less witches on the planet."

I spoke through gritted teeth. "I'm upset that the coven came after *my* pack because of *your* recklessness."

No wonder the witches had attacked the Crescent Pack. If they'd lost thirty-two during that conflict and fifteen had been picked off before that, and yet they'd still had enough to leave... I scanned the room, quickly calculating the injured. Fifty had died in the ambush, and another thirty were injured.

My people's faces superimposed themselves over the shifters that were moaning and holding injuries, several circling the drain and unlikely to make it.

A heavy rock settled in my gut.

Then another thought struck me. "Was it you or one of your men who shot me in the back, you fucking coward?"

Frank paled, and that, combined with the vibes I'd gotten from Sam, was confession enough for me. No wonder he'd acted strange. He'd either thought I'd died or that no one could kill me. Considering it was so different from the witches' traps and arrows, I should've realized earlier that the two were unrelated.

Nothing would give me more pleasure than disposing of Frank right here in front of all his people, so they could see him for who he truly was.

But then I sensed a vibration against my thigh and heard the ringtone I now despised.

I tossed Frank to the ground and called for Mikal to take him to the basement and shackle him so I could deal with him later. Then I charged out the nearest door and answered the phone. "You have ten minutes to get to Solitude Stone. A witch will be awaiting your arrival. If she senses anyone else with you, she'll leave, and you'll never see your mate again.

Once you're fitted with a silver collar to prevent shifting, my sister will portal you to our location."

My pride baulked at the mention of the collar. They wanted to treat me like a junkyard dog, just yank the chain to get him to behave?

"Before any negotiations take place, I need to see for myself that Kerrigan's..." *Alive.* The word lodged in my throat, the gravity of the situation not allowing me to say it. "Safe and sound."

"Cooperate, and I'll grant you that one kindness. A word of warning, however. This is your one and only shot, so I suggest you don't blow it. Dr. Ryan's life *literally* depends on it."

Every cell in my body reacted, cranking the frenetic energy tasering my insides to high. Someone else would have to deal with Frank and help Sabine attend to his injured pack members. I rushed toward the Jeep, flung open the door, and noted the time on the dash as I fired up the engine.

"Tick-tock, wolf. Your timer just hit nine minutes..."

CHAPTER FORTY-ONE

THOSE SAME FUCHSIA fingernails that'd raked pain across my neck dug into the tender skin under my chin, not piercing, just applying a menacing amount of pressure. "Don't worry, Cinderella. Your Prince Charming is coming for you."

Under other circumstances, I might cheerily say, *Hey, we're totes on the same wavelength! I compared myself to Cinderella just the other day.*

But I didn't want to have anything in common with the woman the other witches referred to as Andromeda. Judging from what I'd seen so far, she was head of the coven holding me hostage. How *dare* they use me to get to Conall and the pack members I'd begun to consider family?

Intent on showing her she couldn't break me, I amped up the defiance. "What? No ball gown and glass slippers? Talk about a shitty fairy godmother." In spite of my efforts to remain tough, my eyes burned with the urge to cry. I wanted my purple-haired fairy godmother who cared whether I lived or died.

The long, metal nail I'd pried from the unfinished

basement wall dug into my palm. Did I use it now? Save it for later?

A storm brewed within me, bred of malice and devotion. The witches would pay for the hurt they'd caused Conall, both past and present. With the same steady hand I used to save animals, I'd drive the nail into Andromeda's jugular with precision. As she bled out, I'd antagonize her like she'd done to me in the living room of my own house. Nothing would bring me more joy, and suddenly I understood Conall's barbaric side more than I ever wanted to.

"Careful." Andromeda clamped my chin tighter as she hauled me to my feet. "Or I'll strip you naked and create an outfit entirely of your own blood."

It'd probably be an improvement. Not that I had access to a mirror, but I *felt* how rough I looked. Matted hair, furrowed scabs scoring my throat, and blood crusted down the front of my soiled shirt. Once Conall saw me, he'd go ballistic, something they were obviously counting on.

If only I knew their plans for him.

Do I strike now? It's the first time anyone's come within arm's reach. My only other contact had been with Talia, a flaxen-haired witch who left trays of food at the bottom of the dimly lit staircase. Afraid it might be poisoned, I'd held out.

On a cheery note, perhaps the grumbling of my stomach would cloak the noise of an attack.

Alone, I don't stand a chance at escape. As soon as Conall arrives, together we'll find a way.

Ignoring the bite of the slightly rusted edges, I curled the nail tighter in my hand and conceded to being led upstairs. As Andromeda extracted a key to unlock the door, I slipped my makeshift weapon into my back pocket.

Blinding light seared my retinas, and I flinched as I waited for my eyes to adjust. The instant they did, I immediately wanted to hit the undo button. I expected a gothic castle with blacks and reds and ended up in Barbie's grown-up dreamhouse with Pepto-pink walls instead.

So glad they'd kept the dank basement on the stereotypical doom and gloom side.

Question after question tumbled through my head, but I'd be punished for voicing them, so zipped lips seemed the best way to go. For now.

"Seriously, Mother?" Talia sat in a silken wingback chair that only emphasized her ethereal beauty.

Here and there, I'd overheard the witches referring to one another as sister. I supposed it was possible they referred to their leader as "mother," but given the similarities between the two, I doubted it. They shared a face shape, hair color, and unique lips with Cupid's bows on top and bottom. Andromeda was a slightly older version, although she either had an excellent plastic surgeon or used magic-laden facelifts.

Talia continued to gape at my bedraggled appearance. "Shouldn't we at least allow her to shower and change before the werewolf's arrival?" If I didn't know better, I'd think that was concern crinkling her forehead.

The gleam of the overhead lights caused her hair to glow gold, reminding me of the molten flash that rolled over Conall's irises whenever he went full alpha.

Sharp pricks bloomed in my chest, growing bigger the longer I watered them with our shared memories. I added them to the flammable pile that fueled my hate fire and clenched my fists. "She wants me to look like I've been to hell and back. As if that'll be enough to defeat Conall."

A cruel smile curved Andromeda's lips. "You're smarter than I expected."

Yep. Smarter and not as pretty, that was me.

The creases in Talia's forehead deepened. "Which proves that you might've jumped to the wrong conclusion about Conall and his pack. I still think there's another wa—"

"It's already been decided, dear daughter." Venom

dripped from the words, the *dear daughter* sounding more like a threat than an endearment. As determined as I was not to let my fear of Andromeda show, I had to force myself not to step back at the angry gleam in her eye. "We've gone through countless scenarios over the past few months, and this is our best chance."

"We're out of time anyway." Andromeda's attention shot to the center of the room, and Talia stood. Were they planning on fighting in their Grecian goddess gowns? What a waste, wearing those gorgeous dresses for Conall to shred and bloody, but that was on them.

An incandescent pool of blue formed in the center of the room, and my heart skipped a beat as two dark figures took shape, one petite and female, and a burly form I'd recognize anywhere.

The blaze intensified, and then there stood Conall. A bulky silver collar ringed his neck, the skin around it sizzling and red. Regardless if my poor werewolf remained perfectly still, it scalded and blistered. While he bore it well, indignation flared on his behalf.

"Kerrigan," he said, his relief so palpable it echoed within my chest.

My feet propelled me toward him, and he rushed toward me as well. He stretched out his arm, and I reached for him...

Our fingertips brushed for one blissful fraction of a second, and then an invisible force hurtled me backward.

I hit the wall hard enough that every ounce of oxygen whooshed from my lungs before I slid into an aching heap on the floor.

At Andromeda's shrill laugh, Conall's muscles and bones roiled under the surface, bunching and stretching taut. Smoke billowed beneath the silver collar, and the scent of charred flesh filled the air.

With her cackle bouncing around the room, I regretted my

earlier restraint. I should've killed the hateful witch back in the basement, even if it ended up being my last act on earth.

Conall tore across the room and dropped to his knees in front of me. My head throbbed from the smack against the wall, and as he gently cupped my cheek, my vision separated into two fuzzy versions of the man I loved. "I'm so sorry, sweetheart," he said. "I should've never gotten you into this mess."

"You have nothing to be sorry for." I circled my fingers around his wrist, clinging to him while I had the chance, although, yeah, I could use the support right now, too. "I knew you'd come for me."

Conall lowered his lips to mine in the gentlest kiss we'd ever shared. "I'd burn the earth to the ground to find you."

"Ah, true love. How precious," Andromeda condescendingly said, throwing a hand over her heart, and Conall spun on his knees, putting his body between me and her. Talia and the portal witch flanked their leader, their confident expressions only strengthening my resolve.

Go ahead and enjoy the show. I used the distraction to grope for the weapon in my pocket. I wrapped an arm around Conall's shoulder and chest in a pose more fitting of an engagement photo than an escape and whispered, "Stall, and I'll get this hunk of junk off you."

"Not precious enough for you to try to ruin it, the way you try to destroy everything you can't have," Conall said, drawing all the focus. "Is that it? No one loved you? Ever think it might be your awful personality?"

The second of stunned silence left me curious about the expressions on the witches' faces, but I couldn't concentrate on them. Grams once lost the key to her handcuffs—don't ask — and called me in to help free her "special friend" from the headboard. Chatting with a gray-haired man in a prone position with nothing but a pillow strategically placed over his, um, nether region inspired me to practice so it'd never take that long again.

I was about as rusty at picking locks as the nail, but luckily, the mechanism on the collar wasn't complicated. I jabbed in the tip, feeling for the piece that'd trigger its release.

"If you think this will help negotiations, wolf," Andromeda spat, "you're sorely mistaken."

"You promised me no further harm would come to Kerrigan, and then you threw her against a wall, so forgive me if I don't trust your bullshit negotiations."

While there were obviously other fish to fry, I nearly dropped the nail over his use of *forgive me.* Fake or not, I was impressed his stubborn side allowed him to force out the words.

Almost... The *click* echoed through the room, and I quickly yanked off the heavy collar. I shot to my feet as Conall burst into wolf form.

Three witches rushed us at once.

Conall dodged a strange spark of light from the portal witch and knocked her aside like she was nothing. She hit the wall with a crunch of bones, and while he went after Andromeda, I set my sights on Talia.

Releasing a guttural yell, I chucked the heavy collar at her, tempted to celebrate like a quarterback when it slammed into her skull. More, she crumpled to the ground and stayed there. *Holy shit. Not only did that work, she's out cold.*

Conall roared, and my jaw dropped at the amalgamation of human and wolf he'd become. Andromeda flung up her hand, muttering some incantation, but before she could finish it, he clamped a gnarled, clawed fist around her throat. The cruel smile she'd worn since our first unfortunate meeting faded as he lifted her in the air. Her legs aimlessly kicked out for purchase, and who knew someone else's terror could taste so sweet?

"Wait," she wheezed, and the veins in his arm bulged as he squeezed tighter.

"Like you did, when you attacked me two seconds into our meeting?"

"Your pack..." She pried at his fingers to no avail. "I have people posted..." Her gaze moved to the desk in the corner, and a sleek object flashed as it skittered across the surface and soared directly for me.

Before I could react, the sharp tip of a letter opener hovered a centimeter from my eye. I flattened myself to the wall, wishing I'd put more space between it and me so I could attempt to duck, but too late now.

All the blood rushed to my head, my rapid pulse causing it to throb behind my temples, and was this the point where my life flashed before me?

"I'll drive it through her eye and right into her brain if you don't set me down," Andromeda said. "Talia, could you help instead of merely gaping in horror?"

In the peripheral vision I hoped to keep, I caught movement: Talia pushing to her feet with a groan.

Conall opened his fist, and Andromeda stumbled backward, clutching her neck the same way I'd done after she'd *cut mine open* with her witchy talons. How nice to only be missing a little oxygen and not a fucking pint of blood.

Talia plucked the letter opener out of the air, the jerk of her arm muscle leading me to believe it'd taken considerable effort. She repositioned the sharp tip above my carotid artery, increasing the hysterical rush beneath the surface. If she'd ever felt any sympathy for me and my plight, the oozing gash on her forehead had erased any and all traces.

Andromeda sighed, as if annoyed at us for causing such trouble. "Look around, you two. Haven't you noticed how few of my sisters are here with us?"

As if I knew how many witches comprised a coven. I

glanced at Conall to gauge his thoughts on the subject, only to find him as stoic and expressionless as Sasquatch.

"My coven, along with another we've recently formed an alliance with, have your compound surrounded. If I give the command, you'll lose hundreds of pack members. You'd be wise to remember that before you engage in any more theatrics." She narrowed her eyes on me, and I did my best to hide my surge of fear. At least we'd tried. But we'd also failed, hard, and hearing the pack was in danger... "I take back what I said about you being smart. Step out of line again, Dr. Ryan, and I'll take one eye as a warning."

At her mother's raised eyebrow, Talia jabbed the tip of the letter opener into my skin, hard enough a trickle of blood escaped to join the rest dried to my chest and shirt. Much more of this, and I'd be the one needing a transfusion.

"Understood," I said through gritted teeth.

Andromeda typed something into her phone and held it up for Conall. "There. If they don't hear good news from me within the next fifteen minutes, they'll attack. They have you two to thank for that."

Defeat crept along the line of Conall's shoulders, his stony facade giving way to utter despair. All I could do was sit across from Andromeda as instructed.

I'd been plenty afraid during the past twenty-four hours. Witnessing the moment Conall forced himself to surrender to a witch, however, broke me, effectively sucking the wind out of my tattered sails.

"Let's get right to the point, shall we? In a minute, I'll detail the terms, the whys, and the hows. But since I want you to listen with an open mind, we'll start with the stakes, so you're fully aware that you don't actually have a choice in the matter..."

The certainty in her voice grated, her victorious demeanor provoking me to rebel, no matter the cost, and regardless of how futile.

"You will marry my daughter, Talia, and form an alliance with us, the Oldenwilde Coven. Or"—one side of Andromeda's mouth twisted up, a cruel accent to how succinctly she was about to annihilate the last of my hopes and dreams—"Dr. Kerrigan Ryan will die."

CHAPTER FORTY-TWO

Kerrigan

THE LETTERS BLURRED TOGETHER as I scanned the long list of names, my burning eyes no longer wanting to cooperate. At least it was the last appointment scheduled for the day, and by squinting one eye closed, I managed to make out the name.

"Josiah Harris."

The two people seated along the wall of the large community room stood, the man leaning most of his weight on the woman as she helped him into my curtained-off medical office. Once Conall and I returned to the compound, there'd been no time for mourning what we'd lost.

He departed to update his men; I had dozens of patients to attend to; and there was a wedding to throw together in a matter of days.

A wedding. The word reverberated through my head, and my vision blurred for a different reason than merely being tired. I quickly blinked away the tears, the same way I'd been forcing myself to do for the last four days.

Four days spent treating injuries, from most to least severe. Part of the bargain with the witches included lifting the hex on shifters who couldn't regenerate anymore, but they weren't going to release everyone until after Conall followed through on his promise. Andromeda acted as if she were being so generous, bestowing him with the ability to choose five werewolves who might not make it to the day of the wedding otherwise.

In reality, it was a malicious power play, aimed at pitting the Bridgewater and Crescent packs against each other. Also so she could lord it over him, that she was the one pulling the strings.

There was another spell involved, one placed on me, but it was yet another thing I did my best to pretend didn't exist so I could get through my day. One minute at a time, one hour at a time.

I clutched my chest, the dull shoveling ache continuing to carve up my insides.

"Are you okay?" Sabine asked. "I can handle this if you need a break."

Clenching my jaw so tightly I was surprised my teeth didn't crack, I forced my resolve to overtake the misery. At least I pretended, as my overwhelming grief wasn't that easy to shove aside. "I'm okay."

Funny how one short week ago, Sabine's skepticism wouldn't have contained an ounce of compassion, and yet she'd aimed a steady beam my way since my return. Sasquatch stood nearby, as stoic as ever, watching every move like a hawk that knew it'd eventually have to swoop in and catch me when I cracked.

"I could use more coffee if you get a chance. Please and thank you." Sleep hadn't come for so many nights I couldn't keep track of how long it'd been, so there was no reason to pretend I'd be able to doze off tonight. The thing about having your own life hanging over you, a constant threat that hinged on letting go of what you wanted most, was that it turned you into a pessimistic, bitter mess.

"I'll get it." The deep voice ignited every nerve ending in

my body and shattered my heart in a million little pieces. As desperate as I was to soak in Conall's profile or experience even a light brush of his fingers, the tears clogging my throat warned that if I gave in, I'd come unraveled.

Just make it through this last exam, and then you can head to Gina's place and cry till your eyes swell shut. I'd rather not have my sight tomorrow anyway. How was I supposed to watch as the man I loved married another woman?

A fucking witch.

As we'd sat across from Andromeda, she explained they were under attack on two fronts. Werewolves on one side, and vampires on the other. Given everything I'd been through, the news about the vampires barely caused a blip.

Conall pointed out the coven's quarrel was with the Crescent Pack, as they were responsible for the raids, and that he already planned to draw up and quarter their alpha for another betrayal.

But she didn't care.

In order to save her coven, along with the other they'd aligned with, she and her sisterhood wanted to form an alliance that couldn't be easily broken. And it involved her daughter, Talia, wedding the strongest alpha werewolf in the nation—Conall, naturally.

"A true uniting of the werewolves and witches," she'd said, "where children will be born with both magic and the capacity to shift, ensuring the safety of our people for generations and centuries to come."

I'd sat there vigorously shaking my head, wondering why Conall hadn't been doing the same. Especially as conditions about fidelity and a literal till-death-do-you-part clause were covered. If he broke any of the stipulations, the Oldenwilde Coven would be awarded half of everything the Bridgewater Pack owned, as well as the land.

The terms Andromeda detailed wrote themselves across the paper, the words appearing like, well, magic.

On Saturday next, the alpha of the Bridgewater Pack pledges to marry Natalia Burroughs of the Oldenwilde Coven. If he fails to do so, the Sisterhood will view this as a declaration of war and will retract the offer to grant shifters their regenerative abilities, along with their truce and protection. Dr. Kerrigan Ryan's life will be forfeit, and the entire terms of this contract will be null and void.

Vulnerability hung heavy in Conall's features as he stretched out his hand and took hold of mine. "It's the only way I can keep you alive, Kerrigan. The only way I can ensure my pack's welfare. I love you and I'll always want you, and in a different world, you'd be my mate and that'd be it. The freedom to choose is a big part of why I formed the Bridgewater Pack the way I did. But I'm afraid we don't quite live in that world yet."

I'd tried to argue, my objections tenuous at best. For the first time, I wished Conall was weaker and not an alpha or even a werewolf.

"One last condition," Andromeda had said, and I'd wanted to lunge across the desk, shake the triumphant expression off her face, and tell her that someday, somehow, I'd find a way to destroy her myself.

But that'd endanger the lives of too many werewolves I considered part of my family.

It hit me then that Conall was right. Making the deal *was* the only way to protect his people, along with my life and his. When it came down to it, losing any of his pack members would destroy all those big and little pieces that made him who he was. Those pieces also made him the man I'd fallen so desperately in love with that I didn't think there was a tunnel, much less a light at the end of it.

"Call it extra insurance. Only when *I* have what I most want will you be granted what you most want—your mate's safety. Or your former mate's, as the case may be." The glee radiating from Andromeda fueled my hatred, and as the last clause scribbled itself across the bottom of the contract, she mentioned the failsafe spell would be similar to the one she placed on some private investigator. While her statement didn't mean much to me, Conall turned so deathly pale I feared he might pass out.

Ironically, a spell like that required my consent—as if anything about Conall and my time in Andromeda's house consisted of free will. Thoroughly dejected, we signed our names and added the requisite drops of blood.

An awful darkness slunk through me as Andromeda cast the spell, and the final line of the contract had seared itself into my memory:

When—and only when—an heir is born with both alpha shifter and high priestess blood will Dr. Kerrigan Ryan be completely free of the hex on her life. Until that point in time, the Oldenwilde Coven is also at liberty to call upon her, for the purposes of help, medical or otherwise, and/or to assure the alpha's cooperation in protecting the sisterhood.

The dam on my emotions shuddered, my hands trembling as I labored to open the antiseptic. *Get it together. You're so close to patching up the last werewolf.*

After tomorrow, they'll be able to regenerate all by themselves, and you'll... I literally heard Sebastian the crab in my head say, *Just be...just be miserable for the rest of your life.*

So yeah, doing a bang-up job of distracting myself. Sabine relieved me of the antiseptic and cleaned out the gash in Josiah's leg. As I threaded a needle, I pulled myself together. Then I stitched up his wound and gave him antibiotic ointment and pills for the pain.

Right as I was sending him on his way, a steaming mug was thrust under my nose. I inhaled, frowned at the unexpected aroma, and then took a sip. "That's not coffee."

"See, this is why I maintained you were the right doctor for us," Conall said. "You pay attention to detail."

I summoned up the best dirty look I could under the

exhausted circumstance, but due to all the sorrow, it came out watery and pathetic.

He cupped the mug over my hands and tipped it to my lips again. "It's some of your hippie tea—stress-relieve-something-or-other. I learned from the best."

"Sneaky bastard."

Conall granted me the first genuine smile I'd seen on his face since everything went to shit, and how many times could one prevent themselves from bursting into tears in a day? *Not* asking for a friend. He placed a hand on the small of my back, and I leaned into the embrace like the masochist I'd become. "Sabine, will you close up shop for the day? I think Doc needs some R-and-R."

A protest traveled up my throat but didn't make it to the tip of my tongue. I drank the rest of the tea and set the mug on a random table as Conall propelled me away from the makeshift medical unit. As soon as we stepped outside, he scooped me into his arms.

"I can walk," I weakly protested.

"Not very well. And that's on a normal day."

I smacked his chest but without my usual heat behind it. Not that any of my smacks affected the giant werewolf carrying me in the classic bridal stance—a comparison I wished I hadn't made.

The giant hollow canyon that'd overtaken my chest shuddered, yawning wider to allow for the extra misery filling the gap.

Life wasn't fair. It was a cold, hard fact. But did it have to crank up the unfairness to agonizing?

"Do you...?" The muscles along Conall's jaw flexed. His gaze implored mine, so unguarded and full of longing that my heart snagged on its beats, too afraid to take any full thumps in case his next words caused it to crumble apart. "I know I shouldn't ask, and it'll probably only make tomorrow that much harder, but if you want to spend the night with me—"

"Yes." I slanted my lips over his, kissing him with all the built-up hunger going without had caused. I placed my hand on the side of his face, enjoying the tickle of scruff against my palm. The sense of security I felt in his arms was unlike anything else, and I wasn't ready to call it a day yet.

I'd never be ready, but that was a problem for my future self.

"I can say, without a shadow of a doubt, that I'd regret it forever if I didn't spend one last night with you before..." Finishing the statement would hurt too much, so I planted my lips on his and reiterated my first response. "We have one last night together, and I vote we make it count."

CHAPTER FORTY-THREE

Kerrigan

EVIDENTLY, Conall was as eager as I was, because he used his preternatural skills to reach his place in record speed. Same went for the bedroom. The living room passed by in a blur, and then I was being tossed onto an enormous mattress.

As I sank into the cushy comforter and pillows, I decided the bed was where it was at anyway. The linens smelled like him, too, and I turned my head and inhaled, reminding myself to savor every second, every nuance, every everything.

Conall stripped off his shirt and stood over me, and I propped myself up on my elbows and soaked in the sexy view. "I know you haven't been sleeping," he said. "If you'd rather rest up first, I'm happy to let you take a nap before I wake you up with my head between your legs."

The apex of my thighs throbbed to life, and I pushed myself up, snagged the waistband of his pants, and hauled him to the edge of the bed. "As nice as that sounds, my body's gone way too long without yours. I can't wait any longer. Seriously, if you don't get that thick cock inside me within the next few minutes, I'll..." I paused to conjure a proper threat, and he simply watched me with an amused expression. "I'll do bad things. But not, like, the bad things that you'll enjoy."

Conall braced a hand on either side of my hips and brushed a too-quick kiss across my lips. "Afraid that's not going to work. Just putting you and bad things in the same sentence is making me horny." He sucked on the spot at the base of my neck. "I get off on bad things."

"Then I'll only do extremely proper and nice things." I tapped my lip. "Maybe request a cuppa tea. Force you to watch me drink it while fully clothed and seated at least six feet away."

Conall scowled down at me, the expression softened by the slight quirk in the corner of his mouth. "Why, Dr. Ryan, how can you possibly so unreasonable?"

I gasped and jabbed a finger into his firm chest. "How *dare* you? That's *my* line, and you know it."

He chuckled and snagged the hem of my shirt. He peeled the fabric up and over, a prickle zipping across my scalp when my hair momentarily caught the buttons. My pants went next, followed by my bra and my panties, and then he raked his heated gaze over me.

A thought concerning this being our very last chance to have sex flitted through my mind, and I promptly shoved it away—tonight was ours and ours alone.

Soft lips and rough scruff made for a heady combination, and goose bumps spread across my skin as Conall sniffed me, dragging the tip of his nose and tongue up the column of my neck. God, I was going to miss that. Who would've guessed that being inhaled could be so damn sexy?

As he carried on with the delicious showering of affection, I roamed the dips and grooves of his torso with my fingers, grinning at the way his muscles twitched under my touch. By the time I made it to the waistband of his jeans, his ever-growing bulge was stretched to the limit, leaving the pants tight enough they wouldn't come undone without a fight. Although, I'd be the one to win this battle in the end.

A sigh of relief escaped him as he sprang free of the tight fabric, and I quickly shucked off the denim, a thrill going through me at his lack of underwear.

"Easy access, am I right?" I muttered, and his deep laugh vibrated through me. As I sat up, the same cock that'd dangled in front of my face the night we met was hard and ready.

I skirted my touch down his happy trail, and his arousal bobbed with my movements, doing its damnedest to reach for my palm. Same way the throbbing bundle of nerves between my thighs always sought out his touch—it was about time I gave him a taste of his own medicine.

Power replaced the blood in my veins and, featherlight, I drifted a fingertip along the top of his shaft. "I know that things between us won't be the same after tomorrow, and that we'll never get to be this way again. But tell me you're still mine, that you'll *always* be mine."

Conall cupped my chin and angled my face toward his. Our eyes locked, the intensity within the depths as exquisite as it was catastrophic. "I'm fucking yours, sweetheart. I've been yours since the night you saved my life." He crashed his mouth to mine, claiming it with a possessive kiss. "I'll always be yours, no matter what."

Tears burned my eyes. I did my best to blink them back, telling myself not to think about the after, only to appreciate the gift of getting one last night together. "And my heart will always belong to you, just like every other part of me does."

This amazing man loved me, in a monumentally different way than anyone had ever loved me before. I considered it an undisputable fact, in the same way I knew that an octopus had three hearts. While I only possessed one of the life-giving organs, it felt as though the love I felt for Conall would fill three.

He was willing to relinquish everything he wanted just to keep the people he loved safe.

It was time for me to give now, and my mouth watered as I eyed the object of my obsession.

I nudged his shoulder, applying pressure until his back hit the bed. Then I straddled him, the awe I experienced as I studied his body riling me into a state of needy devotion. I worshiped his pecs with my mouth, traced a line down his abs with my tongue, and lapped at the *V* of his obliques.

His fingers drove into my hair, and tingles zipped across my scalp as he wound the strands around his fist and tugged. After torturing him for a minute or so by swiping my tongue excruciating close to the base of his arousal, I slowly licked my way up.

He groaned, and his eyes rolled back in his head. I poised my mouth over the head of his cock, opened wide, and sucked him into my mouth, nice and deep. His hips jerked, his breaths spilling out in huffs as I continued licking and sucking.

Conall propped himself up on his elbows, watching me for several steamy seconds, his eyes so dark I could no longer make out his pupils. The muscles I'd committed to memory tensed, each one of them popping out. I conducted my own experiment, seeing what part of his torso corresponded to what I was doing with my lips and tongue.

Then he leaned over and dug his long fingers into my hips.

"Wait, I'm not finished," I complained, the words coming out muffled.

"Yeah, me neither," he said, picking me up and swiveling my body around so that my pussy landed on his mouth.

A wanton noise burst from me as he licked up the seam of me, all the way to my clit, and wetness pooled between my thighs. Satisfaction rumbled through his throat as I renewed my blow-job efforts.

He ate me out, the languid swipes too much and yet not enough. If I didn't come soon, I feared I might die from want.

My nipples tightened along with all my muscles as he circled my clit with his tongue. Tremors formed, the scratch of his whiskers on my inner thighs amplifying the myriad of euphoric sensations claiming my body.

"I've gotta drink you up while I can," Conall muttered against my sensitive flesh. I rode his face as I alternated between sucking and swirling my tongue around his hard length.

Pressure built and built, a kettle rocking and ready to blow. He brushed his thumbs over the lips of my sex, and just like that, the tightly coiled tension burst and left me screaming Conall's name.

Gravity shifted, no longer holding me to the earth but sending me soaring through the air, and I pressed my cheek against his erection, unable to focus on giving it the requisite attention while I was flying through time and space.

Gradually my soul returned to my body, and an overly pleased werewolf flipped me on my back and flashed me an ear-to-ear grin.

He flung back the comforter, slid his arm beneath my waist, and maneuvered my boneless body onto the feather-soft sheets. His chest brushed mine as he leaned over me to snag a foil square from his bedside table. Riveted, I watched, mesmerized by the rolling of latex, the twitch of his muscles, and extra definition of his veins. The smattering of hair on his chest and thighs, and the general massiveness of a man who'd been beyond tender with me. Exhale, inhale, exhale, inhale...

Eagerly awaiting the moment he and I would be teetering together on the brink of mutual bliss.

CHAPTER FORTY-FOUR

Conall

NEVER IN MY life had I seen anything as glorious and gorgeous as Kerrigan Ryan sprawled out beneath me for the taking. Her skin was flushed from her orgasm, and her half-lidded eyes contained a covetous gleam.

Watching her come undone, all that unbridled passion flickering across her features, had taken me from hard to rock hard. My dick strained toward the slice of heaven between her thighs, as if I needed a compass to show me the way.

I crawled over her, bracing my forearms on either side of her head and caging her in.

Not that I thought she'd try to get away. I notched myself at her entrance, not plunging inside, but coating myself in her slick heat. Her moan spurred me on, and I groaned, allowing desire to build between us until it crested and crashed over us in a tantalizing wave. I kissed her deeply, my tongue mimicking the plunge my hips would soon be making, playing sadist and masochist until my cock wept with need.

Then I drove into Kerrigan and began pistoning my hips. Sweat beaded our bodies, and our breaths sawed in and out of our mouths. I thrust deeper and deeper, basking in the slap of flesh.

With every withdrawal, her walls clamped onto me as if they were begging me to stay, increasing and intensifying a multitude of intoxicating sensations. As I continued to pump in and out of her, I reached between us and pressed the pad of my thumb to her clit. Her keening noise told me I'd found the right spot, and I pounded into her, all the way to the hilt.

"Holy shit, I'm already close," Kerrigan murmured, bracing a hand on the headboard behind her and sinking her teeth into her lower lip.

"That's good, sweetheart. You go ahead and tumble over the edge. I'll catch you."

Using the headboard for leverage, she pushed against me. We circled higher and higher together. She arched her hips to meet mine, and her head lolled back on the pillow.

With a growl, I rammed into her again and again, until black spots danced across my vision. She cried my name as she tumbled over the edge, sheathing me so tightly I had to muster all my self-control to ride out her orgasm.

I gritted my teeth, giving her everything I had and more. The instant she went pliant underneath me, I let go, emptying every last drop.

Totally spent, I fell to the bed at her side. Then I curled her into my arms and kissed the nape of her neck as we both worked to catch our breath.

As the haze around us faded, it invited in too many real-world thoughts. Throughout the endless blur of meetings and planning for the upcoming nuptials—*my* upcoming nuptials—I'd fixated on the safety of Kerrigan, my pack, and werewolves across America instead of everything I was losing.

The blade sharpened now, slicing as I clung to my last hours with my mate. If I had my way, she'd be in my bed every night. Naked next to me like this or wearing sweatpants and fuzzy socks. A tank top and panties or sexy lingerie. Messy hair, curls, ponytails, makeup or fresh- faced

—I didn't care. I wanted all her nights, all her days, and all her tomorrows.

If I closed my eyes, I could envision a future with Kerrigan. Living together and having children and sneaking into the bedroom late at night so we could be alone. My heart expanded with more happiness than I thought myself capable of.

Quickly, I slammed the door on the notion, but not before it shredded my heart and left a bloody mess in the spot where the organ used to reside.

Kerrigan's fingertips skated across the line in my forearm. "You're quiet."

I pressed my lips to her shoulder. "You've always been the chatty one."

"Yeah, if I left the conversation up to you, it'd be ninety percent grunting," she teased, rolling to face me so that her breasts smooshed up against my chest. I kissed the tip of her nose, and she traced her fingertips along my jaw, so I snagged her hand and kissed the center of the palm, too.

A pained noise sounded in her throat, and her chin quivered. "There's got to be some way we can fight this. I've been waiting my entire life to feel like this about someone—to experience this kind of fierce and profound love—only to have it snatched away?" Her voice took on a desperation that made my skin feel too tight. "I don't care if it makes me sound like a little kid, *it's not fair.* What if we could find someone to undo the spell? Are there, like, anti-witches or something?"

I closed my eyes and exhaled. "I'm probably the closest thing to an anti-witch there is. You know how much I despise them. But I saw that spell in action, babe. One minute I was interrogating a guy, and the next, his neck snapped." I placed a hand on the side of her neck and brushed my thumb over the life-giving artery pounding away under the surface. "I'm not willing to let you die. I won't risk it."

"What if...?" The wheels in her brain spun, the same way mine had been doing the last several days, and still I hadn't found a way out that wouldn't lead to too many people I cared getting hurt—or worse. I'd never felt like such a failure in my life. "If Andromeda dies, would that undo the spell?"

Kerrigan propped herself up on her elbow and swept her hair aside, exposing more of her soft creamy skin. "Turn me in to a werewolf. Bite deep into the vein and inject me with the toxin stuff so I can shift and heal and be strong enough to fight."

As implausible as it was, the idea of transforming her beckoned. Not because it'd get us out of our current situation, but because it would make it harder for anyone to ever hurt or abduct her ever again. "The fact that you'd be willing to go through that means the world to me, but I can't ask that of you. More than that, it's not as simple as I made it out to be when we first discussed it."

She blinked at me, so ready to go all in on changing her DNA, along with the rest of her life.

For me.

"There's a lot that can go wrong. If the bite is too shallow or too deep, or if your body's unable to fight off the toxin in time, you might"—my gulp echoed through the quiet—"die."

"Well, I have access to antibiotics, and we can try a transfusion with your blood so that it's a more hospitable environment and—"

I softly kissed her lips. "We're also a whole month away from the full moon, which is another important step in the transformation."

"Okay, then forget using newfound superstrength to sneak up on Andromeda and slit her throat with my claws. I'll just track down a gun, concentrate on how cruel she was when she held me hostage, take aim, and pull the trigger. Yeah. As long as I remind myself what's at stake, I could totally shoot her."

Here she was trying to convince herself. The idea of killing Andromeda was one thing—I wouldn't hesitate myself if it wouldn't put Kerrigan at risk. But the woman I was in love with... she'd struggle to follow through. Even if she managed to pull that trigger, she'd live with the consequences the rest of her life, and whether or not she wanted to believe it, it'd haunt her.

"Kerrigan..."

"No, don't use that defeated tone with me. We can tell the pack our plan, and tomorrow, right before the wedding..." The illuminated lightbulb over her head blinked out, and her face crumpled. "It'd turn into a big bloody conflict and too many werewolves would die in the process, wouldn't they?"

"Afraid so," I said, the words coming out gruff. "And if we failed, you'd die, and that'd kill me."

"But to just give up? How are we supposed to do that?"

"It's not giving up. It's finding a way to survive, to keep on living. Kerrigan, I need you to promise me something..."

Already the stubborn woman I loved was shaking her head, sensing I was about to ask something difficult of her. It wouldn't be easy for me, either, which was why I'd forced myself to stay away the past couple of days while I'd formulated this part of the plan. "You need to move away from here and start a new life. Do your best to forget about me and Guadalupe Falls, and that things like werewolves and witches exist—"

"As if I could actually do that." Not that I'd expected my decree to go over smoothly, but her expression bordered on hostility with a pinch of bafflement. "After losing my mom and my grandma, I finally found a place where I belong, with friends and family and a sense of purpose. You seriously want me to say goodbye to you, Gina, Sasquatch, Elias and Gideon, and the rest of the werewolves? Just leave behind my clinic and everyone I care about?"

"Of course, it's not what I want, but it's the better, safer option for both of us. If you're far away, it'll make it harder for Andromeda to invoke the final clause." Not impossible, unfortunately, but as long as I fell in line, the witch wouldn't feel the necessity for an extra bargaining chip. Not being able to see or talk to Kerrigan would make me downright miserable, but she deserved to have the fullest life she could, one that wasn't constantly threatened as a way to get to me. "As for your clinic, I'll buy it from you and give you whatever else you need to relocate. It's the best way I can think of to take care of you."

A tumultuous storm brewed in her gray-blue eyes, the flash of lightning meaning she was about to spew thunder. "No way. Not only do I not need you to take care of me, paying off the clinic was never part of the deal. I don't even care about that right now."

"Once the dust settles, you will. You're amazing at what you do, and I won't be the reason you don't follow your dreams." I licked my lips, fighting against the urge to hold back the last vital part of the plan. "You can't tell me where you're going, either, because if I know, I'll never be able to stay away, and that'll only endanger the both of us. As well as everyone we love."

Hurt pinched her features, and she opened her mouth, undoubtedly to argue.

"Please, sweetheart." The words scraped on the way out, leaving my chest achy and raw. I bracketed her face in my hands. "Do you hear what I'm saying? I love you so much that I'm stripped bare, begging you to go somewhere you can be safe and happy, and even..." My possessive nature reared its ugly head, and it took every ounce of my determination to expel the rest. "Find someone who'll make you happy, who loves you and can give you everything I no longer can."

That faceless man I longed to strangle would never love her on the same primordial level I did, to the point my heart and soul belonged to her and always would.

But that was probably for the best. Love like that was rare and unruly. It burned fast and furious, igniting both people, leaving ash in its wake, and often came at a price.

My price required letting her go so I could once again be the alpha my pack needed me to be. I skimmed my thumb over her cheekbone. "*Please*, Kerrigan. Promise me you'll at least try."

Tears brimmed her eyes, and the mangled heap that used to be my heart radiated sorrow, head to toe. She sniffed. "Okay."

"Promise," I said, desperate to hear she'd be safe and happy regardless of how much I despised the fact that it wouldn't be with me.

"I promise." With that, she buried her head in my chest and burst into tears. I stroked her hair, fighting the rising lump in my throat and doing my damnedest not to cry myself. I held her like that until her sobs faded, her breaths slowed, and she gradually drifted to sleep.

Then I stared at the ceiling, wishing like hell that tomorrow didn't have to come.

CHAPTER FORTY-FIVE

Conall

TAKING into account that I was already being forced to marry a witch—one I didn't and never would love—it only added insult to injury that I had to do it in a fucking penguin suit.

As I fiddled with the ridiculous bowtie, my gaze kept getting drawn to the copy of the contract Andromeda had handed us as we left, as if this was all some business deal instead of destroying my future with Kerrigan and any chance at happiness in one fell swoop.

Guilt rose, as it'd done several times this week. The agreed-upon alliance was about more than just me. More than just Kerrigan. I'd committed myself to this pack, and I'd never regretted a single second of it.

Until now.

Since the thought wouldn't leave me alone, I picked up the document and skimmed down the page, striving not to let my simmering anger reach the boiling point.

Diego walked in, also in a suit. He wore an equally grim expression, his and my dispositions more suitable for a funeral than a wedding. The way he tugged at his bowtie conveyed he found the ridiculous thing as uncomfortable as I did. "Man, I wish I could do something more than stand at your side and pretend this is a joyous occasion. I feel so damn helpless."

He'd expressed the same thought countless times during our meetings.

The door opened again, and Tyrese and Nissa walked in hand in hand, cuddly and kissy, as if they were about to renew their vows and couldn't wait to get started. Tyrese wore a classic black suit, white shirt, and tie combo, while my beta's pale purple dress flowed into a skirt that highlighted her baby bump and floated an inch or so above the floor. I did my best to conjure some joy for how madly in love they were, but did they have to rub it in my face today of all days? Talk about battery acid on an open wound.

My impending nuptials aren't their *fault*. Still, I appreciated Diego's dour mood and how well it mirrored my own. If I didn't get a proportion of the loathing out now, how the hell was I going to stand in front of two packs and two covens and celebrate ending centuries of fighting?

All so we could breed and battle vampires. Fuck today already.

"Sorry," Nissa said, her smile dropping as she caught sight of me. Assumedly because she could read my facial tics as well as I could read hers. "We were just at the cli—in Guadalupe Falls getting an ultrasound and found out..." She snuggled up to her husband, who kissed her forehead.

"We're having a girl," they said together, and Tyrese lifted Nissa's hand and kissed the back of it, his eyes for her and her alone. "We were both surprised, especially when Kerig— uh, Doc—estimated the due date closer to three months than four, given the size of our baby."

They were tiptoeing around, avoiding saying Kerrigan's name, as if that would prevent hole after hole from being punched clean through me. Since leaving her sleeping in my bed at four a.m., I'd bled misery. The defunct organ in my chest pumped it through my body, infused it with agony, and sent it right back through me in bursts. What good was accelerated healing if it didn't take care of the most pain I'd ever been in?

At the sound of the loud *thwack*, the three of us turned to gape at Diego, who'd just punched a fist through the drywall. "Sorry." He shook his head and then lifted his chin. "Actually, I'm not. Tyrese and Nissa, and you and Kerrigan—you've all found someone you *want* to pledge your life to, and that's so rare. In the beginning, I'll admit I was worried about the relationship and the effect it might have on your decision-making skills, along with the majority of our members. But you've already given up so much for the pack, and most everyone agrees it's unfair you have to do it again, on such an extreme level at that. I've never given a shit about marriage. Hell, one to form an alliance with no expectations besides breeding and keeping two species from tearing each other apart would be more like an ideal arrangement to me."

I whipped my head toward Diego, and he held up his hands.

"Sorry, man. That last part was a fucked-up thing to say."

"Only if you don't mean it," I said, and my three closest friends cast confused looks in my direction. I lifted the contract and reread the last paragraph, paying close attention to every single word.

An idea was forming, one that was ludicrous and risky, and I absolutely shouldn't entertain.

But then I thought of Kerrigan. From her smile, to her wit, to how she never hesitated to put me in my place. Of her scent and driving my hands through her hair, and watching her shatter apart while she was naked and underneath me. I replayed the part of last night where she swept her hair aside and told me to bite her. She'd been willing to go through a painful transformation, track down a gun, and shoot Andromeda, just to be with me.

I didn't deserve her or her unconditional love, but if there was anything I could do— anything at all—wouldn't it be worse not to try?

I scratched at the scruff on my cheek, my mind whirring, and hope I didn't dare give into started to form. "If you're serious, there is one thing you could do. But it's a big thing. We're talking life changing."

Diego strode toward me, fealty and resoluteness setting his jaw. "Anything. Name it, and I'm in."

Was I honestly considering saying the words aloud? Of fighting myself as strongly as I'd have to fight one of my own men? Not just one of my own men, but one of my best friends and the guy who'd been there for me since the year we were both born? In truth, we'd become brothers. We gave each other shit and were competitive to a fault, but at the end of the day, there was love and affection. If you messed with one of us, you'd have to contend with both of us.

"I need you to challenge me for the position of alpha," I said. "Once it starts, our primal instincts are going to take over, especially with the top-ranking position hanging in the balance. Holding back isn't in my DNA, just like it's not in yours. Not to mention that no wolf—from our pack or any other—would respect either of us if we didn't give it our all. The fight'll be ugly and brutal, and there's a high likelihood we'll both limp away."

His jaw hung open, same as Nissa's and Tyrese's. I got it. It wasn't anything I ever thought I'd hear myself say, either. I'd lived for the pack so long that panic welled over not being in charge or controlling each working, moving part as I worked to change the werewolf hierarchy from the inside out.

The creases in Diego's forehead deepened and then smoothed. Gradually, one dark eyebrow winged up, and an ambitious glimmer played across his features. "You...want me to challenge you for the alpha position?"

The paper in my hand crumpled, the fact that he was

obviously interested in the job giving me a moment of hesitation. But that wasn't the point, and it was harder than expected to coerce my ego into taking a backseat. This wasn't about being the biggest or the baddest.

I lifted the contract and tapped the paragraph about Kerrigan's life being bound to the agreement. If the *alpha* of the Bridgewater pack failed to marry Natalia; if the *alpha* failed to produce an heir.

The only way for me to be with Kerrigan was to no longer be the alpha.

"Yes," I said. "If you do this, though, you'll have to swear to follow through with the wedding. Kerrigan's safety won't be guaranteed until you produce an heir—just so you're clear on what becoming the alpha would entail. On what exactly I'm asking of you."

Slowly, Diego nodded, as though he suspected this might be some elaborate trap.

"If you're going to challenge me, it's going to have to be right before the wedding, in front of the packs and covens so they can all stand witness. More than that..." I blew out my breath, picturing Kerrigan in my mind and letting my love for her steel my resolve. "In order for this to work, I need you to win."

CHAPTER FORTY-SIX

Kerrigan

ALL DURING NISSA'S ULTRASOUND, it'd been impossible not to think about Conall and the upcoming wedding at the compound. But at least it'd kept me busy for a snippet of time.

Through the open doorway of the exam room, Sasquatch paced across the lobby of my clinic. I'd actually had to request he go to the lobby because he took up so much space and the anxiety radiating off him amped mine to the level I felt as jittery as if I'd consumed an entire pot of espresso.

Since he'd been ordered not to leave my side, I'd also had to assure him the lobby still counted and that he might as well take the entrance since Tyrese could cover the back.

Right before I'd lowered the wand to Nissa's belly, I'd said, "I'm not sure why the jelly is always cold, but it is. I could warm it up for you if you'd like, but—"

"I've been awake while doctors lifted my intestines out of my stomach," Nissa responded, "so I think I'll live."

For several seconds, I stood frozen, jellied wand in the air. Then I glanced at Tyrese to see if it was a weird joke I didn't understand. The clench of his fists conveyed it wasn't, and

WELCOME TO
BRIDGEWATER

that he held a whole heap of animosity for those who'd hurt his mate.

In a weird way, it meant Nissa and I had something in common. We both joked away upsetting past experiences and current anxieties. Only hers were a hundred times more devastating, and that fortified my determination to keep my sorrow in check. Other people had it worse, after all.

As I was performing the procedure, I'd gnawed on my lower lip, debating whether or not to broach the subject that'd been on my mind for a while. "I've been wondering something since that first night you and I met. If I'm out of line, just say so, and I'll zip my lip."

Nissa tensed, not quite confirming or denying. I assumed that meant she was waiting to hear the question, so I plowed on with it.

"Why'd you help me chain up Conall if you thought there was a possibility I might hurt or experiment on him?"

"Easy. He needed his ego taken down a notch," Nissa said with a laugh, and Tyrese chuckled along. Obviously, I hadn't hidden my concern very well because she aimed a reassuring smile at me. "Only kidding. Like I told you after the last big pack meeting, I consider him my brother. Which is why, that night, I carefully weighed his odds of survival. You landed higher on the list than dragging his unconscious ass to the compound. That decision was all logic, no emotion."

While Nissa talked a tough game, I didn't quite buy it. She was as fiercely protective of Conall as he was of her. In the face of the awful decision he and I were forced to make, at least he'd always have plenty of strong people watching after him. That also comforted me as I deliberated leaving Guadalupe Falls.

"Everything looks great," I said as I swiped the ultrasound wand across Nissa's stomach. "And if we can get a peek right around here..."

Tyrese sandwiched Nissa's hand between both of his, the

couple's excitement so palpable unexpected tears formed in my eyes. I'd like to say it was 100 percent being an amazing, empathetic person, but I had a fleeting thought, one that said, *In another life, that might've been me and Conall in the not-too-distant future.*

"You're having a little girl," I'd told them, and the couple had hugged. With the tightness in my throat reaching the aching point, I'd backed away, ready to excuse myself so they could have their special moment without a side of blubbering from an emotional woman they barely knew.

I'd only made it one step when Nissa reached for my hand.

"Thank you," she said, giving me a quick squeeze. "I wish that I could've grown to call you my sister, but if you ever need anything, you have my number."

I'd nodded, and then they'd rushed off to get ready for Conall and Natalia's wedding, leaving Sasquatch and me and my shattered heart alone in the too-quiet clinic. And with nothing much to do, my thoughts bombarded me, and it required every ounce of strength I had to prevent myself from falling apart.

I organized the vials of medication, the rattle echoing loneliness the way my voice had those first days in the clinic.

When that didn't take as long as expected, I decided it was time to scrub the place down.

"I'll help," Sasquatch said, relieving me of the bucket of soapy water and gesturing for one of the sponges.

The point was for the activity to eat up as much time as possible, and I'd nearly told him as much, but he looked about as helpless as I felt.

So we dropped to hands and knees and got to work.

To sell or to re-open my practice to the more usual animals of Guadalupe Falls, I still hadn't decided.

Suddenly, affection for this tiny building crashed into me in a wave. Yeah, the start had been a bit rocky, but how could

I even consider a future that didn't include this town and a certain werewolf?

Then again, at the thought of staying, the sharp shards of my broken heart sliced me right open. The idea of seeing Conall out and about—or even knowing he was out in the woods without me—and not being able to call him or touch him or kiss him or...

A tear escaped and rolled down my cheek. If the idea was too much to bear, how would I ever survive the reality?

But saying goodbye to him?

Both options left me feeling like I was internally bleeding out, and sadly, there wasn't any surgery or medical procedure to fix it.

I tossed my sponge into the bucket of soap water, swiping my arm across my forehead as I peered out the glass door of the clinic. "Do you know that hawk?" I asked Sasquatch, without fully thinking through the question and how ridiculous it sounded. I crinkled my nose, wishing for the ability to snatch my words out of the air and stuff them back into the recesses of my brain. "Never mind. That was a weird question. I don't, like, think you talk to animals or whatever."

Sasquatch sat back on his heels, a mournful expression on his face that shredded what was left of my poor battered insides. "Not all animals. I can't even talk to her..." He glanced out at the hawk perched on the porch railing to the clinic. "But sometimes I relive our conversations from long ago to remember what it was like when I could."

The raw wound in his voice poured vinegar on my internal injuries, and I recognized it for what it was. Heartbreak. I crossed the room and sat in front of him. "Tell me about her."

Where we still talking about the hawk? I wasn't quite sure. It didn't matter, though.

"She's smart and brave and so beautiful that the first time she spoke to me, I just gawked at her awkwardly."

For the first time all day, a ray of sunshine broke through the storm clouds in my soul. How could I leave Guadalupe Falls? I had Gina, Elias, Gideon, and Sasquatch to look after. I'd also want to look after Conall, but how could I stay and watch him live out the life I once thought I'd have with him? "What happened next?"

"She cracked a joke that was so utterly brilliant, I didn't know whether or not it was a joke. In some ways, your humor reminds me of hers. You'd like her."

"I'm sure I would." Was now the time to ask Sasquatch his real name? Or did I ask for the one that belonged to the woman he loved? Or should I just relish the fact that he'd shared part of his love story with me?

Before I could decide, his phone rang, and he held up a finger, silently requesting a moment to answer it. As he listened to the voice on the other end—one I recognized immediately, despite being unable to make out the words—Sasquatch's pale green gaze moved to me. "Yes, sir."

He hung up the phone, and I held my breath, afraid of what he'd say and afraid of what he wouldn't. Then he hopped to his feet and extended a hand. "Evidently, you and I are going to that wedding after all."

———

What did one wear to a wedding between a witch and one's werewolf ex-boyfriend?

Considering I'd had all of ten minutes to get ready, it ended up being what I already had in the closet. While my little black dress suited my mood, I also wasn't in the mood to draw the ire of any more witches. The blush-colored dress with the glittery scoop neckline didn't hide the deep scratches across the front of my throat, but it was what it was.

After throwing my hair into a loose bun and snagging my heels, Sasquatch drove us into the mountains, so fast that I closed my eyes, held onto the oh-shit handle, and prayed we wouldn't wreck.

Once we arrived at compound, he left me with Gina, Elias, and Gideon and rushed to his house to change.

We walked to a hilltop that opened up to a meadow, and who knew a bunch of werewolves could throw together such a beautiful last-minute wedding?

Rows of chairs had been arranged among tall pines that stretched toward the sky and filled the air with their fresh mountain scent. I was surprised to see a dozen or so men mixed in with the beautiful women seated on the bride's side, leaving me wondering if there were male witches, or if they were family, and how that worked. While a handful of the women wore gothic dresses, complete with corsets and charcoal eyeliner, the majority looked like a mix of woodland fairies and modern women you'd pass on the street.

In Hollywood, anyway. Either they had great skin care routines or performing spells was great for the pores.

Our group settled into the second to last row on the groom's side, saving a seat for Sasquatch on the end. Fairy lights twinkled in the branches over our heads, and since squinting didn't reveal wires and the heights were beyond anything even Sasquatch could reach on a ladder, I assumed there was magic at play. I guess that made them witch lights.

Longing wrapped barbed strings around my heart as I took in the rose petal–strewn aisle that led to an archway made up of a crescent moon and a pentagram.

"Conall's going to hate all the witch symbols," I muttered, more to myself, but Gina wrapped her arm around my shoulders and rested her head against mine.

"I'm so sorry, hon. I know this is as hard for you as it is him."

Shit, I was going to cry. Elias and Gideon spun in their seats and offered hand squeezes and knee pats, and I focused on holding myself together. Deep down, I felt like I shouldn't be here, even though I wanted to see Conall one last time before...

Nope. Don't go there or you will cry.

Still, why had he asked me to come? Did he worry someone might get injured? I wasn't sure, although I feared it proved that the only way the both of us would be able to move on was to be apart.

Sasquatch slid into the seat next to me as a woman announced the ceremony was about to begin. He wore a tweed suit that hearkened back to the early 1900s, with a tie, a vest, a chained gold pocket watch, and a jacket that totally worked for him. I opened my mouth to tell him so, but the commotion up front drew my attention.

My heart ceased beating as Conall, dressed in a white shirt and a black suit with a bowtie, took his place next to the altar, so handsome it literally hurt. Diego and Tyrese lined up next to him, music swelled, and I plummeted into agony as the realization I'd have to leave town—leave him—swallowed me whole.

CHAPTER FORTY-SEVEN

Conall

"I OBJECT," Diego yelled, and I about slapped a hand over my face.

"We're not at that part of the ceremony yet," the witch who was acting as our injustice-of-the-forced-peace said.

If this wasn't an overblown show of the Oldenwilde Coven's power, and I hadn't been coerced into a suit to sing and dance like some kind of monkey, I might feel bad for Natalia Burroughs. I highly doubted this was a dream come true for her, either. Still, she'd walked down the aisle with grace, head held dutifully high, and I supposed that objectively, she even made a beautiful bride.

No one compared to my mate, though. I'd barely caught sight of Kerrigan, but it was enough to debilitate the beating of my heart, even as it fortified the decision I'd made. I could also smell her among the guests, my nose joining every cell in my body that reached for her as my instincts screamed this wedding was all wrong.

I opened and closed my fists, reminding myself I needed to lose this fight. For the record, the "I object" Diego tossed out wasn't the way *I* would've thrown the gauntlet.

He's not going to be able to lead the people. Without me to steer the pack in the right direction, we'll end up in even more danger.

What if he's scared of the Council? They'll never get their boots off our necks. I batted those errant thoughts away. No matter how much I told myself that Diego would do a fine job, my pride or confidence or whatever-the-fuck anyone wanted to call it argued. The idea of letting go of control was akin to ripping out my spine.

Lucky me, I'd have Diego try to do that for me.

Diego stepped out of line, away from Tyrese. He shed his suit jacket and flung it on the grass. "I challenge Conall Shaw for the alpha position of the Bridgewater Pack."

Andromeda shot out of her seat and charged toward the altar. "I'm not sure what you dogs are up to, but I'm not allowing it to happen." Her icy gaze turned to me. "Have you forgotten that Kerrigan's life is tied to our contract?"

"No, I haven't forgotten." I bared my teeth at her. "Trust me, I never will. You and I will always have unfinished business." I discarded my suit coat and unfastened my cufflinks. "When it comes to werewolf business, however, you don't get a say. The contract says the alpha has to marry Natalia and produce an heir. Diego and I are about to fight it out to see who'll be getting hitched this afternoon. Now, step back unless you want to be one of the casualties of our heated, violent challenge. When wolves fight for the top position, it gets ugly."

Andromeda seethed, and I fucking grinned in her face. *Take that, you heartless witch.*

I couldn't get too cocky, though. Adrenaline coursed through my veins, the upcoming fight fueling my animalistic side, and that didn't bode well. It also rankled that if he won, I'd still have to rely on him to produce an heir for Kerrigan to get out of the contract unscathed.

But I'd weighed my options, and one of them was missing Kerrigan's exact weight.

Diego and I kicked off our shoes and removed our shirts while Nissa formed a boundary to prevent anyone else from being caught up in the fray. After I let her, Diego, and Tyrese in on my idea, I asked if she was offended, as she was technically second in line.

She assured me the only thing she cared about was that both Diego and I lived to tell the tale. But as she neared and attempted a smile, I saw the worry in her eyes. "Are you sure this is the only way?" she asked. "Both of you are going to end up severely injured. Or worse."

"Good thing I know a sexy vet who can fix us up after we're done kicking each other's asses."

Not what Nissa wanted to hear, so I appealed to her logical side. "Diego already issued the challenge. Now neither of us can back down without appearing weak."

Her chin quivered the tiniest bit before she threw her arms around me and Diego and wished both of us luck. Then she turned to Tyrese, and the two of them headed away from us.

The wedding guests scattered, leaving their seats to form a giant semi-circle near the archway as we headed toward the open meadow behind it. No reason to ruin the altar that'd be put to evil use after the fight.

"If you win, and you don't marry Natalia, Kerrigan dies," I said to Diego, low enough he should be the only one able to fully make out the words. Not that it was a big secret. The entire pack knew what was at stake. "If you step out on Natalia, same thing. Until you produce an heir, my mate's life is going to be hanging in the balance."

Diego tipped his neck side to side, the move punctuated with the crack of his joints. "I understand." One corner of his mouth twisted up, the same cocky way it did whenever we sparred— before he inevitably lost. "You could always drop your guard first thing, let me get in a solid punch, and then stay down."

I huffed a laugh. "If only that were an option." I might be

able to drop my arms and take that first punch. But after that, my survival instincts would kick in, and the inner wolf would fly off the leash. Everything I wanted to tell him—every tip from all the training we'd done together—whirred through my head. Unfortunately, it wouldn't do any good. We both were too aware of one another's fighting stances, strengths, and weaknesses. Any tips I gave him would remain in my head as soon as the fight started.

But there was no reason we couldn't have some fun while we beat the shit out of each other. I cast Diego a smirk, bounced on the balls of my feet, and wiggled my fingers in the typical *bring it* gesture.

Two seconds later, we exploded into a flash of fur and teeth.

The excited buzz from the crowd lit a match within me, and my words came out gruff through my elongated teeth. "Looks like someone's finally learned how to hold half-form."

In good news, my confidence in Diego's ability to lead the pack just grew; in bad news, I'd never wanted to kick his ass more.

———

It started with growls and bared teeth. I told myself to let Diego get that first hit, but he rushed me, and I instinctually charged right back.

We used the surrounding woods as our boxing ring, launching ourselves off rocks, slamming into tree trunks, only to jump to the next and use them as leverage for an aerial attack. I collided into his body, hard enough all the oxygen whooshed from my lungs. We rolled through grass and dirt, leaving the air thick with debris. Diego's low kick took me by surprise. I tucked into my body, but the hit still sent me rolling end-over-end for a couple of yards. He darted for me, determined to attack before I could recover. I quickly leaped to my feet and threw a jab that caused a crunch of bones and blood to gush from his nose.

I dodged the roundhouse he countered with, grinning at his swing and a miss. He dug his claws into my arms, deep through the muscle and sinew, and bashed the front of his skull into mine.

Pain exploded, along with a stream of blood. Pretty sure that hit split my eyebrow. I squinted against the sanguine stream, no corner man to ice the swelling cut into submission, no medical doctor to declare whether it was safe to proceed.

Werewolf fights were like old-school cage matches, no rules, no bell. No stopping until someone couldn't get up. I snapped my teeth at him, kicking as he lunged. Made contact, but it wasn't enough to prevent his razor-tipped claws from raking stinging heat across my back.

Growls, blood splatters, the snap of teeth.

I whirred around and slashed, taking a decent chunk out of his hide. He stumbled and then kicked my knee, a loud *pop* sounding as my leg bent the wrong way.

Before the adrenaline could fade and the rest of me registered one of my legs didn't work, I dropped the ground on all fours, ducked my head, and barreled into Diego, aiming for the wound in his side.

This time he went down, sliding across his back, right over the top of a rock. His head thunked back, his bared throat exposed, and I saw the kill shot.

All I had to do was sink my teeth into the front of his neck and he'd have no choice to submit or die.

"Conall!"

The voice filtered through the haze of bloodlust and self-preservation, awakening my humane side. I glanced around, my vision a blur of crimson and dust.

Kerrigan rushed forward, breaking away from the crowd, and panic overtook my defenses. Sasquatch snagged her around the waist and hauled her away, and I bared my teeth at him. How *dare* he touch my mate?

The growl that came from beneath me registered way too late. Diego tucked his head, digging it and his claws into my gut as he leaped to his feet and used the momentum to launch me into the air. I hit the ground hard, dragging a path of destruction through the grass, and still I heard Kerrigan's voice.

If I could just see her one more time.

A giant blur of russet fur pinned me to the ground, and fists rained down fury. I ignored the leg that bent at the wrong angle and pulled up my arms, my mind searching for a way out of the pinned position.

But Kerrigan. This fight was for her. My clawed fingers trembled with the desire to grip Diego's shoulder and fling him off me.

Diego...challenging me for the position of alpha.

Because I'd asked him to.

So that I could be with Kerrigan.

"Please, Conall. *Please*," she shouted through the din of the roaring crowd. "You made me promise to stay alive and follow my dreams, and if you don't stop this right now, I'm taking it back."

I jerked my head to find her, so fast it slammed against the ground. "Can't take it back," I snarled.

"Then neither can you," she yelled, punctuating the words with a stomp of her foot that, judging from his expression, managed to shock even Sasquatch.

All I had to do was tap out, and that woman was mine.

She'd always be mine, but this was the type of mine where we got to laugh together and go to dinner and spend nights fucking and mornings cuddling in bed. We'd get to have babies and grow old together...

If I held onto those images, winning seemed like losing.

I stretched out my arm. Lifted it in the air. My muscles and bones revolted at the idea of hitting the ground, and if I didn't do it fast, I wasn't sure I'd be able to. "I yield," I shouted as I smacked the packed dirt two times.

Just like that, the fight came to a grinding halt.

Diego reached for his side, the flap of fur and peeled-open skin exposing a generous portion of his ribs. He heaved a ragged breath that harkened to the day after I'd been riddled with silver bullets and couldn't get as much air as my lungs required.

Slowly, Diego pushed to his feet. His fur, claws, and fangs receded, and what remained of his tattered pants covered up the vital bits. He extended a hand, and I almost slapped it away without thinking. But then I, too, returned to my human form. With a grunt, I accepted his help and let him to tug me to my feet.

Well, one foot. Putting my weight on my broken leg caused it to scream, so I aligned the bones the best I could to facilitate their knitting back together. Diego and I both braced our weight on nearby trees, blood dripping from various parts of our faces and bodies. Our injuries gradually got the message the fight was over, leaving them free to clot and begin the healing process.

Then I smelled her: *my mate*.

I spun right in time for Kerrigan to collide into me, her arms going around my neck as she began cursing me out for being such an idiot, and what were Diego and I fighting over anyway?

Once I started laughing, I could hardly stop, despite the murderous glare on Kerrigan's face. Which prompted her to smack my arm, the move so familiar and reassuring I suddenly understood the idea of turning the other cheek—or arm, as the case may be. "This isn't funny, Conall," she said. "You nearly gave me a heart attack."

I crashed my mouth to hers, ignoring the sting of pain that meant my split lip hadn't fully healed. She kissed me back, urgently and fervently, for all of a handful of seconds before she pulled away and attempted to step out of my embrace. "Um, oopsie. We just sorta kissed in front of your fiancée."

"You mean *my* fiancée," Diego said, flashing her a macabre grin. For a guy who kept his scruff ridiculously groomed, no trace of it showed through the scrapes and gore.

Kerrigan's brow furrowed. Then she shot us a scowl that made it clear she wanted to knock the two of our heads together.

"The contract says that *the alpha* of the Bridgewater Pack must marry Natalia Burroughs of the Oldenwilde Coven," I explained. "Same applies when it comes to producing an heir. Given that Diego challenged me for my position—and won— I'm no longer the alpha." I swiped at the last of the blood dripping from my nose, wishing it'd stop throbbing already. Another minute or two, and I should be fine.

Kerrigan blinked at me, and I saw the moment she allowed hope to spread its wings and fly. "You're saying..." She brought her trembling hands to her mouth. "I'm afraid to say it, more afraid to believe it because I'm not sure my heart can take it if I'm wrong."

I cupped her cheek. "You're not only worth fighting for, Kerrigan Ryan. You're also worth losing for. And if you'll still have me after watching me get my ass kicked—"

"It was hardly an ass-kicking," she said, and I pressed a finger to her lips so I could finish.

"Making a speech here, woman." I cleared my throat. "If you'll still have me, I'd love nothing more than to live out the rest of our days together."

Kerrigan flung her arms around me and peppered my face with kisses that were highly preferrable to the punches I'd received. Then she fused her mouth to mine with such intensity that I rocked back a step, my broken bone letting me know it could use a few more hours before bearing any weight.

Something I didn't bother telling my mate as she wrapped her legs around my waist and hooked her ankles, fully trusting me to hold her up. To ensure I wouldn't let her down, I shifted most of my weight to my uninjured leg, planted my hands on her amazing ass, and squeezed with equal zeal.

Then she smiled against my mouth and said, "Silly, werewolf. I'm already yours."

EPILOGUE

Kerrigan

SWEETIES THAT THEY WERE, the witches granted Diego an hour to heal and clean up before the ceremony.

Okay, so it was probably more a matter of not wanting to be embarrassed by the wedding photos. Whatever the reason, it permitted me time to patch up both Diego and Conall, as well as administer a steroid shot to speed up their healing time even more.

Since I was almost scared to let go of Conall, for fear I'd lose him again or would wake up and discover today had all been a weird roller-coaster of a dream, I had no choice but to join him in the shower. I know, poor me.

By the time we arrived at Diego's house afterward, both of us had damp hair and the sort of grins that only hot shower sex could bring.

As soon as we entered the room with Diego, Tyrese, and Nissa, we had to turn down the wattage on our happiness so it wouldn't feel like we were rubbing it in the groom's face. I'd never chatted much with Diego, and definitely never one-on-one, but I signaled to Conall I wanted a minute. Then I approached the new alpha of the Bridgewater Pack under the guise of helping him with his tie.

"Your face healed so nicely." I winced at my awkward introduction, but Diego merely chuckled.

"Better not say that too loudly, or Conall will start punching it again."

"I heard that," Conall said, and Diego and I shared a laugh.

I raised my voice as I tugged out more fabric on the right half of the black bowtie, working to even up both sides. "Don't worry, babe. I prefer ruggedly handsome to pretty boy." "Pretty boy?" Diego balked, and the rest of the room snickered.

"Oh. Did you not know?" I smoothed the silk into place and repositioned the points of his collar over the black neckband. "I just figured between the bronze skin, dark scruff and eyebrows, and dimples for days, you already knew. If anything, I should've done a worse job patching you up. You don't want to outshine the bride."

"As if that's possible." Diego's gaze drifted toward the window and then to somewhere beyond, to a time and place that didn't exist in the present. "You've seen her, right?"

"Talia?" Actually, it seemed only her coven used the shortened version of her name. "Yeah. Up close and personal while she held the sharp end of a letter opener to my jugular."

That jerked him back to the present, and he cleared his throat, a hint of trepidation creeping into his features. "Sorry about that."

I shrugged a shoulder, which was a bit of a weird blasé reaction after the trauma the witches had caused. Getting to be with the man I loved made it easier not to care. "Not your fault, and seriously, I can't thank you enough." I nodded at my handiwork. "There. All fixed. It's good to know if the doctor thing doesn't work out, I totally have a future in bowties."

Either my joke wasn't funny, or my companions were too anxious to laugh—I chose to assume the former.

Diego stepped in front of the mirror and slipped into his suit coat, wincing slightly at the movement. Undoubtedly a side effect of the fractured rips and gaping hole that'd been ripped out of his hide. "I've never wanted to get hitched, and this isn't even a real marriage, so why am I so damn nervous?"

"It's a real marriage," Conall cut in, scooting to the edge of the seat he occupied. "You told me you understood how serious the terms are."

I waved his statement away, as he was missing the point entirely. It was a good thing I'd come along, as dudes were so bad at emotional pep talks, and Nissa and Tyrese were a bit lost in their own world. "It's a big moment in your life," I told Diego, "even if it's one you never planned for. On top of that, you're now in charge of the future of the pack. That's huge."

Diego blew out a long exhale. "I'm ready." He raised his voice, aiming the next words at my mate. "I am ready, Conall. You don't have to worry. You did all the legwork of forming the pack and getting us to where we are now, but you deserve a break. I also owe you, so I'm happy to take on more of the weight." He pivoted to sit in the windowsill, the setting sun lighting up his profile in gold. "I just didn't expect to feel anything. Now I feel...too many things."

The knock on the door drew all our attention.

Time was up.

Right before we left the room, I hugged Diego around the middle. "Thanks again." Conall gave him a bro-hug with a hard pat on the back, and then they were having a pat-off, as though there hadn't been enough testosterone expelled between them earlier today. They decided it'd be for the best if Conall *wasn't* a groomsman, for obvious reasons, so he and I went to go find a seat.

About ten minutes later, Diego, Tyrese, and Mikal were in

place near the altar, and soft, lilting music began to play—the same song that'd about ripped my soul in two earlier this evening. It caused a pang, not on my behalf but on Diego's.

Conall interlaced our fingers and canted his head toward mine. "One day, in the not-too-distant future when you and I get married, I'll have to restrain myself from racing up the aisle to meet you so I can carry you to the altar before you change your mind."

"As if I'd ever change my mind," I said, wrapping myself around his arm and kissing his cheek. Butterflies fluttered through me as I felt him smile underneath my lips, the forming groove so delicious I couldn't help dipping my tongue into it for a quick taste.

"Yeah, I know. But now that I'm no longer the pack alpha, I was trying humility on for size." He made a sour face. "I don't like it."

I laughed and snuggled closer, enjoying the zing of having his large hand circle my thigh. "That's why I didn't bother asking if I had a say in whether or not we get married."

"You do. As long as you say yes," he teased, twisting his head so that our mouths aligned.

The prelude music changed, and we all stood as the bride marched down the aisle—for the second time today. Poor Natalia probably hated me even more now than she did when I'd pinged her in the head with that heavy silver collar they'd put on Conall.

Wearing an ethereal dress with a plunging neckline and embroidered lace flowers that flowed into a gauzy skirt, she appeared to be floating. Although I couldn't be sure she wasn't, I did catch a peek of peep-toe heels. People gasped as she passed, and I understood why. Statuesque, with loose blond waves that fell to her mid back, she was beyond beautiful. Her expression remained so carefully impassive, as though she were afraid to betray her true feelings, and even after everything that'd happened, my heart went out to her.

As she passed by, it formed the perfect gap for Andromeda to cast me and Conall a death glare. A shiver ran through me, and Conall curled me closer, a low growl rumbling through his throat.

"She can request your help, but I won't let her or anyone else hurt you," Conall said, and I nodded. With him by my side, we'd get through it together. It didn't mean she was going to make it easy on us, or on Diego for that matter.

The witch conducting the ceremony spoke about the union of two souls, and how it'd bring about the uniting of both sects of people who worshipped the moon. It would've been beautiful had the marriage not been the result of coercion.

As they reached the part with the "I wills"—another thing that would be romantic under different circumstances—I held my breath. Conall sucked in a lungful next to me, his fingers tightening around my palm.

"I will," Diego said, and sweet relief flowed through my veins.

The same question was posed to Natalia.

Silence fell over the audience in a thick blanket as she remained perfectly still. Her gaze moved to her mother, and whatever she saw in Andromeda's features had her pivoting back to Diego. Although she stared more through him than at him as she replied with, "I will."

The witch pronounced them husband and wife and mentioned the kiss.

Awkwardness crowded the air. Neither of the newlyweds moved.

Suddenly, every shifter tensed and growled, practically in unison. Conall pulled me to stand along with him, as the entire groom's side also leaped to their feet.

The witches looked at each other, clearly as confused as I was. Then Diego grabbed his new bride's hand and rushed her up the aisle, opposite the way she'd come.

Diego stopped next to me and Conall, tucking Natalia behind him as Conall did the same to me. I glanced at her, as though she'd tell me what was going on, even if she knew. Her wide eyes met mine, and then whispers erupted on the bride's side as several figures took shape.

"Are these unexpected visitors you and your coven's doing?" Diego snapped at Natalia, so harsh that I winced at his tone.

She, on the other hand, remained as stoic as when she'd walked down the aisle. She moved to stand next to Diego, head held high. "No. With all the cloaking spells, they shouldn't have been able to find us, either."

Right as I opened my mouth to demand someone tell me what was going on, a world rumbled through both sides of the aisle, one that turned every one of my organs to stone.

Vampires.

———

Thank you for reading MOONLIGHTING WITH THE WEREWOLF!

Sign up for my **newsletter** for information on my new releases and sales.

For fans of alpha billionaires who think they're unavailable until they meet the heroine, check out my super steamy romantic comedies <u>FOREPLAY WITH THE BOSS</u> and <u>MASTER DEBATER</u>.

My boss is teaching me to be bolder in the boardroom... and the bedroom.

. . .

In order to take over my father's company, I'm going to have to put myself at the mercy of Jameson Stone, billionaire CEO of Craze Advertising. He's as hard and immovable as his name implies and instructs me to *demand* what I want instead of constantly backing down. It's something I've always struggled with—not only at work, but also in the bedroom. There are things I want to try—steamy scenarios I've only read in my romance novels—but have been too afraid to request.

When my boldness lessons turn into foreplay lessons, it's nearly impossible not to fall for the man capable of making my wildest fantasies come true. But if I'm not careful, I'll end up losing everything I've worked for to a man who'll always choose business over me.

Excerpt below...

———

Check out the <u>MEET CUTE SERIES</u>, focused on modern dating and disastrous meet-cutes that go wrong before they go right.

<u>BIG DICK ENERGY</u>
<u>LOVE'S A GLITCH</u>
<u>BANG BUDDIES WITH BENEFITS</u>
<u>MATCHMAKING: DOGGY STYLE</u> (coming soon)

———

And if hockey romances that make you laugh and swoon

are your thing, read <u>GETTING LUCKY NUMBER SEVEN</u> about a shy chemistry nerd who's sick of spending her weekends studying with her cat and wants to check items off her bucket list with her hockey-playing guy friend Beck— starting with mind-blowing sex!

———

FOREPLAY WITH THE BOSS
CHAPTER ONE
KAT

Since it was of vital importance that I not be late today, I'd woken up extra early, scrambled around my makeshift home away from home, had a fight with the too-smart-for-its-own-good coffee maker, and now I was...well, under-caffeinated and running late. *Naturally.* I had the kind of hair that sensed fear, and since I was afraid of everything I was going to face today, the auburn strands refused to cooperate, half curly, half straight, one-hundred percent mess. The extra humidity factor in Boston definitely didn't help.

Is bed-head in style? I certainly hope so, because this is as good as it's going to get.

You know what else sensed fear? Eyeliner. Why I'd decided to pick today of all days to attempt the cat-eye look was beyond me. I thought I'd *try* to make a good impression with my new employer, even though that boat had most likely sailed already, considering my father had made a call to get me the job. Nothing says I'm fully in control of my life and adulting my ass off like having your daddy call in a favor.

All because he thought I wasn't ready to run the company.

To be fair, I wasn't. I'd started working at the office with him the second the ink on my business degree was dry, but I wasn't sure I had a boss-type personality. My whole life I'd been on the timid side of the scale, and I'd gotten walked over plenty because of it. Each time I picked myself up and brushed myself off, I promised that the next time I'd be stronger. But when the next situation arose, all my shiny pep-talks went kamikaze on me, not even taking out the enemy, just dive-bombing the ground around my feet, rocking me in the process. My face would get too hot, and my heart would pound too hard and fast, and my flight response kicked in—I was pretty sure I was missing the fight one.

Apparently, that's no way to run a company or even a department. If JT Stone, CEO of Craze Advertising and Marketing, couldn't train me to be as ruthless and scary of a boss as he was rumored to be, my dad would have "no choice" but to hand over the company that'd been in our family for three generations to a guy who specialized in beardscaping and mansplaining.

I can't let that happen. I can't let my dad down like that.

Using a Q-tip, I turned my failed cat-eye into a smoky eye. It was more evening glam than first-day-at-a-new-job—and possibly even made it look like I was trying too hard—but I didn't have enough time to start over, so it'd have to do.

As I rushed back to the bedroom, I tripped over the sneakers I'd left out after last night's muppet-flail run on the treadmill that'd come with the place. (Getting in shape was also on my list of things I needed to fix about myself.) Kicking the neon shoes aside, I pulled a sheer purple blouse over my black tank-top, smoothed a hand down my black pencil skirt and, after a longing glance at my five-inch black stilettos, slipped on sensible pumps in the same color. I had a weakness for shoes, even though they were also tempting fate with how often I managed to trip over nothing.

I felt more in control when I had them on. The extra height and fact that they could double as a weapon made me feel like I could face anything, but I was told they only reminded the men in the office I was a woman, and I needed to be more serious. Evidently serious women wore blocky three-inch pumps with sole support.

I might as well put on a pair of Crocs. I shuddered at the thought. In my one act of rebellion for the day (my hair shouldn't have all the insubordination fun), I kicked off the sensible shoes and grabbed the stilettos. The rest of me might not make much of an impression, but my shoes sure as hell would.

I caught sight of the time, swore, and rushed toward the door. I grabbed my purse and ran my hand along the bottom. *Where are my keys, where are my keys, where are my keys...?*

Man, I really need to clean out this purse.

The jingle told me I was close, and I finally unearthed them. I got into my car, drove to the station for the commuter rail, and then sprinted, afraid I was going to miss my train. And okay, maybe regretting that I hadn't stuck with the sturdy pumps.

Embarrassing loud gasps came from me as I kicked it up a notch and I couldn't believe I was already winded—I seriously had the stamina of an overweight cat who could hardly make it to his next resting place for another nap.

I stepped onto the train behind a group of dudes, who were talking and laughing and in no hurry to make it up the stairs.

"Excuse me," I tried, but my words were drowned out by theirs.

The doors closed and I felt a tug. The strap of my purse hadn't quite made it into the train, and now the doors had hold of it. I didn't even have room to give it a good yank. Why didn't these guys want to move onto the train and take a cushy seat? Were they going to stand here and talk for the thirty minutes it took to get to the office building downtown? That was going to be fun, standing here, getting jostled at every stop and then praying the opening of the doors wouldn't spill me onto the tracks.

I cleared my throat, and when they didn't get that hint, I gave words another shot. "Pardon me..."

They only talked louder.

I tugged on my purse. *Almost...* It came free, slipped right out of my grip, and landed in the middle of the aisle. Half the contents spilled out because that was the kind of day I was already having.

The group of men glanced at me, brows furrowed, like *I* was the annoying one for daring to accidentally throw my purse past them.

"What's wrong with you? Stop standing there like idiots and move out of her fucking way." The deep voice came from the other side of them, and they scattered like cockroaches after the light's been turned on.

My gaze dropped to my purse, and I reached for it, trying to scoop up everything before it got kicked around the floor and I ended up crawling on my hands and knees to retrieve it.

Other hands joined mine, and I caught a glimpse of a tattoo peeking out of a suit sleeve. I glanced up to thank him —I was sure he was the owner of the rich, deep voice that'd made those guys finally move. Then I froze, a deer in headlights of sexiness, and dropped everything I'd just gathered.

The guy couldn't possibly be real. Dark hair, perfectly styled, blue eyes so clear you could practically see yourself swimming in them, and one of those dimples in the chin that made you want to run your tongue over it.

Whoa. What?

My brain had obviously short-circuited, but I couldn't stop staring. He was rugged and yet refined, chivalrous with an air of dangerousness, and while I'd experienced attraction before, this was on a whole new level. It was consuming and edged with more infatuation than was proper to have for a perfect stranger.

I didn't consider myself an improper kind of gal, but one hot look from this guy and I was pretty sure everyone attracted to the male species would have indecent thoughts.

"Are you okay?" he asked, extending...a couple of tampons. Of course. No sexy red lipstick or sleek pens, because my luck was too shitty for that.

"Yes, thank you." I snatched the tampons out of his hand and shoved them back in my purse, then gathered the rest as quickly as I could.

He stood and extended a hand, and I took it—when else was I going to get to touch a man this hot without him taking a restraining order out on me?

"Why don't you come over and take a seat by me?"

"Yes. A thousand times yes," I said, and unfortunately, not just in my head. Luckily, he merely looked amused by my overly enthusiastic response. *Let's work on employing the filter, okay? Or that restraining order will be filed before we reach our destination.*

He led me to the set of seats opposite the door I'd come in through. I slid into one, and he sat across from me. I noticed the open laptop on the seat next to him.

I tried to think of something clever to say, but then I was imagining licking his jaw like the sexual deviant I'd suddenly become, and my tongue stuck to the roof of my mouth as my pulse raced through my body.

He glanced at his laptop and then back to me.

"Oh," I said. "If you're, uh, working, don't let me stop you."

"Why didn't you tell those guys to move out of your way?" There was an edge to his

words, like my failure to do so irritated him, and the question even felt a little like a scolding. "I tried. They didn't hear me."

His dark eyebrows scrunched together like I'd said something that didn't make sense.

"Tried?"

"Twice." I lifted two fingers like he wouldn't understand otherwise, because clearly I was suffering some kind of lust-fueled stroke.

The creases in his forehead deepened.

Speaking of trying, I was trying not to squirm under his intense scrutiny. I crossed my legs, and his eyes tracked the movement. When his attention snagged on the heels, I decided wearing them was the smartest decision I'd ever made.

Slowly, his gaze ran back up my body, heating me as it did. "Next time, I suggest demanding they move in a loud voice and adding a shove if they're too dumb to understand that."

"I'll keep that in mind," I said, "but I'm hoping that most people are polite enough that there won't be a next time."

"Oh, there'll be a next time," he said, but instead of sounding like something bad, his delicious voice made me think that I'd deal with rude people all day long if it meant a few minutes sitting across from him.

CONTINUE READING <u>FOREPLAY WITH THE BOSS NOW!</u>

ABOUT THE AUTHOR

Cindi Madsen is a USA Today bestselling author of contemporary romance and young adult novels. She sits at her computer every chance she gets, plotting, revising, and falling in love with her characters. She loves music and dancing and wishes summer lasted all year long. She lives in Colorado (where summer is most definitely NOT all year long) with her husband and three children. She and her family also take their Marvel addiction very seriously, as their one-eyed cat, Agent Fury, and their kitty named Valkyrie can attest.

facebook.com/CindiMadsenBooks

instagram.com/cindimadsenbooks

tiktok.com/@cindimadsen

x.com/CindiMadsen

pinterest.com/cindimadsen

amazon.com/stores/Cindi-Madsen/author/B005UTG1Y0

bookbub.com/authors/cindi-madsen